MW00946388

# THE ROSE OF SHANHASSON

## THE SHANHASSON TRILOGY - BOOK 1

### JOELY SUE BURKHART

# THE ROSE OF SHANHASSON

The Shanhasson Trilogy Book One
A *Blood & Shadows* story
PUBLISHED BY:
Joely Sue Burkhart

Copyright © 2011-2018 Joely Sue Burkhart
Cover Art by Dark Imaginarium
Formatting by Tattered Quill Designs

All rights reserved. No part of this book may be reproduced, scanned, or distributed in print or electronic form without the express, written permission of the author.

This is a work of fiction. Names, characters, places and incidents are the product of the author's imagination and any resemblance to any organization, event, or person, living or dead, is purely coincidental.

Adult Reading Material

# THE ROSE OF SHANHASSON

By Joely Sue Burkhart

As Our Blessed Lady's last daughter, Shannari must rule as High Queen or the Green Lands will fall into eternal darkness. Her destiny is to shine against the Shadow, protect the land and people with her magic, and keep the Blackest Heart of Darkness imprisoned. Her blood is the key, powered by the love in her heart. However, Shannari's heart is broken, her magic is crippled, and the nobles must have forgotten the dire prophesies, because everyone wants her dead.

Only love can restore her magic, but her scars testify how love can be corrupted. So when a barbarian warlord conquers her army and professes a love like no other, Shannari's first instinct is to kill the mighty Khul. Even worse, one of the Khul's guards used to be an assassin–a very skilled assassin, if the darkness in the Blood's eyes is any indication. The same darkness festers deep in her heart and draws her to the wickedly dangerous man as inexorably as his Khul's unshakable honor. Her weakening heart is not only torn between love and duty, but also between two magnificent warriors.

Yet neither warrior will be able to help her when Shadow calls her name.

A Complete Reverse Harem Epic Fantasy
    Book 1: Beginning of a menage

Book 2: Menage

Book 3: Full harem

*Warning: two of the men in the harem die (one in book 2, one in book 3), though everyone is reunited at the end.*

"The Rose of Shanhasson is a superb blend of fully-realized fantasy and scorching romance. Joely Sue Burkhart dropped me into her fantasy world and left me breathless. *The Rose of Shanhasson* is one of the best fantasy romances I've read in years!" Larissa Ione, NY Times and USA Today bestselling author of the "Demonica" series.

# DEDICATION

*For my Beloved Sister*

*The gods have many faces and many names,*
*yet no matter their guise,*
*one eternal truth remains.*

*Love is the greatest gift of all, and the greatest sacrifice.*

*In every age and every land, they consign their Chosen*
*to manifest their heart's desire in the world,*
*that all people may bear witness.*

*Love's sacrifice conquers even the blackest Shadow of evil.*

B*lessed Lady above, why have You forsaken me?*

Scanning the chilly gray waters of Dalden Bay, Shannari searched for even a small sign of hope. She stood on the holiest ground in the Green Lands and had offered ceaseless prayers throughout the night for naught. Our Blessed Lady's silvered full moon mocked her with its silence.

The thick bayside air tasted like tears. Shoulders drooping, she swallowed the choking lump of misery. She rubbed her aching, dry eyes and turned away from the mist-covered bay. Power pulsed with the gentle moonlight, resonating in her blood. Her skin tingled with the sweet melody, her heart aching, yearning to use that inborn gift.

*If only I could find some way to restore my magic...*

But no. That was another failure entirely. *My heart is dead.*

Waiting at the last column, the High Priest took her chilled hands between his own. Father Aran's snowy white hair and beard gleamed against his scarlet robes. "Our Blessed Lady has heard your prayers, Your Majesty."

Shame clawed her chest and she dropped her gaze. "Please, don't call me that."

"I've known since your birth that you would be the next High Queen. I saw the Rose Crown on your head even in the cradle."

"So you say." Shannari jerked her hands free and clenched them into fists at her sides. "You also told me of the great power I would have as the Lady's Last Daughter. Yet here I am, my magic crippled, my country surrounded by enemies, and betrothed to Prince Theo, the one person who most wants me dead." Her voice broke. She would never forget the malice in the Crown Prince's eyes, nor the suffocating horror that had come over her when he'd touched her. "I'm trapped."

The High Priest flinched. "The mistake was mine, Your Majesty, I—"

"How can I refuse to marry him now without starting a civil war?"

"Our Blessed Lady wants Her tainted son removed from the High Throne at all cost." The High Priest stared through her, deeper, seeing beyond to some future that made his eyes flash with hope. "A way will be provided."

Shannari refused to let that gleam of hope move her. She'd seen the same look in his eyes too many times to no avail. Seeing a possible future and knowing the Lady's prophesy didn't make it happen.

"Dark at times, clouded with Shadow and fraught with peril, your path is steep and treacherous with ravines on either side. If you fall, all the Green Lands will fall with you. This I know in my heart. Yet hope comes, though from where I cannot See."

She knew all too well the dark prophesy of doom waiting for her people if she failed. Other children grew up on nursery rhymes and fairytales; she'd learned a destiny of blood, and darkness, and death with her mother's murder. Death loomed closer than ever in these dark times.

Inwardly sighing, she joined her waiting father, King Valche. Surrounded by guards, they walked toward the village curved along the shoreline. Chittering raucously, gulls fought for scraps on the beach of sand and broken shells and the stench of rotting fish made her stomach churn.

Vessels ranging from local fishing boats to sea-worthy trading ships lined the docks. From crates full of rare spices from the jungles of Mambia, to exotic furs from the frigid ice of Jjord in the extreme north, exotic goods from all over the world came through this port,. Without Dalden Bay, Allandor's tables might miss the sea's natural bounty, but the largest blow would be felt in the merchants' pockets.

Shannari ran through her options again and came to the same conclusion. Surely an alliance with Allandor's greatest enemy was worth the risk to herself if it would save the Green Lands. Shivering, she rubbed the nape of her neck. She had the nasty feeling that an invisible axe loomed over her head.

"I despise Stephan," King Valche muttered beneath his breath. "I hate his clingy, sneaky ways, how he always cozies up to Theo, oozing snake oil promises."

"Tell me any other way, Father, and I'll do it."

King Valche sighed heavily and ran a hand through his silvered hair. "We need him, slime or no."

Dressed in Allandor's regalia of midnight blue trimmed in gold braid, he presented the perfect image of control and regal civility. Ruefully, Shannari wondered what image she projected in her leathers and chain mail, sword within easy reach at her side. Her father had begged her to wear a court gown to emphasize her lineage and legitimate claim to the High Throne. Nevertheless, Last Daughter of the Blessed Lady or not, she went nowhere unarmed, even when escorted with a full contingent of guards. She'd learned that lesson at a very young age.

"Let's try polite conversation first and see where we stand

with Stephan," King Valche said. "Maybe he'll surprise us. Maybe he'll take a stand against Theo for once and do what's right."

"No, I'm afraid not. Stephan knows nothing but taking. The only bargaining chip we have is Dalden Bay." Well, that wasn't entirely true. Lightly, she touched the hidden scar on the left side of her chest above her breast. "I'll marry him if I must. Anyone's better than Prince Theo."

A silent warning shrilled in her head and ice chilled her blood. Her heart pounded as adrenaline surged through her. Crippled and stunted her magic might be, but she knew a warning from the Lady when she felt it.

Struggling to maintain a normal demeanor, Shannari looked about them, her hand nonchalantly stroking her sword hilt. While the docks were busy this early in the morning, the main cobblestone street was deserted. The appointed meeting place, the best inn in Dalden Bay, towered above the smaller shops and houses of the villagers on the corner.

Flanked by guards, she couldn't identify a visible threat, but the chill increased. Her teeth chattered and her fingers cramped on the hilt. Danger approached, but from where?

An alley opened up on her right. As they walked past, the shadow of deadly intent raised the hairs on the base of her neck. *If I raise the alarm, the assassin might slip away only to try again. I have to stop him now.*

Choking back a cry, she took another step, waiting, waiting...

Behind her, steel whispered in the crisp dawn air. Shannari whirled and drew the sword. The nearest guard reached for his, too, turning too late. Slipping around him, the assassin rushed the last few steps, closing quickly so she couldn't entirely block his thrusting blade. She fouled his aim and the knife slammed into her right side.

An iron fist of pain exploded in her ribcage. Grunting, she took a quick step back to gain some space. Thank the Lady for chain mail. Swinging the sword in a hard arc, she slit the assassin's throat.

Blinking in shock, the man fell to his knees, his hands wrapped around the gaping wound in his neck. His mouth opened and closed wordlessly and he pitched face first onto the ground.

Eventually, she would fail. A knife would find her back, this time slicing her heart beyond repair, just like her mother. She would never forget the dark pool of blood spreading on the floor, her beautiful mother shattered like a porcelain doll.

*I must wrest the High Throne from Theo soon, before one of his assassins succeeds in killing me.*

King Valche bellowed, his face dark with fury. Shamefaced Guardsmen crowded closer, their swords at the ready. More soldiers raced down the street led by the always reliable Sergeant Fenton. The baker across the way poked his head out the door.

Firm but polite, Sergeant Fenton brought the baker outside his shop. "Do you know this man? Did you see anyone about this morning?"

Shannari pushed the assassin over onto his back with her boot.

The baker recoiled and shook his head, wringing his hands in his apron. "No one, sir, other than the King when he passed right at dawn. I heard the guards about at The Slumbering Lion, but nothing else."

Turning her attention to the body, Shannari dismissed the witness with a nod.

The assassin stared upward with glazed brown eyes. He was perhaps thirty years of age with nondescript features. She didn't recognize him. His brown coat and breeches were clean and cut from quality cloth but not extravagant. His boots were serviceable and scuffed but well made. He wore no jewelry or insignia. Anyone could have sent him.

So many enemies, so much blood on her hands. Her ribs ached and she resisted the urge to hunch over in pain. Wincing, she bent down and wiped her sword and hands on the dead man's coat. At least the blood hadn't splattered her leather pants too badly.

"Are you hurt?" King Valche's voice quivered with rage. "Should we cancel the meeting?"

She stood and sheathed her sword. "We can't wait, Father. We need the Duke now more than ever."

"This attempt could very well be his doing."

"He won't assassinate me before he learns how much we might offer. I'll do whatever is necessary to secure this treaty."

"I wish there was another way." King Valche stared down the street at The Slumbering Lion, his jaw clenched. "I've delayed with every tactic I know. High King Rikard has every right to demand your presence in Shanhasson. If we don't gain enough support, he'll send an army large enough that we'll be forced to accept his terms. Allandor is strong, but could we stand against the entire might of the Green Lands?"

He turned his tired, concerned gaze to Shannari. "I did my best. The betrothal bought us a little time, but I wish I could keep you from bartering away your life and your hand in marriage for a crown, even the Rose Crown of all the Green Lands. Your mother *chose* me and our love instead of the High Throne. I hoped you could have both. I failed you, Daughter, just as I failed to keep her safe."

Years ago, Shannari had almost made the same mistake as her mother. She'd foolishly believed that love's power would make her magic invincible. Instead, she now bore the vicious scar that proved love could never be trusted. "Oh, Father, we haven't failed. Father Aran said Our Blessed Lady will provide a way. We have to believe."

"What I believe is that Theo would rather see you dead than beside him on the High Throne."

The pulse of ice through her veins echoed the assassination warning and confirmed her father's fears. Shannari hardened her voice to steel. "Then Lady help me, I'll see him dead first."

Stephan waited in the inn's private dining room. Sitting across from him at the wooden table laid out for breakfast, Shannari scrutinized the Duke of Pella and Allandor's sworn enemy.

Every inch the nobleman, he was dressed smartly in a dark blue coat and breeches, his hands well manicured, his fingers bearing several expensive but tasteful rings. His dark shoulder-length hair was neatly pulled back in a queue.

Despite his gentlemanly appearance, fierce cunning glinted in his light gray eyes and his mouth reflected a hard slant of cruelty. He didn't rise when she and the King of Allandor came into the room.

His message was clear.

Her palms dampened and she carefully kept her hand near her sword when she sat down at the table. This man was dangerous in ways that Theo would never comprehend. No doubt Stephan had a knife or two hidden on his person, while she'd be forced to clear the table before unsheathing her sword if he attacked. She hated the disadvantage but couldn't bring herself to carry a knife. Not yet. Murderers carried knives, assassins in the streets, shadows in the hallway leaping out to kill her mother. She wasn't quite ready to stoop so low, but with Stephan sitting smugly across from her, she was sorely tempted. "Thank you for agreeing to this meeting, my lord Duke."

Stephan inclined his head slightly. "Princess, Your Majesty."

With such blatant disdain, the situation required a full-on

assault. A quick glance to her father confirmed the change in plan.

No one performed the political waltz as well as King Valche. "You and I have shared many disagreements over the years, Duke, mostly over this very port. In exchange for meeting with us today, I propose to sign Dalden Bay completely over to Pella."

Stephan leaned back in his chair and propped his boot in the chair beside him. He took a long drink from the heavy cup in his hand—his own, of course, for he would never trust anyone enough to allow unknown food or drink to pass his lips —before answering. "You must desire a very great boon from me."

Ignoring the fluttering of nerves in her stomach, Shannari matched his flippant tone. "I desire the High Throne, and I want you to help me."

"Marry the Crown Prince as you agreed two years ago and the High Throne is yours."

"I will rule the Green Lands alone."

A small smile played about his lips. "What you speak of is treason."

Damn him. Her lips compressed, and she fought to keep her calm, political mask. He knew exactly how crucial his country's support would be in her bid for the High Throne. "Treason? When I am the Blessed Lady's Last Daughter; when more royal blood flows in my veins than in those of the Crown Prince Theo?"

"I care nothing about Leesha's Last Daughter or how much of Her blood you might claim."

"What do you care about?" King Valche demanded. "If Shannari's on the High Throne, she'll be a true protector of the lands, not simply a royal brat with too many perversions to count."

"I am loyal to my liege. He has rewarded me richly over the years."

Her laughter wiped the smugness off his face. "Come now, Duke. You and I both know who your true liege is."

Stephan paled. He reached for the cup again and his hand trembled.

She spared a quick glance at her father and he shook his head imperceptibly. Interesting. Where else did Stephan owe allegiance? "Pella and the North Forest have long been allies. With King Challon's support, the entire north would follow."

Stephan's tension eased and his mouth quirked with amusement. "If I present your cause to my great uncle, I'm sure he would seriously consider giving you his support. What you ask is unreasonable, though, without a great deal of protection and assurances. I've been a loyal subject to the royal family and to Crown Prince Theo personally for many years. What can you do for me that the Crown Prince can't?"

Clenching her jaw, Shannari wanted to punch the arrogant smirk off his face. All he cared about was more power, always more power, while people died and their homeland slid a little further into Shadow with each passing day.

She slammed her palms flat on the table and pushed to her feet. "The High Priest publicly refuses to coronate Crown Prince Theo, and Leesha's Temple in Shanhasson is closed. If we sit back and allow Theo to rule the Green Lands, we doom our people to disease, starvation and suffering unlike anything we've ever seen before. How can you—"

A queer look flickered across Stephan's face. "Why Princess Shannari, whatever do you have on your hands?"

Following his gaze, she glanced down. Blood crusted her fingernails and stained the grooves of her knuckles. She shrugged and raised her gaze back to Stephan's. "Someone tried to assassinate me."

His chair scraped on the floor and he rose slowly to his feet, his gaze still locked on her hands.

Cold chills raced down her spine, raising goose bumps on her arms. Dread rolled in her stomach like a cold ball of lead. The Lady's warning screamed through her a hundred times more desperately than before. She felt ill, as disgusted and terrified as when Theo had touched her at their betrothal. She snatched her hands off the table and took a wary step backward.

Stephan raised his gaze to her face and she recoiled. Lust darkened his eyes. "How much blood is on your hands, Shannari? How many men have you killed? I look at your hands and see blood dripping to the floor. An endless ocean of blood, all from you."

She unsheathed her sword and pointed it warningly at his chest. The table's width was suddenly quite inadequate. "Touch me and die."

"I'm yours. Make your offer and Pella will become your closest ally. I'll defy Crown Prince Theo and the High King. I'll bring King Challon to your side. All I ask..."

Panic flooded her heart, racing so hard and fast that black spots floated into her vision. She hated using herself as chattel. She hated arranging her marriage like some stablehand plotting a breeding program for a blooded mare. She hated the thought of living her entire life trapped with a man like Stephan or Theo, cringing each time he touched her. Rubbing her skin raw afterward in a futile attempt to remove his stench and foulness. Hating herself more and more every day.

"Marry me instead of Theo. I'll even kill him for you if you wish, although it will be much more entertaining if you do it yourself." Stephan leaned across the table, the ghastly light from his pale eyes flashing like blades. "And for that, my lovely High Queen, I want to taste the blood on your hands each time you kill."

Horror roared in her ears and she swayed. Shadow threatened to overwhelm her, always waiting for her to stumble, to relax her guard for just a moment. Blood and darkness already stained her soul, but she would never murder for the sole desire for blood.

*Would I? Will all the killing—even in self defense—add up over the years until I'm as corrupt as Theo and Stephan both?*

Her father tugged on her arm, trying to remove her from the room, but all she could do was stare at the hunger on Stephan's face. Stare and wonder if the same foulness would someday twist her soul as well. She tightened her fingers on the sword, adjusting the hilt in her sweaty palm. *I'll kill him before he touches me.*

If she killed him, she would lose everything. King Challon would never support her claim for the High Throne. Even the full might of Allandor's Guard could not stand against Crown Prince Theo if the North Forest and Pella both supported him.

She was good with a sword, but not that good. Eventually, the assassins would succeed. Without enough allies, Allandor would be razed to the ground.

Stephan licked his lips, and she shuddered. Desperation squeezed her throat and lungs so tightly she couldn't breathe.

*There must be some other way. Blessed Lady, help me!*

Sergeant Fenton charged into the room and went to one knee before her. "Captain, Dalden Bay is under attack by the Sha'Kae al'Dan!"

King Valche tightened his grip on her arm and pulled her toward the door. "What, here? The barbarians haven't left their Plains for generations!"

Stephan came around the table toward them. "I brought three hundred of my finest soldiers with me."

Yanking her arm free, Shannari gripped the sword before her with both hands. Stephan didn't carry a sword and his men waited outside. She could eliminate him in one blow. "Get out of the way, Fenton, so I can end this."

The grizzled Sergeant looked into her face and paled. Instead of moving aside as she ordered, he stood and took position before her.

"Shannari, please." Stephan smiled, holding his hands up before him soothingly, well away from the jeweled dagger at his waist. "Accept my troth and I'll drive these barbarians from your land. Then we'll march to Shanhasson and the High Throne will be yours. My life on it."

Fenton drew his sword free, his voice carefully polite. "You will refer to her as Princess Shannari or Our Lady's Daughter."

Stephan sneered. "You call her Captain, do you not? We ridicule the Allandorian Guard for letting a woman lead them."

"She is the finest Captain in the Green Lands. Under her leadership the Guard has never been defeated, yet we've certainly defeated your pitiful excuse for an army numerous times. Remove yourself from Dalden Bay, or I'll personally skewer you and save her the trouble. *My* life on it."

Mocking her with a full court bow, Stephan exited through the opposite door, but tension still screamed through her body. Shannari rolled her shoulders to loosen some of the strain. One enemy retreated but would inevitably regroup with the Crown Prince, while a foreign army advanced on her country.

Waiting until she could no longer hear the Duke's retreat, she turned to Fenton. "How bad is it?"

"Bad, Captain. Two hundred barbarians mounted on massive warhorses. I don't know how long our infantry lines will hold."

"I expected trouble, but not from the south." King Valche rubbed a hand over his weary face. "How many troops did we bring?"

"Five hundred." Sheathing her sword, she headed for the door with Fenton. Ordinarily she would scoff at the odds. Fenton didn't exaggerate the Guard's fame and success. If he was worried, then they faced one hell of a battle. "I want the front line doubled with half our men in reserve behind them."

"Shannari, please, don't lead the Guard today." Shedding his normal regal reserve, King Valche clutched her hand. "If you're killed in battle, the Green Lands are doomed."

Shocked by his plea, in front of witnesses no less, she drew herself up proudly. "You made me Captain, Father. You enabled me to learn and practice strategy and battle techniques all these years. You've never once tried to keep me out of battle. Do you suddenly doubt my ability to protect our homeland?"

King Valche sighed heavily and released her. "I've just been reminded of exactly how twisted our enemies are. You're precious to the Green Lands, but you're my daughter, first. Lady help me, I wish I could spare you from all danger."

Shannari smiled but she feared it was a grim look of expected death and agony. She needed no one to remind her of her responsibilities as the Blessed Lady's Last Daughter, least of all the father who'd drilled her ceaselessly in politics and strategy ever since she could remember. "If Allandor falls to barbarians then all our work over the years is for nothing. I know my duty, Father, perhaps better than you. I'll do what I must."

*No matter the price.*

"Have you ever seen such green grass?"

Shaken to silence, Rhaekhar, Khul of the Nine Camps of the Sha'Kae al'Dan, could only answer his nearest Blood with a nod. Instead of rolling hills of tall golden-brown grass, startlingly brilliant green fields stretched as far as he could see, dotted here and there with squares of rich black earth. As brightly colored as the emerald *memsha* about his hips, the grass must also be flavorful. His warhorse took every opportunity to snatch a muzzle full each time he loosened the reins.

"Even the air smells strange and foreign," Varne continued, a frown creasing his forehead. The other eight Blood fanned out around them. "I hope we don't tarry long in these Green Lands."

To his left, Gregar asked, "Where, Khul?"

"In a dream." Rhaekhar cleared his throat, his mouth dry. He never knew which would be quicker, Gregar's mouth or his blade, so the last thing he expected was solemn reverence on the Blood's face. "I saw bright green grass like this in a vision from Vulkar nearly twenty years ago."

A trick of the sunrise made flames dance in the Blood's dark eyes. "A green valley with a special tree?"

Rhaekhar's heart pounded so loudly that his ears roared with rushing winds. He'd never forgotten the wondrous things he'd seen as a fifteen-year-old lad camping alone in the foothills of Vulkar's Mountain. Details of the dream had faded over the years, but the sense of hope remained with him always. "A tree with a bone-white trunk and leaves both black and red."

The Blood rode closer, his low voice pitched for Rhaekhar's ears alone. "And the lake of fire in the heart of the Mountain?"

Squeezing his eyes shut, he saw again the fiery lake, smoldering black rock, and the Great Wind Stallion wreathed in flames. "Aye."

"What did He give you?"

Glancing again at Gregar's serious face, Rhaekhar hesitated. He'd never told anyone but *Kae'Shaman* about the vision's promise. Besides, it was the Dark Mare, not Vulkar, who had shown him the green fields, shimmering white walls and the garden inside where he would find his own beloved. "A Rose."

The Blood smirked, his eyes flashing as he lightly touched the wicked six-inch knife sheathed on his hip. "All I found was my ivory *rahke*."

"Where is this thing?" Varne demanded.

"I don't know exactly." Truth be told, Rhaekhar had almost despaired of ever finding the Rose. The permanent dwellings lining the bay before them didn't resemble the protective white walls of his dream. "I suspect I shall find the Rose somewhere in these Green Lands."

"I would rather have Gregar's *rahke*." Varne stole a longing glance at the blade on the other Blood's hip. "I shall win it from you yet."

Gregar laughed softly. "I would take the Rose in a heartbeat."

"You speak of a woman?" Varne gave the other Blood a dark look of irritation. Gregar only laughed. "Khul, I don't know who you might find here, but surely you don't expect to take an outlander woman home to the Plains. There's already enough dissent among the Nine Camps. An outlander woman would split the Sha'Kae al'Dan asunder!"

Rhaekhar tightened his grip on the reins, but he couldn't dispute the Blood's words. His enemies were quite vocal in their disapproval of this journey to the Green Lands. Bringing home an outlander mate would be like oil cast on wildfire. "The Great Wind Stallion promised me a love like no other. The Rose of Shanhasson will be my Khul'lanna. I simply must find her first."

Drawing rein, Gregar nodded toward a force amassed against them outside the village. "If the approaching outlanders are any indication, Khul, all you will find at this time is a *kae'don*."

Rhaekhar shaded his eyes to estimate how many outlanders gathered against them. Easily ten fists of men awaited his warriors' charge. "Great Vulkar, they're on foot!"

"There will be no honor in this *kae'don*," Varne muttered gloomily.

Even with their greater numbers, the outlanders had no chance on foot, not against the *na'kindren*. Higher at the withers than the outlanders stood tall, the warhorses would crush them beneath churning hooves until the ground ran red with blood.

"I almost feel sorry for them." Gregar shook his head. "Let us finish this quickly, Khul, so you may find your Rose."

## 2

A *little battle is good for the blood.*

Kneeing his stallion forward, Rhaekhar pressed the ragged line of outlanders even harder. His golden warhorse plunged and another outlander screamed as he disappeared beneath the massive hooves.

The raw, thick scent of blood and death filled the air, and his warriors whooped with pure battle joy. Dodging a wild, desperate thrust, Rhaekhar slipped the point of his sword through the shoulder joint of the closest outlander's metal clothing.

The man dropped his sword and ran, glancing back over his shoulder, only to be trampled from the side by one of the Blood. Gregar's eyes flashed with dark pleasure as he saluted Rhaekhar with his sword.

More outlanders turned and ran, discarding their swords on the field. One man cowered on the ground, his arms over his head, wailing like a lost child. All across the green fields, the outlanders' defenses trembled and shattered in the wake of powerful *na'kindren*.

Disgusted, Rhaekhar shook his head. What honor could his warriors expect to find against these pitifully inferior outlanders? They knew nothing of honor. Killing them was a wasteful blood sacrifice, bringing no glory to the Great Wind Stallion.

Rhaekhar decided to end the battle without further delay and reined Khan toward the outlander leader. Only this man's determination had prevented the outlanders from scattering within moments of battle. Mounted on a small pony, the leader might provide at least some entertainment in this *kae'don*.

Sheathing his sword, Rhaekhar drew the smaller blade on his hip. The outlander deserved at least some honor in death, so he would sacrifice the leader's blood with *rahke* only.

With fiercely bared teeth and punishing hooves, his warhorse shouldered through the panicked outlanders. They parted like silk, giving him a clear path to their leader. Khan reared, screaming a challenge.

The outlander's red pony shied and squealed with terror. Another outlander on foot grabbed the leader's leg and gestured frantically toward the village. Rhaekhar expected the leader to drop his sword and gallop to safety like his men, but he adamantly shook his head. The two outlanders argued briefly, but the one on foot finally nodded. He sheathed his sword, stood aside, and shot a fierce glance at Rhaekhar.

The outlanders' leader raised his sword, his gaze steady. Rhaekhar nodded back respectfully. Good. The leader understood the challenge and accepted. Some small honor might be found in this *kae'don* after all.

The leader leaned forward and the red pony charged.

Anticipation surged in Rhaekhar's veins. Khan laid his ears back and pawed the ground, waiting for the signal to attack, but he held the snorting warhorse in place with a firm hand on the reins.

Stretching out well beyond his defenses to compensate for his inferior mount, the leader swiped at Rhaekhar's chest. He easily leaned aside to avoid the blow. It would be ridiculously easy to slit the leader's throat as he galloped by, but Rhaekhar stayed his hand. He wanted to see exactly how much heart this outlander might have.

Pivoting, Khan struck viciously with both front hooves. The weary pony stumbled and fell to its knees, and the leader flew out of the saddle. Tucking his head, he rolled and thumped across the torn ground. He struggled to his feet and pushed off the metal covering his face.

Rhaekhar's heart raced, and his hands clenched on the reins so hard his stallion reared again. *Great Vulkar, a woman!*

A black braid as thick as his wrist tumbled past her waist. She stared up at him, her dark blue eyes shining with fierce determination. Even defeated, unhorsed and unarmed, she stood before him with more courage than any of her men.

Facing insurmountable odds. Battling his warriors when she had no hope of victory. Challenging him, Khul of all the Nine Camps, with a glint in her eye and pride in her heart.

Such courage—he had never seen her match.

Emotion crashed through him. Bands of iron tightened about his chest until he could barely breathe. His whole body resonated, tuning toward her with vicious, single-minded joy. *At last, I've found my Rose.*

Sucking in a long, deep breath, he sought her scent over the rawness of mud, blood and terror. Too far away to identify her from the remembered dream. Still, heat twisted his gut, muscles tightening, bracing for battle. Surely she was his Rose, but he couldn't know for certain until he stood close enough to breathe her scent.

Twenty mounted men galloped out of the village and slid to a halt behind the woman. She walked toward them, and blinding panic nearly sent him charging after her. How could he claim this outlander woman for his own when he knew nothing of her customs?

The nine Blood rode close, Gregar and Varne on either side of him as usual.

"Will another outlander step forward in challenge?" Varne asked. "Or do you think they've had enough?"

Irrational yet adamant, every instinct urged Rhaekhar to haul her up on Khan's back and gallop for the Plains without delay. "It matters not. For her, I'll fight them all one by one if I must."

"Please, Captain, ride for Rashan," Fenton pleaded. "Let me take your place in the surrender."

Defeated. Under her leadership, the Guard had never lost. Until today.

The morning sun had barely climbed midway into the sky, yet sweat trickled down her spine. Her arms were so tired she feared she wouldn't be able to lift her sword again. All her plans, all the years of careful political maneuverings, for nothing. "You know I can't, Sergeant. I'm responsible for our soldiers. I led them, and I failed them. It's my duty and my right to stand in their place."

"It's your duty to live!" King Valche retorted. "Lady only knows what these barbarians will do to you if you surrender to them. Think, Shannari! Think of the Lady's Green Lands devastated by plagues, war, and famine. You're the Lady's Last Daughter. You must not die!"

"What else can I do?"

"I agree with Fenton. Someone must take your place. You can't do this!"

Fury raged through her, and she clenched her hands into fists. "I will not run! How could I ever sit on the High Throne and demand the full respect of our people if I did such a thing?"

"Sweet Lady above, what if they don't execute you? What if they torture you first? Or rape you? Please, Daughter—"

Her stomach rolled queasily. "They could have slaughtered us to a man without even breaking a sweat. You saw how easily their warlord waltzed through our lines. I was foolish enough to accept his direct challenge, and he toyed with me. He could have killed me at any time, but he acted honorably. Besides, I can't believe Our Blessed Lady would abandon us. Father Aran said She heard my prayers this morning."

"What are you going to do?" King Valche's voice broke with his sorrow. "What can I do?"

"Pray for me. Keep the faith that Our Lady will intervene. Otherwise, I'll do my best to die with honor."

Choking back tears, Shannari turned and walked toward the waiting barbarians. She fought another battle now, to keep her shoulders squared and her chin high. She refused to reveal how much the fearsome barbarians intimidated her. There was nothing she could do to hide her shaking hands.

The barbarians watched her approach with hooded eyes and fierce expressions. All of them were well over six feet tall—giants by Green Land standards. The warlord's implacable face was carved from granite and he gripped a vicious dagger at his waist.

Halting before the warlord, she held her sword as loosely as she dared in her sweaty palm, blade down. She'd never seen such magnificent warriors before, and their horses were equally impressive. She didn't know how to fight massive warhorses that plowed over her infantry. If she lived long enough, she would rectify that deficiency in the Guard's defenses.

The warlord stared back at her, his golden gaze strangely intense. His long brown hair was intricately braided at each temple, heavy with colored beads and rings. The only clothing he wore was a green cloth wrapped about his hips, leaving his legs from mid-thigh completely bare.

His immense chest gleamed like polished bronze in the sunlight, crisscrossed with white scars. In fact, his entire body bore such fine lines, all except his chiseled face. Bands of gold, leather and horsehair encircled his biceps. A broadsword nearly as long as she was tall hung across his back, thankfully sheathed. She would have no hope of deflecting this warrior's blows if and when he decided to kill her.

She stopped as close as she dared, close enough to smell him. A barbarian had no right to smell so divine. No unwashed stench wafted from him, but the mouthwatering smell of baking bread and flowers of all things, combined with the raw, earthy scent of horses, leather and warrior. Swallowing the sudden moisture in her mouth, she tried to think of something to say. What did he expect? An introduction, a confession? "My men..."

"They are free to go."

His low, rough voice thrummed through her body. Trembling, she nodded and the sick knot in the pit of her stomach loosened a bit. Her soldiers would be spared.

"I'm Rhaekhar, Khul of the Nine Camps of the Sha'Kae al'Dan."

The barbarian spoke slowly in her language, heavily accented but understandable. His shoulders were tight, his jaw clenched, his fist locked about the knife on his hip. He looked like he was on the verge of tearing someone apart. Hopefully not her. Worried, Shannari waited silently for the rest of his demands.

"Do you yield to me?"

She nodded, barely daring to breathe. Her father and Fenton stepped up on either side to face the Khul with her. Grateful for their moral support, she prayed they didn't interfere with the inevitable sentencing. "What are your surrender terms?"

"One fist of my warriors will remain in this village to prevent further outlander encroachment on our Plains."

Keeping her features smooth, Shannari resisted the urge to

turn and question her father. The Madre Desert served as a forbidding barrier to the huge fields of grass that lay beyond the burning sands. To her knowledge, Allandor never intruded on the Plains.

"Agreed," King Valche answered.

The barbarian's attention whipped to her father. "Who is this man? Why does he agree to the terms your Camp must accept?"

"I'm King Valche of Allandor, and this is my daughter, Shannari dal'Dainari. She's Captain of the Guard, Princess of Allandor and Our Blessed Lady's Last Daughter. Someday she will rule all the Green Lands as High Queen."

Heat blaze across her cheeks. Standing defeated before the mighty warriors, she struggled not to drop her gaze to the ground. The litany of titles was embarrassing, especially when she'd lost the battle, but he hoped to sway the barbarian toward ransom instead of execution.

The big Khul stepped closer to her, golden eyes blazing like the sun. He seized her chin in strong fingers, tilting her face upward. "Do they also call you the Rose of Shanhasson?"

The simple caress of his fingers on her face exploded through her starved body. Belatedly, she regretted her refusal to take another lover after Devin had died.

Too late, she tried to jerk her head free, but he merely tightened his grip. She raised her sword, but he casually knocked her blade aside with his forearm, never looking away from her face.

In a husky whisper, he repeated, "Are you the Rose of Shanhasson?"

"No!"

Leaning down until his mouth hovered above hers, he breathed deeply. Tilting her head slightly, he sniffed at her neck. His long hair trailed across her face, sweet hay and flowers.

"I know your scent, Shannari. Vulkar help me, I recognize you. You are the Rose I seek."

So close, so tempting, his scent and words and threats. Breathing shallowly to avoid his alluring scent, she brought the sword up between their bodies and pushed the flat of the blade against his chest.

He didn't budge.

"You must be mistaken, Khul Rhaekhar. I've never been called the Rose of Shanhasson. In fact, I've only been to Shanhasson once in my entire life."

Closing his eyes, the barbarian breathed deeply, still close enough to kiss. A smile suddenly broke the guarded expression on his face. The transformation from formidable warlord to seductive danger stole her breath. Full lips curved, baring strong, white teeth which softened the hard planes of his face. "You recognize me, too, or at least your body does."

Her pulse raced, her heart thudded, and a hot coil of desire tightened deep in her stomach. Her body remembered the touch and weight of a man in her bed, and it yearned for this man, this barbarian. Fiercely. *How does he know?*

Clenching her teeth with determination, she slid the sword up his body, deliberately digging the point into his neck. "I have no idea of what you speak."

Ignoring the deadly weapon at his throat, he smiled and pressed closer. Blood dripped down his bronzed chest. His scent intensified, flooding her senses. His thigh brushed hers, his arm slipped around her waist, and it was all she could do to keep from falling wholeheartedly into the barbarian's embrace.

Warningly, she said, "I will kill you."

"Wait!" Father Aran pushed his way through the Guardsmen. "She is the Rose of Shanhasson!"

Bewildered, she turned her head toward the High Priest. The barbarian released her. "How could you?"

Father Aran knelt before her and took her right hand, kissing the knuckles. "Princess Shannari belongs in Shanhasson with the

Rose Crown of Leesha on her head. As Our Lady's Last Daughter, she is truly the Rose of Shanhasson."

"You are mine, then, *na'lanna*. You will come with me without delay."

Terror and dismay roiled in her mixed with betrayal. She stared into the High Priest's face as tears trickled down her cheeks.

What would become of Allandor and her people if she left them to Theo's merciless care? What of the darkness Father Aran prophesied for the Green Lands if she failed? Carried off by barbarians to the ends of the earth, she would never be able to wrest the High Throne from Theo. "What have you done?"

Father Aran pressed the back of her hand against his forehead and then stood, his face lined with guilt and sympathy. "Forgive me, Your Majesty, but the way has been provided."

"I don't understand," she whispered, brushing the tears away impatiently. "How—"

The High Priest turned to the barbarian and raised her hand to him. Wrapping his large, calloused palm around her fist, still gripping the sword stained with his blood, Rhaekhar kissed her knuckles, too. She shuddered, swallowing the moan that threatened to escape.

"Will you let me claim you here and now?"

From the heated thickness in his voice, she dreaded asking for an explanation. "Claim?"

"Gregar, what is the proper word?"

"Marry, wed, consummate, pleasure, mate, copulate, tup," the dark-haired warrior replied with a wicked smile of delight.

Her eyes widened at the progressively coarser descriptions of intimate activities. She jerked her hand free and stepped backward, giving herself room to fight. "Absolutely not!"

"This is an outrage!" Usually the calmest head during the most heated negotiation, King Valche was so angry that a vein thumped on his forehead. He glared at Father Aran. "Our own High Priest hands my daughter over like common chattel to a barbarian, who then demands she wed him on the spot! Are you forgetting the betrothal ceremony in which you promised her hand in marriage to the Crown Prince?"

Rhaekhar shrugged. "The man is not here to protect what is his. I'm warrior enough to take what I want and keep it. If this Crown Prince wants to challenge me, let him come."

"Do you want the might of the Green Lands marching into your Sea of Grass?" King Valche retorted. "If you take the Lady's Last Daughter into your Plains, the Crown Prince won't challenge you. He'll send his armies to murder her!"

The barbarian's face darkened and he gripped the knife at his waist. "Anyone who attempts to harm her will suffer my wrath."

"Silence!" Shannari raised her voice, her head thumping with alarm and their shouts. "Arguing is pointless. Our Lady's will—"

King Valche broke in. "How can you trust the High Priest after he handed you over to the enemy? He could be lying! What if he's secretly trying to eliminate you as a threat to Theo?"

"Impossible," Father Aran retorted. "May the Lady strike me down if I lie!"

"It doesn't matter." Numbness filled her, for which she was truly grateful. So much arguing and political posturing left her feeling empty and sick. "I'm tired of being moved on the board like a pawn."

She looked into the barbarian's ruggedly handsome face and sorrow pierced what was left of her crippled heart. She would never be free, never marry for love nor bear children without plotting to secure a throne and ensure the continuance of a dying royal line. He still dreamed that happiness, while she was surrounded by death. "While I appreciate your proposal, Khul Rhaekhar, I must decline. Although few nobles recall the truth of the legends, I must rule as High Queen or the Green Lands will fall into darkness. It's my destiny and my duty. I can't come with you."

Rhaekhar's voice echoed with silky menace. "As leader of these outlanders, you yielded to me."

More barbarians fanned out behind and around him. Steel rang as swords were drawn. Cries echoed behind her from the Guardsmen. King Valche cursed and whipped out his own purely ceremonial sword.

Fear tightened her stomach and she shifted the hilt against her palm, her fingers cold and tingling. Her gaze darted from the big Khul to his guards, the massive warriors behind him, and back to his implacable face.

Nothing she did could save her father and her soldiers. Either she accepted the barbarian's demands and left her people to die at Theo's whim, or she died now with a sword in her hand. Either way, Shadow would swallow the Lady's Green and Beautiful Lands. *What else can I do?* "Execute me, Khul, and leave my soldiers alone."

"I don't want your death. I want you. If you won't come with me willingly, then I'll take you by force."

"Please, Your Majesty," Father Aran said. "Don't make this any more difficult than necessary!"

"Difficult?" Shannari bit off the word. "You truly expect me to go meekly to some foreign land, leaving my country and my throne for which I've fought my entire life?"

"It doesn't have to be this way." The High Priest's tears startled her. "I didn't See suffering or unhappiness, or I never would have given your hand to him. I See only love."

Phantom pain blazed over her scarred heart. She laughed bitterly. "And you didn't See suffering?"

"Love is the greatest gift of all," Rhaekhar said, his manner carefully unthreatening.

"I know what love is, Khul. It's simply another way for the Gods to torment us. I will sooner kill you than love you."

"You are welcome to try."

The smug, condescending look on his face pushed her over the edge. Fury raged to life, blazing away the numbing fear holding her captive. With a roar, she swung the sword at his head.

## 3

Teeth bared, she swung the sword directly at Rhaekhar's head with enough force to slice him nigh in half. Gliding in front of him, Varne unsheathed his *rahke*, while Gregar caught her sword on his ivory blade and swung her blow wide.

Rhaekhar didn't even flinch. The Blood would die before allowing another to draw his blood. Unless he wished it, of course.

Gregar laughed. "Khul, I believe she wishes to challenge you once more."

She straightened her shoulders and lifted her chin, staring Rhaekhar in the eye. Beneath her courageous demeanor, though, her scent trembled and tears glittered in her eyes. Despite her proud, confident stance, she was as fragile as delicate hand-blown glass. One wrong move might shatter her into a million irretrievable pieces.

She'd had her fill of entreaties and arguing. Perhaps some

physical action would put her more at ease with him. "Aye, I accept her challenge. I shall demand a kiss this time."

Her gaze dropped to his mouth and her lush scent ripened, heating with physical attraction. Surging desire blazed through his body and joy swept away his concern. She desired him. She couldn't hide such a thing from him, not when she was *na'lanna*.

"No kissing!"

"Then you must win this challenge. Let us come to an agreement on terms. I shall lead my warriors back to the Plains empty handed if you draw my blood first. Otherwise, you will come with me this very day of your own accord, but I shall not make love to you until you ask."

She made a rude noise that did Gregar justice. The aforementioned Blood grinned with approval. "You'll wait a very long time then."

Rhaekhar gave her a deliberately smoldering smile. "If I disarm you, I win a kiss. Agreed?"

"And if I defeat you?"

"You may kill me if you so desire."

"What about them?" Shannari inclined her head toward the Blood. "I don't believe they'll simply let me walk away after I cut out your heart."

This time Gregar snorted. "You're welcome to try."

"You're next," she retorted.

The trickster Blood grinned, his dark eyes dancing with mischief.

Groaning, Rhaekhar shook his head. She had no idea what would happen if she made a direct challenge to the Blood, especially Gregar.

"Khul, may I ask for a kiss as well?"

Shannari spluttered, and this time even Varne laughed out loud.

Great Vulkar, she was beautiful. Her brilliant eyes sparkled like jewels, her color high and full of fire. Rhaekhar decided he would rile her as often as possible. "I'm the only warrior who will be kissed this day."

"Only if you win." She pointed her sword at Gregar. "Back off."

The Blood took a step closer, pressing the sword tip into his body. Her jaw tightened with determination and she pushed a little harder, puncturing his chest. Smiling with anticipation, Gregar pushed back. A little closer, a little more steel pressing into his body.

She shifted her grip on the hilt, fully prepared to skewer him. A coldness settled on her features that told Rhaekhar she'd killed before and often. Very impressive. He liked a hint of danger in a woman.

Evidently, so did Gregar. "Go ahead," he taunted, his low voice echoing with amusement and his trademark wickedness. Shannari shivered and her eyes widened. "Run me through. I shall greatly enjoy it."

Her gaze flickered to the smaller wound she dealt to Rhaekhar's neck earlier. "Are you all crazy?"

"Gregar is... special. He used to be a Death Rider." At the blank look on her face, Rhaekhar added, "An assassin. Death Riders delight in sacrificing blood to the Great Wind Stallion. Blood sacrifice is a very great honor among us."

She jerked her sword away. Gregar wiped his hand across his chest and licked the blood from his fingers. "Would you like a taste?"

A turbulent rush of unease flooded the fledgling *na'lanna* bond. "Blessed Lady!"

"Let the challenge begin," Rhaekhar said hurriedly. Pale and trembling, she looked like she might bolt. He slipped his sheathed sword over his head, handed the weapon to Varne for safekeeping, and unsheathed his *rahke*.

"Is that your choice of weapons?" Shannari asked doubtfully. "A knife against my sword?"

"Aye. Are you ready?"

She spared a wary glance at the Blood. Laughing, Gregar held up his hands and backed away to join Varne several paces behind Rhaekhar. Her people backed away as well, forming a makeshift ring for their challenge.

She took a deep, calming breath and closed her eyes.

Goose bumps raced down Rhaekhar's arms as if he'd jumped headfirst into icy water. When she opened her eyes, he swore they were changed, luminescent, like the full moon on the Silver Lake at the foot of Vulkar's Mountain.

She advanced and he had no time to contemplate further. Curious to see exactly how much skill she possessed, he made no attempt to disarm her. She swung the sword in a measured, controlled attack, carefully offensive without leaving herself vulnerable. He met each stroke as gently as possible, sparing her the full brunt of his considerable strength.

Her mouth tightened and she shot him a glare of indignation. She possessed a warrior's sense of honor, which he had just gravely insulted. At his unapologetic shrug, she quickened her attack, forcing him to step lively a few times to avoid her sword.

Well pleased with her skill, he grinned widely. He didn't know a single Sha'Kae al'Dan woman who would raise a sword against a warrior, let alone hold her own.

She fought him fearlessly, but the effort cost her, especially after the earlier *kae'don*. Sweat streaked her face and she breathed heavily. Her strokes slowed and her arm trembled each time he countered her less graceful swings.

He pressed her, trying to sneak his *rahke* beneath her defenses. A little blood must be shed to honor her courage. She blocked his first strike, grunting with effort, and stumbled sideways. Slipping his *rahke* above her drooping sword, he tenderly placed a shallow cut at the base of her neck.

She leaped backward and touched a finger to the wound. Blood smeared her skin, mesmerizing him. For a moment, he was a lad once more, standing in the heart of the Mountain over a lake of fire.

*Draped in shadows, a single Rose dripped blood onto a stone floor.*

Her scent filled his heart, a rich complex aroma of sultry summer nights and spicy sweet flowers. His mouth watered and he longed to seal their *na'lanna* bond, binding her to him forever.

Burning pain dissolved the vision. He shifted sideways, and her sword slid across his abdomen, leaving a shallow, long cut instead of spilling his intestines. His heart sang with pride. What a strong, proud warrior woman he had found. She would kill him, taking advantage of his momentary weakness to eliminate her sworn enemy without hesitation or guilt.

Turning to keep him fully in her sights, she stared at the wound she'd given him. Ashen, she opened her mouth as if she might apologize and then shook her head. Perhaps she wouldn't kill him without guilt after all. The thought gave him hope that she could come to love him despite their differences.

Renewing her determination, she tightened her grip on the sword and shifted to a defensive stance. Without warning, he charged toward her. She whirled to avoid his attack. Instead of striking with his *rahke*, he grabbed her from behind. Knocking the sword out of her hand, he wrapped his arm around her neck and hauled her tight against him.

Wild with terror, she clawed at his forearm about her throat. He lifted her off her feet in an effort to calm her struggles. Flailing, she let loose a piercing wail of mindless panic that sliced his heart in two.

He could not bear such fear in her. "Peace, *na'lanna*. I would rather cut off my right hand than harm you."

Her chest heaving, she gulped for air. "Release me!"

"Do you concede this challenge?"

Calmer now, she tested his grip, squirming against him to see if she could break free.

He felt the wild tumult in her heart as his own. Great Vulkar, she inflamed him. Pressing his mouth to her ear, he whispered, "You are mine, Shannari dal'Dainari, Rose of Shanhasson. You can't deny me."

Tension drained out of her and her shoulders slumped. "You won. Again."

Sliding his mouth down the graceful column of her neck, he grazed her with his teeth. "Aye."

She jumped as if he'd bitten a chunk out of her, and her scent smoked hotter.

Chuckling, he released her. "I'm prepared to accept my first winning from this challenge."

"A kiss," she muttered darkly. Dropping her gaze to her bloody sword on the ground, she heaved a huge sigh. "Let's get it over with."

Despite her words, the pulse leapt in her throat and desire trembled through her scent. Suppressing his amusement, Rhaekhar cupped her cheek and tilted her face up to his.

Reluctant and mulish, she tried to hide the quiver of her chin and failed miserably.

"You have no wish to kiss me?" Closing her eyes, she tried to turn her head, but he held her steady. "No hiding, na'lanna."

She scowled at him. "What does that mean anyway?"

Lowering his mouth toward hers, he breathed the words against her lips. "My beloved."

Averting her mouth as much as he would allow, she closed her eyes, her jaw clenching. "You have no right to call me some foolish endearment. You don't know me. You certainly don't know what I'm capable of."

"Do you not feel it, Shannari?" He brushed his mouth against her straining jaw and she flinched. Fisting a hand around her thick braid, he gently tugged her head backward to bare her throat. "Do you not hear my heart whispering to yours?"

He swept his tongue across the small cut. The taste of her sweet blood hit him like a *na'kindre* kick in the stomach. Drumming hooves thundered in his head, and his ears roared with rushing wind. Her blood slid down his throat, blazing a path of fire through his body.

Sagging in his arms, she whimpered. Horrified, he realized he had smashed her against him with his mouth locked on her throat hard enough he would likely leave teeth marks in her skin. Breathing hard, he concentrated on regaining control.

Great Vulkar, what had he done? She wouldn't understand how tempting her blood was to him. Such a raw, base hunger very likely re-affirmed her belief that he was only a barbarian. A violent savage who thirsted for blood and ravaged her with no thought of her pleasure.

She made another low, ragged sound, shredding his heart with regret. He eased the punishing grip on her shoulders, laved the small wound once more with his tongue to ease the sting of his teeth, and slowly lifted his head.

Shannari seized handfuls of his hair and dragged his mouth down to hers.

Silken lips opened immediately, inviting her entrance. His hair, softer and finer than any man's had a right to be, caressed her face. Smoky and smooth, his taste rolled on her tongue. And she drank him down as though she died of thirst.

Had kissing always been this explosive? This dangerous?

Sucking her bottom lip into his mouth, he raked his teeth

back and forth. Blessed Lady, the man knew how to use his teeth. The blood on her neck... and the rich, inviting scent of his blood...

Shame flooded her, souring her stomach and plunging a knife in her heart.

She shoved Rhaekhar in the chest and twisted from his grasp. Panting, she closed her eyes a moment. Control. She had to stay in control lest she become a monster as dark and perverted as Stephan. Or Theo.

"Shannari, what is it?"

She kept her back to him, struggling to smooth the longing and shame from her features. "I'm sorry, Khul Rhaekhar. I forgot myself."

"Then I shall pray you forget again very soon."

When he'd held her pressed to him, she'd felt exactly how much he'd enjoyed her kiss. He wanted her as badly as she wanted him. Fire coursed through her body, weakening her knees all over again. Weakening her resolve. Kissing would eventually lead to other more dangerous activities. Blessed Lady above, how could she resist his advances if she left with him as he demanded?

"The first portion of my challenge bet has been most adequately satisfied."

She didn't respond to his lighter tone, for she knew very well what he was about. His easy jesting had worked earlier to distract her, but it wouldn't help him now. Not with this.

Taking her hand, he tugged her around to face him. She met his gaze briefly, but didn't dare let him see too deeply. She dropped her gaze to his chest, tracing the trail of blood down from the small cut on his neck to the ugly jagged wound on his side. Still bleeding freely, the wound filled the air with the thick, metallic bite of blood, enhancing the scent of sweet hay, horses, and wildflowers.

Swallowing hard, she averted her gaze to the ground. So much blood. So much temptation. Her sword lay discarded at her feet. She picked it up, grateful for the distraction of cleaning the weapon.

"I feared I'd made a grave error, *na'lanna*." He spoke softly enough she doubted her father, still arguing with the High Priest, heard him. "Forgive me for tasting your blood so quickly without explaining my people's ways. As I said, blood sacrifice is a very great honor among us."

Her heart pounded harder. Torn between hope and shame, she couldn't meet his gaze. If he looked at her the same way as Stephan had, she would hate herself even more. "My people consider tasting blood an abomination."

"To me, it is a thing of great honor to be enjoyed and treasured. Tasting your blood was not a thing of darkness." He hesitated and touched her arm lightly. "You—"

She turned away, trying to decide how much to admit. Perhaps it would be best to scare him away now. If he knew how honor could be tarnished, how she would inevitably corrupt him, how love could be used to destroy, then perhaps he would leave her in Allandor without a backward glance.

"Shannari, you may trust me with your life."

The fool believed in love. Of course he believed in trust as well. The two weaknesses went hand in hand.

Facing him, she looked him squarely in the eye and let all the dead coldness in her heart reflect in her gaze. "This morning, someone tried to assassinate me. I killed him and then met with another man, my country's closest enemy, to form an alliance. I would have married him despite my hatred in order to secure the alliance for my country. Instead, this man asked to taste the blood on my hands."

Stiffening, the barbarian wiped all expression from his face. "Who have you shared blood with?"

The remembered lust on Stephan's face made her stomach heave. She swallowed the rising bile back down. "No one. He disgusted me."

Rhaekhar flinched as if she'd buried her sword in his stomach.

Her poor scarred heart ached, surprising her. She didn't know him well enough to regret his loss, but Leesha forgive her, she couldn't let him think she felt the same way about him. "You do not."

Relief eased his stony expression and he took a step toward her. Immediately, she backpedaled out of his reach.

*He deserves to know the truth.*

The wall locking away that old, shameful memory quivered, threatening to splinter away and leave her drowning in an endless sea of regret and humiliation. Forcing the words out, she whispered, "I'm afraid you will be disgusted by me."

He stared at her silently as if he weighed and measured her heart. What was he thinking?

The argument between King Valche and Father Aran had escalated to the point of shouts and threats. Rhaekhar glared at them and then at the handful of other barbarians who never seemed to let him out of their sight. "Can you not quiet them so I might have this discussion in peace?"

A hopeful smile brightened the dark-headed barbarian's face. "Permanently?"

"Nay," Rhaekhar snapped. "Great Vulkar, what else do they require before we can return to the Plains?"

Barely daring to breathe for fear of bursting into tears, Shannari wasn't sure if he spoke to her or not. Had she succeeded?

"You!"

Both arguing men jumped and turned their attention to the irate barbarian. Rhaekhar seized her hand in a punishing grip and marched her over to the King's party. "What else do you want?"

Always the consummate tactician, King Valche's mouth fell open with shock.

"Well? I wish to retire without delay. We return to the Plains at first light on the morrow."

King Valche's gaze flickered back and forth between her and the barbarian. "You— you're not invading Allandor?"

"Great Vulkar, what would I do with your Green Lands?"

"But you defeated us! We surrendered! Don't you want anything else?"

Rhaekhar headed toward the main street of Dalden Bay, dragging her along. "This village is mine. The Rose of Shanhasson is mine. I have all that I want."

She was too stunned to argue or protest. If the blazing heat in his eyes was any indication, she'd failed to scare him off. In fact, she'd accomplished the opposite. Inwardly groaning, she tried not to think about what the barbarian might wish to do in privacy.

"Shannari!"

She glanced back over her shoulder at her stricken father. "Promote Fenton to Captain and send him with a few hundred troops to make sure the Duke and his soldiers leave Allandor without trouble."

"But—" King Valche ran his hand through his hair. "What am I going to do without you? There must be a way we can prevent this travesty!"

"Our Blessed Lady hears your prayers, Your Majesty." Frail and shrunken, Father Aran had aged twenty years since dawn. "Never doubt Her hand in your life. I know you don't understand, but remember this. Sometimes She washes our eyes with tears so we may See Her truth."

The High Priest walked away, leaving her father alone in the street, lost and forlorn. "What can I do to help you?"

She made a low sound of anguish. Her father, her country, her people. She couldn't bear abandoning them.

Rhaekhar drew her against his side. "Shannari is my concern now. You may tell her goodbye on the morrow."

Defeated, she contemplated her options. The barbarian was unlike any man she'd ever known before. She threatened him and he laughed. She defied him and he let her try to gut him. He apologized for offending her and she nearly devoured him. He apparently enjoyed the corruption she tried so hard to suppress. The worst mockery though, was that he truly believed in love.

My beloved.

The knife in her heart twisted deeper.

*It would be so much easier if he simply killed me as I deserve.*

"How does a June wedding sound to you, Theo?" High King Rikard asked, his ancient voice a dry rasp that set the younger man's teeth on edge.

Crown Prince Theo dan'Regis dan'Rikard glared at the doddering old man. Dry and leathery, his skin had sagged into wrinkles and pockets of flesh. Dark brown age spots splotched his shaved head, completely bald except for the royal lock at the base of his skull. Yellowed with age, the lanky rope curled into a disgusting pile on the throne beside him.

*Theo's* throne, not this thin, withered, incompetent old man who should have died years ago. "Are you finally demanding the bitch show up for our wedding as she promised two years ago?"

High King Rikard cackled. "Ah, youth is wasted on the young. You have no idea what to do with a woman like her. If I were even twenty years younger, I would wed her myself."

"She's an arrogant whore, and I refuse to share the High Throne with her."

"Then you'll not have my throne at all." The old man's voice sharpened, his pale eyes gleaming. Rikard's body might be infirm, but his mind was as sharp and twisted as ever. "We've been through this, Theo. You'll marry Shannari or I'll name her my sole heir."

Rage pulsed through Theo, dark and icy hot. "Why must I marry her? I'm your grandson! I've done everything you asked."

"As well as dozens of vile things behind my back that would turn all of the Green Lands against you like a pack of starving wolves."

Theo gritted his teeth but remained silent. His grandfather might pretend outrage, but the old man had his own dark pleasures. He might be too decrepit to sneak down into the prison cells, but that didn't stop him from having the guards bring certain young prisoners to the secret room in his private quarters.

"You need her, boy. Valche's an incredible strategist and he's taught her everything he knows. If she's not legally bound to you, some noble will always be willing to turn on you for her hand. The Rose Crown is a heady lure, and it's hers by law. No one but a Daughter can wear the Rose Crown and live."

The endless talking and postulating on this and that alliance made him want to scream. Once the High Throne was his—as his rightful due—he would ensure the high and mighty princess met a most suitable end.

With her gleaming, flawless skin and luscious body, she was made for a man's pleasure. He might despise her, but he couldn't deny the near violent desire he felt for her.

The things he would do to her...

He wanted to own her, debase her, ruin her in every way possible.

Rikard cackled again. "I see you like the thought immensely."

Theo made no effort to conceal the bulge in his breeches. "Who knows, she might like my dungeon room. Some women do."

"If she's anything like her mother, she'll run as fast and far as she can. More's the pity."

"Then why are you talking about a wedding again?"

"Our very good friend in Pella has agreed to approach her and Valche with my latest threats. They met in Dalden Bay sometime this morning. I expect confirmation from Stephan very, very soon."

Theo wanted to wail and kick someone into a bloody pulp. Stephan was his most trusted confidante. Why had he made a secret arrangement with the High King and not told him? He was supposed to be working on a way for Theo to eliminate the old fool without causing any repercussions.

"A messenger, Your Majesty." The Lion Guard at the door let in a travel-stained man who hurried down the red-carpeted aisle and dropped to his knees before the dais.

"Your Majesty, I have urgent news from Dalden Bay."

Rikard took the sealed parchment, his beady eyes flitting over the words. "Leesha's tits!"

Smiling with nasty glee, Theo very nearly laughed out loud. The arrogant princess and her father must have rejected his grandfather yet again. The only way they were going to get Shannari out of Allandor was to invade, just as Stephan kept telling him.

Rikard pounded his bony thigh with a fist. "After nearly two hundred years, the barbarians come out of the Plains and ruin everything! The Sha'Kae al'Dan defeated the Allandor Guard this morning. Shannari herself surrendered to them! According to Stephan, the barbarian warlord was very taken with her. He's carrying her off to the Plains first thing in the morning."

"Good riddance."

"Are you a Leesha-damned fool? If Shannari's not married to you, she'd best be dead."

Biting back a petulant response at the tone of his grandfather's voice, Theo took the parchment and scanned the Duke's brief missive. "What does it matter? This way, she's out of the picture. She can't stir up the nobles, and she certainly can't make a bid for the High Throne."

Rikard rubbed his eyes wearily. "I sometimes despair of ever teaching you anything. The first thing that warlord is going to do is rape her. She's an attractive young woman, certainly finer than anything a barbarian has ever seen, with enough fire to fight him tooth and nail. He'll use her again and again and again, until he tires of her or breaks her spirit."

Theo reached over his shoulder and pulled his royal lock in front of him. He absently tugged on the thick shank of hair. Shannari was *his* to ruin, *his* to break. Now, some barbarian would spoil her before he ever had a chance.

He jerked harder, letting the fury build inside him. His hands trembled and he snarled under his breath.

Rikard's breathing became shallow and difficult. "We can't risk a pregnancy outside of the bloodline. Surely you understand."

Maybe the old man would keel over right here. "What are you going to do?"

"We were so close." Rikard sighed, shaking his head regretfully. "Now we have no choice. Shannari dal'Dainari must die."

## 4

J erking awake, Shannari automatically reached for the sword beside her on the bed. The familiar leather sheath calmed her enough to allow her to recall her surroundings.

After the battle, surrender, and subsequent challenge, the barbarian had dragged her away only to pause in the middle of the street, confused by the sights and sounds of the village. Not willing to sleep on the ground when a bed was available, she'd brought him to The Slumbering Lion and ordered a bath and food. As soon as the hot water arrived, he'd left her to her privacy. Clean and relaxed from the bath, she'd lain down on the bed, intending to rest just a moment, but the previous night's long vigil had taken its toll after so much fighting.

The darkened room indicated she must have slept for hours. A low fire and candles on the table gave a soft, comforting glow to the simple room.

Water sloshed. Naked, the barbarian stood washing himself beside the copper tub. Thick slabs of muscle banded his back and waist. Damp hair slicked midway down his back. His buttocks were firm and round, his thighs columned granite. He raised an arm to wash beneath, drawing her gaze up broad shoulder, bulging biceps, corded forearm to his large warrior hand, fingers curled against his palm.

For such a massive, powerful man, he moved with a predatory grace that stole her breath. Heat flared between her legs, every muscle tightening. Her hands itched to explore that muscular body to see if his skin was as soft as it looked.

Averting her gaze from temptation, she noted the two other barbarians always close to Rhaekhar. Silent and unobtrusive, they sat on the floor against the wall near the door. The darker-headed barbarian flashed a smile at her but said nothing.

"There's food on the table."

Startled, she glanced back at Rhaekhar. He continued his bath, his back to her. Her stomach growled loudly, gnawing with hunger. When was the last time she'd eaten?

The covered platters on the table beckoned. Steam rose invitingly from the mugs. She edged toward the side of the bed, the sword still in her hand. Would he let her remain armed in his presence? She certainly wouldn't if she were the victor.

Hesitating, she wished she were dressed more satisfactorily. A clean linen shirt and pantalettes were as far as she'd dressed before weariness had swept her away. He likely wouldn't let her keep her clothing for long anyway. The heat in his gaze was as unmistakable as the bulge when he'd kissed her earlier.

Her heart pounded heavily. Trembling, she squeezed her thighs together, trying to still the growing fire. She couldn't pretend disinterest in him, not when everything about him attracted her. Perhaps a quick, hard session with him would ease this insane attraction.

He picked up a towel, its size thoroughly inadequate for his large body. Still with his back to her, he bent at the waist and dried his legs. "Did you sleep well?"

Awed, she stared at his ass, her mouth falling open. Dear sweet Lady above, why did she keep looking at him? She wasn't made of iron. In fact, she felt like a puddle of melted butter.

The smart-mouthed guard snickered under his breath. Embarrassed, she jerked her gaze away from the tantalizing view. Determined to continue her charade of indifference, she slipped out of bed and walked to the table with as much grace and arrogance as she could muster. Not another peep came from the shadows.

The steaming cup's aroma confirmed her hopes. She sat down and drew the mug to her, cuddling the warm stoneware in her hands. Thank the Lady, somebody in the kitchens remembered her love for caffe. She would reward them with a queen's ransom if she ever returned here alive and free.

Rhaekhar padded about the room, she supposed still nude, so she concentrated intently on the lovely hot brew in her cup and a thick slice of nutty brown bread she ate so quickly she hardly tasted it. Lady, she was hungry. Cheese and meat on another slice barely made a dent in her appetite.

Considering the small amount of food left, she hesitated. The barbarian might not have eaten yet.

He came up behind her and touched her shoulder. "Go ahead, Shannari. I ate while you slept."

Panic closed her throat. She stiffened, half drawing the sword free. Why must he continue threatening her from her blind spot?

The barbarian did nothing further to alarm her. His touch was casual, not intimate. "I can feel your hunger, na'lanna. Eat your fill."

Re-sheathing the sword, she left it in her lap and helped herself to another slice of bread. "How is that possible?"

He didn't answer her question as he touched her braid. "Your hair is still damp."

She shrugged, making her way through another stack of meat and cheese. Her hair was long, and thick enough that it took forever to dry.

He untied the end of the braid and began unraveling it. She froze, her mouth full.

"Come sit before the fire to dry your hair."

She swallowed the food in a gulp and reached for her drink to wash it down. "It's much too long to leave loose. It will tangle into an utter mess."

Picking up her mug, he walked over to the glowing coals in the fireplace. "I shall brush it for you. Come."

She followed, watching him warily. At least he was dressed, if the cloth about his hips could be called clothing. It was entirely too small in her opinion, especially now that she'd had a glimpse of what hid beneath.

He sat on the thick woolen rug before the fire. When she hesitated, he reached up and took her hand, drawing her down in front of him. She couldn't bear sitting there with her back to him, a possible threat no matter how carefully he pretended otherwise, so she turned sideways as she sat.

"You don't need a sword to protect yourself from me."

She hadn't even realized she'd brought it with her. "My mother was killed by an assassin when I was only three. I've carried some kind of weapon ever since."

"Even to sleep?"

"Most especially to sleep." Rage and hurt made her voice shrill. She lightened her tone. "Assassins prefer to strike when you're least prepared and the most vulnerable."

He returned to his work, gently unraveling her hair from the braid. It took him a while. Never cut her entire life, her hair reached the back of her thighs when loose. He worked silently, his fingers firm, his manner unthreatening. She relaxed enough to sip from her mug.

Spreading her hair out like a cloak about her shoulders, he picked up the brush. He started at the ends with small strokes, moving to longer, more sure strokes when her hair was free of tangles. Smoothing his free hand through her hair with each stroke, not once did he jerk her head. She should pray her maid learned the same technique.

"I suppose you don't have Blood here to guard you."

What an interesting name for guards. "Oh, I've grown up with guards all around me. But none ever come into my room where I sleep. They certainly can't keep someone from poisoning my drink."

She didn't turn her head, but she sensed his sudden intensity. His fingers closed about hers on the cup and he lifted the drink to his mouth. He sniffed it suspiciously. "It certainly smells vile."

She drew her mug free and held it closer to her chest protectively. "Caffe is my favorite drink."

"If you say so." He continued brushing her hair. "The Blood are more than my guards. They swore their lives to me. If you were to unsheathe your sword in a threatening manner, one of them would reach you and prevent you from harming me. If he couldn't disarm you, he would put his body in the way of your sword. He would die if need be to keep me safe."

Scoffing, she shook her head and set the mug aside to lay her hand on the sword hilt. The two Blood still sat on the opposite side of the room. She could plunge the sword into his stomach before they—

A hand closed about hers on the sword. "Do you think so?"

She flinched back from the formidable Blood. Silent as a ghost, he'd come to protect his Khul impossibly fast.

"This is Varne, my nearest Blood."

A cold heavy weight pressed against her shoulders, sucking the warmth out of her until she shivered. "Nearest?"

"He's the last line of defense, the nearest to me at all times. This is Gregar, my shadowed Blood who used to be a Death Rider."

So cold. She opened her mouth to ask where he was, her teeth chattering harder. A blade touched her neck and she froze. Blessed Lady, the Blood was close enough to hold a knife to her throat while she sat here, oblivious until he touched her with steel. As always when threatened from her blind spot, terror screamed through her body. Muscles bunched, her fingers locking on the hilt, her heart thundering in her ribcage. Her fear only intensified the sense of bone-chilling cold rolling off the Blood.

Varne removed his hand from hers and stood at Rhaekhar's side protectively. Automatically, she started to draw the sword. Helpless with a knife at her throat, she couldn't just sit here and—

The wickedly sharp blade lifted her chin higher and the sudden press of bare flesh against her back scalded her. The Blood whispered against her ear. "Shall I draw a bit more of your sweet blood for Khul?"

G regar hovered against her back, barely visible in thick, black shadows. As a Death Rider, he could wrap the cold Shadow of Death about himself and disappear. He could slit Shannari's throat before she even knew he was there, and the knowledge shook her to the core. Silently, Rhaekhar waited for her to look to him for assistance.

The Blood whispered something to her too low for him to hear. Her jaw clenched and she stiffened, her fingers tight on the sword's hilt. Shadows draped across her shoulders, darkening her face.

A sudden and irrational urge demanded he drag her away from the Blood. In his heart he knew the Blood would never hurt her, but he couldn't ease the trepidation. The shadows wanted to suck her down and drown her in a sea of blood and agony.

Gregar raised his head, his dark eyes glittering like black ice in the shadows. At his familiar smirk, Rhaekhar loosened the tension straining his shoulders.

"Or perhaps I shall draw Khul's blood for you."

Her gaze leaped to Rhaekhar's face, her eyes wide with fear and reluctant desire. The surge of hunger through their *na'lanna* bond at the thought of tasting his blood very nearly sent him plunging over the cliff into raging, uncontrollable lust. Why did she fear his disgust when he would like nothing better than to give his blood to her?

"Leave us," he said in a voice thick and heavy to his own ears.

Gregar drew his *rahke* up her neck, trailing the blade across her cheek in an odd, dangerous caress, but he stood and backed away.

Varne didn't move. Using the silent hand language of the Blood, he signed, *I don't trust her.*

*Na'lanna must be trusted.*

*Not with your life.*

Rhaekhar sighed. His word might be law on the Plains, but the Blood protected him as they chose. A direct order wouldn't please his nearest Blood at all, and he most likely wouldn't heed it anyway.

"Do you think I'll try to kill him?" Shannari's voice quivered from the interaction with Gregar, but otherwise she faced Varne confidently. "I surrendered to him. I may not like it—in fact, I hate it—but my honor dictates that I do as he commands."

Varne shrugged, still refusing to leave. "Women have no honor."

"If it weren't for my honor, I would gut you for such a ridiculous statement." Her lips tightened, her beautiful eyes flashing, her chin inching up even higher. Such pride. "Not all men have honor, either. I may not understand your code of conduct yet, but when I give my word I don't break it. If your Khul tries to hurt me or force me to do something that violates my beliefs, I'll fight him with formal warning according to your custom. May Leesha strike me down if I lie."

Pride swelled in Rhaekhar's heart until his chest ached. "Challenge me as you wish, *na'lanna*. I shall meet you with pride and honor."

She met his gaze, her eyes dark gleaming pools. Her lush scent filled the room with smoldering flowers. Her tongue darted out to moisten her bottom lip, and his stomach clenched so hard a small groan escaped.

He had best get rid of the Blood without delay. He didn't know all he needed to understand at this time, but he'd have a better chance of tasting that sweet mouth again if they were alone. "Leave us, Varne, but remain close. If my woman gets too unruly, I shall beg your help."

Gregar bent over laughing and slapping his thighs. "Nay, call me if you need assistance, Khul. It's an honor to serve."

Shannari studied the sword in her lap as though she'd never seen it before, refusing to look up until they were gone.

Fighting down his desire, Rhaekhar took a deep calming breath and began brushing her hair once more. "The Blood have saved my life many times in the past five years. Shall I tell you how they became Blood?"

She inclined her head a bit but said nothing.

"After a special kind of *kae'don*, or battle, I was named Khul of all Nine Camps. I chose one warrior from each Camp to serve in my Blood. Standing before the gathered people with *Kae'Shaman* to illuminate Vulkar's will, I sacrificed my blood for them."

She straightened, listening hard.

"I used my *rahke* to make a cut on my arm, here." He held his left forearm before her, and she trailed a finger across the diagonal white scar. The small touch seared his skin, and his voice dropped another notch. "Then each of them tasted my blood."

She sucked in her breath and held herself very still.

"It connected me to them in an unbreakable bond. My blood in their veins enables them to feel me, deep inside themselves. They feel my emotions. If I'm in danger, they sense it before the attack. The Great Wind Stallion blessed us, giving them great gifts for their sacrifice."

She turned the sword over in her hands, her fingers tracing the whorls in the hilt aimlessly. "What sacrifice did they make?"

"They swore to sacrifice every last drop of their blood in my protection. The greatest honor for a Blood is to die in Khul's defense."

"But they didn't actually sacrifice blood for you. I mean, you didn't taste theirs."

"Nay, the Blood bond does not work in such a way." Burying his fingers in her thick, soft hair, he grasped the back of her neck and massaged gently. He could almost hear the frantic whirl of her thoughts. "But the *na'lanna* bond does."

She bowed her head, letting him work on her neck. "I thought it was just an endearment."

"You asked how I knew you were hungry." He leaned closer, sharing the heat of his body without actually pressing himself against her. "I knew because I felt your hunger in my stomach, even though I myself had already eaten."

She breathed shallowly, not with fear, exactly, but wonder and anticipation. A small tremor shook her.

"I felt the moment you awakened. I felt your gaze on my body and your reaction. Only a warrior's *na'lanna* can form a bond that allows them to share their hearts and minds through blood. The more blood you share with me, the stronger the bond will become. According to legend, before long I shall be able to find you anywhere on the Plains."

Her scent heated, growing need pulsing through her. Every instinct urged him to kiss her. To force her to admit the desire raging in her. To claim and mark her as his own.

But he wanted more. He wanted this princess to choose him of her own accord, not because he tormented her with need when she was vulnerable. He wanted this outlander Captain to accept him with love, not because she'd surrendered to him on the battlefield.

Pulling her hair over one shoulder, he bared the side of her neck. Sliding his hands across her shoulders, he continued massaging the tension from her body without pressing a more sensual advantage.

"Do you— do you actually want to—"

"Oh, aye," he breathed roughly against her ear. "Whatever you're willing to share with me, I shall take, gladly. I want your blood as much as your body, as much as your heart, as much as your trust."

"If you speak truthfully, then you already know how I feel." She sighed shakily, hunching her shoulders against his soothing caress. "When I look at you, when you tasted my blood, I can't deny that I... I liked it. But I can't give you my heart or my trust. I have none to give."

Rhaekhar felt her certainty and regret through the bond. He lay down beside her on his back without touching her. "Why?"

Pain speared her heart, wounding his in turn. With trembling hands, she reached over and picked up the empty cup, absently raising it toward her mouth. He gently took the cup from her and set it aside. He reached for the sword in her lap, but she clutched it tighter.

"Someone butchered my heart."

Fury sharpened his voice. "Do you give me his name and I shall cut his heart out for him."

"He's already dead."

Had this lover abused her? Had she shared blood with him? Did she still mourn for him? Why did she hide the natural inclinations and desires of her body with shame in her heart?

Letting out a long, slow breath, she loosened her grip on the sword and allowed him to draw it out of her lap. Showing his trust in her, he set it beside them within easy reach.

"There is a way you could know my heart, *na'lanna*. You could know my feelings as your own. You would know if I lied, what deceptions I might use to ensnare you. Already, you feel some of my emotions through the bond."

She started to shake her head but hesitated, tilting her head as though she listened.

Deliberately, he thought about pushing open the thin cloth covering her breasts. Of kissing her neck, perhaps biting her shoulder, experimenting with the right pressure to see what pleased her the most. Need roared in his blood, and he growled beneath his breath, forcing his hands to remain unthreatening at his side. "What am I feeling now, *na'lanna?*"

Clutching her hands together in her lap, she laughed roughly. "That's not all that hard to guess, not from the way you've been looking at me."

He touched the newly stitched wound on his side, drawing her gaze to his body, reminding her of his blood. "You honored me greatly by drawing my blood. Few have done as well in a *kae'rahke* against me. Although Varne thought this needed a few stitches to ensure it healed properly, I shall wear your scar with pride and honor."

Her gaze lingered on the wound then drifted lower to his groin. After bathing, he'd purposely left off the loincloth he typically wore beneath the *memsha* to make riding more comfortable. His erection was quite evident, and her breath rushed out in a raw needy moan. The scent of flowers thickened in the room, rich with the spicy musk of her need.

Smiling, he unsheathed his *rahke* and trailed the tip just above the cloth. He slowly drew the *rahke* up his stomach. Watching, she held her breath.

"I want to sacrifice blood for you. I want to strengthen the bond with you so that you may know my heart at all times. I want to feel pleasure roar through your body, the same as I felt when I tasted yours."

She started to turn her face away, her jaw and shoulders straining. With a flick of his wrist, he cut his chest just above his left nipple.

Shuddering, she made another ragged cry, raising her hand toward him, but still she hesitated.

The intensity of her fear and shame made his heart ache. "Please, Shannari."

"I might... hurt you. Your Blood..."

"You cannot hurt me, *na'lanna*, and the Blood will only come if I call them. I desire this greatly, as greatly as I desire to breathe."

She placed her palm on his stomach, her gaze locked on the seeping blood. "Get rid of the sword and your knife so there are no... temptations or accidents."

His heart pounded with anticipation. He slid the weapons as far away as possible. "The thought of your mouth on me drives me mad."

"*You* drive me mad," she growled, leaning over him. "I swore I would never do this again."

Closing his hands on her shoulders, he held her away a

moment. "I must warn you. Sharing blood can be a very arousing thing, for both of us. I must know now, before you taste me, whether you truly—"

"I want to taste you," she said, forcing her mouth lower. She looked up at him, her brilliant eyes dark with need and rising hunger. "And then, I want all of you, as hard and as fast as you can."

## 5

Wrapping his hands in her hair, the barbarian hauled her mouth down to his chest. The taste of his blood erupted on her tongue, metallic, but strong and rich. Mixed with his scent, the blood intoxicated her. Her head buzzed and roared and her heart thundered like reverberating drums. Her fears and guilt floated away, and the world dwindled to this man beneath her.

His blood burned a path of fire through her body. Lower, from her mouth to her stomach to between her thighs. The desire she'd felt earlier was nothing compared to this heavy, aching need. Bathed in fire, she felt a primitive urge to sink her teeth deeply into the muscle over his heart.

Fighting for control, she tried to lift her mouth, but he held her so tightly against him she could barely breathe. Fed by his blood, his delicious scent and the incredible rock-hard press of muscle, tension coiled in her stomach. She swallowed another mouthful. Deep inside, she felt a swelling bloom of pleasure.

Horrified at how quickly he'd brought her to the verge of

climax, she jerked against his grip. Not a kiss, not an intimate caress—her undoing proved to be his blood. A tidal wave roared through her.

Shuddering, she came hard. Need rushed through her, cresting higher.

With a rumbling growl, Rhaekhar rolled, pinning her to the floor beneath him. He gripped her wrists over her head with one hand and tugged at her pantalettes with the other while he mashed her lips with his own. The taste of his mouth was as good as his blood, wild and raw.

Releasing her mouth, he moved lower to press biting kisses against her neck. Each time his teeth touched her skin, a surge of heat and wetness pulsed in her groin. Arching against him, she tried to force him along. The damned barbarian didn't seem to be in as much of a hurry as she.

"Patience, *na'lanna*."

His deep warrior voice vibrated his chest against her, a strumming pulse she felt clear to her spine. "No patience!"

Laughing, he sat up, straddling her hips and trapping her legs between his. He looked down at her, stark possession and hunger darkening his golden eyes. Squirming in an effort to ease the intolerable ache he'd stirred, she wanted to scream with frustration.

At least he'd released her hands. She slid her palms up his muscular thighs, reveling in the strength and power in him. Blessed Lady, he was so big and rough and muscled. The thought of his full might driving into her...

He was close enough to touch, but not close enough to kiss or bite. Groaning, she tried to buck him off her. With scrambling fingers, she caught the cloth he wore and jerked it away.

What a mistake.

The barbarian wanted her. She was more than willing. Why did he wait?

"What is this cloth called?"

Sweat trickled down her forehead, burning her eyes. She strained harder, using his thighs for leverage, but he would not be moved. Panting, she said, "Linen shirt."

He fingered the carved bone buttons as though he'd never seen such a marvel. While she lay beneath him burning up with need and naked from the waist down.

Rage quaked through her. Growling at him, she seized the neck of her shirt and ripped it open. Linen tore; buttons flew. Breathing hard, she glared up at him. Then she remembered the hideous scar on her chest. What would he think of it?

Heavy lidded with lust, Rhaekhar licked his lips, his white teeth flashing against his full bottom lip. His golden gaze settled on her breasts, lingering a moment on the scar without a flinch. No tightening about his eyes that might reveal disgust. "If you want my hands on you, all you need do is ask."

"Damn you," she whispered, her voice breaking. She'd known this was a mistake. She didn't want an arrogant, bossy man ordering her about. A man like him decided that once he'd bedded a woman, she was his to command like a serving wench. If he could make her beg for his attention like a starving dog whining for a scrap of meat, all the better.

Those rugged, glorious hands remained stationary on his thighs. "You know what I want."

Swearing beneath her breath, she gnashed her teeth. He wanted her to beg. "Never!"

"I recall someone swearing she would never ask me to make love to her as well." An arrogant smile curved his lips. "I can see how much fortitude that oath contained."

Her cheeks flamed. Asking was different than begging, but to be perfectly honest, she hadn't exactly asked, either. She'd ordered him. "Bastard."

"You want this to be hard and fast, full of raw need and meaningless, like a stallion maddened by the scent of a stray mare in heat." He leaned down and tenderly brushed away a lock of hair plastered to her face. "But I want more from you than your body, Shannari. This stallion intends to drive all others away with hooves and teeth, because I will keep my mare forever."

"You won't break me."

"Breaking you is the last thing on my mind. I treasure your courage, your strength and your pride. Nay, I want to love you. There's a difference."

Not in her mind.

He was a man, a man who wanted her fiercely. Obviously stronger, he thought to corner her, overwhelming her senses to the point of weakness and surrender.

*So I'll play along.*

She allowed her eyes to flutter shut and released a hopefully pitiful sound. Biting her lip, she feigned shyness and averted her face.

"Shannari, *na'lanna,* let me love you. Let me show you exactly how it might be between us. Bend your pride to me in this small thing, and I shall never give you cause to regret it."

A surge of tenderness and warmth from him wrapped around her like a blanket. Hiccupping another fake cry, she slipped her hands down the floor slowly, avoiding his arms and chest, then raising her palms carefully without touching his stomach or thighs.

She closed her hands around that impressive erection and squeezed.

A shudder wracked his big body against hers, his breath rushing out on a groaning roar. He fell forward, bracing himself on his elbows on either side of her. Breathing raggedly, he laughed. "I'm no untried lad, but a warrior with a warrior's control. While I greatly appreciate your caress, I still must hear you plead most sweetly for what you hold in your hands."

She couldn't resist giving him a smug, sultry smile. "What I hold in my hands is just as hungry and desperate as I."

Shifting, he thrust into her hands. The glide of velvet and marble between her palms made her eyes roll back into her head, wiping away her confident smile.

He pulled back, slowly, drawing every inch through her clutching fingers. "Wouldn't this feel much better inside you, *na'lanna?*"

She nearly sobbed. Every muscle in her body clenched with longing.

He rocked his hips again and again, dripping sweat on her, his breathing rough, his muscled body flexing above her. "I feel your need. You're so tight, so close, my smallest finger slipping inside would bring you screaming and clawing with pleasure."

The thought alone was almost enough to send her soaring again. Desperate, she raised her head and pressed her face against his neck and chest. All hot warrior and sweet hay baking in the summer sun, his scent only increased her torment. She longed to sink her teeth into him, gnawing through the muscle and his relentless control.

She dropped her head back to the floor and bit her lip to the point of drawing blood to keep from begging him. *Shannari dal'-Dainari never runs. She certainly never begs!*

He dropped his forehead against hers. "Great Vulkar, woman, your pride will kill me."

It was the abject longing in his voice combined with the fierce, overwhelming ache of desire she felt through their bond that defeated her. He truly was on the edge of release. Only his phenomenal control prevented him from spilling on her stomach.

He ached as badly as she did. She knew it, deep in her heart where she couldn't lie, even to herself. This man suffered when he could have commanded. He waited when he could have taken what he wanted. He refused her careless, crass offer of fulfillment despite his own physical need, because the emotional need of his heart was greater.

Blessed Lady above, the barbarian already believed he loved her.

Wrapping her arms about his shoulders, she threw back her head, drowning in emotion. Frustration, because she ached so badly. Despair, because she could never love like he did. Agony, simply because she wished she could. "Please!"

He trembled against her. "Are you sure, Shannari? Once we are joined, I cannot—"

She wrapped her fists in his hair and jerked firmly to quiet him. "Blessed Lady, yes!"

Kneeing her thighs apart, he demanded, "Say my name."

"Rhaekhar," she whispered against his lips. "Please."

He pressed against her, and his size snared her breath in her throat. Despite her need, her tightness prevented him from thrusting as deeply as she wanted. Blowing hard and straining to keep from hurting her, he twisted his hips and eased bit by bit into her.

Too slow! Groaning at the fullness, she arched against him. The near pain stalled her orgasm. Until he gripped her shoulder with his teeth.

Her spine bowed. The blood she'd tasted from him earlier flared and ignited inside her. Bubbling upward, erupting like a volcano, pleasure spilled from her on a silent scream of agonized pleasure. Grinding his hips against her, he plunged deeper, driving the molten explosion even higher.

"Mine," he growled around a mouthful of her flesh.

When his teeth broke her skin, the fresh blood shattered his control, flaming through him as wildly as her own release had flamed through her. Something deep inside her snapped, clicking into place as if it had always belonged. An interwoven binding gleamed in the secret darkness of her heart.

Sliding into oblivion, her last thought was one of regret. *I should have bitten him as hard.*

Dreaming, *Shannari floated on her back. The full Moon above gleamed as brightly as the noonday sun. Cool water cradled her, carrying her away from her troubles.*

The moon took on a reddish tinge. Curious, she let her feet sink so she bobbed upright.

She saw these calm silvery waters in her mind every time she held a weapon. When she faced battle of any kind, she pictured this lake in her mind and pushed all her thoughts and fears below the calm waters to improve her concentration.

Why was she here? She held no weapon. She didn't face a battle. She didn't even have any clothes.

The sandy bottom firmed beneath her feet closer to the misty shore. A formidable black mountain towered above the lake. Three jagged peaks crowned by a glowing red center pulsated like a living heart. Sparks and flames shot to the heavens and distant thunder rumbled the ground, casting ripples through the mirrored waters.

Silent power weighed upon her, humbling her soul. The moon seemed larger than ever, taking up the entire velvet sky. The air reverberated with a sweet, haunting melody she could sense but not hear. Her soul knew majesty was all around, but she was blind and deaf.

SHANNARI, DAUGHTER OF MY BLOOD.

The ringing, melodious voice danced over the waters, filled with all the joy and love and warmth in the world. She recognized this voice, too, although she'd never actually heard it before. She was in the presence of the Blessed Lady, Leesha.

Shannari glared up at the gorgeous silvered moon. "Why? Why didn't you save me? I'm your last Daughter. If I die, Your land and people will perish into Darkness forever. Your own priest has told me these things. Yet You allowed barbarians to conquer my army."

Silence was her answer.

Hurt rage filled her, burning her cheeks like acid. "Why have you forsaken me? I've always tried to do Your will. I've fought for the Rose Crown my entire life so I can protect Your people. And my reward is captivity with a barbarian warlord who... who..."

She couldn't voice the truth shrilling in her heart. Rhaekhar made her *feel*. He made her wish—that she had a softer, gentler heart, that she could trust and love with passionate abandon like he wanted. Like he deserved. Instead, her heart was frozen, wounded by death and blackened by blood.

Her heart shattered, shards of glass and ice piercing her with pain. Gasping, she cupped her palm over the aching scar. "You never heard my prayers."

I HAVE NEVER FORSAKEN YOU.

Falling to her knees in the crystal waters, Shannari cried harder.

I SPEAK, AND YOU DO NOT HEAR. I ILLUMINATE YOUR MIND, BUT YOU DO NOT SEE. I THAW YOUR HEART, AND YOU REFUSE TO FEEL.

"Forgive me, Leesha. I want to see. I want to hear. Help me, I beg you. Save me from the barbarian. If this is a test, spare me, please. I can't bear it."

WE SENT HIM. HE WAS BORN TO PROTECT YOU, MY DAUGHTER. HE WAS BORN TO LOVE YOU. HE WAS BORN TO SAVE YOU.

"Love," Shannari whispered, closing her eyes with shame. "Love nearly killed me.

DO NOT BE AFRAID TO LOVE, MY CHILD. LOVE IS MY

GREATEST GIFT TO YOU. LOVE AS WE MEANT YOU TO LOVE. HE WILL NEVER WOUND YOUR HEART.

Mist rolled across the lake, concealing the mirrored waters. The full moon disappeared behind a cloud, and shadows closed all around her.

She had so many questions, so many doubts, so many... "Wait, please! You said, 'we.' Who else sent Rhaekhar? How will he save me?"

Faintly, the Lady's final words whispered in her heart.

*COME TO ME, HERE, AT MY SILVER LAKE. I WILL BE WAITING FOR YOU.*

W atching her sleep, Rhaekhar couldn't keep the grin off his face. Such a Rose, such a warrior, such a lover. He couldn't ask for a more perfect mate. With her desire for his blood and her fearless passion, Shannari had solidified their *na'lanna* bond in one glorious joining he would never forget. *She'll never be quit of me now.*

Reveling in the connection they now shared, he closed his eyes and breathed deeply of her scent. She was dreaming, although what he couldn't tell. Her heart felt very far away. He stroked her back lightly, listening to her steady, deep breathing. Her natural fragrance of hot summer nights and enthralling flowers soaked into him, easing his loneliness.

The rhythm of her breathing changed, and his heartbeat quickened with anticipation. He wanted to stroke and kiss every inch of her body, imprinting each hollow and curve in his memory. He would take her slowly this time, giving her pleasure after pleasure until she couldn't move, and then—

She shot upward and her fist caught him underneath the jaw. His head snapped back and his teeth crashed together hard enough to make his jaw ache. Through the pain, he caught a glimpse of wild eyes and pale, strained face before she whirled away in a flurry of black hair.

Scooping up her sword as she moved, she crouched in a corner, blade held before her in both hands. She breathed heavily, but her hands didn't tremble. She scanned the room quickly and then stared at him, eyes narrowed and braced for battle. Her scent was as sharp and hard as the sword in her hands.

He sat up slowly so as not to alarm her into trying to chop off his head again.

"What the hell did you do?"

He moved his jaw side to side to make sure it still worked. "I was breathing your scent, and watching you sleep, and... I think I touched your back."

"I don't like to be touched. Not when I'm asleep."

"All right." He would have to work on that one. He would like nothing better than to sleep wrapped around her body. He allowed his voice to heat. "Why don't you come back and lie down with me?"

She stood and walked away, deliberately putting the table between them. "How long did I sleep?"

Astonishment and confusion warred inside him. After the love they'd shared, why would she distance herself? "Not long. We have a very long night ahead of us yet, na'lanna."

Raising an eyebrow, she gave him a long, pointed stare. "I really don't like for you to call me that. Besides, haven't you had enough for awhile? Aren't you... satisfied?"

Perhaps she had no understanding of a warrior's control. She didn't understand his burning need to touch her, to cover her with his body and kiss her the whole night through. "Can outlanders only make love once a night?"

She blinked and the corner of her mouth quirked. "Once a week is more like it. Or longer. Why, I've heard at court that some nobles don't visit their wives' beds more than once a year."

Great Vulkar, once a year? He nearly choked and cursed and challenged every outlander he could find at the very thought. Until he caught the wry amusement softening her scent. "Come kiss me, Shannari, and I'll show you what I think of once per week."

"Is that an order?"

Frowning, he sat up straighter. Did she honestly believe he would order her to his blankets? "Nay, a warrior rarely orders his mate, and certainly never to his own pleasure."

She poured herself another cup of that bitter-smelling brew, even though it must be cold. "Truly?"

His stomach felt queasy and not from the thought of her vile drink. Surely she didn't think he would use her in such a way. "What honor would I earn by commanding you to my pleasure? I shall only command you for your protection."

Her indelicate snort offended his warrior sensibility.

"If I give you an order, Shannari, I expect it to be followed without question. Your life may very well depend on it."

"My thanks, Khul, but I think I'll protect myself. I've done it nearly all my life."

"You will—" He hesitated when he realized his voice had lowered to a rough growl, echoing with command.

She glared at him, stark naked, her glorious hair hanging about her shoulders like a velvet cloak. "Yes? I will what?"

Vulkar, she moved his heart like no woman he'd ever known.

"I will refrain from disagreeing with arrogant bastards who believe they may command me like a common slave? I will kiss you whenever you wish and spread my legs for you as often as you desire without question? Is that what you expect from me?"

He stood with a roar. "Nay!"

How had he gone from longing to pleasure her the many hours remaining until sunrise, to wishing to seize her and smash her unruly mouth with his own until she submitted? He never lost control of his emotions.

"You're *na'lanna*, my beloved, my mate. I want to make you scream your pleasure so loudly that all Nine Camps will hear of our great love. I want to love you, and I want—"

Her face closed, her jaw firmed, and her scent... Vulkar help him, the stark, resigned scent of agony and betrayal nigh tore his heart from his chest.

"You defeated my army, and I surrendered to you. You spared my soldiers, my country, my very life, and so I'll go with you as you demand to your Plains. I won't try to kill you unless you try to kill me first. We're obviously compatible bed partners and I'm not opposed to sharing such pleasures with you. But I will not love you. I don't want your protection, your tenderness, or your promises. I certainly don't want your love."

Stricken, he clenched his jaw and closed his hands into fists. He couldn't touch her, else risk seizing her and dragging her down to the floor for hard, bloody, rough lovemaking in an attempt to defeat her all over again. He took a deep breath, struggling to calm his pounding heart. Every muscle braced for battle, screaming to fight and claim what was his.

Her scent was a torment. Lush, hot, smoking even as she glared at him with those flashing eyes of fury.

He didn't want her lust. Vulkar help him, all he wanted was her heart.

The one thing she refused to give.

## 6

W ithout a word, the barbarian picked up his scrap of clothing, wrapped it around his hips, and walked stiffly from the room. To his credit, he didn't slam the door behind him.

Shannari collapsed into a chair. Her heart still raced after the shock of waking. Leesha help her, sleeping with someone again was going to be pure hell. The barbarian was extremely lucky her sword had not been as close as she usually kept it, beneath her pillow. She'd learned quickly to kill before she was fully awake.

What was she going to do? How was she going to survive the next days, weeks, months—or more—with a man who tempted her so badly?

Groaning, she folded her arms and dropped her forehead down onto the table. The thought of those big, rough hands gliding over her skin while he kissed her slowly and thoroughly had melted every little bit of defiance she had built against him. Yet, her crude words had offended his honor. Although she regretted her success, her resolve to withstand him did nothing to deter her returning desire.

The man was all explosive power, massive and muscled and untamed, but curiously tender at the same time. Leesha help her, she wanted him. The sex had only intensified her attraction.

*Do not be afraid to love.*

The dream...

She'd forgotten all about it when the barbarian startled her from sleep. Dreams tormented her all the time, usually of thick suffocating shadows. In the worst, she had been locked in utter darkness in a tiny cell and she knew she was going to die. After that dream, she'd barely slept for a week.

Her dreams had always haunted her; they felt so terribly real. This one... Part of her wanted to believe the Lady truly had visited her dreams. But if Leesha had not spoken to her at the Sentinel after a night of prayer, why would She speak in a dream that could easily be forgotten? Or discredited? In a way, this dream was worse than a nightmare. Falling in love with anyone, let alone a barbarian from the distant Plains, was surely the worst thing she could do.

Love had nearly murdered her before. She had too much at risk now to make such a mistake based on a dream she might have made up entirely out of desperation and fear.

Straightening, she drained the cold caffe from the cup in one long drink. Work always helped calm her when fears and doubts assailed her. Some tiny detail of obtaining a throne always existed, even in the wee hours of the morning.

With a heavy sigh, she pushed to her feet and went in search of parchment and ink. Stephan must be dealt with, now more carefully because of her absence. She'd exposed her plans to him, played her hand, and lost the game. She couldn't lose Allandor to him. Fenton would need to increase the troops at Fort Mintor on the Pellan border.

Which reminded her of something else she'd promised to address. With fresh parchment filched from her travel bag, she wrote a letter to the Steward of Far Illione.

She knew better than to ask Rhaekhar for horses like his mount. Theft of the magnificent, sacred horses had been the cause of the last war. Allandor was lucky that this time the Sha'Kae al'Dan planned to return to their Plains with so little bloodshed.

If she couldn't acquire warhorses to match the Sha'Kae al'Dan mounts, perhaps the Keldari would be interested in trading some of their desert mounts. Rawboned, ugly and rumored to be as savage as their *dra'gwar* riders, the horses survived the worst desert conditions on nothing but briny water and scraggly tumbleweed. Thank the Lady, Allandor's coffers could spare the gold to purchase a few hundred head of such horses. Rather, she had enough gold to purchase the wagons of timber from woodcutters necessary to trade to the Keldari for the horses.

Living in a desert where the tallest trees were mere shrubs, the Keldari could not resist the temptation of fine lumber. What they did with such lumber on the other hand was a complete and utter mystery. Supposedly, there were no cities to be found in the barren wasteland. Although no one in recent years had survived a journey into the forbidden territory to find out. Who knew what secrets lay in Keldar?

A knock sounded at the door, too light and undemanding to be one of the barbarians. She glanced at the window. The rising sun surprised her. Rhaekhar hadn't returned all night. Refusing to feel guilty despite the pang in her chest, she decided it was safe to answer the door in her robe.

A young boy stood just outside, shifting from foot to foot.

"Yes?"

"Prin— Princess Shannari?"

She smiled to gentle her usual intimidating demeanor. "Yes, I'm Shannari. Do you have a message?"

The boy held out a parchment, his small hand trembling. "I was told to wait for your response."

"Thank you." Recognizing the seal, she frowned and raised her gaze to the boy. Who was this young man to hand deliver a message from the Duke of Pella? "What's your name?"

The boy gulped and nearly bolted. "Brandon, ma'am. I mean, Your Highness. Pa runs the inn."

She nodded absently, trying to decide whether she wanted to read the message or simply burn it. "When were you given this?"

"Just after supper, ma'am, I mean—"

She waved away his worry about formality and nodded, encouraging him to continue. The poor boy couldn't be more than ten years old.

"I was outside in the stable when a man asked me to deliver this to you, but not until this morning. He said that was very important. At dawn, I was to bring this to you as soon as you were alone."

"The man—was he dressed in a fancy blue coat?"

"Yes, ma'am. He rode with the Pellans."

The boy practically spat the last word and Shannari smiled. No worries then that this boy or his family secretly supported the Duke.

"They were harsh with Ma because she didn't bring their ale fast enough for supper. They" —The boy hesitated, his face twisting with rage— "One of them hit her. Pa cursed them, but there weren't nothing he could do. Pa refused to take their gold for the rooms, even though they made a terrible mess." Brandon dropped his gaze, abashed. "I almost threw the message away, but I thought—I thought you might need it. Or at least, you should know."

Shannari made a mental note to ask her father to reimburse the innkeeper. "I agree, Brandon, the Pellans are not my friends, either. That's why I can't decide whether I want to read this or not."

"Begging your pardon, Princess, but Ma says you'll protect us from the likes of them. Is that true?"

The weight of the world pressed on her shoulders, but she smiled gravely at the boy and nodded. "Someday I'll be the High Queen. Then I'll make sure people like the Duke of Pella never hurt anyone again."

The boy grinned. "Then I did right in bringing you the message from that Pellan rubbish."

She couldn't agree more with the boy's assessment of Stephan. She needed to know her enemies as well as her friends, and she had to keep those enemies closer. With a sigh, she broke the Duke's seal and opened the parchment.

*Dearest Shannari,*

*It was with deepest regret that I heard of your surrender to the barbarians. I understand your hesitancy to call on my country for aid after the many years of our disagreements, but I swear on all I hold dear that I stand ready to aid you in any way possible. Do not fear that Pella will invade Allandor during this time of difficulty. My troops will await your command. Please, Shannari, let me help you. Join me. Only you can cleanse this darkness from my soul.*

*Yours,*

*Stephan, Duke of Pella*

She felt ill just from holding the paper in her hands. The look of lust and raw hunger she'd seen in his eyes twisted her stomach into knots. Why did he disgust her so badly, when the barbarian did not?

Rhaekhar had tasted her blood, and she'd nearly come apart in his arms right there on the battlefield. She hungered for his blood, just as Stephan eyed the stains on her hands, but somehow with Rhaekhar it was more. More than horror, more than disgust, more than darkness. Too much more, in fact, which is why she feared the barbarian as much as she did Stephan, albeit for different reasons.

Whatever the barbarian planned for her, though, she couldn't forget her destiny. The Rose Crown and the High Throne of Shanhasson must be hers one day. Theo must be deposed. This was her sole purpose in life. To that end, Stephan could not be dismissed, not after making such a concession to her.

His troops awaited her command! Relief and distrust battled inside her, just as their two countries had fought for generations. If she could trust Stephan, then at least she knew Allandor would be safe until she returned. If she couldn't trust Stephan, then nothing had really changed. She didn't trust him now.

If he invaded, the Guard would turn him back. They had defeated Pella several times already, and Fenton was more than capable of leading the troops. Stephan could run to Prince Theo or High King Rikard with tales of Allandor's treachery, but again, what could Shanhasson do? Invade? Rikard wanted civil war as little as she did.

Perhaps it would be best to cooperate somewhat with the Duke. If he spoke truthfully, he would be the key to her success without war. He might even be used to win her freedom from the barbarian.

Ah, now that was a thought. Smiling, she sat down at the desk and quickly scribbled a reply.

*My Lord Duke:*

> *I appreciate your offer and will consider your words carefully. The*
> *barbarians are a formidable opponent and easily defeated the Guard. Help*
> *me, I beg you! He leaves warriors in Dalden Bay, so beware.*
>     Shannari dal'Dainari
>     *Rose of Shanhasson*

She debated that last line but added it anyway. It would pique Stephan's interest, for no one in the Green Lands had ever referred to her by such a title, although it certainly made sense.

Asking for assistance nearly made her throw up; begging for the Duke's help made her want to draw steel and gut someone. If Pella and the Sha'Kae al'Dan could be baited into fighting over Dalden Bay like a pack of dogs, then a few belly-curdling lies were nothing.

She would lie, cheat, steal, and murder if necessary. Or endure explosive, dangerously tempting lovemaking with a barbarian intent on claiming her heart and soul. What would Rhaekhar do once he finally understood she had no heart or soul to give?

Perhaps she deserved Stephan after all.

R haekhar shaded his eyes against the rising sun and surveyed the green fields to the east and then the river to the southwest. "I'll leave a fist of my warriors here to maintain control. They can camp across the river closer to the desert without disturbing the outlanders."

Varne nodded. "As you say, Khul. Who do you leave in command?"

"Athgart. He's used to command and one of the best scouts. I want the blasted lands beyond the river patrolled regularly. No more outlanders will move in the desert without alerting us immediately."

Turning, Rhaekhar headed back toward the village. The wooden and stone buildings sat side by side along the muddy stone track. That people lived their entire lives here astonished him. What would Shannari think of the Sha'Kae al'Dan lifestyle, roaming the Sea of Grass as the herds demanded, and setting up Camp in a new place nearly each day?

Thinking of her made him clench his jaw with frustration. Desire pulsed through him, which only angered him more. Even now, he wanted her with an intensity that shamed him.

Walking on his left, Varne cleared his throat. "Khul, may I speak with you regarding the woman?"

Despite his inner turmoil, Rhaekhar did not like the note in his nearest Blood's tone. "You may speak to me of *na'lanna* Shannari."

"I know what you feel for this woman, but... The vision you spoke of from Vulkar, you had it when you were just a lad. Could you be mistaken?"

"Nay, I recognize her scent, I know her blood. She's mine, Varne. I know it."

"I don't like her." His nearest Blood had never been one to mince words. "I don't like how she insults you. It will only get worse, Khul. She delights in tormenting you."

"She's *na'lanna*."

"So you say. But is she worth risking your position, your Camp, all Nine Camps?"

Rhaekhar tried to casually brush aside his Blood's words, but his stomach tightened with unease. Before the Great Wind Stallion, he'd sworn to lead the Nine Camps and to protect the Plains at all cost. Surely the gift of *na'lanna* would not compromise his sworn duty. "Vulkar and the Dark Mare promised her to me."

"Then They have committed you to the Three Hells. Tehark will use her against you to improve his standing with the other

Camps. None of the khuls will appreciate an outlander in their midst, let alone one you threaten to make Khul'lanna. If she loved you, it would be different, Khul, but her animosity is obvious. Even more, I See..."

Each Blood gained special gifts from the Great Wind Stallion when they tasted Khul's blood sacrifice. Varne's gift was inner sight, a sense of two paths diverging and which should be taken. "What? What have you seen?"

"Shadows." The formidable Blood whispered, his face pale as though he saw a great horror. "Shadows hang all about her."

"Like Gregar's?"

"Nay, not exactly. These are... darker."

"Aye," Gregar answered softly from Rhaekhar's other side. He spoke with a keen edge to his voice. As if in a dream, he unsheathed his ivory *rahke* and rolled it back and forth on his palm, stroking it lovingly. "Darkness is strongly attracted to her. Her blood Calls to Shadow."

Varne stepped forward, unsheathing his *rahke*. "Including you?"

Rhaekhar sucked in his breath and carefully kept his place between the two of them. He didn't care to see which Blood would be victorious if they came to blows. He needed them both too much.

Still rolling the *rahke* in his hand, Gregar met Varne's gaze briefly and then looked into Rhaekhar's eyes. The day darkened. The rising sun slipped behind a bank of clouds and silence hung heavy in the air. "Aye."

Goose bumps raced down Rhaekhar's arms and his scalp itched, hair prickling. Adrenaline pumped through his body. His chest rumbled a growl of aggression, male to male. Every muscle in his body bunched, tensing, ready to prove his dominance.

Another warrior sniffed around his woman. A woman who

openly professed she would never love, him or any other for that matter.

Warriors killed each other for lesser offenses.

"Khul, do you want me to challenge him?" Varne's voice echoed with silky menace.

Gregar smiled, his eyes swallowed by shadows.

Gripping his *rahke*, fighting the urge to carve out the Blood's heart for admitting interest in Shannari, Rhaekhar deliberately bit his tongue and the inside of his cheek. The coppery taste of blood sharpened his senses and the small pain cleared some of the red haze. "Don't be a fool, Varne. If I want his blood, I will challenge him myself."

Gregar said nothing, but met his gaze unflinchingly. Shadows lengthened on the ground and the silence became oppressive.

Ice dripped down Rhaekhar's spine. Gregar was Death. He carried Vulkar's gift of Shadow. If he had truly wanted Khul dead, Rhaekhar would be gasping and bleeding on the ground already. "You said earlier you would rather have the Rose. You knew of whom I spoke even then."

"Aye."

Shadows thickened in the air until Rhaekhar couldn't breathe. Agony shredded his heart. *Mine, the dream of the Rose is mine!* "What vision were you given of her?"

Gregar shook his head. "Forgive me, Khul, but I shall not say, not unless it will save her life or yours."

"You're Blood!" Varne retorted, his face a mask of fury. "You swore to sacrifice every single drop of your blood for Khul. If he asks, you will answer him, so I say as nearest Blood."

"No oath I ever swore, on Khul's blood or any other, demands I share my personal torment and shame." Gregar's voice dripped with disdain. "Let alone with you."

At least the rising challenge between his two Blood kept his own fighting instinct in check. Rhaekhar pushed Varne in the chest, keeping him back. All these years, Gregar had followed Varne's lead as nearest Blood without question. One night in the Green Lands and they were ready to challenge each other. "Varne, enough! This is my decision."

"As you will, Khul," Varne bit off each word as he grudgingly retreated a step. "It's an honor to serve, even if some have forgotten."

"I forget nothing," Gregar whispered. He held Rhaekhar's gaze a moment longer, and then deliberately bowed his head. "You are my honor, Khul, and I serve you still. The only difference is that I would serve Shannari with honor as well."

Jealousy roared through Rhaekhar's veins. His neck corded, his shoulders strained, and he ached to pound this threat into a bloody pulp. Gregar was one of his oldest, most trusted friends, but no warrior relished such competition. If the Blood hadn't said, "with honor" or had continued staring him in the eyes, then Rhaekhar would have challenged him on the spot. His honor would have accepted nothing less than blood.

"See what damage she's wrought?" Varne shook his head. "She'll tear the Nine Camps apart, just as she tears you and your Blood apart. The darkness inside her demands it."

"There is no darkness without light," Gregar said softly, carefully raising his gaze with lowered shoulders and softer voice to minimize the challenge. "Your love can be the light for her, Khul, and keep her from falling into Shadow. She bleeds in Shadow and none can save her from her own battles. But you can give her love where otherwise she would know only betrayal and death."

Shaken, Rhaekhar concentrated on letting his body relax, dropping his shoulders and breathing more freely. The promise of a love like no other was still his and his alone, yet the Blood must have seen many of the same things shown to Rhaekhar in whatever vision he had received of Shannari. Why him instead of Gregar? "Would you have given her betrayal?"

"Nay." Gregar glared down at the ivory *rahke* in his hand, his lip curling with hatred. "I shall never betray you, Khul, nor her."

Somehow, Gregar would have brought her death.

Rhaekhar's blood chilled.

This time, he couldn't resist unsheathing his *rahke*. He wouldn't challenge Gregar out of jealousy, but he would challenge him to ensure Shannari's safety.

"She's safe from me now, Khul." Gregar shrugged but kept his gaze averted. "The oath I swore on your blood ensures it."

"I still say we should leave her here where she belongs and return to the Plains at once," Varne said. "You accomplished your goal and none can dispute this *kae'don*. Bring that woman home, though, and the disputes will worsen."

"Only a fool would suggest leaving behind *na'lanna*." Instead of Gregar's usual humor, the underlying ache of loss in his voice stirred pity in Rhaekhar's heart.

Just the thought of returning to the Plains without Shannari made his heart thunder in his chest and his stomach twist. "Never. Where I go, she goes. If there are any *kae'don* to fight or disputes to settle, I shall do so gladly. If I cannot keep her and win her love, then I'm no warrior."

"Keep her safe, Khul."

The unspoken threat, *Or I shall*, hung in the silence. This threat, though, Rhaekhar could tolerate, even approve. Shannari came first. He would dismiss the complication of Gregar's affections, unless... Gritting his teeth, he pushed the thought away. She came first, in everything. He would do what he must. To signal his acceptance, Rhaekhar sheathed his *rahke*. "If I had decided to leave without her, what would you have done?"

Gregar laughed and re-sheathed the *rahke* on his hip. At last, the sun broke through the clouds and the air brightened considerably. The intolerable weight of Death withdrew. "You would have had only eight Blood."

"Because I would have killed you." Varne tried to match the other Blood's lighter tone and failed.

Gregar smiled, a fierce baring of teeth. "Then you would have had only seven Blood, Khul."

As soon as Shannari stepped outside The Sleeping Lion, her father rushed forward. King Valche clutched her hand, searched her face a moment, and then dragged her into his embrace. Stunned, she hesitated a moment and then squeezed him back just as hard. Her father rarely showed affection and certainly not in public.

"Did he rape you?" He asked against her ear. "Are you hurt? By Leesha, I swear—"

"No, Father, truly. I'm fine."

"There's a fresh wound on his chest. I thought—" He eased back a step and she avoided his gaze. She didn't want him to see the turmoil in her own eyes. The shame. The fresh wound was hers, in a way, but not like her father thought.

Her gaze fell on the barbarians standing a few feet away. Rhaekhar stood with his back to her, talking with his Blood. They passed around some flask, each drinking several long gulps. By the tension in his shoulders, he was aware of her presence.

He was still angry. No, furious. She could read it in his body and his determined absence. Most men would shout and rant their fury at the source, but not the barbarian. Cold, controlled and calm, he kept an iron grip on his emotions. Interesting. What would it take to break that arrogant control?

"Your letter was sent to Pella safely," King Valche whispered with a wary eye at the barbarians. "Lady above, Daughter, why did you contact him?"

"He promised not to invade Allandor in my absence. Of course I contacted him. I'd do anything to ensure your safety and

Allandor's until I can return. Which reminds me; please compensate the innkeeper extremely well. I owe his family a great deal and they refused to accept the Pellans' gold."

"But how—"

"And the other letter?"

"It will be done, Daughter, but I'm not convinced horses will make much difference. Not without you here to lead."

Rhaekhar turned and waved her over impatiently. Shannari ground her teeth together with frustration. The gall of the man! She wanted to march over and feed him a few inches of steel. "As Leesha is my witness, I will find a way to come home as soon as possible."

When she neared, Rhaekhar's hard golden eyes drilled into her, his face a cold mask. "We ride within the hour."

Deeper, though, she felt searing heat. A need to haul her against him and imprint his will on every inch of her.

How was it possible? His external demeanor proclaimed arrogant coldness without a single sign of such volatile desire. The bond he'd spoken of earlier—even if he spoke truthfully, she'd never expected to feel anything herself. But how else could she sense the desire he held carefully in check?

Her mind whirling, she nodded. The barbarian turned back to his men without another word. Braced for injured masculine pride and frustrated arguments, she stood a moment staring at him.

She realized she wanted to spar with him. She wanted him to voice his anger at her earlier, deliberate insults. To give her a chance to poke at his honor some more. And yes, she wanted to relieve some of the guilt she felt. The man had made incredible, passionate love to her, and she'd insulted him badly.

Furious at herself, she decided to spend a few more moments with her father for contingency planning. She turned away only to be jerked back around and pressed against a solid wall of muscle.

"Where's my kiss this morning?"

Hot, velvet skin, rich sweet-hay scent and rough, tender warrior hands swamped her senses. Desire poured through her, followed by a rush of adrenaline. He did nothing but hold her, letting her absorb his heat and scent. Blessed Lady, this man was dangerous. He knew if he forced her, she would be happy to fight him. Sensual warfare, though... "Forget it."

His breathing was ragged against her ear, his breath hot, and his lips seared her skin. His fingers brushed the base of her neck and the curve of her shoulder where he'd bitten her, and she cried out. Not pain but fire flooded through her, stirring her memory of his frantic body, his fierceness, his mouth locked to her shoulder to taste every last drop of blood.

"No kiss?"

His teeth grazed her earlobe, and she shuddered. "Never!"

"Ah, you challenge me once more. I say you will kiss me by sunset."

Peeling herself away from the tempting expanse of his body, she tried for an airy, confident tone. "Only in your dreams, Khul."

She failed. Even she heard the sultry quaver in her voice.

"Always, na'lanna. My dreams are yours."

The short walk back to her father felt suspiciously like full blown retreat.

## 7

The barbarian rode to where Shannari stood with her father. Blessed Lady above, the warhorse was huge. Relief surged through her again at the thought of how badly the battle could have gone yesterday. "Where's my horse?"

Rhaekhar grinned and reached down his hand. "You're riding with me."

Shaking her head, she backed away. "You must be jesting. There's no way in hell I'm riding with you."

"You must, *na'lanna*. Your outlander pony will not survive our pace through the blasted lands, and none of our *na'kindren* will carry you alone."

Narrowing her eyes, she nibbled her lip and stared at him doubtfully. He seemed honestly concerned but she felt an odd twinge through the newly-formed connection with him. A twinge of conscience, perhaps?

He leaned down further, seized her hand and hauled her up before him. She tried to wriggle away, but his arms locked her against him. Even through her clothes, she could feel him. A whole day of traveling, pressed up against him like this? She was in serious trouble.

"Ah, you like that."

"Get out of my head!"

"I don't need to hear your thoughts to know you want me, Shannari. Imagine what else we might have learned about each other last night. What we shall learn this night."

"Unless I refuse you. I can refuse you, right?"

Stiffening, he sat upright and reined his horse toward the group of waiting barbarians. Cold fury roared through the fledgling bond, mixed with hurt. "Aye."

Shannari rolled her eyes. One night with the man and he wanted her to proclaim undying love. She had no idea how to soothe hurt masculine pride even if she had wanted to, so she changed the subject. "How many warriors will you leave to hold Dalden Bay?"

She honestly didn't expect him to answer. No general in his right mind would share such information with the enemy.

"A fist, fifty warriors."

"So few?" She barely stifled the rush of glee. Even her defeated Guard could handle fifty warriors with the right strategy. With enough time, Fenton should be able to devise the right blend of surprise to—

"Of course, your soldiers will not attack while I hold you captive."

She started to retort that her soldiers would never be so foolishly hindered, but she hesitated. His threat had merit. A threat against the Princess held hostage on their Plains and the barbarians could definitely be assured of peace from Allandor.

Did Rhaekhar mean to use her in such a way? Had that been his plan all along despite his words and promises of love? She suddenly thought better of him. "You would kill me if the Guard attacked your men?"

"Nay, I would sooner cut off my right hand than harm you in any way. But the outlanders don't know this."

True. Even if she were able to communicate the truth to her father or Fenton in some way, they'd still hesitate for fear of repercussion. If all Rhaekhar wanted was Dalden Bay, he would have it uncontested as far as Allandor was concerned, as long as she remained safe.

She was now even more thankful that Stephan had contacted her. She might need to use Pella as a diversion. He would have no hesitation to attack Dalden Bay.

"Of course even if there is an attack, I can return in a day's hard ride with hundreds of fists at my command."

"You have thousands of warriors?" Her stomach rolled and her voice quavered. Two hundred Sha'Kae al'Dan had made minced meat of her Allandor Guard; thousands of barbarians could march on Shanhasson and beyond.

"Aye. The Nine Camps are mighty, and our herds are vast. When the Great Wind Stallion Calls us to battle in the Last Days, we shall be ready." Rhaekhar drew the stallion to a halt and addressed his waiting men. "You are charged with keeping Dalden Bay for the Sha'Kae al'Dan. Do not molest the outlanders in any way. Trade with them if you desire, but allow none to enter the blasted lands or our Plains beyond. Ride for my Camp at the slightest threat of attack. I am Khul of the Nine Camps. None shall take from me what I claim for the Sha'Kae al'Dan."

The barbarians roared their approval and saluted Rhaekhar with their right fists over their hearts.

He wheeled his horse back around to face her father, still standing in the street.

"Do you have any last goodbyes you wish to give your father?"

The compassion in his voice made her tighten her jaw. Lines of worry marked King Valche's face and his eyes glistened suspiciously. Blessed Lady, if he wept, she'd never forgive him. She refused to cry in front of this arrogant Khul.

"May Leesha protect you, Daughter." Her father's voice broke, and Shannari closed her eyes, struggling to contain her tears.

Fear and worry rolled through her, leaving her shaking. What if she never escaped the barbarian? What would happen to her family, her country, her people?

"Khul Rhaekhar, I beg you once more. Please. Release my daughter. I will give you anything my country possesses to keep her safe."

She couldn't stop the tears, not when her regal father humbled himself before the barbarians and Allandorians alike.

"The Rose of Shanhasson is mine. Mine to take; mine to protect. I shall protect her with my life, Valche, but don't force my hand to violence by attacking this village or my warriors. Retribution will be swift and silent."

Despite the agony shredding her heart, she had to admit that was masterfully done. He never directly said he would use her as a hostage, but he knew very well that her people would believe it to be true. Even if she objected now, the thought would linger in her father's mind.

King Valche glared up at Rhaekhar, hatred darkening his eyes. "Know this, Khul. If a single hair on her head is harmed, I'll find a way to pay you back in kind. I swear it on my beloved Queen's grave. Shannari will return to me safe and well or I'll kill you."

Rhaekhar shrugged and signaled his horse into a trot. "As Vulkar wills."

With a whoop, the remaining barbarians rode after them. Shannari struggled to look back over his shoulder for one last glance of her father, but all she could see were the green fields and the storm-gray waters of the bay.

Home. Turning back around, she looked straight ahead and

let the tears stream silently down her cheeks. *Will I ever see my homeland again?*

The Khul had spoken truly when he said her Green Land mount wouldn't survive the trip. She couldn't believe the punishing pace he set to return to his Plains. The massive horses maintained a hard trot for hours on end without slowing.

The lush green grass of the lowlands faded to tall yellowed hay that eventually turned to clumps of brown, withered stalks. The trees twisted in agony, their branches gnarled pitifully and bleached as white as bones. Sand and black, sharp rock replaced the rich dark loam of the fertile fields of Allandor. The deafening, uneasy silence was interrupted only by the creak of leather and the occasional scrape of hoof on rock on their somber passage through the wastelands.

A deep uneasiness welled up in her heart that had nothing to do with the growing homesickness in her heart. She wanted to cover her eyes and ears from the pain. The land seemed to scream to her, and her eyes burned with tears. Some deep, secret part of her longed to reach out and heal these broken, blasted lands. "Why is everything so dead and barren?"

"It's a reminder," Rhaekhar answered solemnly. "The Great Wind Stallion caused this destruction to punish us for failing to protect His greatest gift. If we fail again, the entire Plains will be destroyed, just as the land here was destroyed generations ago.

"Once this was part of the Sea of Grass stretching as far as the eyes could see. We cared for *na'kindren* on these Plains, and we honored Vulkar, the Great Wind Stallion. Then outlanders came and brought their strange customs to our Plains. They asked us to show them how to train their ponies for war. We opened our tents to them, learned their languages, shared our food, and showed them our ways. But the lowland horses had no spirit, no *sangral*. They couldn't be taught the Sha'Kae al'Dan ways.

"The outlanders wanted to buy *na'kindren* so they could breed their own herds. They didn't understand when we refused. How could we sell Vulkar's Own Children? The outlanders were angry and loud with their curses as they rode away on their ponies, but we forgot about them and their puny warriors.

"We shouldn't have forgotten them. We should have guarded *na'kindren* closer instead. The outlanders hid in the tall grass until the warriors were in their tents and then they torched the grass between us and the herd. *Na'kindren* scattered. Some were captured by the outlanders and stolen from the Plains. Many others were killed, trapped by the flames.

"We followed the outlanders to their Green Lands and waged war until every last *na'kindre* was found and brought home to the Plains. We even took the lowland mares that carried the seed of *na'kindre* so not a single drop of *sangral* blood was left in the Green Lands. We swore that *na'kindren* would never fall into the hands of an outlander again.

"Only a handful of Vulkar's Children survived, a fraction of the great herd that had roamed the Sea of Grass in freedom and joy. Vulkar exploded with fury! His hooves sunk into the ground to melt the stone beneath until it ran red across the Plains. He killed the grasses, burned and split the earth, and created a wasteland of desert to protect the few *na'kindren* that were left to us. They fled to Vulkar's Mountain in the Clouds where they would be safe."

She wiped away tears at the desolate loss in his voice. "But you have *na'kindren* now, don't you? Isn't that what you call these horses?"

"This stallion I ride isn't a *na'kindre* of the true spirit and blood. He's descended from the lowland mares that were brought back round with *na'kindren* seed. The blood of Vulkar runs thinly in our *na'kindren* now. But they're still our brothers, and we shall die to protect them."

What kind of horses had the true *na'kindren* been if these majestic beasts carried only a fraction of the true blood? How would his people accept her—a pale-skinned outlander—when her people had brought such distrust and devastation to his land?

The Sha'Kae al'Dan invasion made even less sense. Why on earth would he want to capture Dalden Bay when they obviously had great reason to distrust and even hate her people? "You must have strict laws against allowing my people into your Plains ever again."

"Aye. The punishment for unauthorized entry to our Plains is death."

She couldn't suppress a shiver at the flat, cold tone in his voice. She didn't imagine death at the barbarians' hands would be painless and quick. "Have you killed many of my people?"

"More in recent months than entire decades before," Rhaekhar admitted. "We've always welcomed traders willing to brave the blasted lands on the edge of the Plains as long as they follow our laws. Tents always camp near the border to meet and escort traders if necessary. More and more, though, we've found travelers deeper in our territory. Since Dalden Bay is the only outlander Camp near the Plains, we decided to end all encroach-ment directly."

"Allandorians aren't the trespassers. My father and I would know of it, I assure you. My family visits the village at least once a month and we have many strong contacts there. Invasion of your Plains is the last thing on our minds."

He shrugged against her back. "I hear your words, *na'lanna*, but I can only tell you what we've seen. The outlanders are coming from somewhere. If blocking Dalden Bay doesn't prevent this encroachment, then I shall pursue other options. As Khul of the Nine Camps, it's my duty to ensure the safety of the Plains at all cost."

He pressed closer, rubbing his cheek affectionately against hers. Clenching her jaw, Shannari barely suppressed the low groan. His left arm tightened about her waist, his broad chest covered her back, and his thighs encased her on either side. Surrounded by his heat and strength, she couldn't help but remember his passion. His touch. His powerful body. The heady rich taste of his blood.

"As Khul, I felt in my heart that the Great Wind Stallion wished us to act now, without delay, to keep outlanders from the Plains. To Him I'm more grateful than I can say, for His will brought me to you. *Na'lanna*, my beloved, my heart beats for you."

Deliberately ignoring the fluttering in her stomach at his words, Shannari set the hook for her plan. "I wouldn't be surprised if Stephan has been sending spies into your Plains. I know he has spies in Allandor and Dalden Bay itself. We've warred over Dalden Bay numerous times already, and I was prepared to hand it over to him in exchange for his help. You might find Dalden Bay difficult to hold, Khul."

Straightening, Rhaekhar laughed softly beneath his breath. "Have no worries, *na'lanna*. A warrior takes what he wants and then keeps it. Dalden Bay—and you—are safe in my hands."

She let a hard, grim smile curve her lips since he couldn't see her reaction. His insufferable warrior arrogance would make it impossible for him to ignore any attack on Dalden Bay. With luck, Stephan would organize a strike against the barbarians left behind within a month, two at most. Rhaekhar would be forced to respond with due force. And when she saw the green fertile fields of home again, she'd

What? She'd never run from anything in her life. Running

from the barbarian seemed especially cowardly given the fool-hardy attachment he already felt for her. He might just hold to his oath, too, and hunt her down wherever she went. Nothing short of bloodshed might convince him to leave her behind. Even then, she might have to kill him.

*Best I keep my sword close at all times.*


H er scent was a sweet torment, begging him to bury his face into the curve of her neck. Her body brushed his in pure torture. Yet Rhaekhar resisted the urge to drag her tight against him. She expected him to push his advantage in sensual warfare. She hoped he would be all Khul, arrogant, demanding and invincible.

But even the mightiest Khul on the Plains knew a challenge loss was sometimes worth the small cost of pride.

So he kept his hands to himself as much as possible. He couldn't help cradling her hips with his thighs and didn't want to stop the almost-innocent brush of his arm against hers. The smallest touch was enough to make her shiver against him delightfully.

How he longed to feel her bare skin against his instead of the leathers and metal encasing her body. "You must be very hot in such clothing, *na'lanna*. You would be much more comfortable in Sha'Kae al'Dan clothing."

She glanced at him askance over her shoulder. "If your women wear as little as you do, then you can forget such a ridiculous notion."

"Aye, the women wear a *memshai* around their hips like the warriors' *memshas*, but the women knot theirs."

"Knot it?" He didn't need to see her face to know she frowned. "Why?"

He let all the heat he felt warm his voice. "Do you remember how easily my *memsha* was removed last night? Our women like to make their warriors work for such treasures."

"Oh." Very carefully, she kept her back to him, but he felt the surge of heat and embarrassment, both, through the bond. "They wear nothing else?"

Rhaekhar closed his eyes and concentrated on breathing. The image of this outlander woman with only a *memshai* about her hips sent his heart pounding like a herd of stampeding *na'kindren*. "The women also wear vests." His voice sounded thick and strained to his ears. Very strained. Even thoughts of a vest cupping her luscious breasts were torment. "Loose, comfortable, very cool. I think you would like it."

"I can't imagine such... freedom. I've worn chain mail ever since I can remember, heavier every year for the best protection I could carry."

"You will be safe with me, Shannari. On my honor, you will have no need for chain mail."

She laughed softly and shook her head. "My apologies, Khul, but somehow, I don't believe you. You have no idea how many assassins have come after me over the years. More than I can count. Turmoil and upheaval follow me everywhere. The last time Father and I traveled to Taza there was an assassination attempt on my life every single day. It was ridiculous."

Rhaekhar stroked the hilt of the *rahke* on his hip. Not ridiculous, in his opinion, but grievous. How could Valche allow her to face such constant danger? These outlanders had no concept of honor. "Why do so many of your people want you dead?"

Her scent sharpened, cold and deadly like steel. "Only a Daughter of Our Blessed Lady may wear the Rose Crown and protect the land, and I'm the Last. The land and the Lady are one. I fear for all of the Green Lands if Theo sits on the High Throne."

"This is the man you were promised to?"

She nodded. "He's the only other direct descendant of the

Lady, although I carry more of Her blood than does he. Theo is evil, though. The rumors we hear about Shanhasson—torture, people disappearing—it's madness."

A fist-full of *rahkes* twisted in Rhaekhar's gut. Why would such an honorable, courageous woman bind herself to such a foul cur? It made no sense to him. He couldn't even think of a reasonable response, for every warrior instinct he possessed told him to whirl Khan and gallop toward Shanhasson, never stopping until Theo's blood darkened his sword.

She must have sensed his disquiet. "Politically, my marriage to Theo made perfect sense. Once he touched me, though..." She shivered and pressed back against him. That told him more than anything how much she abhorred the man. "I couldn't do it. I won't. I'll kill him first."

"Nay." Rhaekhar wrapped his arm around her, clamping her tight against his chest. "When I lay eyes on the outlander Theo, I shall kill him. So says Khul of the Nine Camps of the Sha'Kae al'Dan. I swear it on my honor."

8

Dusk painted rose and lavender across the darkening
sky, yet still the warhorses charged onward into the
night. Shannari stretched carefully, trying to avoid
rubbing up against the barbarian. She winced. She'd always
considered herself an accomplished rider, but she'd never spent
so many hours in the saddle before.

Rhaekhar heaved a huge sigh behind her. "I suppose I have
lost your challenge."

"What challenge?"

"That you would kiss me before this night."

She couldn't help it. She laughed. The arrogant, insufferable
Khul actually sounded chagrined. "I told you I wouldn't
kiss you."

"You are indeed a formidable opponent, *na'lanna*. You rebuff
every tenderness and affection I would give you."

Ouch. Why didn't he just come right out and tell her she was
a cold-hearted bitch? She supposed she was. With no heart and
no lasting hope for such foolishness, what else could she be? It

was too late for her to daydream about things she could never have.

Things she didn't even want to have.

*Then why do I ache at the desolation in his voice?*

"Let us decide my challenge loss. What would you like in payment?"

Her response came out sharper than she intended. "I want nothing from you."

"I must pay for the loss of this challenge. My honor demands it." The barbarian vibrated with tension behind her and his fingers turned white from his fierce grip on the reins. "You must allow me to make amends."

"I never accepted your fool challenge," she retorted. "You owe me nothing!"

The dark-haired Blood reined his horse closer. She'd noticed the guards riding about them all day, but this was the first any of them had approached for conversation. "I have a suggestion, Khul."

Rhaekhar didn't seem too pleased if the biting growl in his voice was any indication. "This is none of your concern, Gregar."

The Blood smirked, totally undeterred by the menace rumbling from the big barbarian. "As you say, Khul, but if I remember correctly, the oasis where we camped on the way to the Green Lands had one very attractive quality. Perhaps Shannari would accept a bath from you in payment for your challenge loss."

Rhaekhar relaxed behind her enough to actually chuckle. His burly forearm came around her again to hug her close. She kept her back as stiff as possible, but the barbarian refused to release her from the intimate contact. "Aye, now I know exactly what my challenge loss shall be."

Alarm sent Shannari's voice shooting up an octave. "What?"

The Blood gave her a wide, knowing smile, his white teeth

flashing against his face. Gregar was darker skinned than the Khul's bronzed gold, bringing to mind a fresh, hot cup of caffe with just a little cream. With his mischievous grin and dark eyes gleaming with wickedness, Gregar was quite something to look at. The devil himself.

"While a dip in the small pool won't be as warm and relaxing as our steamtents, I believe you'll enjoy the bath just the same," Gregar said. "I'm sure Khul can give you a most acceptable bath."

His wording sent her pulse skittering faster. "I'll need privacy for my bath. Complete and utter privacy."

"Of course," Rhaekhar purred against her ear. "The pool is secluded from the main campsite, and the Blood will ensure we aren't disturbed. Won't you, Gregar?"

"Oh, aye, Khul. Not a soul will intrude on your challenge loss. I swear it on my honor."

In his own way, the Blood was just as disturbing as his Khul. She couldn't forget how Gregar had scared her the previous night, the blade held to her throat before she'd even known he was there.

Oddly, he seemed familiar somehow. Some resonance, a secret memory she couldn't recall. Impossible, she knew, just as she could no longer fear him, even knowing what he was.

Death Rider. Assassin. Knife to her throat. Bone-chilling coldness. Shadows. Death waited in his dark, shining eyes.

Yet she felt no urge to reach for her sword. In fact, she hadn't reached for her sword all day. Was she already so comfortable with the Sha'Kae al'Dan that she no longer considered them enemies?

Pushing that troubling thought away, she tried to think of a way to remove the barbarian from any participation in bathing. After the heat of the desert, she smelled horrid and her hair was caked with dust. A bath would be lovely. But—

"I shall enjoy this challenge loss immensely." Rhaekhar's

lips brushed her ear, sending goose bumps shooting down her arms. "To fully repay my debt to you, I shall dry you with my tongue."

The short, high-pitched sound that came out of her mouth could only be called a yelp. "Absolutely not!"

"My honor demands it, *na'lanna*. I must repay this loss with the utmost of my ability."

Heat curled inside her at the thought. Oh, Blessed Lady, her body could imagine only too well what the "utmost of his ability" might be. From the events of last night, she guessed the barbarian would be devastatingly skilled in the bedchamber if given half a chance to demonstrate. "Keep your bloody hands to yourself!"

Rhaekhar held his palms up before them to examine his hands. "Bloody? Ah. You wish for my blood, too. Very well, *na'lanna*. I am most pleased to comply. Bath and blood. I can hardly wait to repay this debt."

Laughing, the Blood reined his horse back toward his guarding position several paces away.

"Gregar."

The Blood paused, some of the teasing grin fading from his face. Something silent and deep passed between the two barbarians, but she had no idea what or why.

"My thanks."

Gregar smirked and nodded, then turned those flashing eyes of wickedness on her. "Call on me if you need assistance, Khul. It's an honor to serve you both."

Once again the terrain changed as the obsidian rocks and warped trees began to yield to normal desert vegetation. The sand gleamed golden white in the pale moonlight, clean and beautiful instead of angry and sharp.

Strange plants lifted crooked arms to the sky, their leathery green skin covered with spikes and delicate pink blossoms.

The daytime heat dissipated and the chilly evening air made her thankful for the barbarian's body against hers. He radiated heat like an oven, all velvet skin and baked bread and hay.

Pure temptation.

Surprisingly, though, he remained a gentleman the rest of the evening with only the slight intimacies expected when two people shared a horse, even one so large as this. His unexpected reserve mattered not a bit to her traitorous body. Desire kindled inside her at every movement. The slightest memory of last night. The faintest whiff of his mouth-watering scent.

If she let her imagination drift for even a moment to what the barbarian planned at the oasis...

How could she not think about his gorgeous, muscular body when she half sat in his lap? No matter how carefully she tried to maintain a modest distance, her back and buttocks pressed up against his stomach and groin.

Hell, pure hell.

The warhorse suddenly charged forward, throwing her back against the barbarian's chest. After hours of their exhausting pace, the horses quickened to a canter and then to an all out gallop. Then she, too, could smell it—sweet, pure water in the middle of this barren land. Tall, gracious trees marked the natural springs and the air grew cooler and sweeter beneath their shade.

The barbarians didn't make much of a camp. A fire, a flask passed around, some kind of smoked meat, hard bread. Usual travel or military rations. Shannari couldn't count the number of times she'd eaten such food in the field. What she didn't understand was why she couldn't take her eyes off the man beside her.

Sitting on the ground, surrounded by his warriors, Rhaekhar laughed and talked easily. They respected him. He led them by example, not by right of blood or might of wealth as in the Green Lands. He was a warrior's warrior—bigger, stronger, and smarter than those who followed him. Men who would gladly give their lives for him.

She respected him, too, but that wasn't why she was so fascinated. He laughed with his wicked jokester Blood, his golden eyes warm and shining. Such a smile, wide and open and honest. Such loyalty. None of these men were scheming to overthrow him. He trusted them all implicitly. She saw such trust as a weakness, a failing, but with him...

He was so strong, so invincible, that it didn't matter. She kept trying to analyze his politics, his strategy, but it came down to simple loyalty and trust. They trusted him to lead them; he trusted them to follow.

Astounding.

One of the other Blood told a story about Gregar, and the other warriors howled with laughter. Since they spoke in their own language, she had no idea what was so amusing. The only word she understood was *memsha*, the cloth the warriors wore about their hips.

The other Blood, Varne, she thought, said something including her name. The warriors cheered louder, but Gregar went very, very still. The temperature dropped suddenly, and his eyes... She swore they had gone darker, nearly black.

Shivering, she rubbed her arms. "What did he say?"

"Varne suggested you could be the judge," Rhaekhar answered. He slapped Gregar on the back, and the spreading darkness in the Blood's gaze faded.

"The judge of what?"

Varne laughed, a short, harsh burst of forced amusement. "Gregar's famous for turning everything into an arse competition."

For the first time, she felt some malicious undercurrent

among Rhaekhar's warriors. She'd assumed the two Blood were friends, but perhaps she was mistaken.

Gregar smirked. "A competition I always win."

Rhaekhar laughed, his manner unchanged. Yet the current of tension still vibrated between his two Blood. "What say you, Shannari?"

He had to be jesting. "You want me to judge... arses? Gregar's and..."

Rhaekhar smiled, a hard show of teeth and dominance. "Mine."

She couldn't help the blush stealing across her cheeks. They wore so very little clothing already—did they even have any sort of underclothes on beneath their *memshas*? Inwardly groaning, she couldn't even believe she contemplated such a thing.

Gregar laughed so hard he bent over his knees, gasping for breath. Varne gave him a disgusted look and turned back to the other warriors for more stories.

Very carefully, she kept from looking at either the Khul or his Blood. She didn't want to let her mind begin imagining...

Rhaekhar sat down beside her and leaned in against her side, his incredible warmth soaking into her even through her leathers. For her ears alone, he whispered, "I shall be most pleased to remove my *memsha* so you may see what I wear beneath."

Damned bond. She hated him sensing everything, especially such embarrassing questions. "No, no thank you."

"As you wish, *na'lanna*."

She thought the subject dropped until he picked up her left hand. He kissed her palm, his tongue swirling against her skin. And then he pressed her hand against his thigh.

Ever so slowly, he eased her hand higher, beneath the *memsha*, to his hip where another much smaller cloth wrapped tightly beneath the green material. His breath was hot and moist against her ear. "Loincloth."

His tongue probed her ear canal, and she moaned. So quickly, so effortlessly, he stirred such overwhelming need in her. Need to stroke his body, to feel his heat, his strength, his hands.

He shifted beside her, long, powerful muscle moving beneath her hand. "I don't always wear one, but riding is much more comfortable with a loincloth holding everything secure."

Nearly panting now, she couldn't help but think about "everything" so close to her hand. He released her hand, giving her plenty of space to move away, but she couldn't. She didn't want to.

Inching her fingers across his abdomen, she worked deeper beneath the loincloth. Of her own accord, she turned into his embrace, dropping her head against his chest. Hot silken skin beneath her mouth, his scent musky and rich.

He drew her closer, and she was lost. When he picked her up and carried her away from the whooping warriors, she made no protest. She was too busy tasting his skin.

"Wait but a moment, na'lanna, and let me wash the grime away."

"I don't mind," she whispered against his skin. Salt, sweat, dirt, warrior. It didn't matter. He tasted wonderful. The broad expanse of skin and muscle beckoned. She suddenly wanted to sink her teeth into him, find the rich, spicy blood beneath, and leave the imprint of her teeth deep in his skin.

"Aye, bite me. Put your mark upon me so all may see our passion."

S hannari suddenly pitched backward in his arms. Striding through the trees as fast as possible in the dark, Rhaekhar stumbled and nearly fell flat on his back. She recoiled from him, where moments before she had been eating him alive, much to his great delight.

The *na'lanna* bond flooded him with dark emotions: rage, betrayal, and blackest shame. Her memory was so strong that he saw it as his own. A man in her bed, her hesitant desire blooming. He felt her youth, realized she was just a girl, barely a woman. She bit the outlander on the neck, harder, need rising after the initial pain of his entry.

Rhaekhar tasted the barest hint of blood in his mouth, felt her response, pleasure humming nigh to completion, and then...

The outlander shoved her aside and struck her. The cur actually hit her in the face while shouting obscenities.

Growling with fury, Rhaekhar seized her chin and pulled her higher in his arms. She fought wildly, trying to escape, him or the memory, he couldn't tell. Her sense of shame drowned him, only increasing his rage.

"Listen to me." He leaned down so their noses were touching, forcing her to look into his eyes. "I'm not this cur who would strike you. I shall never turn from you or your needs, whatever they may be. It's impossible for you to repulse me, for you are my very heart. What you need, I need. What you enjoy, I enjoy. To harm you in any way would destroy me. If I ever lay eyes on this cur who hurt you, I shall cut off his cock and make him eat it before I strangle him with my bare hands. Do you understand?"

Chest heaving, tears pouring from her eyes, she stared back at him. She swallowed hard, trying to force the words out. "If I lose control..."

"I want you to lose control. I relish your passion, no matter how wild, or raw, or bloody. It's impossible for you to hurt me."

She closed her eyes, laughing raggedly, and the sound nigh tore his heart in half. "You have no idea what I'm capable of."

"I know your heart, your mind, your soul, your body. You cannot hide anything from me. Listen to me—*my* feelings, *my* desire—and forget this other man. I am your warrior. Any other must come through me to you, even this outlander's memory, and I deny him. I deny him."

His last words were vehement, ringing between them. If only he could deny all who had interest in her, but his honor wouldn't allow him to shirk his duty to his woman. He hadn't mistaken or imagined the sliver of interest she felt for his Shadowed Blood.

If she needed, he provided, whatever it might be. And now, she most needed to forget this memory that tormented her.

Clamping his hand at the base of her neck, he kissed her with all the passion and longing that burned in him. The command and dominance that roared in his blood. Her head fell back beneath his onslaught, her mouth opening beneath his. He claimed every inch of her mouth, possessed it, took her very breath and gave her air from his own lungs, until she was limp in his arms.

On the sandy bank of the pool, he set her down on her feet, carefully steadying her. Swaying, she blinked, her eyes dazed, her lips swollen and soft. He silently swore to kiss her often and hard. She needed both conqueror and tender lover. The trick would be deciding when she needed one and not the other.

She made no objection when he stripped off the leather and metal keeping her body hidden from him. Even her sword. Dazed lushness fled from her face when he began removing his boots. Challenge gleamed in her midnight eyes, sparking for a skirmish when he yanked off the cloth about his waist.

Instead of hauling her into the water, he tossed the *memsha* and loincloth into a heap on his boots and strode into the water without a backward glance.

He didn't need to see her eyes locked on him; he could feel her desire flaring through the bond like wildfire. Perhaps he could provide Gregar some competition after all. "Are you going to stare at my arse all night or join me in the water?"

## 9

**D**eliciously cool, the water lapped at Shannari's legs as she waded deeper. She averted her gaze from the gloriously nude temptation almost within hand's reach and concentrated on washing the grime from her body.

She felt fragile and raw, as if she'd rolled about on punishing sand and sharp rock. She'd never intended to share that horrible memory with anyone, let alone another lover. Even with Devin, she'd kept that secret tightly concealed. Not that it helped. She'd never so much as nibbled on him, yet he'd still turned on her.

*Everyone turns on me sooner or later. Best I remember it.*

"This Devin—he's the one who broke your heart?"

Startled, she faced the barbarian before she could stop herself. He had his back to her, so she let her gaze linger on his magnificent body.

A thick mane of golden-brown hair cascaded over brawny shoulders and down his broad back, teasing her eyes lower to his firm, rounded ass. She'd never been interested in looking at a man's backside before, but Leesha help her, he had a fine one. "How did you know his name?"

"The bond."

For such a giant of a man, his movements were graceful and carefully controlled, even while doing something so mundane. Her eyes traced the lines of muscle and ligament from his thick warrior neck to his tremendous shoulders, down his wide chest to his chiseled waist.

"Is he the one who struck you?"

Only two lovers in her whole life before the barbarian, and both of them had ended badly. Very badly indeed. "No." *Not exactly.*

"Is this one dead, too, or will I have the pleasure of exacting my justice?"

"I have no idea whether Jared lives or not. It was many years ago. Would you truly strangle someone with your bare hands?"

"Aye. Strangulation is the worst possible death sentence on the Plains. You were little more than a girl, correct?"

Embarrassment made her hunker down in the water up to her chin. Discussing her previous lovers was disconcerting to say the least. "I was a woman." Technically. Her monthly flows had started. "It was necessary."

"Why?"

How to explain something she didn't fully understand herself? Besides, the whole event was a nightmare gone wrong from the very beginning.

The barbarian turned and looked at her expectantly. Sighing, she tried to explain. "As a direct descendant of Our Blessed Lady Leesha, I'm supposed to have power. Magic. I'm supposed to use it to help our people and protect our lands from evil. According to legend, this magic is awoken through love. But it didn't work for me."

Rhaekhar seemed more intrigued than alarmed by her failures. "We believe much the same thing. We carry the Great Wind Stallion's blood in our veins, and we're charged with protecting the Sea of Grass and His Children, the *na'kindren*. He often gives us great gifts to carry out our duty."

Moving closer, he pulled the heavy braid over her shoulder and began unraveling it. Since she really was filthy, she made no protest. The sensation of his powerful hands moving through her hair was incredible, though. How such a mighty warrior could be so unfailing gentle—when he chose —astounded her.

"You have magic, *na'lanna*. I feel it."

"Oh, some, I suppose, but nothing like I'm supposed to wield as High Queen." She couldn't keep the wistfulness out of her voice. So many times, she'd dreamed about uniting the Green Lands into a strong republic instead of loose, squabbling countries always currying political favor with enemies and allies alike. No disease, famine, drought. No injustice. In her foolish fable, no one suffered or went without in a land of plenty and happiness as the Lady intended. "Now, it's too late."

"Why?"

"Love awakens the magic."

"And you believe you will never love again." His tone of voice wasn't accusatory or threatening, merely curious. "Did you love Devin very much, then?"

She started to hunch deeper into the water, until she realized that put her on a level with the barbarian's navel. Closing her eyes, she concentrated hard on keeping her secrets buried very, very deep. "Not so much, no."

"Then why do you believe you will never love again?"

"Love nearly killed me," she answered flatly. "I'm the Lady's Last Daughter. If I die, no one stands between my people and the greatest evil of all."

Lygon, the Lord of Darkness. He waited for her in dreams, shadows sucking her down to agony and endless pain. Nightmare upon nightmare upon nightmare. Trapped, locked away from the sun, she would die there, and He would be free.

Rhaekhar touched the scar on her chest, his fingers tender. Terror screamed through her. She jerked back, tried to turn away, to hide, but his hand in her hair held her firm. *Oh, Lady, please don't make me live that nightmare again!*

He drew her against his chest, swamping her fear with his rich scent and the warmth of his skin. "Shhh, my heart. You're not ready to tell me about him, so I shall not ask. Tell me instead of the one who struck you. I must understand how your magic should awaken."

With his arms gentle around her and his muscled chest beneath her cheek, she couldn't find the strength to refuse. "Usually the High Priest chooses the man who can awaken the Daughter of Leesha, or at least approves her choice. But Father Aran was delayed in Shanhasson. We were at war with Pella, and it was going badly. Our Captain was wounded, our troops disheartened, and Dalden Bay was on the verge of collapse. We needed help, and we thought my power would save us all. So my father selected one of his most trusted advisors for me. Our joining... Well. You saw how it ended."

"The man was wrong for hurting you, but I consider it a greater wrong that your father forced you to share your blankets with this man with no love, no tenderness, no shared desire between you. No wonder it ended badly, Shannari."

She tried to remember the nervous but excited young woman who'd taken Jared to her bed. He was a good looking man, distinguished, well liked, with a nice smile. She'd been pleased enough with her father's choice. The fault was hers. "No one forced me. I was willing, but I felt nothing afterward. No enjoyment, no happiness, no pleasure, no love." Shame welled up in her heart, and aching sadness. Oh, how she failed. "No magic."

"Nay." Rhaekhar's voice was harsh as he tilted her chin up to meet her gaze. "I shall give you all the love and care and pleasure you will ever need, Shannari. I shall give you my honor, my very life if need be. I shall even find a way to heal your wounded heart. And perhaps my love will awaken your magic as well."

He pressed his lips to hers in a soft, gentle kiss that stole the arguments and doubts and fears from her mind. This conquering barbarian could have used her vilely. Beaten, raped, tortured, starved, she would be powerless to stop him short of death.

Instead, he touched her with such gentleness, such passion, that he stole her very breath. For the first time, she actually let herself consider that he might very well succeed.

Enthralling her with slow, deep kisses, Rhaekhar eased her down to the waiting blankets. He settled against her, between her thighs, and she trembled beneath him. She pulled at his hair, her lips demanding, her body rising up to meet his, urging him to greater speed.

His answer was to move away from her mouth, pressing soft, moist kisses across her jaw, down her neck. And then he began licking beads of water from her skin.

"You're not actually going to... to..."

"Lick you dry? Of course I am. I must." Her skin tasted like summer fruits and cream, silken and velvet beneath his mouth. "I wanted to do this the moment I recognized you."

"Don't be ridiculous," she retorted. She fought him, wiggling and struggling to free herself from beneath his weight. Not because she had no desire for him; on the contrary, she wanted him to hurry. "I never accepted your challenge or this so-called loss. Besides, how on earth could you recognize me when we've never met?" She paused, suddenly noticing the blanket beneath them. "Where did this come from?"

"Aye, I did recognize you. A warrior always recognizes *na'lanna*. I smelled you, and I knew. My heart knew." He decided not to mention the Great Wind Stallion's vision he'd received as a lad. She would likely think him even more foolish. "The Blood spread my blankets while we were otherwise occupied."

Unease trickled through the bond and she froze beneath him. "Are the Blood here even now? Watching?"

To distract her, he gripped her throat with his teeth briefly, letting her remember the thrill of his bite the previous night. "Watching for danger, not us. Don't even think of them."

She surged up again in one last desperate attempt to flip him over. "I want to be on top."

"Another night it will be my great pleasure to let you love me however you wish. This night, however, lie still and let me care for you. You need do nothing but enjoy it."

Uneasy, she stilled beneath him, her body vibrating with tension. He spared several strokes of his tongue against his mark at the base of her neck. Too much attention to the bite would arouse her too quickly for what he intended, but he couldn't resist.

Arching up against him, she clutched his shoulders. "Why does it feel like that?"

"Like what?" He pressed his open mouth over the entire mark, reveling in her response. Lush and hot, her scent spiked with rising desire. "Like my tongue is reaching deep inside your body? Like my heart is moving toward yours?"

She whimpered softly, winding her fists into his hair to hold him close. "Melting."

"Aye, melt for me, *na'lanna*."

Swirling his tongue, he moved across her shoulder, down her arm. Here and there, he grazed her with his teeth. Not a bite, just a reminder. A promise. He laved the crook of her arm, nibbled his way down to her hand, and sucked each finger into the heat of his mouth one by one. By the time he pressed his mouth to her palm, the last bit of unease had bled out of her.

He picked up her other hand and gave it the same loving care, working his way back to her shoulder. By the time he finished lavishing attention on her breasts, her every breath caught on a soft little moan.

"That's quite enough." Shannari panted, tightening her fingers in his hair. "Really."

Ignoring her pleading tugs, he licked a path of fire down the valley between her breasts to her navel. "Nay, it's not nearly enough."

"You don't have to do this."

Sliding lower on her body, he allowed all the need and hunger he felt to roughen his voice. "I want to breathe your scent, taste your desire, feel your heat against my mouth. I want you to near rip out my hair with your passion. I want you to yell so loudly the Blood will wonder if I'm killing you. And then, my heart, I want you to ask me to do it all over again."

Her cheeks colored and her eyes flashed in the moonlight. "It's indecent for them to be so close. We're not far from the others, either. I wouldn't be surprised if they hear our voices, let alone... er..."

He let a wide, confident smile spread across his face. "Indeed, I'm counting on it. Now let me draw some very sweet music from your lips."

Her mouth clamped shut and her jaw tightened.

Shaking his head, he trailed his fingers across the tender skin of her lower abdomen. "You challenge me again, *na'lanna*. Think you I cannot make you scream with pleasure?"

"Not with an audience," she ground out.

"Ah, but on the Plains, we shall camp in the center of

hundreds of tents. The Blood share my tent with me, and often we share with guests. Think you I cannot make you forget them as well?"

Her appalled expression made him laugh out loud. "Never. It's indecent!"

"Well, I'm merely a barbarian after all. Perhaps I shall only make you scream once this night to help break you of this unfortunate reticence."

"Twice, Khul."

The low voice came from the shadows a few feet away. Shannari jerked with alarm at the Blood's nearness.

"Aye, Gregar, I accept your challenge. Now, see what you've done, Shannari? You must scream twice this night or I shall owe another challenge loss to my Blood." He leaned closer, deliberately breathing on her flesh, but she was tense, closed, trying to push him away where moments before she'd tried to pull him closer.

Raising his gaze, he stared into her face. "Tell me no and I'll roll over and go to sleep."

"I'm not saying no, but can't we be… quieter?"

Grinning, he sat up and whispered, "Aye, you can try. Do you want me to stop?"

She bit her lip, thinking, and finally shook her head. When he shackled her ankle and lifted her foot toward his mouth, she glared at him. He tickled the sole of her foot with his tongue, and she muttered a curse beneath her breath.

Nibbling his way up her leg, he licked and kissed the back of her knee until her legs lay completely open to him once more. Up past her knee, nipping as he went, until he traced the crease of her inner thigh with his tongue.

A muffled cry escaped her lips. Amused, he noted that she released his hair to press her hand over her mouth. Next time, he must remember to give her something to hold so she would forget about quieting her cries.

He kissed and licked a path up over her pelvic bone, across her belly, and back down the other side. So hot, so ready, he could smell her desire, feel her muscles trembling with longing. He felt her rising need through the bond, the spreading ache deep inside. Her scent spiced, blazing like humid summer nights.

She cursed again, low and raw, her hips lifting in invitation.

"Not yet, my heart, not yet." Sitting back up, he turned his attention to her other foot, dragging his head back and forth to trail his hair across her skin as he kissed her.

The bond screamed at him, while she remained silent except for the rare strangled cry. Fighting his own desire, he lingered at her thigh. He opened his mouth wide to take as much muscle and skin as his mouth could hold, gripping her firmly with his jaws. He left teeth marks in her skin, so he licked them away, soothing the sting.

Her scrambling fingers found his hair again, jerking his head higher. "Don't— don't make me— beg. Oh, bloody hell."

He slid his palms beneath her, tilting her hips upward, yet he refused to move his mouth higher. "Louder, Shannari. You must be louder or I'll lose the challenge."

Restless, she twisted her hips, desperate to urge him onward. He was more than happy to oblige, sliding a finger deep into her. Clenching his jaw, he fought back his own urges. To thrust as hard and deep as he could, imprinting himself on her for all time. To flip her over and take her like a stallion takes a mare, all domination, teeth and hooves.

Her pride would be the death of him.

**B**lessed Lady above. The barbarian was just as devastatingly skilled as she'd feared.

His mouth. He wouldn't stop tormenting her, using teeth, tongue, lips to obliterate her will, her thoughts, her pride. She couldn't think beyond the thundering need roaring in her body.

Silken hair trailed across her thighs, tangled in her hands. His unbelievably broad shoulders spread her thighs further apart, his rugged hands gripping her hips, dragging her to just the right position. His breath, so hot against her skin.

So close, but so far away.

Lady, she'd never felt such need before. Such agonizing pleasure. Aching emptiness ate a black hole in her defenses until she couldn't bear it any longer.

"Please!"

Immediately, he set his mouth on her, sliding his tongue deep and dragging it the full length of her. Shannari pressed the heel of her hand against her mouth, fighting back her cries. She knew the Blood were nearby, knew it should horrify her, knew she should shove the barbarian off her and demand some privacy. Somehow, though, she couldn't make herself care.

Licking. His tongue swirling flat, dragging over every sensitive, swollen inch. Sucking. Drawing her flesh into the heat of his mouth. Biting. Teeth raking back and forth, followed by his tongue to soothe and tease.

Not to mention his fingers. First one, then two, filling her up, stroking inside while he tormented her with his mouth. She tasted blood, felt pain in her hand, and finally let the cry escape even as the climax reduced her to a trembling, moaning wreck.

He wrung every sound possible from her, drawing out the contractions pulsing through her until she wound her hands tighter in his hair and finally yanked his mouth away. Even then, he came up her body slowly, nipping and kissing his way from her stomach, to her breasts.

To the scar on her chest.

Something speared through her from his mouth, through that hateful scar, straight to her heart.

"Thank you, Shannari." He joined their bodies in one smooth, slow thrust. In, in, so slow, until she was so full it was almost pain, almost too much. Then he withdrew just as slowly.

After tormenting her for so long, how could he be so casually controlled now? She'd expected a wild, rutting, fully aroused barbarian, not this tender, slow, merciless attack. The savage sounds shredding her throat sounded more barbaric than anything he did or said. She tried to tell him to hurry, she needed more, so much more. But all that came out was "harder!" Mixed with more appallingly loud, embarrassingly pleading cries.

"Louder, na'lanna." He plunged deeper, harder as she asked, and Lady help her, she cried out louder just as he demanded. "Make sure all my warriors hear you."

His scent enveloped her, sweet hay, baking bread, and warrior. So much warrior. She ran her hands up and down his corded arms and shoulders, his chest, the flat planes of his stomach. He was built like a god of war, all rock-hard muscle and satin skin begging for her hands. How she'd love to lay this man out and explore his magnificent body at her leisure.

"Any night, my heart. My body is yours, however you wish." Nuzzling her neck, he found the bite he had given her the previous night. His tongue stroked over that strangely sensitive mark in time with his thrusts and a surge of heat pulsed through her body. Too much, by the Lady's Moon, it was too much to bear.

And then his teeth dragged across her skin. Clawing his back, she clamped her jaw hard to keep the scream from roaring out of her throat. He didn't have to bite her again; just the memory was enough while he touched that spot.

His scent deepened with complexity, spiced by his blood. She knew the taste of that blood, now, the scent, and it worsened her desire to a fevered pitch.

"Aye," he growled, raking his teeth up her neck to her ear. "Bleed me. Bite *me* to suppress your cries instead of your hand."

His scent smoked hotter, a tremor shook his body against hers, and a powerful wave of raw lust flooded her. Not hers, his. The bond. He truly did want her to hurt him.

One big hand slid down her flank to draw her leg up higher against him, even while he lowered his chest more fully against her, giving her more of his weight. "You can't hurt me, Shannari. On my honor, I love it."

She rubbed her face against the velvety skin of his shoulder, and a tremor shook his body. She brushed her lips against him, and his breathing quickened. Just a hint of teeth, and his phenomenal control cracked. He slammed against her, filling her to the hilt, body flexing, growl rumbling through him.

Scream with pleasure, or bite him and hope a mouthful of muscle stifled her cries. Those were her options. Digging her fingernails into his lower back, she sank her teeth deep into the muscle running across the top of his shoulder.

His massive arms and shoulders bunched, his body heaved, and he uttered a single raw, guttural word.

"Mine!"

She didn't dare bite him hard enough to taste blood, not after her past experience. Maybe if she had, she wouldn't have hurt her own eardrums. She barely caught her breath, and he was rolling over and dragging her up onto his chest. His big hands smoothed her hair, cuddling her close.

Despite the pleasure still humming in her veins, her stomach fluttered, all hollow and nervous. "I can't sleep like this."

"Of course you can," he answered easily. "You're on top. I'm not pinning you in any way. There's no danger. All nine Blood will die before anyone gets through them."

Shifting on him, she tried to find a comfortable spot that didn't have her sprawled all over his incredible body. She failed. She couldn't possibly relax enough to fall asleep like this.

His powerful hands slid down her back, so gentle. His scent soaked into her. His body heated hers better than any blanket.

"Sweet dreams, *na'lanna.*"

He fell asleep almost immediately. Listening to the steady, strong beat of his heart, she stared up at the waning moon. She tried to soak in some of the Lady's peace, but her thoughts tangled helplessly. She felt vulnerable, shaken, and not simply because of the lack of clothing. With her sword forgotten on the bank of the pool, she didn't have a weapon. There weren't any walls or castles or soldiers to keep the assassins at bay. When had she ever lost her mind so completely that she'd left her sword unattended and out of reach?

Something darker than the night rustled, drawing her attention a few feet to the left. Her sword slid across the grass, a silver gleam in the moonlight, close enough she could grab it in an emergency.

*Gregar*, she thought, the deadly Blood who used to be a Death Rider. Surely an assassin would be a better guard than simple stone walls. At least she knew he wouldn't hesitate to kill.

She hadn't realized how truly near the Blood sat. Fire blazed across her cheeks and she turned her face away. Her stomach pitched queasily and she tried to slip out of Rhaekhar's arms.

Murmuring, he slid a hand into her hair to hold her close, his fingers gentle even in his sleep. His rich scent filled her nose. Why did he have to smell so good? Breathing sweet hay and roasting grains, she felt the knots in her stomach loosen bit by bit.

Out here in the wilderness, far from the constant demands of politics and duty, she could almost relax. She could almost let herself believe she would be safe and happy with this barbarian. She could almost let herself love him.

A very dangerous trap. The scar on her heart twinged, a constant reminder of how love could be used against her.

As she drifted off to sleep, the moon sank behind a darkening bank of clouds.

## 10

Theo threw himself flat on the massive bed. No matter how hard he tried, he couldn't stop thinking about her. The woman he hated. The Princess his grandfather would force him to wed.

The woman he lusted for like no other.

Bunching his pillow beneath his head, he tried to fall asleep. But as soon as he closed his eyes, he saw her. Flawless, ivory skin gleaming with the pearly light of the Lady's Moon. Heavy black hair hanging down her back. Midnight blue eyes flashing with disdain and pride.

Silk sheets stroked his naked flesh, inflaming him more.

"Shannari."

*Theo opened the heavy oaken door and lust blazed through his body.*

*She was bent over a rough, stained altar. Her hands were chained to the wall, stretching her feminine but* muscled body in a fine line. Spread-eagled, her ankles were chained to the floor, completely exposing her for a variety of vile acts. All of which he dreamed of doing to her for a very long time.

Her heavy black hair hung down her back, clothing her like a velvet mantle. He pushed that luxurious hair aside, and her bare skin gleamed, smooth and unmarred.

I CAN GIVE HER TO YOU.

He looked around the room, startled. No one was there. "She's already mine."

THEN WHY IS SHE WITH THE HORSE SPAWN? WHY IS IT HE INSTEAD OF YOU WHO TOUCHES HER GLEAMING WHITE SKIN?

Rage unexpectedly roared through him, leaving him shaking and breathing hard. *She's my fiancée! Mine! Mine to ruin!* "What do you want?"

YOUR FAVORITE TOY THIRSTS FOR PERFECT SKIN. LET ME SEE WHAT YOUR DARKEST, MOST SECRET DESIRE WILL DO TO THIS WOMAN WHEN SHE'S YOURS.

He reached out and took the wicked nine-tailed whip from the wall, lovingly trailing the leather straps through his hand. She whimpered softly, begging and weeping. Her fear pleased him.

Gently, he flicked the leather straps against her skin. Only a warning, a promise. The cat-o'-nine-tails didn't even redden her skin. Not yet. But she strained violently at the chains, struggling until her wrists were bloody.

He ran his free hand down that smooth, slender back. Her skin was unbelievably soft and fine, supple and warm like living silk. She struggled harder, panicky animal-like sounds tearing from her throat. Her midnight blue eyes flashed up at him wildly, shining with fear. Fear of him.

Power pulsed through his body, raw and violent and dark.

Smiling, he struck her beautiful back viciously and the leather bit into that perfect skin.

She screamed and screamed and screamed until her voice was ragged and hoarse. Delicate tracings of blood dripped down her back, down her luscious buttocks, dripping in fine lines down her thighs like gossamer spider webs of blood.

He smeared his hand in her blood, delighting in her pain and fear. Lady, he was so hard, so completely aroused, and he'd only just begun. How many times could he find pleasure in her torture before raping her?

YOU MAY DO ANYTHING YOU WISH TO HER. YOU MAY KEEP HER AS YOUR TOY FOR AS LONG AS YOU DESIRE. BUT THEN, I REQUIRE HER DEATH. I WANT HER BLOOD SPILLED ON THE GREAT SEAL ABOVE AS SHE TAKES HER LAST BREATH. THAT IS ALL. GIVE ME HER SACRIFICE AFTER YOU TIRE OF HER. THEN I'LL REWARD YOU IN WAYS YOU HAVEN'T EVEN DREAMED.

YOU WILL RULE THE GREEN LANDS FOREVER.

His breath caught in his throat. Forever? He could be High King forever; never have to share that power with her? He could torture her, ruin her, and then have the pleasure of killing her too? Without repercussion? He looked at her, dripping with blood, screaming with terror.

He'd do anything to have her like this. "Who are you?"

I AM LORD OF ALL THAT IS DARK

I AM THE ENDLESS NIGHT, THE DEATH OF MORNING.

I AM THE NEVERENDING WINTER THAT BUTCHERS THE FRAGILE HOPE OF NEW SPRING.

I AM THE SHADOW OF DEATH THAT POISONS THE HEART OF EVERY MAN.

I AM HATE, LUST, VIOLENCE, TORTURE, DEATH.

I AM THE BLACKEST HEART OF DARKNESS.

KNEEL HERE AT MY ALTAR, SWEAR TO KILL THIS

WOMAN FOR ME, AND YOU SHALL HAVE YOUR MOST SECRET DESIRE.

Theo tugged on his prince's lock, jerking his head slightly. His knees trembled, weakening, and he fell before the altar heavily. Shannari chained for his torture or the High Throne forever? Which did he want the most? "What would you have me do?"

*IT'S TIME FOR A NEW HIGH KING TO RULE THE GREEN LANDS.*

Theo jerked awake, panting, struggling against the tangled sweaty sheets. A dream, only a dream.

But what exhilarating possibilities.

He'd wearied of Stephan's endless maneuverings, his interest in Allandor and Shannari herself. Theo didn't need either Stephan or Shannari to rule the Green Lands. Not if Rikard died while Stephan and Shannari were away from Shanhasson.

It wouldn't be easy. The old fool was terrified of assassination. Nothing passed his lips that hadn't been tasted by another. He had weaknesses though. Weaknesses only Theo knew. *Because I share them.*

Shivering in the darkness, he sat up and hugged his knees to his chest. He waited to feel guilt or even fear, but he felt nothing but anticipation.

*It's not like I haven't killed before.*

L ocked away in darkness, Shannari found herself in a prison cell barely large enough for her to pace a few steps in either direction.

Cold, dank air clung to her skin like greasy oil, and the smell... Rotten and dead and foul. Shadows oozed with thick power as if the light of the sun never touched these depths.

She knew this nightmare well.

The cell door swung open, screeching in agony. Outside, more suffocating shadows waited, hungry, cold, writhing with glee and hatred.

Something hit her back. Cold stone. Heart racing, she realized she'd stumbled back against the wall as far away from the door as possible.

Where else could she go? What choice did she have? The greatest evil the world had ever known waited for her. He was always there, waiting for her to slip or weaken.

She reached for her sword, but it was gone. In fact, she was naked. Pain seared her back, as if strips of flesh had been torn away. Naked, unarmed, injured, and alone.

"Lady, help me!"

Nothing. No melodious voice promising salvation, no well-spring of power, no light, no hope. Only cold emptiness and black shadows.

Laughing with despair, she drew herself upright and slipped through the waiting door. She refused to cower, no matter what waited ahead. She certainly couldn't run. Not from her destiny. Not from the darkness already eating away inside her.

Following the stench, she crept down the dark tunnel as quietly as possible. A light flickered ahead, drawing her forward. Shadow and flame-light writhed on the stone, revealing a heavy oaken door locked by ancient chains as thick as her thighs.

Foulness wafted from a tiny barred window in the door, along with low, wickedly pleased laughter, all the more horrific because it was so genteel and elegant. Something moved behind the bars, a hint of motion and shadow blacker than the darkness. Laughter slithered through the bars again, rumbling through her body until her bones hurt. Still silky but crawling with malevolence.

Evil. Pure, unadulterated evil.

Her internal alarms blared with urgency. "I know you."

I AM YOUR GREATEST NIGHTMARE. YOU AND I ARE OLD FRIENDS, SHANNARI.

The voice writhed in her mind like maggots in a corpse. Cold fear flooded her from head to foot and her heart nearly pounded out of her ribcage. She cast her gaze about the cavern, searching for a weapon, anything she could use to protect herself.

Shadows moved, soul chilling and heavy with evil. They rose up above her, behind her, beneath her, wrapping around her arms and legs. Covering her eyes. Tightening around her neck. She opened her mouth to scream but choked as the darkness slithered down her throat.

YOUR LADY ABANDONS YOU. THE HORSE KING FAILS YOU. EVEN THE SHADOWED KILLER IS HELPLESS TO SAVE YOU, WEAKENED BY HIS OWN HEART'S DESIRE. WHO SHALL WOUND YOUR HEART THIS TIME? WHICH OF YOUR LOVES SHALL I CORRUPT NEXT?

No, no, it couldn't end this way! Always before she'd found a way to escape, to fight. But how could she fight now, alone and unarmed? Straining to draw breath, she froze when a new voice penetrated her struggles.

"Shannari."

Devin. Stars above, no, not him. Never again. Her heart stuttered, agony spearing through her chest.

*"I've been waiting for you."*

R haekhar jerked awake. Shannari thrashed in his arms, and a horrible whimpering, choking sound escaped her mouth. A sound so foreign from this strong, proud warrior woman that he immediately knew something was very, very wrong.

*"Na'lanna!"*

An arm came around her neck and jerked her out of his grasp. Varne hauled her backward, his *rahke* to her throat.

"Release her!"

"The Shadow I see within her grows stronger." Her flailing arm caught the Blood in the face. Unrelenting, Varne didn't flinch as her nails tore down the side of his face. "She's a threat to you."

An ivory *rahke* flashed in the night, suddenly lifting the Blood's chin higher. "Give me a reason to let you live."

Even Rhaekhar shivered at the ice in Gregar's voice. Shadows draped the two Blood, nearly obscuring them even with the full moon blazing in the night sky.

Varne slowly removed his arm, letting her crumple to the ground. "I protect Khul, not her."

Crawling over to her, Rhaekhar pressed his ear to her chest. He couldn't hear her heart beating. Her skin was like ice. "Great Vulkar, she's not breathing!"

Gregar shoved the other Blood aside and then knelt beside Shannari. His dark eyes burned with flames, gleaming with sympathy, and something else. Something darker. Death. Hunger. It made Rhaekhar's skin crawl to see another look at her like that, let alone one of his most trusted friends.

"She fights Shadow."

Varne hovered at Rhaekhar's back, a wall of protection against any threat. "In her dreams?"

He didn't have to look at his nearest Blood to hear the sneer in his voice. If Shannari didn't need him so badly, he would be tempted to use his own *rahke* on Varne to teach him some respect.

Staring down at her, Gregar picked up her left hand and a shudder passed through her, although she still didn't breathe. "Events in dreams can be more devastating than any living action."

His voice was flat and cold, so achingly distant and devoid of emotion that Rhaekhar wondered what terrors the Blood had survived in his own dreams. *Or committed.*

He pulled her lifeless body into his lap to warm her with his own body heat. Stroking her cheek, calling her name, he tried to reach her through the bond. All he felt was cold darkness and terror from her. Faint, so faint, as if she traveled seas of time and space.

"If she fails, the Endless Night will roam the Plains once more."

Rhaekhar sucked in a shaking breath. The thought of *na'lanna* battling such evil, alone, sliced his heart and stomach to ribbons.

Such a battle was for the Gods, not his woman. "What can we do to help her?"

"I could go after her, but the risk to her would be just as great." At the confusion that must be visible on Rhaekhar's face, the Blood continued, but refused to meet his eyes. "As a Death Rider, I could enter her dream, but on my last precious honor, Khul, she would be better off dead."

Rhaekhar couldn't stop his teeth chattering. Death Riders walked in dreams? Shannari, better off dead, at his own Blood's hands? The Blood who loved her? He clutched her harder against his chest. "How can I help her?"

Gregar tucked his ivory *rahke* into her hand. "She needs a weapon. And she needs to bleed."

"Nay," Rhaekhar whispered, his entire body shaking.

"It's best if you do it, Khul." Gregar met his gaze. His mouth twisted in that trademark smirk, but agony glittered in his dark eyes. "I would draw too much."

She went rigid, her body vibrating from head to toe.

"Hurry, Khul." Gregar's voice softened and a dreamy peace smoothed the pain from his face. He cradled her hand gripping the *rahke* in both of his palms and lifted the blade to his chest. "A little blood will be sufficient."

Silently, Varne offered his *rahke*. Rhaekhar shook his head. "Mine."

Another Blood appeared beside them, Khul's *rahke* in his hand. Rhaekhar took his *rahke* and lifted the wickedly sharp edge to her fragile skin. He chose the scar over her heart, the scar he wished to obliterate. Closing his eyes, he whispered a quick prayer, and then made a small incision.

Light blinded him. For a moment, he couldn't tell where it came from. The ivory *rahke* in her hand glowed like a captured star, shining in the night like a beacon. In the many years he had called Gregar friend, Rhaekhar had never seen such a marvel.

Shannari took a long, shuddering breath. Her eyes flew open. And with a low, vicious cry, she buried the *rahke* in Gregar's chest.

The dark-haired Blood with the wicked smile fell forward slowly, the knife in his chest still in her hand. Horrified, Shannari tried to pull back, but his hands gripped hers in a vise, pressing the blade deeper.

He fell on her, staring into her eyes. No surprise, no reprisals, no pain. His gaze was heavy lidded, smoldering with desire, pleasure, raw hunger, death. Blood gushed from the wound, searing her skin.

"Thank you," Gregar whispered, his voice thick. "You honor me."

One of the other Blood she didn't know gently lifted his weight from her and lay him on the ground beside her. Gregar never took his gaze from hers, even as the blade slid out of his flesh. No pain flashed in his dark gleaming eyes.

His chest glowed like the knife in her hand. Light pulsed in the wound, a liquid rainbow flashing in the night. Before her eyes, the wound closed until only a scar remained. A scar over his heart to match hers.

"Oh, Lady, I didn't mean to—" Her teeth chattered so badly she could hardly speak. The knife dropped from her nerveless fingers and the light faded. "What happened? What did I do?"

Rhaekhar bowed his head against her chest, his arms squeezing her so tightly she made a small sound of pain. Immediately, he loosened his grip, but he didn't raise his head. "You were dreaming. You stopped breathing, *na'lanna*. I couldn't wake you."

Shivering, she fought back the overwhelming horror of the dream. The nightmare tormented her often, but she'd never hurt anybody. Then again, she'd never been so desperate before. Her stomach heaved. Rolling away, she barely avoided vomiting on the barbarian.

So sick, so scared. She could still feel thick, foul shadows writhing like snakes inside her. She could still taste rotting death. Shaking, she swiped a hand across her mouth, smearing her lips with Gregar's blood.

His blood was still warm. The spicy taste on her lips washed away the foulness. So good, heating her stomach, chasing away some of the bone-chilling shadows deep inside. Before she could think, she slipped a finger in her mouth. Another. It shamed her how good his blood tasted. She truly was tainted, corrupted, ruined, just as the Nightmare had told her in the dream.

"Nay." Gregar touched her back lightly. "As I said, Shannari, you honor me."

"Too much," Rhaekhar retorted. "What were you thinking? She could have killed you."

While the two barbarians argued, Shannari staggered over to the pool and scrubbed the blood off. Her hands trembled. So much blood. Bad enough that she seemed to hunger for Rhaekhar's blood. At least he professed to love her. But why on earth would Gregar's blood tempt her?

"Are you well?" Rhaekhar asked, his voice low.

Turning slowly, she studied his face, trying to judge his emotions. The bond between them was quiet. Careful. Hesitant. He didn't seem angry or jealous, at least not now. Deep down, he seemed more resigned than surprised.

He should be furious. If tasting blood was a great honor to his people, then she'd just accidentally given great precedence to his friend.

Miserably, she whispered, "I'm sorry."

"There's no reason for your regret, *na'lanna*. I'm relieved that you survived the darkness you battled."

Carefully, she stole a glance at Gregar on his left. He watched her, his manner oddly expectant. He seemed to suffer no ill effects from having had a knife buried in his chest. That didn't make her feel any better. "How did you know?"

"Gregar felt the Shadow in your dream."

Varne shifted uneasily on Rhaekhar's right. His cheek was scored by what looked like her fingernails. When had she done that?

"Do you want to taste Varne's blood too?" Rhaekhar asked solemnly.

Shaking her head hard, she quickly looked away from the glowering Blood. That's the last thing she wanted to do. Gregar snickered, drawing her gaze to him again. Why were they acting so careful and strange? She'd stabbed the man, and they walked on eggshells around her. It didn't make any sense.

After giving her another disapproving glare, Varne left, disappearing into the shadows around the pool.

"Why's he upset? If anyone should be angry, it's you two."

"Varne has no sense of humor." Gregar hunkered down in front of her and winked suggestively, his teeth flashing white in a wide smile. "I'm not angry."

"I'm not angry either, na'lanna." Rhaekhar watched her, then Gregar. He didn't rant or rage. No fury flowed through the bond. If anything, he seemed to have accepted whatever hesitation he experienced earlier. "Do you want anything else from Gregar at this time?"

Suddenly, she realized she was stark naked. Chilly water or not, she scrambled into the pool and made a great show of washing. With her back to them. "Some clothes would be nice."

The wicked Blood laughed again. "It's an honor to serve, Shannari."

She glanced over her shoulder. "Gregar?"

Pausing, he faced her. Heavy and solemn, the night waited

silently, shadows draping over his face. Again, she had that haunting sense of familiarity, of recognition. Some dark dream, forbidden, shadowed, blood and temptation.

"How did you know you wouldn't die?"

His mouth quirked, his dark eyes gleaming in the moonlight. "I didn't."

She had no idea what she'd done.

A blood bond with another warrior. Not just any warrior, but one of his Blood. And not just any of his Blood, but the one who carried the Shadow of Death. Who feared to draw the smallest amount of her blood lest he take too much.

The Blood who loved her enough to die for her.

He braced for the raging jealousy to drive him to challenge his best friend, but he felt only... Relief. She was alive. Gregar had helped save her. Whatever she wanted, Rhaekhar would provide it, as long as she was safe. Apparently, all she wanted at this time from Gregar—rather reluctantly—was blood.

A hard, grim smile curved Rhaekhar's lips. Blood he could certainly provide, either his or Gregar's, whichever she preferred. He would use every weapon at his disposal in this *kae'don*. Even if he must share her bond with each of his Blood, he would use any and all of them to keep her safe. If need be, he would knock Varne senseless and hold him down for her. Another bond would be another lifeline dragging her back from the bowels of darkness.

Rhaekhar waited for her to finish hiding in the water, drawing on the bond to fully explore her emotions. Embarrassment, shame, terror so great it sent his own heart thumping faster. Then a growing sense of withdrawal. The small amount of trust and tenderness he'd earned turned to stone, hard and unrelenting.

She feared for his life, for Gregar, for any and all who neared her.

Silently, Rhaekhar watched her wade to shore, her arms clutched about her chest. He would accuse any other woman of shyness, but she merely tried to hide the scar—not her breasts —from him.

Rubbing aimlessly at the old puncture wound, she hesitated, her gaze flickering up to his and then skittering away. "I'm not sure I should sleep again, even if I could. I should have my own sleeping place, away from yours so no more accidents can happen."

Ah. She would push him away, deny his hard-won encroachment on her heart. He hardened his voice. "Is that how you received the scar on your breast? An accident?"

She flinched and turned away.

He seized her, dragging her into his arms. Heat swirled within her, stirred by the blood she'd consumed, her fear, the press of his body against hers. Whatever her words, her body wanted comforting. She needed to feel safe and warm and loved.

Releasing some of his frustration, his worry, aye, even his jealousy, he kissed her thoroughly, claiming her mouth, her lips, her tongue. He gave her no time to argue or fight or worry.

Need hammered through the bond as he carried her back to their blankets. Hers, to lose herself and her fears if for only a while; his, to lay claim to what was threatened. He slid into her warmth in one hard thrust, and she groaned with pleasure.

"There's no Shadow here, *na'lanna*. No dark dreams. No terror. Only my love, my honor, my blood."

She spoke as much with her eyes as with her words, dark with desire and fear, both. "Everything is touched by Shadow. Everything is corrupted eventually."

"Not me," he growled. He slammed back into her, drawing another low cry from her. "Every night when we come together, you will feel my love. You will know my honor. You will taste my blood. My blood binds you to me, and I refuse to let you go. Do you understand? My honor and my love are unshakeable. Hold to me, Shannari, and I shall fight to keep your Shadow at bay."

She averted her face. Misery swirled through her scent like the Shadow she claimed stained her soul. "Blood feeds the darkness in me."

"Nay. Blood and honor are entwined. Blood shed as willing sacrifice is an honor that Shadow cannot touch. For you, I give my blood, willingly and gladly. Take me, taste me, carry my honor inside you. Strengthen our bond with my blood, and I shall drive your nightmares away forever."

Rhaekhar slid his palm across the ground until he found his *rahke*. Making another shallow wound high on his chest above his heart, he waited for her to taste his blood. He wouldn't force her, no matter his selfish wish to reaffirm her desire for his blood after she tasted another's.

"Unshakeable," she whispered, her voice breaking. "I don't know what that means."

He gathered her closer, pressing her scarred heart against his. "It means I'm yours, forever. When you open your eyes, I'm here. When you close them, I'm in your heart. If you seek me in dreams, you will find me, always. If you need me, reach through the bond and meld your heart to mine. Nothing can break our bond, *na'lanna*, not even the Endless Night, not even death itself."

"I might kill you. I don't even know why Gregar's still alive."

"I know why." She searched his face for an answer, but he shook his head. "You must discover it for yourself. But know this. You could bury my *rahke* in my heart this very moment without fear. I don't believe I would die, not after what I saw with Gregar earlier this night. But if I did, I would go to Vulkar's Clouds with a smile on my face."

"Why?"

"Because my love for you will never die. There's nothing you could do or say that can change the way I feel. When I die, I shall wait for you to join me, and then, *na'lanna*, we shall ride like the wind across the Plains forever."

Hope and longing flickered across her face a moment, before it was wiped away by a tidal wave of pain centered about the old wound on her chest. Agony crashed through the bond with such force he couldn't breathe.

"I don't love you." Her voice was ragged, her face pale, but she didn't weep. Not his warrior woman. "I can't. Not like you want."

"I know." *Then why does she fear for me? For Gregar?* She swore her heart was dead, yet nothing truly dead ached so badly. "Take my blood anyway."

She closed her eyes, her jaw clenching. He thought she would refuse, and his heart sank. Blood was his hope, strengthening the bond, drawing her tighter to him day by day. Until his very thoughts echoed in her mind and heart and she could deny him no longer.

With a rough cry, she wrapped her fists in his hair and locked her mouth to the wound. He felt the rising pleasure swirl through her, golden and pure, driving back the darkness still lingering about her.

He didn't even attempt to control his own response. Hard, pounding, claiming, he drove into her body, pushing her pleasure higher. She threw her head back, crying out, and he matched her hoarse cry on his own release.

She murmured a protest when he rolled over and pulled her close in his arms. Throwing a leg over her, he ignored her half-hearted attempt to remove herself from his embrace. With a sigh that tugged on his heart, she buried her face deeper against his chest and fell asleep.

For the remaining hours till daybreak, he held her, listening to the bond and guarding her dreams from danger. Darkness hunted her, doubts tormented her, and she fought him at every turn. She rejected his tenderness, pushed him to dominance and aggression, shredded his heart with a word or look. Yet he felt the connection between them, soul deep and searing. He knew in his heart she was *na'lanna*, and he feared for her. How could he battle the Endless Night and her doubts at the same time?

She craved his blood and his body. If only she craved his love.

T he morning ride passed uneventfully. Shannari tried not to think about last night. The nightmare. The blood. She stole a careful glance to the left, trying to see where Gregar rode without being obvious.

The wretched Blood winked at her. He rode closer today than at any time yesterday. On their right, Varne rode like a silent thundercloud. Every time she glanced at him, he glowered and trotted ahead. Only to fall back because Gregar never left, and for whatever reason, Varne refused to let the other Blood remain close to Khul if he wasn't there.

At her back, Rhaekhar wasn't much better. Reserved and contemplative, he said very little all morning other than his insistence that she learn as much of his language as quickly as possible. The dynamics were obvious to someone trained in politics, although the details and wherefores escaped her. Somehow, she'd offended Varne, and Rhaekhar and Gregar felt some obligation to her, both of them, which the other Blood despised.

It must be because she'd stabbed Gregar. Perhaps she should stab the other Blood and see if that put him in a better mood.

Varne growled beneath his breath while Gregar laughed as if she'd made a great joke. "You can stab me again whenever you wish, but I wouldn't recommend trying Varne. His blood isn't nearly as tasty as mine and Khul's."

Shannari lifted her chin higher, although she couldn't stop the flush from staining her cheeks. "How do you know what I'm thinking?"

"The Blood bond."

Blessed Lady above, did they hear every thought in her head? Her pulse fluttered uneasily. Rhaekhar's invasive bond was bad enough. If the Blood listened inside her head, she might just draw the sword and prepare to fight to the death. "You're my... my... Blood now?"

Varne snarled what must be a Sha'Kae al'Dan curse and galloped ahead. Gregar laughed so hard he nearly fell off his horse.

It was true. Grasping the hilt of her sword, she tried to blank her mind. Perhaps irrational, but Rhaekhar's silence infuriated her. "Why aren't you doing something?"

"What would you have me do, *na'lanna*? My word is law on the Plains, but the Blood are a law among themselves." Laughing softly, he tightened his arms around her and rubbed her cheek with his. "Only Khul has Blood, and Gregar's mine. Each of the Blood feels me through my blood sacrifice, and so they feel you through our *na'lanna* bond. Even Varne."

He hesitated, sharing some silent look with Gregar that she couldn't decipher. "Gregar shares a blood bond with you separate from mine now. If you wish, you should be able to feel him. Like you feel me."

The last part came out rather choked to her ears. She did feel Rhaekhar, *na'lanna* bond or some other reason. Now, she swore she felt a surge of... of... jealousy from him. The thought made her heart go cold and heavy in her chest.

*My beloved.* Did Gregar think that she...

*I ruin everything I touch.*

What if she tore Rhaekhar and his Blood apart? What if they came to blows over some foolish jealousy, when she could never love either of them?

"What is meant to be, will be." Gregar dared a touch to the back of her hand where she clutched a handful of mane. She'd never seen the joking Blood so solemn. "No matter how we may wish otherwise. I'm bound with honor, now. Khul's honor, his very blood. I shall not fail him, and I shall not fail you."

His words tickled her memory of the horrible dream last night. "Shadowed Killer."

"Aye."

His voice sent cold chills down her spine. She reached down and gripped the hilt of her sword, but she didn't draw it. If a knife to the heart didn't kill him, she didn't figure a sword would do much good unless she took his head. Staring into his dark, gleaming eyes, she didn't want to try. She wasn't afraid, not really. "What's your heart's desire?"

He laughed, but pain cramped across the scar on her chest, matching his. *I can feel him.* Stunned, she held herself very, very still.

"Something I can never have."

Rhaekhar dropped his chin against her shoulder, hugging her. "We shall see, my friend. You have my acceptance and my approval."

Gregar actually looked surprised, and then a genuine smile spread across his face. Despite the warrior behind her who swore his love and honor were unshakeable, something fragile unfurled deep inside her while staring into the Blood's bottomless eyes. Jerking her gaze away, she refused to look at him.

"My blood is yours, Khul. And my blood is yours, Shannari, any time you wish. However—"

Another pain stabbed through her chest and she flinched. Rhaekhar tightened his arms, holding her close to his body, but the jealousy was gone. He held her for comfort, not possessively, which made no sense to her whatsoever.

"I can never have my heart's desire. I would rather be dead than risk it." With that, Gregar's black horse shot ahead and passed Varne.

Her eyes burned, her throat tightened, and for Leesha only knew what reason, she wanted to call after him. *Come back, stay with us, never ever die.*

"Such honor," Rhaekhar whispered. "Such sacrifice. You've chosen well, *na'lanna.*"

Bewildered, upset, even angry that she felt so badly and didn't understand why, Shannari craned her head around to look back at him. Immediately, he lifted her, turning her so she sat in his lap and could easily search his face.

What she saw there made even less sense. He was pleased, if the smug smile was any indication. "I don't understand."

Smiling wider, he tugged gently on her braid and pressed a light kiss to her lips. "Give us time to explain, then."

"Explain what? Why can't you just tell me? It was an accident. Stabbing him, his blood, everything. I won't—"

He shushed her by stroking his thumb back and forth over her bottom lip. "Take his blood. Every single time he offers it, you take it. He's worthy of the honor, and so are you. I'm warrior enough to allow it. Nay, I encourage it."

Wordlessly, she shook her head. Tasting Gregar's blood had been a mistake. She shouldn't even taste Rhaekhar's, but she couldn't resist it when he offered. Weak, she was too weak, and needy, and, oh, Blessed Lady above, just sitting like this was enough to stir her lust again.

His nostrils flared and his burnished gold eyes flared like the sun. "Are you telling me that you don't want my blood? That you don't want me?"

Closing her eyes, she swallowed hard. Lie, court her enemies, even kill, all activities she was willing to do to claim the High Throne and save her people. But she couldn't find it in her poor, crippled heart to lie to this barbarian. "You know I do."

"Then don't lie to me about Gregar. More, don't lie to him or yourself."

His big hand clamped on the back of her neck, hauling her closer for a soul-searing kiss that left her draped all over his magnificent body and regretting how many hours must pass before nightfall.

"I love you, na'lanna. What you need, I need. What you want, I want. You already carry a piece of Gregar in your heart. You're tied to him by his sacrifice and his blood. If you want anything from Gregar, anything at all, then my honor—our honor—demands nothing less than that you will take it."

She must be entirely mistaken. He couldn't possibly mean that she... that he... let alone the wicked, laughing Blood... Heat flared across her face and it was all she could do not to squirm on the barbarian's lap. She'd never thought of Gregar in such a way. Let alone that Rhaekhar would... would...

Chuckling, he picked her up and swung her back around. "Anything at all, na'lanna. Now, take your first look at the Sea of Grass."

The warhorse trotted up the crest of the hill, and Rhaekhar drew rein. All her uneasiness and turmoil fled as she gazed at his homeland in wonder.

Rolling hills of tall golden grass stretched as far as she could see. Clouds filled the wide, azure sky, casting shadows like horses galloping across the hills. The air was hot but not as dry as the desert, and the aroma coming up from the waving grass smelled like baking bread, just like Rhaekhar. Warm, rich, nutty, something fresh and tasty to sink her teeth into.

He made that low growling rumble of pleasure against her ear, his teeth nipping at her earlobe. "You tease me, *na'lanna*, and never fulfill such a delightful threat."

"I don't want to hurt you."

He sighed dramatically. "Shannari, how many times have I said that you cannot hurt me? The thought of your teeth drives me insane." Emphasizing his words, his erection ground into her back. "Bite me all you want."

Pushing back against him, she suddenly regretted the leathers covering her skin, preventing her from feeling the full breadth and might of him. "Maybe I'll make up for it tonight."

Instead of rising heat, she felt a surge of caution through the bond. Why would he be cautious after driving her crazy with his kiss and the hard proof of his need?

"I need to speak to you about Camp."

"All right," she replied slowly. "You mentioned tents before. Don't worry, I've spent plenty of time in the field. I'm not going to fall apart like a spoiled noble who's never gone without three-course dinners or a bath for a few days."

Rhaekhar didn't immediately respond. He urged his horse into a smooth, rocking canter down the slope. So tall, the grass came well up the mighty stallion's chest. The breeze rippled the swaying grass until it really did resemble waves upon the ocean. The Sea of Grass. She could easily imagine her outlander ancestors hiding in the grass, waiting until dark to set the fires and steal the magnificent herd.

"Don't worry about a lack of bathing. Our steamtents will be different, of course, but you may actually prefer them."

His seriousness didn't bode well. "I know very well that you bathe regularly, Khul. You smell better than any noble I ever met in Shanhasson."

Still, he didn't laugh. "It will be very different in Camp. Different than what you're used to."

"I know." Blessed Lady, how bad could it be? "So, what's so terrible you don't want to tell me? You howl at the moon? Run stark naked through the tents? I've seen it all. Soldiers always do bizarre things after surviving battle."

Pressing his mouth to her neck, he whispered huskily, "You can run through my tent stark naked any time you wish."

"Don't change the subject," she retorted, shrugging him away. "Tell me before we get there so I'm prepared."

He heaved a long sigh again. "You're an outlander."

"Really," Shannari said dryly. "That's the huge secret?"

"My people may not welcome you as heartily as I wish. At least initially. Never fear, though, *na'lanna*. I'm Khul and my word is law. In time, they'll accept you, for I allow no other alternative."

She rolled her eyes at his arrogance. "People never like me much. As long as they don't try to kill me, then I don't really care one way or the other."

Fury roared through the bond, and he crushed her against his rock-hard body. "No one would dare lay a hand on you."

"Everybody wants me dead sooner or later." She let him hold her without trying to break his grip. It felt nice to be protected for once, even if she didn't need it. "Don't worry about me. I'll try not to insult anyone, but most people react more like Varne than you when they meet me."

Finally, Rhaekhar laughed and eased his punishing grip. "Promise me one thing, *na'lanna*. Don't try to chop any other warrior's head off when first you meet."

Her answer was a jab with her elbow hard enough he actually grunted. "You deserved it."

"Aye, I did. There's more you should know, too much for me to explain, for here's my Camp now."

Indeed, riders raced toward them from a huge encampment of multi-colored tents nestled between hills. So many; she'd had no idea the Camp would be so large. A herd of grazing horses dotted the hills beyond the hundreds of tents.

"Usually my Camp isn't so very large unless we are riding to the Summer Gathering. This is representative of four Camps. Mine and Drendon's are the largest of the Nine. Even now, this isn't all of our tents. Some were too deep in the Plains to come quickly when I sent messengers calling for warriors."

Her mind whirled with possibilities and political ramifications. "You can call warriors from all the Camps?"

"Not exactly. When the Nine Camps are united as we were before the Fire, then aye, I'll be able to call hundreds of fists from all Camps. Now, though, I limit my request to my three strongest allies. These khuls are in agreement with me, and readily gathered tents."

"Each Camp has a Khul?"

"Each Camp has a khul who leads their tents. I am khul of my Camp. As Khul of all Nine, I try to unite us as much as possible, resolve disputes, and strengthen our numbers of *na'kindren* and warriors in preparation for the Last Days."

"How many Camps stand against you?"

"Only three openly." Rhaekhar shrugged and turned his attention to the riders sliding to a halt before them. "Don't worry, *na'lanna*. I have more than enough warriors of my own to repel any who challenge me."

The warrior saluted with fist over his heart. "Khul, welcome home!"

"All is well, I hope?"

"Aye, Khul. Your Camp most anxiously awaits the stories of your victory."

"Shannari, this is my Second, Casson. Casson, this is *na'lanna* Shannari."

The warrior's eyes widened with surprise, but he nodded to her politely. "Welcome to Khul's Camp, Shannari."

They rode onward to the tents, Casson filling Rhaekhar in on various Camp duties, most of which went over her head. So many *na'kindren* in training, so many warriors arrived after he'd left for the Green Lands, so and so would ask for a *kae'don* to decide water and grazing rights.

More and more people came out of the tents. They welcomed their Khul with wide happy smiles and cheers until they took note of her. Confusion, then reserve guarded most of their expressions. A few took on a harder look more like Varne's. Though the Fire had happened over a hundred years ago, they remembered all too well what damage outlanders wrought.

The most open disapproval came from the khuls Rhaekhar introduced. While Brenn gave her a hearty smile, she saw through his veneer of civility easily. He was a merchant at heart, and she could see the wheels and scales adjusting in his head even while he nodded and smiled. The other khul, Tomai, jerked his head once, then whirled and walked away as quickly as possible.

Rhaekhar swung down off his horse and lifted her down beside him. As soon as she was down, he turned to another waiting warrior and actually hugged him. The two mighty warriors laughed, pounding each other on the back. Thankfully, by the time he turned back to her for introductions, she had managed to wipe the amused shock off her face.

"This khul is Drendon, my very good friend, and his mate, Alea. He's like a brother to me. While my Camp is First, his Camp is a very close Second of the Nine. Drendon, my friend, this is *na'lanna* Shannari."

Eyebrows raised, eyes guarded, the warrior nodded to her and also introduced his mate formally. Alea immediately offered to show her to the steamtents, for which Shannari was grateful. She grabbed her small bag from one of the Blood and followed the tall brunette deeper into Camp.

Despite such a rousing display of loyalty and friendship, she couldn't help but wonder. If Drendon's Camp was a close Second, there must be some undercurrent of maneuvering, no matter how subtle, to make his own Camp First of the Nine. If something happened to Rhaekhar, would Drendon become Khul? She decided to ask some careful questions and find out.

W ater sizzled and steam rose up so thick and moist in the tiny tent that Shannari could hardly breathe. Steamy heat sank into her skin, easing her muscle soreness from the unaccustomed hours in the saddle. Unusual by her Green Land standards, but the steam was quite nice. It also helped to hide the scars. In the past, she'd accepted a maid only if the girl didn't visibly flinch or pass out when her mistress stripped for a bath.

"I hope your journey across the blasted lands wasn't too unbearable," Alea said. She offered what she might think resembled an encouraging smile, but her disdain was obvious.

Shannari shrugged casually. "Hot. Dusty. But not unbearable."

"This must be very different from what you're used to."

She merely smiled.

It must not have been a very pleasant smile, for the false one Alea wore slipped. Her gaze sharpened, as if she was only now realizing the outlander might be a more worthy opponent.

"Don't tell me you believe all Green Landers are sneaky, weak, deceitful wretches."

Alea blinked innocently. "Aren't they?"

Unbraiding her hair, Shannari laughed. "Yes, actually, most are, unfortunately. Other than my father and Our Blessed Lady's priests, I wouldn't trust a Green Lander further than I could throw him."

"And you, Shannari. Are you trustworthy?"

She felt her face blank into the careful, cold mask she wore for politics. "If I give my word, yes. I'm here now only because I gave my word to your Khul that I would come with him as long as my people were spared."

"So Khul demanded you come with him."

Watching the other woman to see how she used a small dipper to pour hot water over her hair, Shannari nodded. "It's a long story, one I'm sure he'll want to brag about tonight."

Despite her dislike, Alea laughed in agreement. "Aye, warriors love to brag about themselves. We'll sit around the fire until morning hearing all about it."

She scooped a handful of soft foam from a copper pot and passed it to Shannari. The mixture was slimy but sweet smelling. When the other woman coated her hair and body with the slick soap, she finally recognized the smell. Flowers, the sweet fragrance that seemed so out of place on her big barbarian.

"Do you love him?"

Shannari blinked, surprised by such a probing question. She decided she liked the woman's forthright attitude much better than the false civilities she was used to in the Green Lands. However, that didn't make her situation any easier. "No."

"Yet you expect him to make you Khul'lanna?"

Putting two and two together, Shannari decided that must be the title for Khul's mate. "I have no such expectations. In fact, I must return to the Green Lands as soon as possible."

"Indeed. Does Khul know this?"

The glint in the woman's eyes surprised her. Shannari prided herself on reading people well, but she had no idea why this woman might be angry at her honesty. Perhaps she played too openly after all. "As much as he will hear."

"My mate and Khul have been friends ever since they can remember. They're as close as brothers." Alea stood, her brown eyes snapping with fury. "I love Khul as a brother. I won't see him hurt or dishonored, especially by some sniveling outlander lady with less sense than an addled prairie grouse."

Shannari laughed, shaking her head. "Oh, yes, of course I believe in your undying loyalty. Rhaekhar mentioned your Camp is a close Second, so Drendon is a close second to him, yes? You'll use my ignorance of custom to further your own agenda."

Alea retorted, "What agenda?"

"You want to be Khul'lanna."

The blood drained from the woman's face and she stumbled back a step, another. She reached out, her hand flailing, and found the tent flap. "Never. You have no idea what you accuse me of. None."

Whirling, the woman fled, leaving Shannari even more confused. She swore the other woman had been weeping. She certainly looked horrified at the accusation.

Rhaekhar was like a king to these people. He admitted three Camps stood against him openly, so she knew politics were a part of the Sha'Kae al'Dan lifestyle. Uneasy, she decided she needed more information to fully understand the powers at play before plucking them to suit her plans. If his own people demanded he get rid of the outlander, surely he would release her. A supremely arrogant, powerful warrior like Rhaekhar would never abdicate just to keep a woman.

He had to release her of his own will or she'd be forced to break her word. Or worse.

After experiencing his tenderness, the exquisite skill he used to love her, even his urging to taste his blood, she wasn't sure she could kill him. Even though her freedom—and all of the Green Lands—was at stake.

"**I**'m relieved your *kae'don* was resolved so quickly," Drendon said, his forehead creased with worry. "Tehark has been very vocal in your absence. You will have trouble, and soon."

Sitting before the roaring central fire, Rhaekhar tried to concentrate on his friend. The important Plains news. His enemy. But Shannari tugged on his bond, unknowingly, aye, but distracting just the same.

Her mind worried over competition between Camps, which she couldn't possibly fathom yet. From the beginning, he'd understood that his proud, strong warrior woman was a formidable opponent in strategy. Now, though, he could only grin and shake his head while imagining the damage she would plan for the troublesome Camps once she fully understood Plains standing.

"I hesitate to even bring this up, Khul, but someone must. Your choice for Khul'lanna couldn't be worse."

Sharpening his gaze on his friend, Rhaekhar settled his hand on his *rahke*. "Any who opposes my choice may challenge me. I shall be most pleased to instruct them otherwise."

"You cannot possibly plan to challenge every warrior in Tehark's Camp," Drendon retorted. "Besides, an outlander wouldn't be worth the effort."

Rage tightened Rhaekhar's face and he clamped his jaw hard to stifle the harsh words threatening to boil out of his mouth. Always easygoing and cheerful, Drendon was fast to anger yet as ready to forgive and forget. Usually Rhaekhar was slow to anger and just as slow to forget any slight or dishonor. They balanced each other, and when the two strongest Camps were in agreement, it provided balanced leadership on the Plains.

Unfortunately, he'd never felt closer to formal challenge. Without taking his gaze from his friend's, he let the pounding fury roll through his body, reflecting on his face a moment like a thundercloud. Then he answered in a cold, flat voice that his friend would recognize despite never hearing directed at him. "I would die for her."

Drendon jumped to his feet. "An outlander? What say your Blood?"

"They have no say. My heart knows her."

"I was hoping you could talk him out of this ridiculous choice." Varne heaved a sigh, shaking his head, his face grim. "Her darkness will tear us apart."

Rolling his ivory *rahke* back and forth across his palm, Gregar laughed. "Always doom and gloom, Varne. Darkness came to the Plains with the Endless Night, not Shannari. She's hunted, aye, but it's our great honor to protect her."

"Would you shelter Shadow within our very tents?"

"Aye, why not?" Gregar's teeth flashed as white as his *rahke*. "We shelter you, do we not?"

Varne harrumphed and turned back to Drendon. "You can see what evil she has wrought already if Khul's Blood fight amongst ourselves."

"Enough." Rhaekhar growled, his hands tightening into fists. "I've heard enough from you, Varne. I understand your vision of darkness, yet Gregar is correct. If the Endless Night hunts a thing, I must save it or I can call myself no warrior."

"What have you seen?" Drendon asked the nearest Blood.

"No matter," Rhaekhar interrupted. He glared at Varne to silence him, and then his friend. "Shannari's *na'lanna*, and she's in danger. Argue all you wish; disagree with me if you feel the need. But you had best bring your *rahke* and plenty of your blood to satisfy me."

Growling, Drendon glared off toward his tent. "Something has upset Alea. Or someone."

"No guesses needed to determine who," Varne muttered.

Rhaekhar deliberately directed some of his ire through the bond, and the Blood had the grace to look embarrassed.

"Perhaps we should sleep in my tent this night," Rhaekhar said.

"You would dishonor me?" Drendon whirled back around, torn between rushing off to see to his mate and arguing with Khul. "This first night in Camp, you must share our tent. If you refuse, everyone will think you're displeased with my Camp. We would lose face. Tehark isn't that far behind me, Khul. Enough dishonor, and his Camp will be Second."

Considering his options, Rhaekhar tried to think of a valid excuse. While his friend exaggerated the importance of opening his tent to Khul the first night back in Camp, the other khuls would indeed take note. However, all in Camp anticipated how well he would made love to Shannari this night. How many times her voice would break the night in pleasure.

And if they were forced to share a tent with not only his Blood but others as well...

"You could overcome her hesitations if you push hard enough." Gregar studied the *rahke* in his hand, smoothing his thumb up and down the razor-sharp edge. He kept his voice low enough that Varne didn't even look in their direction. "Pick your *kae'don* well, Khul, for she'll certainly fight back."

"Aye." Rhaekhar frowned, trying to decide how best to approach her modesty. She wasn't shy, not exactly; she merely didn't care for others to be a party to her emotions. She didn't even want him to know the depth of her desire for him, let alone everyone in Camp. "Even my tent won't be easy at first, not with Blood inside."

Gregar laughed softly. "Only you can decide, Khul, but one or two nights of misery and whispers among your people will be put to rest soon enough when she surrenders to the need she feels for you. The *kae'don* of her heart must be won before you can present her as Khul'lanna."

"Indeed, all whispers and doubts will be set to rest soon enough." He felt Shannari coming toward him before he noted her walking with Alea into the firelight. Louder, for both her and Drendon's benefit, Rhaekhar added, "Aye, Shannari and I shall honor you by staying in your tent this night as custom."

Alea was pale, her face strained. Shannari sat beside him, her body bristling for battle. Leaning close to him, she whispered, "Then you can forget any sort of intimate activities."

"As you wish, *na'lanna.*" Her scent rolled over him, fresh and clean and sultry from her bath. It wasn't difficult to allow an edge of need to roughen his voice. "I shall suffer this night."

She muttered something that he couldn't understand, but her emotions were obvious. As frustrated and needy as he, she trembled at his nearness. Spoiling for a battle to relieve some of the tension tormenting her, she retorted, "Every night."

This time, he chose to ignore her challenge for the moment. "Did you and Alea get along?"

Shannari shrugged. "Well enough. I upset her, but I don't know why. I accused her of wishing her mate was Khul instead of you."

Choking back appalled laughter, Rhaekhar drew her closer to his side, both to torment her and offer his protection. Drendon wouldn't be pleased by such a slight to his honor and loyalty. "For another to be Khul, I would have to be dead. You accused her mate, my long-time friend, of plotting to assassinate me."

"Oh." She thought a moment, watching the other couple. Alea laid her head on Drendon's shoulder, clinging to him for comfort, still obviously upset. "Are they?"

He couldn't keep the shock off his face. "Never."

Hardness glinted in her eyes, her lovely face drawn and lined with weariness. Not physical, but emotional. Great Vulkar above, how many times had her trust been betrayed? Her life threatened by a friend? "I've learned one thing and one thing only. Never trust anybody. Ever."

"I would trust Drendon with your life."

She turned away, staring into the fire. "The only thing trust earns is a knife in the back."

"Or the chest?" Rhaekhar asked softly. She flinched but didn't look at him. "You can trust me, *na'lanna*."

A grim smile curved her lips. "Of course I can. I can love you, too, yes? And not a soul here would ever dream of trying to assassinate me."

Cupping her chin in his hand, he turned her face back toward him. With all the fire in his blood and the love in his heart, he let his eyes blaze with emotion. Frustration, desire, rage, love. "Aye, love me. Trust me. I shall kill anyone who lays a hand on you."

V arne thrust his face so close to Shannari's that their noses bumped. His belligerent smile was viciously pleased. "You've dishonored Khul. He's the laughing-stock of Camp this morning, all because of you."

Lady, how she'd love to take this arrogant bastard down a notch or two. She'd hardly slept a wink last night. How could she with so much embarrassing, amorous activity happening just a blanket away? Her head ached abominably. "How did I dishonor him?"

"You didn't love him last night. All in Camp know of your disdain for him, your wicked delight in shaming him, your blatant disregard for his honor."

Squinting against the too-bright sun, she longed for a fresh hot cup of caffe. "Because I refused to engage in bedchamber activities last night, your Khul suffered dishonor?"

"Exactly," Varne retorted, his dark eyes flashing with ire and glee both. "Everyone expected him to beat Drendon last night, or at least earn a white *kae'al*. Instead, you refused him utterly. He'll have so many challengers lining up to take a piece of his honor, he won't have a hand's span of unscathed flesh left. You risk everything, his position, his honor, his very life."

"Beat Drendon? At what?" She stared at Varne blearily, surprised when his cheeks darkened with either fury or embarrassment. He was already mad, so... "Are you blushing?"

"Go back to the Green Lands where you belong. I shall even fetch you a mount. Leave Khul's Camp, leave his honor intact, and I'll ensure he frees you."

Shannari rubbed her eyes, running through options. Likely, Varne would set her up to escape, and then laugh his ass off when she was captured and punished. She glanced about them, looking for a second party to verify his accusations. Someone she could trust enough to learn the truth about this honor and love-making and *kae'als*, whatever that was.

She took a step around Varne, who grumbled but didn't dare lay a hand on her. Rhaekhar stood a short distance away at a small cooking fire, his Blood gathered about as usual. Drendon was also present and Alea served them. Who to trust?

Just as she walked up to them, Rhaekhar handed his cup back to Alea. "Let us leave within the hour."

Drendon shot a glare at Shannari and whirled on his heel. "Aye, Khul."

Rhaekhar smiled at her as if nothing was wrong. "Did you sleep well, *na'lanna?*"

"Actually, no. I slept horribly. It was too noisy."

Rhaekhar chuckled, the dark-haired wicked Blood bent over laughing, and Varne glowered. Business as usual.

Rhaekhar leaned down and kissed her lightly. "We shall sleep in my tent this night."

The heat of his mouth, the barest taste of him, the scent of baked bread and sweet hay rolling off him—Shannari groaned. It required all her willpower to keep her hands fisted at her side instead of seizing his head and dragging his lips back to hers. Or grabbing his arm and hauling him off somewhere private. "Your tent will be no better if your Blood are inside, too."

"Don't even think of them." His golden eyes blazed with heat. She felt a surge of physical need from him so sharp she sucked in a hard breath. "You won't remember them when I get my hands on you this night."

Shaking her head, she whispered, "Are you angry today? Because of... last night?"

"Do I feel angry through the bond?"

"No. You feel—" She couldn't help herself. She let her gaze drop to his *memsha*. He must have a loincloth on beneath the cloth because she saw no evidence of an erection, but his blazing desire was unmistakable. Heat flooded her face, her chest, until she was surely glowing.

"Exactly." He laughed, moving off with the Blood in his wake. "I'll be occupied all day as the tents disperse. Ask anyone where my tent is and try to get some rest."

She still didn't have confirmation of Varne's accusations. She needed information.

Gregar walked by, winking at her as usual. She hesitated, trying to decide what the repercussions would be. If she talked to him, would that encourage him in any way? Besides, this was likely going to be rather private and embarrassing.

"My favorite kind of discussion." He laughed softly. "Ask, Shannari. It's an honor to serve."

"Will Khul mind if you stay behind?" Worried, she sought Rhaekhar again, but he was already out of sight. People hurried everywhere, carrying loads, leading horses, shouting to each other as they prepared to leave the main Camp. She'd never find him.

"Why should he?"

Sighing, she turned a wary eye on the laughing lecherous Blood. "Varne accused me of deliberately dishonoring Khul."

"That certainly sounds like Varne."

"Did I?"

Gregar shrugged. "Not deliberately."

"But I did dishonor him?" At her insistence, the Blood nodded. "How?"

"Let us find a quieter spot for this discussion." He grasped her arm at her elbow, but she dug in her heels. The last thing she wanted to risk was private time with him. After everything that had happened, she couldn't encourage him in any way. The last thing she needed was two barbarians fighting over her.

Gregar snorted. "There will be no fighting, Shannari."

"I hate it when you do that." Grumbling, she gave in and went with him. "My head hurts, I didn't get any sleep last night, I miss my caffe, everybody hates me, and I really, really wish that I could have some privacy with Rhaekhar tonight."

"Ask me."

"Ask you what?"

"Ask me to help you with the Blood."

"Why should I ask you? You just heard me complain about the lack of privacy."

"Because." He chuckled, leaning closer so his hair tickled her face. Oddly, he even smelled like caffe. She must really be missing her morning brew. "If you ask for my assistance, you'll owe me. We can trade demands."

Politics, barbarian style. She rolled her eyes. "Gregar, can you keep the Blood out of Khul's tent tonight and every night?"

"The Blood will guard outside Khul's tent indefinitely, unless your safety demands otherwise."

Narrowing her eyes, she sharpened her voice. "And your price?"

"If Khul or I ever offer blood, you'll taste it, without question or hesitation. Any time, any place, no matter who watches."

Her stomach rolled with nausea. Not at the thought of tasting their blood, but because she feared she truly was tainted with Shadow.

"It will honor us greatly, Shannari. Everyone in Camp will recognize such a great honor. Tasting blood is not a thing of darkness here, but of honor."

"Yours too?"

He nodded, his eyes darkening with the shadow he carried.

She shivered, her voice shaking. "Okay."

"Very good. Have no worries this night about loving Khul. Now, let us discuss *kae'valda*, or honor."

"And *kae'als*, particularly white ones."

Gregar's teeth flashed in a huge grin. "Aye, white ones. It'll be a very great pleasure."

"Oh, no," Shannari groaned. "Why did you bring me here? To her?"

Gregar scratched on the flap of Drendon's tent, and Alea called out a welcome. "You very likely won't believe my word alone. You already know how Alea feels. If she agrees with me, you'll believe." He winked at her over his shoulder as he ducked inside. "I hope."

Shannari had no choice but to follow him inside the tent and face Alea's dislike. To remember the appalling night lying in Rhaekhar's arms, burning up with need but restraining herself, with sounds of lovemaking just feet away. The rustle of clothing and blankets. The Bloods' eyes flashing all around them. And still, the desire blazing in her that demanded she seal her mouth over her barbarian's and love him anyway.

Civil yet reserved, Alea welcomed them both. Despite her drawn face and frown in Shannari's direction, the other woman cracked the barest of smiles for the Blood. The joking, laughing Blood soon had her smiling wider, more relaxed. Everybody liked him, it seemed.

"I hope you can assist me with a very important discussion for Shannari's benefit."

Alea shot a hard look in her direction but inclined her head. "What do you need?"

Gregar turned his attention to Shannari. "I need you to confirm what I'm about to tell her."

She couldn't help but shiver. His eyes gleamed like bottomless pools at midnight with the full moon above, shining like a mirror.

"You asked me if you dishonored Khul this past night. Why?"

Alea started, sitting up straighter, her gaze narrowing.

"Varne was gloating as if his dislike was at last proved. He told me I risked Khul's position and his life."

"Do you remember the night at the oasis?" Gregar asked softly. His voice lowered, his eyes darkened. "Before your dream?"

Hot embarrassment flooded her face. She knew what he meant. The night Rhaekhar worked so diligently to draw every horrid sound out of her as possible for the benefit of his warriors.

"Do you understand why Khul made you cry out?"

She shook her head. She couldn't meet his gaze nor Alea's. "Everybody heard."

"Exactly."

Shannari jerked her gaze up to his, surprised by the extreme satisfaction in his voice. He smiled, not his normal joking grin, but a cold, calculating smile of utter confidence and foresight. She remembered him challenging Rhaekhar to make her cry out not once but twice. "You did that on purpose?"

"Of course. So did Khul. Do you think he would lose any challenge lightly, even to you? He's the mightiest warrior on the Plains. He's never lost a challenge."

She looked to Alea for confirmation. "Never?"

"That's true, Shannari. I've never seen Khul lose a *kae'rahke*, other than when he and Drendon fought in the *Kae'Khul*. Drendon bested him in the *rahke* portion, but it was very, very close. Khul beat him in the *kae'don* and so was declared the victor. Otherwise, he's never lost, not even a bet."

"He manipulated me." Stunned, she played back that day. How reserved he'd been. How openly disappointed he was to lose. "He played me like a fiddle."

Gregar shared a confused glance with Alea but nodded. "I have no idea what a fiddle is, Shannari, but he knew exactly what he was about. Khul always does."

"He pretended a challenge loss, and then pushed it into an advantage. Something felt off, but I had no idea." She shook her head, quirking her mouth with admiration. "It was brilliant."

"He needed to break your hesitation to make love while others were close. He also needed to make sure his warriors understood how much he loved you before we arrived in Camp."

"And you? Why was twice so important?"

Gregar grinned. "I wanted to hear your sweet voice break the night in pleasure as much as possible, and I knew Khul was more than capable."

Her face was so hot and tight she fanned herself. She couldn't meet the Blood's gaze. Alea snickered and then laughed out loud, harder, until she sagged against Gregar.

All the dislike was gone from her face, Shannari noted, when she finally dared to look at them both. "You have to understand. In my culture, such a thing is very, very private. We have stone walls, thick doors." She waved a hand at the flimsy tent walls. "We certainly don't listen to other's lovemaking."

"Ah, but here, Shannari, we take pride in our love for one another. Each time your voice breaks the night, Khul's honor increases."

"Literally?"

"Aye. That's what the white *kae'als* signify. Each of the beads in Khul's hair signifies his great honor. His *kae'valda*."

"I thought they were merely decorations." She pictured Rhaekhar, his two braids heavy with beads and rings, strings of more beads braided into his hair. "Is his honor so very great?"

"He carries more *kae'valda* than any warrior on the Plains," Alea said proudly. "He's Khul, and none can match him. Whether his *kae'rahke* skills, how he leads his warriors in a *kae'don*, his persuasion and compromise skills with the other khuls."

"Even in the blankets with his woman," Gregar added. "He's Khul. We expect him to be the best. We expect your voice to keep us up late into the night, often, loud and frantic."

Embarrassment warred with horror in Shannari's heart, and she buried her face in her hands. So hot, her face felt on fire. "You know how I feel about him."

"Aye," Gregar replied. "I know your fears. I know you believe you must leave him and return to your Green Lands. You believe you'll kill him, or me, or anyone who nears you. You believe your heart is so wounded, so crippled, that you will never love again. I say it's too late, Shannari. You already love him. You simply refuse to believe it."

How could she make them understand? "If I stay here, my homeland is doomed to Shadow and death. My people will die. If I stay here, your people will start to die. It's inevitable. Eventually, no matter what Rhaekhar says, someone will try to kill me. It happens everywhere I go. I've killed someone in every country and province of the Green Lands. Are you going to let me kill?"

"Nay." Gregar tenderly cupped her chin and turned her gaze

up to his. "I'm going to kill for you. I'm Blood. It's my honor and duty to kill in your defense."

"I might kill him," she whispered, tears burning her eyes. "You saw what happened. I stabbed you. It might happen again. If the dreams—"

"You won't kill him. I swear it."

"You can't—"

"I can," Gregar interrupted firmly. His dark eyes gleamed like chips of black ice. "I am Blood. I am Death. If you dream of Shadow, I shall know. I shall put my body before Khul's. You can stab me over and over, as many times as you wish. Besides, why do you fear Khul's death when you Healed me?"

"Healed?" Her heart froze, stuttering in her chest. "I can't Heal. I don't have any magic."

Gregar lifted her hand and placed her palm on the fresh scar over his heart. "How else am I alive, Shannari? You punctured my heart with my own *rahke*. Of course you Healed me. You'll do the same for Khul if I fail for some reason. But I shall not fail. I'm the Shadowed Blood and I shall stalk your dreams."

He leaned closer, deliberately trailing his hair over her arm. She sucked in her breath, tasting his scent of dark, rich caffe.

"Stab me all you want. I love it. And you know what I'll ask."

She swallowed and nodded. Despite her fears and misgivings, her mouth watered. His blood...

"So." Alea broke in, her voice hard and determined. "You made a mistake last night, Shannari. Understandable, I admit, but a mistake. Khul has lost face. What are you going to do to fix it?"

Shannari tore her gaze away from the dangerous Blood so close and studied the other woman. Understanding flickered between them. Alea still didn't like her, but Shannari could live with that. At least the other woman knew her actions hadn't been deliberately malicious last night.

"I'm going to win him some white beads tonight."

"An outlander woman!" Tomai continued, shaking his head. "Khul, what were you thinking?"

Rhaekhar ground his teeth but said nothing.

"Obviously not thinking at all. With his head, at least." Brenn laughed, slapping Rhaekhar on the back. "I admit, she's quite beautiful, Khul. In my Camp's travels, we've heard all manner of strange tales about the Green Landers. If she's truly a princess of their land, you should send her back. The last time we had any dealings with the royal blood of that land, well, you remember how that ended."

Aye. Everyone in Camp made sure he remembered. Rhaekhar gave the other khul a hard smile. "I remember well. That disaster is why your Camp hasn't been First in generations."

Brenn flushed at the dishonor but could do nothing about the insult. He was a trader, not a warrior. The Khul during the time of Loss and Fire was khul of his Camp. Many accused that Khul of single handedly bringing the disaster down on the Sea of Grass in his arrogance. Now, his Camp claimed position through the goods they obtained, not their *kae'don* or *rahke* skills.

"Shannari is *na'lanna*," Rhaekhar repeated, his hard tone of voice broking no dispute. "She will be my Khul'lanna as soon as I can claim her."

"You must be mistaken," Tomai retorted.

"How can a warrior mistake such a gift from Vulkar?" Rhaekhar smiled wider, gripping the *rahke* on his hip until his hand hurt. "She's *na'lanna*. I shall fight for her. I shall bleed for her. I shall kill for her. If you don't wish to see her as Khul'lanna, challenge me."

"Do you know how many warriors Tehark will send to do just that?" Tomai shook his head. "You open yourself up for fierce competition. Already, the Camps are whispering, jostling for position. Your Camp has lost face. You've lost face. All for an outlander woman. Is she worth your very life?"

"Aye."

Shaking their heads, all the khuls left but Drendon. He opened his mouth, whether to agree with the others or not, Rhaekhar didn't care. "Friends we may be, but I've heard enough disagreements for the day."

"Perhaps you would enjoy a *kae'rahke* this night. A little friendly blood and competition."

Now that was a true friend. Rhaekhar nodded his thanks. Everyone on the Plains knew that Drendon was the only warrior who'd ever bested him in a *kae'rahke*. A challenge from his friend would delay some of the other warriors who might not have the best memory of his skills. Assuming, of course, that he won.

"Blood and competition, my two favorite things," Gregar said, joining them.

"Where have you been?" Varne glared at the other Blood. "Khul has need of his Blood at all times."

Rhaekhar knew, but wondered just the same. Shannari was up to something, but what, he didn't know. Not exactly. Gregar had helped her in some way, though, for which he was truly grateful.

Gregar shrugged. "Merely at Camp. Could you not handle Khul's protection alone? He appears fine to me. Of course, there are seven other Blood standing here, too."

"I'm nearest Blood. Of course he's fine! What would you care, though? You were too busy dallying with Khul's woman!"

"And Drendon's woman." Drendon gave the dark-haired Blood a shove, and Gregar laughed. "Alea's instructing Shannari on Camp life."

Drendon groaned. "I had best return to Camp with gifts, then. Many gifts."

Silently, Rhaekhar agreed. The two women didn't exactly get along. Perhaps some Sha'Kae al'Dan clothing would tempt Shannari. And he also needed to find one particular gift she would greatly appreciate, more than clothing he was sure. If anyone possessed it, Brenn's Camp would.

"Speaking of blood and competition, I would like to make a bet." Gregar winked at Varne, arching an eyebrow at the nearest Blood's frown. "Since Khul will participate in a *kae'rahke* this night against Drendon, I bet Shannari will taste Khul's blood at the fire."

Drendon's eyes lit up. "Khul, will she truly? Such an honor. Even if she's shy in your blankets, sharing blood is a great honor. Many women would refuse such a display."

Varne shook his head. "Not before the entire Camp. She hates it."

Gregar laughed, shaking his head. "You have no understanding of Shannari. Is it a bet, then?"

"Khul cannot persuade or trick her into it. She must taste his blood willingly."

"Aye." Gregar shared a knowing smile with Rhaekhar. "He won't even have to touch her. His blood alone will be enough temptation. Agreed?"

Rhaekhar shook his head, smiling. He didn't know what the Blood was up to. Aye, Shannari enjoyed his blood, but before all the people? When she felt such reluctance? When tasting his blood was enough to bring her pleasure? She couldn't bear for others to hear her cries, let alone watch her quiver and shake in his arms.

Varne looked from him to the Blood and back, his gaze narrowing.

"If I lose, you may have my ivory *rahke*."

"Done," Varne said. "She'll never taste Khul's blood in public."

"I say she will. She will indeed."

"And what do you require if she does?"

Shadows thickened about Gregar, creeping across the ground toward the other Blood. Varne actually glanced up at the sky, searching for clouds across the sun. "The Blood leave Khul to privacy in his tent."

"Never! You would leave Khul unprotected, alone, with *her?*"

Rhaekhar swore the shadows wrapped around Varne's neck. Still, he hesitated to interfere. Gregar was trying to help Shannari in some way. As long as neither Blood drew his *rahke*...

"Unless there's danger, the Blood will remain outside Khul's tent. I shall know if Shadow touches her. Khul will know, too, and so then even you will sense her danger. If you have any forewarning of another threat, then we can protect inside as well. But while there's no danger, Shannari needs privacy."

"I'll do nothing for her," Varne retorted.

"Not even for Khul's honor?" Gregar asked softly, his voice echoing with menace. "You were so thoughtful to describe in full detail how she damaged Khul's honor this past night. Surely you agree that she should be given the opportunity to repair her mistake?"

Fury roared in Rhaekhar's veins. He took a step toward his nearest Blood, hands clenched into fists. "You insulted her? Again?"

"Nay, Khul." Varne shook his head in frustration, "I merely spoke the truth."

"Then I speak the truth now." Rhaekhar stepped closer and deliberately dropped his hand to his *rahke*. "I tolerate no one insulting her, not even you."

"Truth is not insult," Varne replied flatly. He didn't touch his *rahke*, and Rhaekhar knew where his honor lay. Varne was wholly Blood, the nearest, the last defense. He would never risk his position or honor by challenging Khul.

"Gregar and I shall instruct her in our ways. We have no need of your assistance in this matter."

"Very well," Varne said, inclining his head stiffly. "As you will."

Rhaekhar sighed. So far, he'd alienated the few khuls supporting him, given his enemies a valid argument to vocally and physically use against him, and angered the nearest Blood who protected his life. All for a woman who openly professed she would never love him.

All it took was a moment's concentration through the bond, a touch against her mind, a whisper of her desire, her courage, her fears, and he would risk all for her, time and again. *Na'lanna.*

"**A**re you sure you want to go through with this?" Alea asked doubtfully. "You don't look very comfortable."

Shannari tugged at the impossibly short cloth about her hips and fought to tone down the raging heat in her face. She likely glowed as fiercely as the bonfire ahead. A sultry summer breeze whipped up the back of the cloth and sent her meager gown fluttering wildly. Hold the vest shut or push down the thing Alea called a *memshai*?

Gritting her teeth, she stopped, closed her eyes, and concentrated on finding herself and her courage. Yes, her underthings usually covered up more than this outfit. Yes, she felt extremely vulnerable with her hair loose down her back and no armor. But she still wore a sword on her hip and every warrior in Camp was armed. Rhaekhar and his Blood—at least Gregar—swore no harm would come to her here.

For the first time in her life, she was trying to trust someone else to protect her.

It certainly didn't come easily.

The familiar lake spread through her mind. Cool, crystal waters, mirrored surface, peace. Just as she would concentrate before battle, she pushed all her fears and doubts into those smooth waters. The image calmed her turbulent thoughts. Centered and focused, she raised her chin, opened her eyes, and dropped her hands.

"I'm fine. Let's go—we're late."

Alea led the way to her usual spot at the fire with her mate. The men waited for them, laughing and talking loudly, surrounded by Blood and other trusted friends.

Seated before the bonfire beside Drendon, Rhaekhar turned his head and froze. His eyes turned molten gold, flaming immediately at the sight of her. He didn't rise, didn't move, just stared at her, his muscles coiling, prepared to strike.

The other warriors fell silent, some looking at her, some—Gregar—laughing softly at Khul's whole-hearted stare. She concentrated on Rhaekhar, ignoring the others. The heat in his eyes and the flaring need through the bond was worth the embarrassment she felt at wearing such brazen attire.

As soon as she came within arm's length, he drew her down toward him. Only her own persistence put her beside him instead of in his lap. He drew her close, pressing his mouth to ear.

"You torture me, woman. After last night, I'm hard enough to nigh rip this loincloth in half."

His heat engulfed her, all baking bread scent and warrior brawn. She laughed breathlessly and tried to pull back for a little space. "You like?"

"Three Hells, aye, I like." He trailed his fingers down her jaw, her neck, to the gaping front of the vest that did its best to bare as much of her breasts as possible. "Seeing you in our clothing makes me yearn to claim you now so I may wrap you in my *kae'valda.*"

"In your tent, later."

"I mean forever, Shannari." He buried his face in her neck, his hands hard on her shoulders. His big body actually shuddered against her. "Hells."

Releasing her, he sat upright, trying to gather his control. She couldn't help but glance down at his *memsha.* Oh, definitely, he was sincere in his desire. Not even the loincloth could conceal his need. "I'm not going to marry you. I can't. We've been over this before."

"Aye, so you say." His smoldering gaze nearly seared the flimsy clothes right off her body. "I say otherwise. If you want me enough, you will." He took a long, deep breath and smiled, his nostrils flaring. "And you'll want me enough. I'll make sure of it."

What did he smell that sent the flames shooting higher in his eyes?

Turning his attention back to the warriors surrounding them, he slid an arm around her back, drew her into his side, and leaned down to whisper. "I smell your heat, woman. Hot summer nights and a flower. No flower I've ever seen but in a dream ages ago. Your Rose, I believe. The more you want me, the thicker and sweeter the fragrance in your scent. Your scent is all flowers right now."

Sitting beside him, thigh to thigh, his powerful arm wrapped around her, was torment. She'd never been fully dressed before and yet still able to feel a man's skin like this. He radiated heat, searing her everywhere they touched. And the damned barbarian made sure they touched.

She had no memory of what they ate. What people said. All she could do was concentrate on keeping her hands to herself and longing for his tent. She just hoped the Blood kept his promise.

"**A**re you ready for our challenge, Khul?" Drendon asked, his eyes bright with excitement. "I'm certainly eager to draw your blood."

Concerned, Shannari turned to Rhaekhar. Was this her fault? His own friend challenging him, threatening to hurt him?

He stood and offered a hand to draw her to her feet. "Merely a demonstration between friends. For every wound he gives me, I shall return one in kind."

"Isn't he the only one who ever beat you in a challenge?"

His eyes flared with surprise and he nodded. "Aye, once. Don't concern yourself, *na'lanna*. I shall not lose this challenge."

"How do you know?"

"Because I fight for you."

Dread and guilt rolled through her. Why couldn't he have just left her in the Green Lands? Why did he have to bring her here, ruin his life, his Camp, his friendships? *I tried to warn him. Shadow follows me wherever I go.*

"There's one thing you could do that would help me win."

She ran through her options. With the sword at her hip, she could fight, definitely, but he'd already defeated her not once but twice. Drendon must be nearly as good if not more so. Why didn't the Blood refuse to allow this fight? "What?"

His voice thickened and heat surged through the bond. "You could let me taste your blood. For luck. For strength. For love."

Hardening her face, she nodded. The answering blaze in his eyes drew a small moan from her. "For luck and strength, yes."

The lust burning in his burnished gold eyes didn't diminish. With a quick yank, he removed the cloth about his hips, standing before her clad only in his loincloth. Despite the crowd, she couldn't help but drink in his body. The loincloth enhanced the shape of his genitals and buttocks, leaving nothing to her imagination. His muscular, sinewy legs appeared longer, even more powerful. His entire body screamed supreme and confident warrior.

She wanted to kiss and bite every inch.

With a low, rumbling growl, he unsheathed his *rahke* and wrapped his other arm around her, drawing her into the heat of his body. "For love," he repeated, his voice rumbling through her. "My love."

Rock-hard muscle against her. Desire roaring off him, his scent flaming, his skin searing. The wicked sharp blade flashed in the firelight, tinged red by the flames. He made sure she saw it, that she thought about him using it on her. He forced her to acknowledge her trust that he wouldn't hurt her, that he wouldn't draw too much blood.

That he wouldn't kill her.

Her heart slammed frantically against her ribcage, and she waited. She waited to feel terror shrilling through her nerves. She waited for the Lady's warning to crash inside her head.

All she felt was aching, trembling need. Need to feel his mouth on her. Need to feel her blood rushing into him, the bond blazing in her mind.

Smiling, he trailed the *rahke* down her neck, nudging open the vest enough to reveal the horrid scar on her left breast. Despite the trust he'd earned, she still tensed and gripped his supporting arm. She fought her instincts, the urge to rip her sword free and drive him back.

He didn't force her. Drowning her in his scent and heat and longing, she made a small pleading sound that he took for acquiescence. A quick pain to her breast, and he pressed his mouth to her skin.

He licked and sucked at the small cut, rumbling with such pleasure and hunger he sounded more beast than man. She wrapped her hands in his hair and held him close, while wave after wave of need rolled through her. How could the simple feel of his mouth drive her insane? Her knees trembled, weakening, opening her legs for him. Her body wanted him hard and fast, now, right now, right here.

Groaning, he set her aside, steadying her when she wobbled. "Thank you, *na'lanna*. With your blood pounding in my veins, I shall never lose to Drendon."

Rhaekhar joined his friend in the circle of warriors, leaving his Blood with her. Varne pointedly ignored her, but Gregar stood on her left, Alea on her right. Struggling to calm her breathing, she didn't protest when the Blood steadied her with a knowing wink.

An elderly man placed a hand on each warrior's chest, and the crowd stilled expectantly.

"Two warriors stand before You, Great Wind Stallion, with fire in their blood. They offer their blood to You in honorable combat. May You strengthen their arms and hearts and show Your Grace on the victor."

Evidently the elderly man was a priest of Vulkar. He removed his hands and took one step back. "Who will take first blood?"

Drendon answered at once. "I shall."

"And what do you demand?"

"I'm sure Alea would appreciate a new bow, chosen by Khul's own hand."

"Indeed." Rhaekhar smiled. "And if I draw first blood, I desire a *rahke* for Shannari."

The holy man continued. "Who will be the victor?"

"I shall," Rhaekhar answered immediately. "If I win, I demand one *na'kindre* of my choice from Drendon's herd."

Drendon's eyes narrowed. "If I win, I demand one of my choice of Khul's trained warhorses."

The crowd murmured excitedly while the two warriors stared

each other down. Drendon grinned, obviously excited; Rhaekhar stoic and formidable in his silence. Unshakeable.

"Is this dangerous?" Inwardly, Shannari cringed at the husky, shaky timbre of her voice. Her heart still thudded and a heavy, liquid warmth pooled in her stomach. Giving the barbarian blood felt almost as good as tasting his.

"It can be," Gregar replied. "Otherwise, there would be no honor to gain. Drendon does this to benefit you and Khul."

She thought Drendon hated her. "What do you mean?"

"Drendon is slightly faster than Khul and will most assuredly draw first blood. He knows this. He could have asked for something that would impede Khul's honor. For instance, he could have demanded you and Khul share his tent every single night for a week, a month, indefinitely. Instead, he asked for something he wanted, that would increase his honor, without risking Khul's."

Shannari cringed again at the thought of sharing a tent with the other couple indefinitely. Alea muttered beneath her breath. Evidently, she wasn't too thrilled at such a prospect, either.

"Drendon is a true friend," Gregar said. "He even arranges for your mount. None on the Plains can match the beauty in Drendon's herd. Yet the risk is great. Drendon has long coveted Khul's golden warhorse, Khan. Don't worry, though, Shannari. If Drendon and Khul truly had any grievances, this would be formal challenge. No betting would happen and they'd fight for blood only. This fight is for amusement and blood."

Oh, well, that sounded like fun. She shook her head, her mouth quirking. She tried to imagine such a spectacle at court and failed.

The holy man removed his hands and stepped back to the edge of the crowd. "Let the *kae'rakhe* begin."

The two warriors began a strange, deadly waltz and she couldn't look away. The flames writhed behind them, casting eerie shadows across the ring. They leaped at each other and whirled, the sharp blades a part of their bodies instead of distinct weapons. The excitement of the watchers was palatable, so heavy in the air she found it hard to breathe.

The sound of the two warriors' struggle was loud in the silence. Their rough breathing, the screech of blade on blade, the shredding of the air itself as a *rahke* ripped toward an opponent.

Drendon's blade almost caught Rhaekhar, but he leaped back at the last possible moment, sucking in his stomach tightly to avoid the swinging arc of the rahke. Her heart tried to hammer out of her chest, and her hand hurt from gripping the hilt of her sword. It was all she could do to keep from drawing her own weapon.

Gregar moved closer, a subtle press against her. When the next blow actually did draw Rhaekhar's blood, she leaned into Gregar's side and he squeezed her reassuringly.

"Watch, now. Drendon's slightly faster but shows his emotions easily. He doesn't control his excitement well and has fought wildly and hard. Khul has allowed his friend's excitement to run its course, and the first thrill of the battle has passed. He knew he would probably bleed first, and now he will ruthlessly and systematically attack, his greater endurance and control giving him the advantage."

Indeed, Drendon's *rahke* drew blood several more times, but he soon wore many more wounds than Rhaekhar. Sweat glistened on their bodies in the firelight, smearing with the blood. She knew the tremendous strength in his body, though, and he fought even harder when he sensed his friend's tiredness.

She strained with him, every fiber of her body pushing with him, urging him to move faster, to strike harder. In a sudden flurry of moves that she could barely follow with her eyes, he pushed Drendon across the ring and a *rahke* fell to the ground.

Rhaekhar held his knife up under his opponent's chin, his chest heaving with exertion.

The warriors stomped and clapped, cheering when the holy man stepped back into the makeshift ring. "For blood," the old man said, smiling, and gave each warrior a small black bead. A *kae'al*. After her discussion with Gregar, she now recognized the honor implied.

Rhaekhar slipped the bead onto a leather string in his hair, still talking to his friend. Even from this distance, she could tell his body vibrated with tension. If the fight was over, why was he so stiff and controlled?

Suddenly, she realized everyone was staring at her. The stomping continued, expectant but not quite as enthusiastic.

"What am I supposed to do?"

Gregar leaned closer and whispered, "Remember our agreement." Then louder, as he gave her a little push, he said, "Show us how much you appreciate your warrior and his skills."

Her ears roared, and not from the noisy crowd. Blood. Gregar wanted her to taste the blood running from at least a dozen wounds. Did Rhaekhar want this too?

Definitely, she decided, coming to a stop before him. Hot, blazing need roared in his eyes. The loincloth bulged more than ever. Slick with sweat and blood, high on the fight and his victory, he stared at her like he contemplated dragging her to the ground here and now before all his warriors.

That didn't sound as distressing and humiliating as it should have.

"I made a blood sacrifice to Vulkar this night." His low, rumbling voice was thick and raw, thrumming through her body. "Are you going to waste it?"

Her gaze dropped to his muscled chest, arms, and stomach, examining the wounds. Most were neat and shallow, bleeding freely but not jagged. Only one in his side, gaping across his ribs, likely needed stitches. She was impressed at the skill used to place such wounds so carefully in the heat of a fight.

Which one to use, though, that wouldn't cause him too much pain? That wouldn't embarrass her too much with so many onlookers? She decided the cut high on his shoulder. Stepping closer, she stretched up on her tiptoes to reach it, but his hands settled on her shoulders.

Golden eyes blazing, he pushed hard enough to make his desire known, but gave her a chance to refuse. She hesitated, trying to decide whether a small battle was worth it. Resistance would be stupid when she wanted what he offered just as badly as he did, and allowing him to direct her in this would give him more pleasure. The damned arrogant barbarian certainly enjoyed giving his commands.

Sighing, she allowed her knees to sag. Sliding his hands into her hair, he pushed her to kneel in front of him. Staring at the washboarded planes of his stomach, she knew exactly which wound he wanted her to taste. The knife had caught him just above the loincloth, actually nicking the material slightly in its southerly route. Her face would practically be in his groin.

He liked that thought, oh yes indeed. Breathing hard, he tightened his fingers in her hair, tugging her closer. To keep her balance, she gripped his waist, fingers slipping in the sweat and blood to settle lower on his hips.

*Blood, all he wants to give me is blood. Right?*

Closing her eyes, she let him put her mouth on his stomach exactly where he wanted. Salty skin, rock-hard muscle, hot blood so thick and sweet. She dug her fingers harder into his hips and licked the blood carefully from his skin, even slipping her tongue beneath the loincloth. The blood was hotter, here, richer, scorching down her throat to heat her stomach.

Fire spread through her veins, a pulsing wave.

Drowning, she tried to back away before the inevitable, but

he knew. The bond hummed and strained between them so hard even she felt it. She could almost hear his thoughts with his rough growl.

:*Come for me, my heart.*:

Blessed Lady, she did just that. Forgetting their audience, everything but him and his blood and the gleaming golden threads in her head tying her to him. Crying out against his skin, fingers scrambling for purchase, need scouring the flesh from her bones until she felt so raw, so vulnerable.

So helpless in the onslaught of vicious pleasure.

She hated it, this crushing need. Need that demanded she jerk that ridiculously small cloth away and put her mouth to better use. Need that demanded she beg him to take her now, immediately, before she died. Need that demanded she surrender all pride, all hope, all plans, simply to be with him.

:*Need me, aye. It's one step closer to loving me.*:

Jerking her mouth aside, she would have fallen without his hands closing on her shoulders. He pulled her up against him, another torment, and walked her back toward their spot at the fire as if nothing had happened.

As if she hadn't just climaxed in front of so many people. As if she hadn't gone against her natural inclinations to do something that would please and honor him. As if—

She refused to think it.

Head down, stumbling along beside him, she didn't make any protest when he sat and dragged her into his lap. She couldn't have stood without his help anyway. She couldn't bear to look around, to see the reaction of so many people who must have got quite the eyeful.

He cupped her chin in his palm, but she resisted, burying her face deeper against his chest. She couldn't bear to look at him, at anyone right now. If Gregar mouthed off about their "agreement" or if Varne said one word in disapproval...

"Well done, Shannari."

She didn't know the voice. Reluctantly, she peeked up into the holy man's face. Up close, he looked even older than she'd thought. His face was deeply lined, tanned to leather by long summer suns and age.

Rhaekhar rubbed his thumb across her cheek and chin. "Shannari, this is *Kae'Shaman*, the most honored *shaman* of the Nine Camps of the Sha'Kae al'Dan."

Horrified, she realized she must have blood smeared all over her face. She started to swipe her sleeve across her face, then remembered her clothing. Or rather, the lack thereof. She'd only embarrass herself more if she tried to find a scrap to wipe her face.

Her cheeks flooded with shame and mortification. To meet such a holy man, covered in blood, inner muscles still clenching and aching with need...

Rhaekhar handed her the cloth he normally wore about his waist, and she buried her face in it.

"She's honored to meet you, *Kae'Shaman*, I'm sure." They both laughed, accompanied by Gregar, the perpetual jokester. Her stomach rolled queasily, and Rhaekhar pushed her head lower against her legs.

"I'm most honored to meet a Daughter of Leesha."

Embarrassment or not, that drew her attention. Bracing herself, she raised her gaze to *Kae'Shaman's*.

"I See—" His eyes flashed, his voice singsong, his gaze locked on her, but deeper. As if he saw her heart. "A circle of golden flowers on your head."

"The Rose Crown," she whispered. Her heart raced. The High Priest often received visions from the Lady, but understanding them was difficult at best. "What else?"

"Oh, many things." The old man gave her an enigmatic smile all priests must be taught early by their Gods. He placed something in her hand. "Welcome to the Sea of Grass, Daughter. We've been waiting for you. I hope to give your warrior several of these by morning."

*Kae'Shaman* turned and shambled away. Shannari opened her palm. A white bead.

"Did you obtain the item I asked for?" Rhaekhar asked his Blood.

Varne immediately offered a leather thong a finger length or so. "Aye, Khul."

Shaking his head, Gregar winked at her and offered his own, as long as his forearm. "Perhaps such a thong would have held your white *kae'als*, Varne, but Khul needs one much longer for Shannari. This may be sufficient for a night or two."

She gave the bead to Rhaekhar, her cheeks heating all over again as she watched him slide the bead onto the leather and tie it in his hair. Every time she looked at that damned thing, she'd remember. "How long do these... tallies... continue?"

"Until we're mated," Rhaekhar replied. "Then I'll remove all white *kae'als* not yours and give them back to *Kae'Shaman*. All that are yours I shall treasure forever, but I shall only wear the ones from our claiming from then on."

"Claiming? You mean wedding?" At his nod, she thought through the ramifications. The barbarians actually kept a count of how many...

"Aye." Gregar laughed, slapping Rhaekhar on the back. "I expect Khul to set a new record."

Her ears roared and spots danced before her eyes. Her head was stuffed with cotton. She'd thought the Green Land custom of royal beddings distasteful. "Record?"

"The current record without *drakkar* is only three, is it not?"

Her head started to pound. She had no idea what *drakkar* was, and it sounded like she didn't want to know.

Gregar smiled brightly. "You had best push her head back down Khul."

Indeed, the spots spread, darkening her vision.

Rhaekhar scooped her against his chest and stood. "Or better yet, we shall simply retire to my tent."

"Aye, Khul, you should get a good start on filling the new thong."

## 15

Shannari didn't bother looking around the tent. All her curiosity was centered on the barbarian. At last, they were alone, they had some semblance of walls and privacy, and she was going to have her way with him.

Pushing against his chest, she rolled him over. He went willingly enough. Flat on his back, he stared up at her, golden eyes blazing like the sun, blood drying from a dozen small wounds, sweat and blood and lust overwhelming his normal sweet hay and baking bread scent. Delicious.

"This is supposed to be your night, na'lanna."

"It is." She shrugged out of the vest, enjoying the way his eyes darkened to honeyed ale. Her fingers felt clumsy and desperate enough she couldn't seem to get the knot undone which held the cloth about her hips. "You said any other night you would let me do as I wish. Tonight is my night."

Drawing her closer, he tugged on the knot and tossed the offending material aside. "As you wish. Remember to be as noisy as possible, though, na'lanna. The noisier the better."

Her cheeks blazed with embarrassment all over again. Counting. Listening. Watching. A sound very close to panic escaped her throat.

"Shhh, *na'lanna*. Don't think."

She closed her eyes a moment and took a deep breath. If she could lead warriors in battle, surely she could make love with someone listening. She just wouldn't think about it.

Lady, she'd never seen a man better put together. All warrior, muscle and strength imprinted on every inch of him. His skin was velvety soft with very little hair even on his legs and arms, crisscrossed with so many scars. So much honor.

"I taste even better."

Shivering, she closed her eyes, waiting for the vicious clenching deep inside to ease. She might not last long enough to torment him as she hoped.

"There are other nights, *na'lanna*. Many nights."

"Quit finishing my thoughts for me."

He laughed roughly and trailed his fingers across her thigh. "I cannot help it. You must hear me even better. Are you going to look at me all night?"

"How much latitude will you give me?"

Frowning, he started to sit up, but she pressed her hand in the center of his chest to keep him down. "What do you mean?"

"I mean, if I say don't touch me, will you heed my..." She almost said command and thought better of it. "Wish?"

His eyes narrowed despite the alternative word choice. "Why would you not want me to touch you?"

Leaning down, she brushed her mouth over his, softening his frown until she could draw his bottom lip into her mouth. A few nibbles, and his hands were closing on her head and command vibrated through his powerful body once more.

He was a supreme warrior, an arrogant barbarian, a fearless leader of men used to giving commands to everyone. Even in a kiss, he couldn't help but give commands. Even in the throes of passion, he never fully released his control on his emotions.

"I cannot."

"Why?" She trailed her mouth down his neck, licking and nibbling as she went. Nothing too hard. Yet. "I want you a little wild and crazy."

"Wild and crazy could hurt you. There's no greater wrong a warrior can commit than injuring a woman in his care."

She snorted loudly and deliberately bit his neck harder. "You wouldn't hurt me even when I sliced you open with my sword."

"This is different, *na'lanna*." Already, his voice was thick with rising need. "Only a warrior in bloodlust would ever completely relinquish control."

"Bloodlust." She found the wound on his shoulder and carefully licked it clean. "Sounds good to me."

Groaning, he clenched his hands into fists. "You have no idea of what you speak. A warrior in bloodlust is more likely to rape than to love. Nobody is safe from him, especially his woman."

"That's exactly what I want." Swinging a leg over him, she made herself very comfortable on his lower abdomen. "I want to kiss and nibble every inch of you, but I don't want you to touch me. I don't want you to roll me beneath you and end it until I'm ready. And when you do, I want you to relinquish your control."

Another rumble escaped his throat. "So you want me to use control to avoid touching you while you torment me, only to lose control utterly when you say?"

She smiled wickedly. "Exactly."

Closing his eyes, he muttered, "Gregar must be laughing his arse off."

She didn't want to think of the dark Blood laughing. She didn't even want to think too much about the gorgeous barbarian beneath her. Already she trusted him too much. She enjoyed his body too much. She exposed too many of her secret thoughts and longings, things she'd never dared tell another, let alone a lover.

The clenching this time was of pain, and centered about her heart.

"Aye, I shall do as you wish," Rhaekhar answered. "I shall not touch you until you give me permission."

To prove his point, he very firmly planted his arms at his sides, palms flat on the tent floor.

With narrowed gaze, she searched his face to find the reason for his solemn satisfaction. He was reluctant, yes, but also oddly pleased. "I'm going to take my time."

He trembled beneath her but nodded.

"I want to taste your blood some more. It might hurt."

"I trust you not to hurt me too much."

Scooting a bit lower, she laid her head against his chest. His heart thumped strong and steady beneath her ear. "Why the sudden agreement?"

"Do you really want to talk about whys and wherefores when you could be loving my body?"

The barbarian had a point.

"Besides, if you truly wanted to know my motivations, you could listen through the bond. As much of my blood as you've taken, you should be able to hear my every thought, if that is your desire."

It wasn't, obviously. Involuntarily, she tensed. Had she truly heard him speaking in her head earlier at the fire?

:Aye.:

Gritting her teeth, she concentrated very, very hard on not listening to him.

Sighing, he spoke out loud. "I make one request."

She lifted her head, staring down into his rugged face.

"I want you to mark me."

Heat rose in her at the thought. Her secret desire, her great shame.

"I marked you, remember? And you know how it feels each time I touch it. When I put my mouth upon it. Don't you want the same power over me?"

Closing her eyes, she nodded jerkily. She wanted it, definitely. So much it scared her. She wanted to sink her teeth into his shoulder or neck, feel him shaking helplessly beneath her, while she branded him. As hers.

It wouldn't be fair to mark him and then leave him. She wasn't cruel, not usually, but the thought of another woman with him, touching her mark, her barbarian...

Chuckling, he arched beneath her suggestively. "You are welcome to try leaving me, *na'lanna*. You won't get very far."

"Why is that?"

Golden eyes flashed at her fiercely and he smiled, a deliberate gleam of teeth and dominance. "Even if I didn't have the bond to track you down, I would never surrender what was mine. Never. You're mine, *na'lanna*. Best you remember that. Now get to tormenting me already."

His last words were almost enough to change her mind. The narrowing of her eyes and the stubborn lift of her chin told him clearly what she was thinking.

She planned to leave him. Hells, she'd never intended to come so far. She certainly feared the slight softening of her heart. The weakness. The need.

Need he would use against her.

Deliberately, he breathed deeply, letting heat blaze in his eyes. Great Vulkar, she smelled wonderful, all lush heat and sultry nights. He licked his lips and she shuddered, a soft cry shaking through her.

To distract herself more than torment him, she returned to kissing his chest. She found another wound from the *kae'rahke* and it was all he could do to keep his hands at his side instead of burying them in her hair and holding her close. His blood roared through her, spreading fire he could feel through the bond. Every lick, every taste, bound her tighter to him. Didn't she sense it? Nay, she must not. She would never willingly make herself defenseless in their battle.

Yet her denials still worried him. If she could refuse the whisper of his thoughts in her mind, the touch of his heart against hers, then what chance did he have to force her to examine her own?

Teeth grazed his skin, her tongue probing the cut carefully, and he gritted his teeth. Oh, aye, the Blood was definitely laughing at this intolerable torment.

"I want you."

Her whisper shattered his heart. A small weakness admitted. "Then take me, my heart."

"I don't want to want you," she growled, sitting up. Scooting lower, she lifted herself over him and took him inside. They both groaned out loud.

Agony, to lie here, waiting, refusing to respond to his urge to drive her to pleasure.

"I don't want to need you."

"I know."

She wouldn't allow him to touch her, so he stared up at her, drinking in the glowing flush on her cheeks, the blazing need darkening her gorgeous night-sky eyes. What an incredibly lovely sight to see his woman taking her pleasure in his body, her breasts full and sweetly curved, so close, but so far away.

Her hair fell about her shoulders like a black cape. The

thought of his *kae'valda* wrapped around her made him throw his head back, arching his hips beneath her. "I need you just as much."

She gave a little twist of her hips, grinding against him, and the dam broke inside her. Crying out, she rose up and slammed down again, her sheath gripping him in a vise. When she finally fell back against his chest, he was drenched in sweat and breathing like a *na'kindre* ridden hard and fast and long.

She burrowed her face into his neck. "Want. Need. What are you doing to me?"

"I'm loving you."

"I don't want you to love me. I'll only hurt you. I'll never love you. Don't you understand?"

"Aye." He understood things she refused to consider. Secrets of her heart she refused to examine. "I love you anyway. You forgot something, *na'lanna*."

Pushing up to her elbows, she glared down at him. "Why are you doing this?"

"This?" He moved beneath her, still unbearably hard and aching inside her. Her eyes rolled back in her head and he chuckled. "You were supposed to mark me. And while you're at it, I need a few more screams of pleasure."

"I'll show you screams of pleasure," she muttered. "Do you get beads for your own screams?"

She sank her teeth into the base of his neck, and his answer was lost entirely. Deeper, harder, her jaws gripped his throat until she tasted blood. Quivering, she came again, and with a roaring shout, he found release, too.

And he never put his hands on her.

Breathing hard, she sat up and wiped at her mouth. Her hand trembled, and she stared at her bite on his neck. Shaken. Scared. Solemn. She whispered so low he could barely hear her. "Does it hurt?"

"Nay, my heart. It feels incredible. Touch it."

She slowly reached out and traced her finger around the ring her teeth had left in his skin. Throwing his head back again, every muscle in his body clenched. Need came roaring back to life in him and he hardened inside her.

She shuddered, gulping for air.

"Are you finished?"

She nodded shakily. "I reserve the right to continue later, though."

"Agreed." He rolled her beneath him. "In due time."

He kissed her softly, nibbling, drawing her bottom lip into his mouth to suck on it. He took his time, exploring the dark recesses of her mouth, stroking his tongue along the roof of her mouth and her teeth. A hint of his blood flavored her tongue, and a fierce satisfaction roared through him.

Shannari didn't quite know how to handle this tender exploration. Her hands froze on his back, and she lay stiffly beneath him. She didn't accept the invitation of his open mouth for equal treatment.

Drawing back, he studied her face. Eyes stunned, wide open, her lips parted and trembling. Vulnerable, naked need gleamed in her jeweled eyes like tears. She squeezed her eyes shut and firmed her lips, hiding, but she couldn't hide her heart from him.

He didn't push the advantage. Instead, he gathered her against his chest and simply held her. Bit by bit, she relaxed into his embrace, even playing her fingers up and down his spine.

"Is hugging all you want to do with me?"

"It's enough, for now. I could hold you endlessly, *na'lanna*. I treasure the beat of your heart against mine."

She fell silent, some of her uncertainty and anxiety coming back. She simply didn't know how to handle tenderness from him. Arrogance and dominance she knew. Tenderness left her bewildered and scared.

Deliberately, he used their bond to stroke his thoughts through her mind, another intimacy she couldn't refuse. *:What are you afraid of?:*

She tensed even more beneath him. "I'm not afraid."

Closing his eyes, he sank deeper into her, both body and mind. In his mind's eye, she glowed with pearly moonlight, shadowed here and there by old hurts and doubts. He wrapped his bond, his love, about her, trying to drive those shadows away.

"Hurts," she gasped.

Pain did arc through her, not physical but remembered. Over and over, people she'd trusted had wounded her. Blades sinking into her flesh, crippling her heart. The wounds were real, as the scar on her chest indicated, but they went much deeper. How could he possibly heal these old injuries?

He knew no such magic. There was no enemy for him to defeat. No sword, no *rahke* he possessed could defeat the old wounds still haunting her. For all his strength and honor as Khul of the Nine Camps of the Sha'Kae al'Dan, he couldn't fight this *kae'don* for her.

She really would choose to leave him. If he allowed it.

"Nay," he growled. Plunging hard, he thrust as deeply as he could go, drawing a ragged cry from her. She clawed at his back, tilting her hips to take him even deeper, and he lost all control.

Savage, dark need filled him, pouring over into her. Or perhaps the darkness was hers and she shared it with him. He'd certainly never known such agonizing, mindless need before.

She screamed, and her pleasure slammed into his gut, clenching inside him like a fist. Jerking back to his knees, he withdrew and flipped her over. He'd dreamed of taking her this way. Covering her like a wild stallion, forcing her into submission, teeth in her neck, pounding into her hard and fast.

She pushed backwards to meet him, but he wrapped an arm around her hips to lock her in place. Pressing heavily against her back, he pinned her beneath him. He leaned down to breathe in her ear. "You'll take what I give."

Arching her back, she tried to buck him off to at least regain some control, but she was no match for his size and strength. Frustration boiled through the bond and she jerked her head back, trying to catch him in the face. "You can play dominant herd stallion all you want, but you can't make me love you."

Her accusation slapped him in the face, dowsing the furious need. Recoiling, he almost withdrew completely. At least some of his control returned. "Do you refuse me, then? After the love we've shared this night?"

He waited for her answer, not moving a muscle. Sweat inched down his face, burning his eye, to drip onto her gleaming skin. Very deliberately, he kept his thoughts and emotions under tight control. She didn't want to know his heart. She didn't want the intrusion, the intimacy, the connection of spirit to spirit.

"No," she whispered. "I won't refuse you. But we haven't shared love."

Relief filled him but couldn't entirely erase the fury and desperation in his heart. This was a *kae'don* he couldn't win. *But I must. I must.* "I have. I do. Every time I touch you, I make love to you."

Instead of arguing, she sank her teeth into his forearm braced beside her head.

A spasm raced down his back, blazing flames rushing through him like wildfire. Still, he hesitated. He didn't want her to claim later that she hadn't been fully willing, or that he was too aggressive, too... barbaric.

*:Make me forget that I have no heart.:*

The touch of her mind was faint, faraway, yet oh so precious. Her words made little difference to him, but the bond, and her use of it, meant the world. Perhaps he could make her forget her scarred heart, her fear, and the betrayal that still haunted her. *:My heart is yours,* na'lanna.*:*

He thrust deep, aching to join his heart to hers as well as his body. Harder, her cry coming so soon, too soon, and the fire exploded inside him.

Every muscle trembling, he eased down beside her and wrapped his arms around her, cradling her back against him. Limp and exhausted, she mumbled some protest, he was sure, about sleeping so close to him after her nightmares. *:Sleep well,* na'lanna, *safe in my arms.:*

## 16

Shannari stole another glance at the leather thong hanging so prominently from the thin braid at Rhaekhar's temple. Four more white beads swung at his face while he worked at something near the fire. Her cheeks blazed and she dropped her gaze to her hands clenched in her lap.

If another unknown person hurried by with an armload of tent and supplies and actually smiled at her or wished her a good day, she was going to scream. The attitude in Camp toward her was entirely different today. Even Alea smiled and asked her if she'd slept any at all.

Hardly, Shannari was forced to admit, even to herself. The barbarian had kept her busy most of the night. She was sore enough she rather dreaded climbing on the back of a horse today. But the horses needed fresh grazing, Rhaekhar had told her, and so the Camp must be moved.

"Forgive me, *na'lanna.*"

Involuntarily, she tensed. She heard the laughter in his voice, the smug arrogance of a man who knew he'd done an outstanding job the previous night. Her nose twitched, though, and despite the aching tenderness between her legs, just the sound of his voice and the rich warrior scent rolling off him was enough to make her reconsider how many hours must pass before they retired this evening. Sweet hay, baking bread, flowers, leather, warrior, caffe. Caffe? Was that wretched Blood laughing at her again?

"Perhaps this will help."

She cracked an eye at him and froze at the sight of a steaming cup in his hand.

"I hope I made it correctly."

Snatching the delicate bone china cup from his hand, she cradled it in both palms and simply breathed the rich aroma a moment. "You made this? You found caffe? Here?"

"Brenn's Camp always obtains the best outlander items for trade, even this bitter brew you're so fond of. The trader gave me explicit directions and swore he provided everything you would need, but he did admit that tastes varied."

Touched beyond words, Shannari took a small sip. Heaven. "It's perfect. Not too strong, but not too weak, either. I can't believe you did this. That you found it, here, and made me some." Swallowing another sip, she stared up at Rhaekhar. Her breath hitched. Her eyes burned. "Thank you."

"You're most welcome, na'lanna."

Damnation, the pleased smugness only intensified on his face. It really was a wonderful, thoughtful gift, and she loved it, but she was appalled, too. He'd gone to a great deal of effort to track down this non-Plains item. He obviously cared a great deal about her happiness. *I can't afford to cultivate such tenderness from him.*

He stroked the back of his fingers up and down the curve of her cheek and chin. "I have no ulterior motives in this gift. I hold no strings to entrap you. Simply enjoy it, and think of me."

Oh, that definitely made her feel better. She scowled at him around another sip of caffe. "Speaking of gifts, I assume you'll need to acquire the bow from your loss last night."

"Aye, as soon as we make Camp, I'll visit my friend, Blaine. He always has the best weapons available for trade, both from other Camps and beyond the Plains." He stroked her cheek once more and then grazed his fingers down her shoulder and bare arm. "I'm more pleased than I can say that you continue to wear our clothing. Did Alea provide these for you?"

"She gave me several things yesterday. Can I come with you to see this Blaine?"

"Of course. And then you'll allow me to acquire more clothing for you. I wish to see you dressed in my *kae'valda*."

His voice roughened and he traced the healed mark on her shoulder. Shivering, Shannari fought back the tidal wave of longing that bubbled up inside her. Such a simple touch, but so dangerous.

"I'll also provide your *rahke*."

"I have my sword," she replied, irritated at the huskiness in her voice.

"Everyone on the Plains carries a *rahke*." His eyes blazed with heat, but thankfully he quit touching that sensitive scar so she could think. "I know your skills with a sword, but a *rahke* carries more honor."

"More honor? What do you mean?"

"When I accepted your challenges, I chose to honor your courage and used only my *rahke*. If I cared little for you or your honor, I would have used my sword."

In the battle, the warriors had fought with swords, and her soldiers had been unable to hold the line for more than a few moments before forced to full-scale retreat. Yet when she'd ridden against him, he'd used only his *rahke*.

*Even then, he knew? He cared?* She didn't like the quiver in her stomach.

"I know your honor, *na'lanna*. Perhaps you would allow Gregar to instruct you in our fighting techniques."

She arched a brow at Rhaekhar, suspicious. "Why him?"

He shrugged and smiled. "He's the best."

"You said you've never lost a *kae'rahke* except once to Drendon, yet Gregar's the best? How can that be?"

"I've never challenged Gregar. I've never challenged Varne, either. He's nearly as good, but I think Gregar would best him even without his gift of Shadow." At her frown, he leaned down and kissed her softly. "There are reasons they're Blood, *na'lanna*. They're formidable, deadly weapons, sworn to protect me. Plus, they're my friends. We've never had any reason to challenge one another. From an early age, we knew how we would each be Called to serve Vulkar."

No reason to challenge one another—until she'd come to the Plains. Until she'd tasted Gregar's blood by accident. Until she—

"I shall not give Gregar formal challenge. He and I have already come to an understanding. All that remains are final arrangements."

Sudden panic made her voice climb higher. "What does that mean?"

"When you're ready, we'll explain."

Terror and shame clawed her throat to ribbons. She had done this. The fault was entirely hers. She spread betrayal and death, just as in the Green Lands.

Gripping her shoulders, he gave her a little shake. "Don't worry and don't blame yourself. What is meant to be will be. Vulkar and your Lady have a purpose for you, for me, for Gregar. I shall not challenge him or prevent him from his purpose."

Yes, but Lygon had a purpose too. A purpose to murder her

and to corrupt as many people as possible, spreading Shadow across the world. *What is your most secret heart's desire?*

"To see you alive and well with Khul."

She jerked around to face Gregar, spilling some of the caffe on her hand. He stood close behind her, so close she could feel his body heat, yet the panic she normally felt when someone threatened from her blind spot was absent.

She moved the cup to her other hand and shook off the caffe. Thankfully, it wasn't boiling hot. "That's all?"

"Aye." He winked at her, devilish dark eyes dancing with mischief. He reached out and took her hand in his, lifting it toward his mouth. "For now."

She expected him to check for a burn. Instead, he licked the caffe from her skin. Slowly. Thoroughly. A grip of iron shackled her wrist, even if she could summon enough thought and will to yank her hand away. All she could do was stare at him, stunned, while heat uncurled deep in the pit of her stomach.

He made a pleased, purring sound very much like a smug cat. "Mmmm. Strong. Sweet. Creamy. I like this caffe very much indeed. You should try some, Khul."

Oh, Lady. Horrified embarrassment flooded her cheeks. She tried to tug her hand from the Blood's grasp. Before he released her, though, he bit the heel of her hand. Not hard, but enough to make her wish he had.

She whirled around only to bump her nose into Rhaekhar's chest.

"I must admit that the brew is too bitter for my taste. However, I haven't licked it from this sweet skin before. Perhaps I shall earn a few *kae'als* by licking caffe this night."

"If you need assistance Khul, it's an honor to serve."

After half a day of riding before Rhaekhar on his horse and more hours spent perusing bows and ridiculously short knives—which she ultimately refused—Shannari needed a break. Namely, a physical break. It'd been days since she'd practiced with her sword, since she'd had any sort of physical activity other than bedsport.

*I can't afford to become complacent.*

Rhaekhar disappeared for Camp business and she didn't feel like delivering the bow and dealing with Alea, so Shannari walked away from Camp into the rolling hillside.

She didn't have to go far to find the peace she was looking for. Waving golden grains swept here and there by the breeze truly resembled waves. The sky was endless, a deep, beautiful azure. The wind drove puffy white clouds across the flat bowl of sky. A few hills over, horses grazed. The sun beat down on her head, baking her dark hair and sending sweat trickling down her back and between her breasts. It was a nice heat, though. Not the dry misery of the desert.

The rich smells all around her almost made her hungry. Baking bread, sprinkled with wildflowers, scented lightly with horse and fresh air and sweet hay. Her chest tightened. Unable to stop herself, she closed her eyes a moment and listened for Rhaekhar.

His presence surrounded her, imaginary arms closing around her, his warmth enveloping her. *:My heart. Do you need me?:*

Startled, she opened her eyes, mentally flinching. She hadn't meant to contact him so fully. She hadn't even known it was possible. She felt his arms around her, the heat of his chest against her back, but he wasn't there.

*:Are you well?:*

Swallowing her trepidation, she decided to send him some confirmation to break the connection. Although deep down, she really doubted he would hear her thoughts directly. If she under-stood the *na'lanna* bond correctly, it was strengthened by blood. He'd tasted her blood several times, but was it enough? *:I'm well. Sorry, I didn't mean to distract you.:*

*:I'm pleased you thought of me.:*

Oh, definitely. His arrogant satisfaction was obvious in his mental touch. He was practically purring with pleasure.

*:If you need me, simply call. I shall return to you without delay.:*

He emphasized *need*, all scorching, rumbling desire searing her brain. His imaginary hand slid down her stomach, invisible fingers trying to slip beneath the narrow strip of cloth about her waist.

Her heart raced and her body came alive for him, tingling and tightening with need. *:Enough. I want to drill for a while.:*

Chuckling, he allowed his ghostly arms to disappear. His mental presence evaporated. *:As you wish, my heart.:*

Relieved, she took a deep breath and rolled her shoulders and neck to loosen up. Her mind wouldn't quit thinking about the damned bond, though. With just a random, innocent thought, she'd connected with the barbarian on an intimate level she'd never thought possible. Arms around her when he must be miles away. His words, echoing in her head in his utterly recognizable voice.

The question begged to be answered. Could she do the same with Gregar? Frowning, she tried to dislodge the thought, but she couldn't help but wonder. She supposedly had a blood bond with him. He felt enough of her emotions through Rhaekhar that the Blood might even realize she was thinking about him now. Unless she wanted him to think she was a coward, she had to try her theory.

She brought up the laughing Blood's image in her mind. Long sable hair down to his waist, bottomless dark eyes, his wicked sense of humor.

*:You're no coward, Shannari. I would never think such a thing.:*

She swallowed hard. She was right on both accounts.

*:You can call me if you ever need me. Reach for me, and I shall come.:*

He didn't touch her, not like Rhaekhar had. Perhaps he didn't have enough of a blood bond with her to do it. For whatever reason, she was thankful. It was easier to pull back from Gregar, although she had a lingering sense of his presence.

Now that she was aware of him, of this bond and the relatively small distance between their minds, she felt him. Listening. Hovering. Lightly touching her thoughts. No wonder he overheard everything.

*:I cannot return what you've given me, but I sincerely try not to take advantage. I listen to protect. As Blood, I can do no other.:*

*:Can you touch me like he did?:*

Nothing. Why didn't he respond? She gave a little impatient tug on him, willing him to answer.

*:I cannot hear your thoughts directly, if that is why you are concerned. I have thankfully not tasted your blood, and I must regretfully refuse such an honor even if you offered. But if I'm reading your emotions correctly...:*

Teeth closed on her hand again, exactly as he'd done this morning.

Breathing hard, she pushed him away.

*:Play with your sword, Shannari, and when you're ready to learn real warfare, ask me. I won't even demand anything in return.:*

His wicked laughter echoed in her head, and then he withdrew again.

Arrogant bastards, one and all. Play with her sword indeed. Closing her eyes, she prepared her mind for battle. As always, she pictured the lake in her mind. Its surface was glassy, smooth, silver, glimmering in the light of the full moon above. Peaceful and beautiful as all things of the Lady's, the lake also reminded her of her failure.

She let the crushing wave of guilt, dread, fear, uneasiness, and yes, desire, roll through her, tightening her chest until she couldn't breathe. Then she shoved all that turmoil into those crystal clear waters. Emotion and heartache sank beneath the water without a single ripple. When she opened her eyes, she was completely calm and focused.

Unsheathing the sword, she began a basic drill. She flowed from form to form, the rhythm playing in her mind. Slash, whirl, counter, lunge, choreographed like a waltz. She pushed herself faster, harder, enjoying the sweat and her quickening breathing. The growing tiredness in her muscles had everything to do with exercise and her old world of weapons and protecting herself, and nothing to do with a commanding, arrogant barbarian who looked at her with smoldering eyes while demanding her trust and love.

A shrill iciness suddenly poured over her. Goose bumps raced down her arms despite the sweat and heat of the day. Her stomach cramped.

*:ALARM!:* Gregar bellowed so loudly in her head she winced. *:Beware shadows!:*

She continued the drill in case someone did secretly watch. Searching the tall, swaying grass, she didn't see anything. But the Lady's warning screamed louder through her nerves, shrieking with danger. The Blood's presence in her mind swelled, and she felt him coming as hard as his horse would gallop.

Rhaekhar, too, his fury stealing her breath, his fear twisting her stomach into knots. What were they so afraid of?

A shadow hovered behind her. Icy taint flowed from it, staining the air with foulness. Many assassins had come after her. She'd killed them all. But none had ever felt like this. This stomach-twisting taint felt more like one of her nightmares of Lygon.

The thought made her teeth chatter. Tightening her grip on the sword, she whirled hard and fast, swinging the blade in an arc directly toward the shadow stretching across the grass. She expected to stumble with the force of her blow, for her blade to meet nothing but grass.

The counter of an ivory knife slammed her teeth together and sent her heart hammering against her ribs.

A man—undoubtedly a Sha'Kae al'Dan warrior—nearly as large as Rhaekhar. Shadows clung to him like a cloak. She couldn't see his face at all. He wore a long tunic splotched with gold and brown, remarkably similar to the tall Plains grass.

And his eyes...

Dead. Cold. Gleaming with ice and blackness and malice.

She blocked the *rahke* again, blinking hard to keep her eyes focused on the man and not the shadows obscuring him. After losing the challenge to Rhaekhar, she was very, very worried, despite the obvious advantage she had in her longer sword. This man was just as skilled as Rhaekhar, possibly more. And he wanted to kill her. Badly.

Letting a small smile curve her lips, she went on the offensive. She might be reluctant to kill Rhaekhar, but she had no such hesitation now. Swinging blows at the assassin as quick and hard as possible, she tried to drive him back, to find an opening in his defenses, something she could use to wound him.

The white knife was so fast, though, so deadly. The assassin caught just the tip on her forearm. She leaped back but felt the hot trail of blood on her arm. She couldn't stop to examine it, but she feared it might be serious. It didn't hurt beyond a fiery sting, but blood was definitely pouring from the wound. Already, she felt lightheaded. Her knees quivered. She parried the assassin's blow, forcing the knife away from her heart, but her arm shook.

Two warriors galloped toward her, rumbling with fury, a thunderstorm raging in the deep recesses of her mind. Yet this warrior with eyes of death would drag her into Shadow, and soon. Already, darkness threatened, and it was all she could do to stay on her feet.

*:Where the hell are you?:*

Rhaekhar leaned low over Khan's straining neck and urged him to greater speed. Unmatched in both endurance and speed on the Plains, this day the formidable golden warhorse could not catch Gregar's black *na'kindre*. Shannari weakened enough to call him for help, and desperate fear and rage burned in him.

A Death Rider. Here, in his Camp, committing the unthinkable. A woman was never offered up for sacrifice. Never.

So why had she been marked for termination?

He felt her alarming weakness, flinching the moment the ivory *rahke* bit into her wrist. Her growing fear fed his fury, driving him mad with his need to protect her. He'd given his word she would be safe. On his honor, he'd sworn none would lift a hand against her.

The rest of the Blood rode hard with him. Even Varne was furious, his usually implacable face twisted into a grimace. They'd failed. Khul's blood flowed in her veins, and they'd failed to honor that sacrifice.

Close now, they galloped up the last slope toward her. She was still on her feet. Staggering with blood loss and weariness, she took another strike on her sword and almost fell. The sword dropped from her hand.

Nothing stood between *na'lanna* and certain death.

*Vulkar forgive me, I can't reach her!*

Desperate, he tried to judge the distance between Gregar and the Death Rider. Too far. Not even the Shadowed Blood could cover over twenty paces in a heartbeat.

Gregar hopped up to crouch on the black stallion's back and

launched toward Shannari. Surely an impossible distance, but Rhaekhar strained with him, willing the Blood to fly further. The ivory *rahke* flashed in the sunlight on its downward arc straight toward her heart.

Twisting as he fell, Gregar slipped beneath the *rahke* and wrapped her in his arms. He bore her to the ground beneath him, and her death sentence sank to the hilt in the Blood's right side.

Varne tackled the Death Rider and eliminated him. Leaping off Khan's back, Rhaekhar crouched beside her, quickly scanning her for injuries. The only wound he could see was a deep, vicious slice down her right wrist, but blood poured. Too much blood.

Despite the *rahke* wound in his back, Gregar pushed up to his knees. But Rhaekhar didn't fail to notice how carefully the Blood avoided touching her. Not with the scent of her sweet blood thick in the air.

"Your *memsha*—wrap it around her arm." Gregar's voice was tight, hard, teeth clenched. With pain? Or something worse?

Afraid of the darkness he might see in his friend's eyes, Rhaekhar yanked off his *kae'valda* and wound it tightly around her wrist. Her face was pale and clammy, her eyes wide, her face strained as she struggled for short, shallow breaths.

Varne flashed a silent command at one of the Blood, who raced back to Camp to fetch *Kae'Shaman* to Khul's tent.

"See?" She rasped, laughing mirthlessly. "Everywhere I go."

"Shadow shall not have you this day." Rhaekhar picked her up and ran to Khan's side. At least she hadn't come far from Camp. A few minutes of hard, tense riding, and he swung down at his tent.

Wrapping his gnarled hands around her wounded arm, *Kae'Shaman* didn't wait for Rhaekhar to carry her inside.

She gasped with pain, her eyelids fluttered, and she went limp in his arms.

"Stay with me, Shannari! Don't leave me!"

## 17

F loating. She floated in a gently rocking boat. Darkness all around, but she wasn't afraid. The full moon hung above, glimmering with a peaceful opalescent light.

Voices intruded in the serene beauty of the dream.

"Did we stop the bleeding in time?"

She identified Rhaekhar despite the tight, odd tone in his voice. She'd never heard the invincible warrior sound so shaken.

"Aye, but it was a very near thing. Another cut into her veins or a few more moments, and Vulkar would have Called her home this day."

*Kae'Shaman's* low voice wound around her wrist, soothing away the pain. At one point her arm had been bathed in fire.

"Now, let me see to your wound, Gregar. You've honored Vulkar with enough blood this day. Shannari's out of danger."

Gregar. He had flown out of nowhere, appearing out of the shadows almost like a Death Rider himself. The *rahke...*

*He took the rahke meant for me.*

No one had ever taken a wound to protect her before. No one had ever successfully stood between her body and the assassin. Blinking furiously, she opened her eyes. Rhaekhar leaned over her, his face twisted with worry. She tried to speak, but her tongue felt like a huge wad of cotton.

"Give her a drink of water, Khul, while I see to your Blood."

Rhaekhar tilted a cool flask of water to her lips, and she suddenly realized she was terribly thirsty. Cradling her head, he let her drink her fill, his blazing gold eyes locked on her face. She pulled away a bit and he gently set her head back down. "Is Gregar okay?"

"See for yourself, *na'lanna*."

She turned her head, and Gregar smiled, his dark eyes gleaming with relief and a multitude of emotions she didn't dare identify. He lay on his left side, his head just a foot away from hers. *Kae'Shaman* knelt between them, still chanting softly with his bloody hands against the Blood's side.

"My blood is Khul's, and my blood is yours, Shannari."

Varne stiffened, growling beneath his breath. She studied him a moment, trying to understand why those words would offend him. She listened, too, to Rhaekhar through the bond. All she felt from him was overwhelming gladness that she was alive and a horrible guilt. "It's not your fault. Assassins have hunted me all my life."

"It is my fault," Rhaekhar ground out. "On my honor, I swore none would raise a hand against you. I swore you had no need for weapons in my Camp. Yet without your sword and skill, you would be dead this day. Without Gregar, you would be dead this day. I failed to protect you."

She tried to make light of the injury but he spoke truthfully. Weakness still trembled through her body. "It was only a scratch. I'm fine."

"It was more than a scratch, *na'lanna*. A Death Rider knows exactly where to place a blow that either kills without delay or causes such injury that death soon approaches."

Finished with the Blood's Healing, *Kae'Shaman* added to the explanation. "One of the major veins in your wrist was sliced at least an inch lengthwise, Shannari. If Khul hadn't wrapped his *memsha* around your arm, you would have bled to death before reaching Camp."

"But the veins in the wrist are small. To place a stroke like that in the middle of a fight would be next to impossible."

"Not for a Death Rider," Gregar answered softly.

She turned her attention back to him and shivered at the darkness in the Blood's eyes. So deadly, but not so cold and dead as the other Death Rider's eyes. Flames flickered in Gregar's eyes. Flames that might burn them both.

"As the Great Wind Stallion's Right Hand, his mother's milk is blood and he rides Death like *na'kindre*. Cloaked in Shadow, he lies in wait for his sacrifice, and he does not fail. To face one and still breathe is a gift from Vulkar. I should have..."

His voice shook and he closed his eyes a moment, fighting some inner battle. Opening his eyes, he turned his gaze up to Rhaekhar, composed but resigned. "Her blood Calls. She smells like a mark, Khul, when no sacrifice has been offered. I believed the temptation and shame were mine to bear alone, but I should have known it would affect the others, too. My blood is yours, Khul, but it will be my greatest honor to protect her with my life. Perhaps my blood will erase this dishonor."

Rhaekhar's hands settled on her, hard and desperate as he pulled her into his lap and sheltered her with his body. She was too weak to demand he put her down. "Every Death Rider on the Plains will attempt her as a mark?"

His voice shook with fury and fear, both, and the bond

between them vibrated with tension. She tried to follow their conversation, but she wasn't sure what all the talk of mark and sacrifice meant. It sounded like she had a giant target painted on her back once again, which didn't surprise her in the least.

"I don't know how strong the compulsion will be for the others. The mark of death on her isn't from Vulkar. I don't feel it the same way as a normal mark. I smell it. I sense it in the darkness, something just over the next hill, or the next, that begs me to investigate. They'll come, drawn by her scent and the strangeness of the Call. Vulkar forbid—" Gregar shuddered, averting his gaze from them both. "—they catch a scent of her blood."

"Great Vulkar." Rhaekhar breathed shallowly, shaking, nearly squeezing her to death. Why wait for the assassins to come again? "What can I do? How many Death Riders roam the Plains?"

"At least a fist. Not all of them will be as susceptible to her Call. That which makes us silent in death, the Shadow we use to hide, is what makes us vulnerable to the Endless Night's taint. Those that walk more often in Shadow will be the ones who come. The ones who've killed the most, even for Vulkar."

"The most skilled," Varne said flatly. "The most honored."

"Aye."

Shannari again had the feeling that some nasty barb was hidden in that exchange between Blood. If these Death Riders walked in Shadow, how could they make sacrifices to Vulkar? It didn't make sense to her at all.

"She needs a Blood with her at all times." Rhaekhar's voice and body language vibrated with command. "She carries my blood in her veins."

Varne turned away and paced back and forth. The silence inside the tent became oppressive, and Rhaekhar radiated disappointment and disapproval. Even the holy man frowned at Varne.

"She's not Khul'lanna."

"I shall protect her as my own," Gregar whispered. "I shall be her Blood."

Her heart raced, worry stealing her breath. Oh, Lady, would Rhaekhar take the Blood's offer as a threat? Would they fight now, as she'd feared all along?

But Rhaekhar relaxed immediately, his arms easing their grip on her to merely hold her against him. "Aye, thank you, Gregar. It will be a fearsome attack indeed that overwhelms the Shadowed Blood protecting his own."

Varne stalked outside without a word. Rhaekhar pressed a kiss against her head and then gently lay her back down beside Gregar. "I expect you to never let her out of your sight."

The Blood stared at her, his dark eyes bottomless and full of emotion. Longing, shame, hunger. She shuddered, desperate enough she contemplated begging Rhaekhar to change his mind. "Aye."

Cold chills and fire, both, raced down her spine. This Blood, never letting her out of his sight?

Rhaekhar stared at the tent flap, his brow creased. Through the bond, she felt his sadness and worry for his one-time best friend. Another casualty to the Shadow she carried. "I had to give him the chance to correct his mistake."

"I know, Khul, yet he is blind to everything but his own fears. He most hates that which he fears in his own heart." Gregar laughed, but his eyes, too, were sad.

*:I'm not the only shadowed Blood.:*

She gasped, her mind racing. What did he mean? She didn't feel anything for Varne, not like the dark-haired Blood lying beside her.

Gregar's eyes flashed, his mood lightening. "He won't change even when she becomes Khul'lanna."

"When?" She tried for an offended, sarcastic tone, but the weakness and breathlessness in her voice betrayed her.

"Aye, when." He laughed, the familiar smirk twisting his lips. "I've seen it."

"Vulkar let it be soon," Rhaekhar said fervently. "I shall return shortly. *Kae'Shaman*, can you stay?"

"Aye, Khul. She's out of danger, but I shall stay until you return."

"Rest, *na'lanna*." Rhaekhar ducked beneath the tent flap, leaving her with the Blood and the holy man.

The latter she wasn't worried about at all. He checked her arm, humming softly, and then moved away to sit quietly against the tent wall.

The former... terrified her on levels she hadn't known existed until now.

Gregar edged nearer, his breath fanning her face. "I shall sheathe a *rahke* in my body daily if this is my reward."

Staring into those gleaming obsidian eyes, she felt trapped, exposed, and weak. Oh so weak. "You took a wound for me."

"Aye, I'm Blood. That's what we do. If I can't stop the weapon, I take it into my body instead of allowing it to touch you."

"You could have died."

Gregar shrugged. "Not this day. I've seen the day I shall die, and it won't happen until you carry my ivory *rahke*. As long as you live on that day, I won't mind dying."

Her heart ached, her throat tightening. "I'll Heal you again, remember?"

"When Vulkar Calls me home to His Clouds, not even your Lady's Healing will save me. Not even the temptation of your blood will be able to hold me, no matter how much I long to stay."

A shadowed dream tickled the back of her mind, the nagging sense of familiarity and recognition. "I know you from a dream."

"Aye," he whispered, shuddering. He moved closer, filling her nose with the dark, rich scent of caffe and warrior. "A nightmare."

"Shadows all around, so cold, waiting. I know you're there, but I can't see you. Just like today. I couldn't see the assassin, but I knew he was there."

"Wrapped in Shadow, the Death Rider lies in wait for his mark."

"Was I your mark?"

"You still are." A deadly edge crept into his voice, a cold blade of death and darkness. He sighed, a long, aching breath of air against her cheek that squeezed her heart. "You're my greatest mark, and my greatest shame."

Had they somehow shared those dark, bloody dreams? Did he know how some of the dreams evolved? From dying at the hands of an assassin to lying in his bloody embrace. Lust and pain and blood and—

"My greatest love."

She shook her head frantically, her heart thundering.

"*Na'lanna.*" He laid his cheek softly against hers, whispering their doom and nightmares into her ear. "You can't deny me, just as you can't deny Khul. I would love you, too, but I would kill you in the end. I lived your death a thousand times at my own hands before I ever knew your name."

Panting, short gasps for air. She couldn't seem to catch her breath. "I killed you in some of those dreams."

"Aye, and you loved me, too."

"Never."

His low, ragged chuckle made her shiver. Lips brushed her ear, his hair trailing her face. "Deny me, deny Khul, and the Endless Night shall win this *kae'don.*"

"Love you, love Khul, and I will still lose this *kae'don*," she retorted, turning her face into his. Their noses bumped and he sighed again, as if he relished even such an accidental touch. "You of all people should know that love murders."

"Ah, but do you want to live in Shadow, your heart forever untouched and frozen? Or die with a smile on your face and our love warming your heart?"

"I have no heart."

"So if I kissed you now, you would feel nothing in that scarred, shriveled muscle beating so loudly and so rapidly it sounds like stampeding *na'kindren?*"

Her heart did indeed pound, blood rushing through her veins, chest heaving. She turned away and stared up at the tent ceiling. "Nothing at all. Besides, I have more honor than to dally with Khul's Blood in his own tent when he proclaims a love like no other."

"What do you care if he loves you?" Gregar's voice sharpened, a shockingly cold intensity rolling from him that sent goose bumps racing down her arms. "What do you care if I love you just as much? What do you care of our honor? If he didn't want me here with you, he would challenge me. He certainly wouldn't give me the great honor of protecting you. If he didn't approve, only one of us would pursue your heart. The other would die. He already honors me more than you do with these spiteful insults."

"Spiteful!" She spluttered, trying to come up with a logical argument. "If I wanted to insult you, I would call you a loud-mouthed vulgar bastard."

Gregar laughed. "Those are not insults. Vulgar I am, proudly, but if Khul rejected my intentions, I would cease without delay."

"*I* reject you." She was pleased at the harsh, adamant tone of voice she managed to muster. "*I* wish you'd cease without delay."

"Very well," he breathed into her ear. "I shall not kiss you until you beg me."

She raised her arms to push him away, but the injury pained her, drawing a quick gasp from her throat.

Groaning, Gregar rubbed his cheek against hers and took her hand in his. "You're killing me, woman."

His thumb swirled against her palm, and her voice trembled. "How?"

He drew her bandaged wrist up to his face. "I love soft, fragile little sounds of pain." Breathing deeply and noisily up and down the bandage, he shuddered. "Blood. Your blood... Make that sound again."

He pressed his thumb firmly against the newly-healed wound, his eyes swallowed by shadows. She let a small moan escape again, for it truly did hurt. Watching the flames rise in his eyes, though, was worth it. The small pain and his immediate enjoyment of it fed something in her she didn't know existed. At least outside of the dark, bloody dreams of a shadowed man trying to kill her.

Gripping her wrist in his jaws, he pressed his teeth up and down the bandaged cut, not biting, exactly, but threatening. A rumbling growl of hunger resonated from his chest. The sound of a predator on the hunt.

Every bleating, breathless cry of pain she made only fed his hunger. She didn't think he'd actually hurt her, but the threat was there and real enough that fear rose inside her. The more afraid she became, the harder his teeth dug into the bandage. The thought of his teeth digging into her arm...

"I won't be pleased if you tear open my careful handiwork," *Kae'Shaman* said mildly, reminding them both of his presence.

With her wrist in his mouth, Gregar snarled at the holy man.

"Tell him to release you, Shannari, and he shall without delay."

Gregar rose up to a crouch, muscles bunching along his shoulders, still gripping her wrist in his mouth. She curled her fingers against his cheek, and he jerked his gaze away from the holy man to focus on her. His eyes flashed like faceted obsidian, so dark, yet flickering with flames. Death waited in his gaze, but so did fire. And more, so much more.

Rhaekhar suddenly filled her mind, his iron-clad touch honed to a cutting edge. :*Do you need assistance with him?*:

He wasn't jealous, exactly, but he knew everything. Through him, she became aware of the heat flaring between her thighs, the need spreading through her like wildfire along with her fear. Embarrassed, she gave a tug on her arm. "Let go, Gregar."

He did so immediately and even backed away to give her breathing room. Crouched in the shadows, though, he gazed at her, his eyes gleaming in the darkness of the tent. His teeth flashed in a very wide, cocky smile.

:*Why did you let him do that?*: She tried to be angry at Rhaekhar, at them both, but failed. Tears threatened, and betrayal burned cold like an icicle through her heart. :*Why did you leave me with him?*:

:*You need to know the truth.*: Rhaekhar hugged her hard through the bond. :*We almost lost you this day. No one will get through Gregar to harm you. No one, except possibly himself.*:

"Tell Khul that next time he should stay." Gregar's voice was rougher than usual, but she could still see the white of his teeth in the tent. The wretched Blood was thoroughly pleased with himself. "That was merely fun and games, Shannari. If you ever want to get serious, I insist that Khul remain to ensure your safety."

Shame flooded her and she rolled away from him, cradling her wounded arm to her chest. If she could love Rhaekhar enough, like a normal woman would love such a tremendous warrior, then Gregar wouldn't have a prayer. He wouldn't be here tormenting her now. "There won't be a next time."

*:When you're ready to face the truth, invite him to share our blankets,* na'lanna. *I won't refuse him.:*

*:I'll refuse you both.:*

Instead of being offended, Rhaëkhar chuckled in her mind. Phantom fingers trailed over her shoulder, and the bite mark he gave her nights ago throbbed to life. *:You are welcome to try.:*

W iping his palm on his breeches, Theo crouched in the shadows. Despite the cold stone against his back, sweat dripped into his eyes, drawing a muttered obscenity. *Damn that old man! What's taking him so long?*

He gripped a dagger so tightly his fingers hurt. His stomach rolled and pitched, and he frantically gulped for air, swallowing back the bile. He wouldn't fail. He couldn't. Not when the High Throne of the Green Lands was at stake.

At last, the stone panel embedded in the thick castle wall inched open with a groan. Wheezing, Rikard shuffled inside with a lit candle in his hand. "Damn Valche and his scheming. And damn all barbarians! Ah, well, what's done is done. Too many times over to count. Guard, bring my prisoner inside for questioning."

Suppressing a hysterical giggle, Theo pushed up to his feet but pressed his back tighter into the corner. A Lion Guard dragged in a bound and blindfolded peasant and tossed him on the ground before a rough stone altar in the center of the cell.

The doddering old man gave a small coin purse to the Guard, who bowed and left with secrecy insured. Of course, Theo had already given him twice that to allow him inside this foul chamber.

His own little secret room was much more to his liking.

Rikard bent down and set the candle on the stone floor beside the prisoner. Standing, he groaned.

Theo heard the creak of ancient joints from his hiding place and again nearly gave away his position with a nasty laugh. Easing away from the wall, he carefully crept behind his grandfather. The knife shook in his hand, but his fear was gone. Anticipation surged in him and his heart raced. *This is so much better than shoving someone down the stairs.*

"The day I'm too old to offer sacrifice is the day I die to eternal torment."

Laughing out loud, Theo said, "Today's the day."

Rikard whirled around. "You sniveling, pitiful, disgusting bastard!"

A hard shove was enough to knock the frail old man back onto his altar. His fingers curled like claws, Rikard tried to drive Theo back, but he was weak. So weak.

"I should have done this a long time ago."

The black stone tore open a gash on Rikard's forehead. Shadows thickened in the room and the rough stone soaked up the offering hungrily. A thick shadow slithered around his grandfather's neck.

"It's time for a new High King to rule the Green Lands."

His hand shook, so the gaping wound he made in the old man's neck was jagged and ugly. In his excitement, the knife bit so deeply that steel crunched on the stone altar, notching the blade. A fitting reminder for his first formal sacrifice.

"Please accept this sacrifice, Great Lord of the Dark. May You rule above and below. May You bring Your Endless Night to our world forever!"

Rikard opened his mouth and croaked. Smiling wickedly, Theo leaned down, cocking his head to the side. "What is that, Grandfather?"

"Die."

"You first."

## 19

"Varne." Rhaekhar struggled to keep his voice calm and controlled. Not an easy feat when his woman burned for another warrior and then swore to refuse them both. His face felt stiff and unnatural, carved from stone. The same stone from which Shannari's heart must be carved. "I would speak with you."

"And I you, Khul." Varne stalked out of the shadows, his face a grim mask. "You made a grave error."

"How so?"

"You cannot allow Gregar such freedom with your woman. Why don't you challenge him and be done?"

"Indeed, Shannari's *my* woman. I'll do whatever necessary to see to her safety and happiness."

"Safety?" Varne laughed, shaking his head, his lip curled in an ugly sneer. "You do recall that Gregar was *Kae'Had-Mangus* before he became Blood? The most honored Death Rider. None has ever worn as many red *kae'als* as he."

"I don't doubt Gregar's honor nor his love for Shannari."

Despite his frustration and the instinctive urge demanding he drive all other stallions away from his mare, Rhaekhar could admit that Gregar truly loved her. He loved her enough to die for her. What more could Khul ask of his Blood?

"Then you're a fool."

Rhaekhar stepped closer, gripping his *rahke* but not unsheathing it. "You're the fool, Varne. I'll do anything I must to keep *na'lanna* safe. No one will get through my Shadowed Blood to harm her. No one. It just so happens that she wants him, too, though she'll swear otherwise until she's blue in the face. A blood bond with him keeps her safer. The stronger the bond, the stronger his protection."

"How can you share *na'lanna* with anyone, let alone him?"

"Gregar would sacrifice his life to keep her safe. I can't say the same of you. You accepted the honor of my blood sacrifice. You swore to protect me with the last drop of your blood. Yet you won't protect her after she's honored me so many times by tasting my blood."

Varne turned away, his jaw clenched so tightly a muscle ticked in his cheek. "You hunger for her blood."

"Aye." Rhaekhar closed his eyes a moment, relishing the sweet heady intoxication, the bond pulsing between them, drawing her nigh to his heart. "And she hungers for mine, and Gregar's. I'll use her need to bind her tighter to us."

"What if..." Varne hesitated, refusing to look at him.

Did the nearest Blood shared the same need, and it shamed him? Shannari had no interest in him at all, so Rhaekhar didn't think it likely.

"What if she wants other warriors' blood? What if she draws them to her, the same as these Death Riders are supposedly drawn to her? What will you do then?"

Jealousy surged through him at the thought of any other warrior making his intentions known. He couldn't imagine approving others. Gregar's sacrifice and honor were unquestioned, but any other? Rhaekhar gripped the *rahke* so hard his fingers hurt, each groove and carving in the hilt digging into his palm. *I'll do what I must, but I wouldn't like it.* "If she wants another blood bond, she'll have it. If she wants another warrior, and I can approve of his honor, then she'll have him too. Another warrior is another *rahke* to protect her."

"I see a hard future for you, Khul." Varne shook his head sadly. "She swears she doesn't love you."

"She does," Rhaekhar retorted. "She simply doesn't know it yet."

"As she loves Gregar, right? Indeed, she likely loves me too."

Rhaekhar laughed out loud. Despite his worry she would continue to refuse him, she possessed no affection whatsoever for his nearest Blood. "You have no worries in that regard, Varne. Friends we've been our entire lives. You've protected me with your own blood for years. Yet I tell you this once and never again. I'm Khul of the Nine Camps of the Sha'Kae al'Dan and Shannari is *na'lanna*. You will protect her with your life, as you do me, or I shall find another Blood to replace you. If you ever fail in your duties as my Blood again, I shall give you formal challenge in addition to dismissing you."

"Not even Gregar expected Death Riders to come after her! How can you blame me for failing to protect her?"

"I don't speak of the attack. I speak of your refusal to protect her as Blood. Either you're Blood and you protect all of me— most especially my heart—or you're no longer Blood."

Varne glared at him, jaw working fiercely. Finally, he gritted out, "Aye."

"Gregar shall be nearest to her, but if he falls or—" Even now, the thought of her kissing the Blood, loving him, tasting his blood... His throat convulsed, his heart shredded by his friend's ivory *rahke*. "If he's otherwise occupied, I need to know that you'll protect us both."

"He gives new meaning to nearest Blood," Varne muttered with a scowl. "Aye, you're Khul. She carries your blood in her veins. It's an honor to serve you, Khul, however you wish. I shall do as you say."

Nearest Blood indeed. When Rhaekhar had named his Blood, he'd never expected he would share his blankets with any of them.

He ducked back inside the tent, relieved to see that Gregar had retreated to his normal guarding spot at the wall. Shannari lay curled on her side, sleeping.

Varne took his position inside the tent as well. Sighing, Rhaekhar decided he couldn't order them outside, not after just lecturing his nearest Blood. After such an attack, they naturally wanted to protect inside once more, despite the arrangements Gregar had worked out.

Shannari wouldn't be pleased when she realized the Blood guarded inside. Perhaps Varne's shorter thong would have been sufficient after all.

W aking quickly, Rhaekhar cupped her face and returned her kiss. He sensed the fragility in her, the weakness, the reluctant need. Not for his body, exactly, but for his love. The very thing she hated and feared. If only he could force her to say the words...

"I'm sorry," she whispered against his lips, her fingers tangling in his hair.

"Why?"

"For wakening you."

"What better way can a warrior be awakened than by his woman's kiss?" She didn't realize the Blood were inside the tent.

For once, he was grateful she refused to listen to the blood bonds tying her to both him and Gregar. She would have known immediately that the Blood were close.

To better keep her from discovering the Blood's presence, Rhaekhar gently switched their positions. Leaning down he kissed her with all the tenderness and love in his heart. "I almost lost you this day."

Shivering, she tightened her grip on his hair and pressed her face against his chest. "Don't remind me."

He held her, gently smoothing his hands up and down her back.

"You smell so good." Her scent heated, desire rising in her, but she was content to lie in his arms. "Sweet hay and flowers, baking bread." Sighing, she dropped her voice so low he could barely hear her. "You make me hungry."

"You make me hungry too, my heart. I could breathe in your scent of roses for the rest of my life."

Rubbing her nose back and forth against his chest, she refused to answer. Permanency with him was impossible in her mind.

"Think about it, na'lanna. My arms around you forever. My scent in your nose every single night. My body at your disposal. My every thought directed at your pleasure, your safety, your happiness. My love warming your heart for the rest of your life."

"Impossible," she breathed against his skin. Yet their bond surged with hope and longing.

He moved on top of her, joining his body to hers gently. No thrusting, just body to body, heart to heart contact. "Nay, not impossible. This is all yours if you want it. If you want me."

"I do want you, but..." She trembled beneath him, her hands sliding through his hair, across his shoulders, his back. She found her mark in his neck. The brush of her fingers sent flames shooting through him. Still, he refused to move.

"If you want me, you can keep me. Forever."

Fear washed through her, from so many causes he couldn't sort through them all. Guilt and shame, terror, anger, and bitter longing. She laughed harshly, tears thickening her voice. "Forever doesn't exist."

"I swear to you now that I'm yours forever. Where ever you are, there I shall be."

"Don't make promises you can't keep, Khul." She tugged on his hair, forcing him to raise his head to look into her eyes. What he saw in her stark, forlorn gaze made his heart clutch in agony. "I belong in the Green Lands. I must wear the Rose Crown and rule from Shanhasson or Lygon will break free of His prison. I'm the Last. Don't you know what that means? If I die, if I fail, our world will end. A new age of Shadow will begin. I can only fight out my destiny one day at a time."

"Alone? Why fight alone, Shannari, when you could have me by your side?"

"You'll never leave your Plains, your Camps, to come with me, and I can't stay here. Don't ask me to give up my destiny, my duty, my honor."

"I never asked you to give up anything but this *kae'don* to shield your heart from me." He brushed his lips against hers; giving her a slow, tender thrust that immediately tightened her body around him. "I shall never ask you to give up your destiny. I merely ask that you allow me to share it. To share your life. To protect and love you to the best of my ability."

Pain and anger tinted her scent like blood spreading through a pool of crystal water. "I don't want to want things I can't have!"

"You *can* have me. Love me, Shannari, and we'll find a way."

"A way will be provided," she whispered, her voice breaking.

"Aye. Give me a chance to show you the way."

She said nothing, but she pressed her face deeper into his chest, holding him tightly.

He continued the slow, exquisite stroking, keeping as much of their bodies touching as possible without crushing her beneath him while he flooded their bond with all the love and tenderness in his heart. He didn't try to delay their completion, nor drive her to multiple releases. He didn't command her body's response and restrain his own.

Quivering, she found release with him, softly, silently, but her tears wet his skin. He rolled over and drew her up onto his chest, smoothing his hands up and down her back.

"Maybe you'll give me a child to take home with me."

Fury roared through him, hot and fast, leaving him shaking in its wake. Great Vulkar, she had no idea how she insulted him. That a warrior would give his child to a woman and allow her to leave his protection...

She didn't insult his honor deliberately. When she pushed up on her elbow to search his face, honesty gleaming in her eyes. He read the fragile hope in her heart. She admitted this small hope, a desire to take a piece of him away with her forever.

When such a thing would tear every last *kae'al* from his hair and destroy him. "There will be no child unless we're mated."

"As many times as we've been together, I could be pregnant now."

His jaw clenched so hard his teeth ached. "Nay."

Her gaze narrowed, and he felt her hesitant touch through the bond. "I didn't mean any dishonor."

"I know." Fighting down the rage, he tried to explain. "On the Plains, a warrior would never give his child to a woman unless she carried his honor. Unless she possessed his love, his heart, his protection."

"How can you prevent conception?"

"I drink *drakkar* daily. I swear to you, Shannari, I won't give you my child until the day you allow me to claim you."

Disappointment flickered across her face. To hide it, she lay back down upon his chest, but her sadness ached through the bond. "I wouldn't mind having your child."

"Then stay with me. Allow me to claim you. Become my Khul'lanna. Sleep on my heart like this every single night, safe and loved in my arms with our child nestled against your breast."

Silence was his answer. But she fell asleep in his arms with that exact image held in her mind.

S hannari sat up, clutching a blanket to her chest. The barbarian stood beside her, wrapping his *memsha* about his hips. Through the small window in the roof of the tent, she saw it was barely dawn. "Where are you going so early?"

"I'm participating in a *kae'don* this day."

"Battle? Why?" Suddenly she noticed that two Blood sat inside the tent against the walls. They looked very comfortable. As if they— "Why are they in here?"

"After the attack, they will guard us both more closely. Be pleased that only two wished to sleep inside with us."

Her stomach fluttered queasily. "They were in here last night? All night?"

"Aye." He shrugged. "Don't worry about the *kae'don, na'lanna.* Lyell's warriors can't possibly best mine. How did Gregar say it? This is all fun and games."

Heat flooded her, drowning her in shame and fury. "You tricked me. Last night. We— While they—"

"I have time to make your caffe. Perhaps then you'll be able to finish a complete thought."

She spluttered with shame and fury. "How dare you!"

Gregar laughed as though Rhaekhar had made a great joke, and even Varne's lips twitched toward a smile.

Softening the sting to her pride, Rhaekhar leaned down and kissed her. "You take my breath away when you're angry."

"But— I can't—"

He slapped Gregar on the back and ducked outside with Varne at his heels.

"Bloody hell."

"Sounds good."

She shot a dark look at Gregar and wrapped the blanket tighter about herself. If she'd had any inkling that the Blood protected inside the tent last night, then she never would have kissed the barbarian. Let alone... While the laughing, lecherous Blood watched. "Did you enjoy the show?"

"Aye, very much indeed. You're definitely not your normal cheery self in the mornings without your caffe."

"That's not what I meant."

The grin wiped off his face immediately. "I'm Blood first, Shannari. I've guarded Khul inside his tent for five years with never another thought to what activities he might pursue in his blankets. A Blood doesn't need to eat or sleep, let alone ease physical need with a woman. A Blood's only need is Khul's protection. Unless you invite me to join you with him, I shall remain Blood."

"You can watch and not... feel?"

"Aye. Listen to my bond this night and see for yourself. Unless you deliberately invite me to participate, I shall remain Blood, as unexcited as Varne." His eyebrow rose with obvious expectation, but if he made a joke, she didn't understand it.

She looked about the tent for some privacy. No way in hell she was getting dressed with him ogling her, no matter what he said about being Blood.

"There's a steamtent in the back. Shall I heat it for you?"

"Thank you."

With a cocky grin, the Blood headed for the smaller flap in the rear of the tent. "It's an honor to serve."

She dug through the chest of Sha'Kae al'Dan clothing Rhaekhar had selected for her, trying to find something not so abominably short. None of the pieces even came close to hitting her knees. Nearly all of them were brilliant emerald green, too. She didn't mind green, but she didn't know that she'd wear the color every single day. A few outfits were all gold but ridiculously short. The only other color he'd selected was a deep purple-blue very close to the color of her eyes, and only if the material still bore his green. The two colors were unusual together to say the least.

Heat suddenly wrapped against her back. She froze, waiting for the usual terror to flood her, the urge to reach for the sword that wasn't there. But she felt only the silken muscle of warrior against her.

"My *kae'valda*." Gregar's voice was oddly hushed, and he trembled against her. "He would let you wear my *kae'valda*."

"The color? I thought *kae'valda* was the beads in his hair."

He lowered his chin against her shoulder and hugged her. "Aye, but the color comes first."

Bewildered, she didn't try to break out of his hold. Not yet. "You wear red now."

"When I became Blood I gave up my past *kae'valda*, but he remembered. He honors me more than I dared hope. Wear this on the day you want to invite me to join you and Khul in his blankets."

She whirled away from him and he let her go. Unfortunately, the blanket slipped down her shoulders before she wrestled it tighter.

Gregar gazed at her neck, her right shoulder, his fingers stroking the hilt of his *rahke*. She couldn't figure out what he stared at, until Rhaekhar's bite mark twinged. Shrugging the burning throb away, she jerked the blanket tight and marched for the steamtent in the back.

"Later this day, I wish to offer—"

"I don't want anything from you."

He ruined her flamboyant exit by blocking the flap with his arm. When she gave him a pointed stare, he winked but dropped his arm and allowed her to pass. Trailing his fingers down her back as she marched by, he whispered, "Not even blood?"

Shuddering, she paused a moment. Despite her best efforts, she began to turn her head toward him before regaining control. "Not a chance."

"Ah, you challenge me, woman. I accept."

Escape into the steamtent couldn't stop the sound of his low chuckle. Damned dark-haired lecherous Blood. And damn her treacherous body that anticipated the battle.

## 20

W hen she stepped out of Khul's tent, she found only Gregar waiting for her. "Where is he?"

"Khul was forced to leave so he could prepare for the *kae'don*." Gregar offered her the steaming cup in his hand. "He did have time to prepare this, though. Once you deliver the bow to Alea and visit Market Day, he invites you to come watch his fun and games with Lyell."

Grateful despite Rhaekhar's abandonment with the Blood, she took the cup and sat down in the main tent's shade. "What's Market Day?"

"Three Camps have gathered this day for the *kae'don*. Naturally they wish to trade. Khul instructs you to take whatever you wish from the traders."

Shannari frowned. She hadn't brought much gold at all, and she preferred to keep her private funds in case she needed it for emergency flight. "How are they paid?"

"Gold is a Green Land vice. In our Market Days, goods are

exchanged and a tally is reckoned at the end of the day to equal the Camps based on standing."

"Based on standing? What does that mean?"

"Everything is a competition." Of course, he winked and leered at her, making her wonder what sort of competition he might arrange with Rhaekhar if she ever lost her mind and invited him. "The Nine Camps constantly jostle for standing. Khul's Camp is First, Drendon's is Second, so they get both the best trade items and the best exchange rates. The other Camps expect Khul's Camp to take whatever it needs. They expect you as Khul's woman to take whatever you desire. If not, they'll lose face."

"Are you trying to tell me that if I don't take things, people will be insulted?"

"Aye. If Khul's woman is unsatisfied with their trade goods, then the Market Day will be a failure."

"But I don't want to incur a debt to these other Camps, not until I understand how the prices are determined."

"No debt will be incurred. You must take items as your right. As Khul's right. He's First. He takes First selection. As Khul'lanna, full management of his Camp's trades will be your responsibility. It's best to gain the experience now."

"I'm not his wife, his mate, and I'll never be. I must return to the Green Lands."

Gregar shrugged. "So you say, but here you are."

Fury blazed through her body, leaving her trembling. Not at the Blood, exactly, although she chose to vent her anger on him. At herself, for wishing she could live the impossible. "You're a fool if you think I'll doom the Green Lands to darkness and death for a few romps in Khul's blankets."

His dark eyes gleamed. Shadows gathered around his face, draping along his shoulders. "Ah, but what if those romps can save you, Shannari?"

Hair prickled on the back of her neck. "What do you mean?"

"Love is the greatest gift of all."

Her chest hurt, and she absently rubbed the old scar. "Hard to believe when someone I make love with tries to murder me in my own bed." Horrified she'd let that terrible secret out, she clamped her mouth shut and lurched to her feet, intent on leaving the tent—and the Blood—far behind.

Before she could escape, Gregar's arms closed around her, drawing her back against his chest. "Those were dreams only. On my honor—Khul's own blood—you're safe from me now."

Tears burned her eyes. "I didn't speak of you."

His arms tightened and deadly cold trickled down her arms until she shivered against him. "Tell me."

"Devin made love to me, watched me fall asleep in his arms, and then he put a knife in my heart." Rage washed over her, betrayal, agony. She hated admitting any weakness. "Father Aran rode half the night after a premonition he received from the Lady, and he arrived just in time to Heal me. Otherwise, I would have died years ago in the name of love. Instead—"

She swallowed, forcing the last words out. "With the last of my strength, I killed Devin. I slit his throat, the man I loved. Bleeding to death, we lay in the bed that we'd just—"

"While I live, no one will touch you with steel or blade again. As long as you let me stay close, at your back, like this."

"I can't love again."

"You already do."

Gregar spoke so matter-of-factly, so calmly, while she wanted to hack and slash all about her with a sword. "I know my destiny, Gregar. I must return to the Green Lands."

"Eventually." He rubbed his cheek against hers and then released her. "I know my destiny, too, and Khul's. Your priest isn't the only one who has premonitions. I've seen the day of my death. I've seen the years of happiness it will buy you with Khul. And it's worth the sacrifice."

"I don't—"

"Sacrifice," he whispered, giving her a little shake. "You've never loved someone who was willing to sacrifice for your love. That's the difference. That's the gift. Take what Khul offers with open heart, Shannari. He'd cut off his right hand before harming you."

Blinking back tears, she turned away and noticed two boys standing a few feet away. They whispered among themselves, casting surreptitious glances her way. Closer to young men rather than boys, she decided, and built like warriors.

Gregar stepped around her, bumping her back away from them. Deadly cold radiated from him. "Why are you here?"

The tallest lad's mouth tightened, and his friend tossed his head, shaking long dark auburn hair about his shoulders. "We would like to meet our future Khul'lanna."

"Why?"

Surprised at the Blood's rudeness, Shannari took a step toward the boys. They surely weren't threats to her safety. They didn't even carry swords.

Gregar moved with her, bumping her, using his body to keep her back. Smiling at the boys, she drilled her thumb between his shoulder blades as hard as she could. "I'm Shannari."

She held her hand out to them and Gregar growled.

"What's wrong with you? You're starting to sound like Varne."

With a dark scowl, Gregar let her step forward.

"I'm Dharman of Khul's Camp." Hesitantly, the tall lad took her hand. "It's my great honor to meet you, Shannari."

"Honor," Gregar muttered. "You lads know nothing of honor."

"Not yet," the red-haired lad said cheerfully. "But we will. I'm

Sal. Drendon is my khul, and it's my great honor to meet you, Shannari." He gave a pointed stare at his friend, arching a brow at him until Dharman released her. Sal smiled as he took her hand, revealing an adorable dimple in his cheek.

"Why aren't you drilling?" Gregar said stiffly. "You two need all the practice you can get."

Dharman elbowed his friend who only clutched her hand harder. "Everyone's at the *kae'don*. We thought we might escort Shannari to—"

"I'm her escort. I'm her Blood."

"You're gravely mistaken." For his youthful awkwardness, Dharman stared at Gregar with a hard glint in her eye that surprised her. "You're Khul's Blood and always will be."

Shannari shivered. The sun slipped behind a bank of clouds and shadows crept across the ground toward the boys. Shadows from Gregar.

"Stop it." She had no idea why he so adamantly opposed the young men's presence. Varne insulted her, obviously hated her, yet Gregar laughed in his face. These two young men simply wanted to meet her. "Did you say drill? Perhaps I can come practice with you another day."

The boys grinned enthusiastically and agreed to fetch her at her earliest convenience. While Gregar muttered and glared at them with Death darkening his eyes. They left, already planning her day with them. Tossing his gorgeous hair over his shoulder, Sal gave her a flirtatious grin that showed the dimple in his cheek again.

Oh, dear, that young man was trouble.

Gregar sighed bitterly. Rubbing her arms to chase away the goose bumps, she frowned at him. "What on earth is wrong with you?"

He rolled the ivory knife back and forth across his palm. When had he unsheathed it? "I'm not yet dead."

"No one said you were." Reluctantly, she listened harder to his bond, trying to understand why he was so angry, so bitter, so... hurt. "They're just boys. I didn't mean—"

"Lads, aye. They don't even wear *kae'valda* yet." He raised his gaze to hers, his dark eyes flashing. "Remember *my* honor. Remember me. Don't rush me to my death."

Her throat clogged, painfully tight and raspy. She refused to consider the cause. "Why are you talking about your death?"

"Their arrival tells me..." He closed his eyes and swallowed hard. His hands shook and the razor-sharp knife nicked the fleshy heel of his left hand. "The day of my death comes too quickly."

Tears burned her eyes. She didn't understand why he thought two boys would hasten his death. As on the ride to the Plains, she wanted to throw her arms around him and sob, begging him. *Never leave. Never, ever die. Stay with us forever.*

Soberly, he traced the curve of her cheek with his thumb. "On my honor, I shall be with you forever. Not even death will keep me from you."

Her heart ached, sliced in half, torn to shreds. She'd never asked for this. For two warriors of such unswerving honor and courage to love her. To demand a share of her heart. To tempt her to do the unthinkable.

Dark and rich, the scent of his blood so close twisted the knife in her heart deeper. His obsidian eyes flickered with flames and at last a hint of his wicked smile quirked his lips. "A challenge, remember? Will you succumb to my blood so easily?"

Swallowing hard, she determinedly walked away from the tent. She had no idea where the Market Day was, but she wasn't going to stand there drooling over his blood any longer, either. "I remember. I'm not giving up so easily."

He sighed dramatically and re-sheathed his knife as he caught up. "On the day of my death, will you at least honor me with a kiss?"

Shannari snorted loudly but felt heat creeping through her body. Kiss Gregar? Taste his blood? Next, he really would convince her to—

Gregar laughed softly. "Vulkar let it be soon."

On a hilltop outside Camp, the people gathered for Market Day. Hides spread out on the ground were loaded with supplies and crafts. People milled, talking and laughing, throughout the casual set up.

Shannari swept her gaze over the crowd, quickly taking mental notes of the arrangements. The hides were colored—green, sky blue, and orange—so she quickly realized who belonged to which Camp. The people at the green hides welcomed her with a nod and smile as she walked by. Secure in their position as First Camp, they seemed to know she would automatically find their goods acceptable.

At the sky blue hides, people were friendly but pushier. They needed her approval in some way. If she walked past a hide without taking anything, the owners frowned and tensed, staring across the way at their competition. Since Alea wore sky blue at the fire, these people belonged to Drendon's Camp, and therefore, the orange must be Lyell's. With the hides arranged by content, she could see at a glance why Drendon's Camp was second and Lyell's was evidently lower. Much lower, if the quality of goods was any indication.

She decided to find Alea and deliver the bow first, and then spend a little time browsing. Perhaps she'd find some goods her father might be willing to trade for.

Silent behind her, Gregar placed his palm in the small of her back to draw her attention, nodding toward the right. She saw

Alea immediately and headed in that direction with her best polite smile firmly in place.

The woman shocked the hell out of her by hugging her. "Shannari, welcome! How's your arm?"

"Fine, fine. Your *Kae'Shaman* has a great gift."

"None is better at Healing in all the Nine Camps. I hoped you would stop by before the *kae'don*. The warriors will be rowdy after their fight and will take all the best goods later."

Smiling a little more naturally, Shannari offered the bow. "Khul asked me to deliver this personally. We hope it meets with your approval."

Alea actually squealed and snatched the bow from her hands. "Oh, it's exactly the one I've been watching Blaine make. It's beautiful. Thank you, it's perfect."

Relieved, Shannari glanced down at the other woman's hide. "So what's your specialty?"

"Alea, aren't you going to introduce me?"

The woman's voice would have been pleasant if it weren't sharp with the desperate tone of someone trying very, very hard. She appeared several years younger than both Shannari and Alea. Young and nervous and very desperate. Why? Shannari didn't know, but she smiled kindly at the young woman.

"Shannari, this is Krista, Lyell's mate. Krista, this is Shannari, Khul's woman from the Green Lands."

The young woman seized Shannari's freshly healed arm so hard she winced. "Won't you come to my hide?"

Alea shook her head. "Krista! Give the woman a moment to get to know you before you drag her off to view your goods."

Shannari glanced back at Gregar, cocking an eyebrow at him. What good was a bodyguard if he didn't prevent such annoying situations? The bastard merely grinned.

"We're so happy you came to Market Day, Shannari," Krista gushed, still clutching her arm. "We've worked very hard for months to prepare our best goods. The Summer Gathering is only a few weeks away."

Shannari politely nodded at each good the other woman held up for her perusal, but nothing really caught her fancy. The necklaces were heavily decorated with feathers, which she guessed would be extremely annoying about her neck. The colors were a little too vibrant, too garish, for her taste.

She looked again to Gregar more desperately. What if she couldn't find anything reasonable to take from this poor girl? She couldn't bear to wear such a ridiculous frou-frou item. "Summer Gathering?"

"All Nine Camps will gather at the base of Vulkar's Mountain for a fortnight of trading, competitions and ceremonies," Alea said. "The khuls meet and the Camp statuses are re-affirmed for the year."

Ah. No wonder the younger woman was already nervous. If her Camp was lower status, this was their chance to improve their standing on the Plains. However, if these goods were any indication, it would take more than a few Market Days to impress whoever decided the final standings.

"How about this one, Shannari?" Krista held up an even more extravagant necklace, heavy with feathers both around the neck and dangling from heavy beaded chains. The only purpose the ugly thing might have would be in covering up the embarrassing amount of cleavage the Sha'Kae al'Dan clothing revealed.

"Don't you have anything... simpler?" At the woman's crestfallen look, she tried to explain. "I'm afraid my father despaired of ever making me dress appropriately. I'd rather carry my sword than wear the latest fashions, even at Court. That fact that I'm even wearing something other than my leather pants and armor is quite an achievement."

Both women stared at her blankly. "What is Court?" Alea asked. "Pants? Armor?"

Gregar snickered.

"Never mind," Shannari sighed. "I just want something simple. If you have a necklace that has some green beads in it— no feathers!—then I'll take it."

"No feathers?" Krista actually sniffed and her eyes glistened suspiciously. "It's our Camp's trademark."

"Bloody hell. Fine, one feather. Only if it's green."

Still sniffing with blotchy cheeks, Krista dug through baskets of necklaces, looking for something to suit her. "This has the fewest feathers. I didn't use as many since the colors were so vibrant."

Bracing herself to suppress the groan at what "vibrant" might be after the Court Jester combinations she'd already seen, Shannari took the offered necklace.

The colors—green and dark blue, almost purple. Rhaekhar's and Gregar's *kae'valda*, accented with white.

"It's a sign," Gregar whispered reverently. "Take it, Shannari, I beg you."

"It also has a matching earring," Krista added eagerly.

"I don't have a hole in my ear."

Alea smiled brightly. "That's easy enough to resolve."

Sighing heavily, Shannari nodded. The other two women squealed with excitement and rushed about looking for an appropriate needle. "Are you sure Khul won't mind?"

Gregar latched the necklace for her and stood back to admire it. "Why should he?"

"I can get the earring later." Her face felt tight and her stomach clutched so hard she hunched her shoulders. "I must be late for the *kae'don*."

Immediately, Gregar pressed against her back, scanning the area for danger. "What's wrong?"

"Nothing." Shannari pretended interest in a hide off to the

left. Then the next. If she slipped away quietly, maybe they'd forget entirely. The necklace was enough to avoid insult, and—

Still wrapped about her back, Gregar easily drew her to a halt. Her heart pounded so hard she couldn't breathe, but not with desire. For once, she welcomed the Blood's heat against her back. He drove away some of the cold creeping up her numb fingers.

"You're afraid." Gregar bowed his head close to hers, his soft voice against her ear. "Why? Tell me, Shannari, so I may protect you."

From a great distance, she heard Alea. "We have a needle! Shannari?"

She tried to speak, to beg him, but a solid, thick lump blocked her throat. She was afraid he'd laugh and tease her, that he'd never understand such a blind aversion. Her stomach rolled and pitched and her knees simply gave out.

Effortlessly, Gregar caught her before she crumpled to the ground. "Do you fear the needle?"

Terror shrilled through her, a cold, sharp blade that stiffened her body and drew a gasp of pain. Without questioning her further, the Blood moved away from the women, steadying her in his arms when she couldn't walk alone.

Alea called after them. "Gregar?"

"Shannari wishes to join Khul now."

Tears burned her eyes. Her knees didn't shake quite so badly, yet she clung to the Blood. With his dark, rich scent of caffe in her nose, the sharp gleam of needles didn't torment her. "Thank you."

"It's an honor to serve, Shannari."

He could have teased her. Now he knew her great, silly secret, yet the Blood didn't even quirk a smile at her unreasonable fear.

"If you fear a thing, then it isn't unreasonable. I swore no one would touch you with steel or blade while I'm at your back. A needle is steel. You're safe."

"Are you going to tell Khul?"

Gregar paused at the outer edge of hides, drawing away slightly. The gleam in his dark eyes chased the last of the numbness from her body. "I might. Or I might not. If you care to bargain with me—"

She opened her mouth to retort—

When Gregar slid in front of her, bumping her back from some approaching threat she couldn't see. His body vibrated with tension, his bare back flexing against her face. She stepped away, but he moved with her, reaching behind him to hold her close to the protection of his solid body.

Cold, so cold. A dark chill emanated from him that made her teeth chatter. She tried to see around him, but he kept her firmly locked behind him at his back. Now she better understood his attitude with the boys. That had been only a warning compared to the blatant Death rolling from him now. How could his skin be scalding hot while this bone-chilling cold flooded from him in waves?

"Why aren't you at the *kae'don* with your khul?"

She shivered. The frigid menace in Gregar's voice was horrible to hear. She could only imagine how deadly his face must look, cast in shadows and etched with the promise of death.

"I could ask you the same question."

Shannari jabbed the Blood in the ribs. "Move aside, or next time it'll be my sword."

Chuckling, Gregar stepped slightly to the side, but kept his body carefully angled before her.

A rather small, unimpressive barbarian stood before them. Belligerent and cocky as a young rooster, he sneered at her cool appraisal.

"Who's this little man?"

"I'm Sontache, Second to Lyell, you filthy, outlander whore."

Gregar was gone so quickly she swore he disappeared a moment. He wrapped his hand around the other man's throat and lifted him off his feet. "Shannari carries Khul's blood and holds his heart in her hand. To insult her is to insult Khul."

Gripping the hilt of her sword, she walked over to stand before the gasping red-faced man dangling from the Blood's fist. "What was your plan?"

The barbarian shook his head, gasping for air.

"Sontache!" Krista screamed and ran toward her kinsman, but Alea grabbed her arm and kept her back. "What's wrong? What's happening?"

Shannari hesitated, trying to decide the best course of action. She wanted information, but she didn't want to cause a riot or traumatize the women. She was used to blood and assassins and war, but that didn't mean they were. "I need to know what he planned. Hurt him but don't kill him."

Gregar set the man on his feet, and with a flick of his wrist, bent him over backward with a hand fisted in his hair. "It's an honor to serve."

The Blood smiled, and goose bumps raced down her arms. Wicked pleasure and darkness spread in his eyes.

The ivory knife flashed and the barbarian howled in pain. A woman cried out, and Shannari glanced over her shoulder worriedly. Krista was on the ground, ghostly white, but Alea seemed to be calm and in control.

Blood dripped down Sontache's face. "I was merely going to escort her to the *kae'don!*"

Gregar sliced the man's other cheek open to the bone.

"Somehow, I don't believe an innocent escort is what you planned." Shannari leaned down to give the man a sympathetic smile. His frantic gaze darted from hers to Gregar's dancing black eyes of murder and back. "Maybe you wanted to embarrass me, yes? A little hanky-panky on the way to the battle with some witnesses to spread tales to Khul's enemies?"

Pale and slick with sweat, the barbarian didn't have to answer. The panic in his eyes spoke volumes. "Just a kiss or... If you were willing—"

Gregar growled low and deep in his throat. She spared a glance at his face and blanched. Darkness spread across his face and cold seeped into her bones until she ached. "Don't kill him in front of the women."

He didn't even look at her. "He would have done what I have not."

She shivered harder. "Maybe he has information about his own khul to share. If we kill him—"

Slowly, Gregar turned his head and looked into her face. His eyes were black, flat, and full of death, like the Death Rider who'd nearly killed her. "Khul will want him dead for planning to put his hands on you, let alone his filthy lying mouth."

Krista moaned on the ground and several of the women were crying.

"Wait until we get to the *kae'don*, please."

His expression never changed.

"I'll taste your blood as you wished. Just don't kill him here."

Immediately, the death relented in his gaze and he shot her a wicked smile. "Agreed. I knew I would convince you eventually."

He jerked Sontache upright and marched him down the hill away from the women. The barbarian struggled briefly, until he felt Gregar's *rahke* bite into his side. "Perhaps we'll be too late for you to participate in the *kae'don*, Sontache. Perhaps Khul will let me challenge you."

The barbarian made a sound suspiciously like a whimper.

Gregar chuckled. "I wonder how long I can keep you alive while I carve your meat off your bones strip by strip."

## 21

"What is it you always say before a *kae'don*, Khul?" Lyell smiled tightly and adjusted his grip on his *rahke*. His warhorse shifted and tossed its head, already more than ready to flee the field. "A little blood in battle, aye?"

Rhaekhar didn't allow a matching smile to break the harsh concentration on his face. Lyell was nervous and rightfully so. Why would he even wish to engage the First Camp in a *kae'don*? None could match the sheer dominance of Khul's warriors and warhorses. Only compassion for a fellow warrior would stay his hand and prevent him from thoroughly embarrassing Lyell's entire Camp.

"He says a little battle is good for the blood." Gregar shouted, drawing everyone's attention. "If you're as inept as your Second, be prepared to give Khul all the blood in your body."

Sontache stumbled down the slope with the Blood and Shannari right behind him. The look on their faces chilled Rhaekhar's blood. The Blood's bore the furious jealousy he half feared was on his own face each time he looked at the other warrior, where Shannari's was back to that hard, frozen mask she'd worn in her Green Lands when she'd surrendered to him. Since he'd not felt a single hint of reluctant yearning from her bond all morning, he suspected the worst. Another warrior had tried to touch her.

Only tried, because the Blood would be lying on the ground breathing his last before he'd allow another warrior to lay a finger on her.

Fury exploded in him, but he clenched his jaw and remained silent. He must be Khul of all Nine Camps and not an enraged warrior on the rampage, no matter how much the tight-lipped dread on Shannari's face angered him.

With a hard shove, Gregar sent the other warrior sprawling onto the ground before Khul's warhorse.

"What happened?" Rhaekhar ground out. He ran his gaze quickly over Shannari, but he didn't see any injuries. He regretted shutting down their bond as much as possible while he prepared for battle. "Did he harm you?"

"No," she replied quickly. "I don't think he planned to hurt me."

"Then what?"

"He planned to embarrass you." Her face flooded with color and she gave the Blood an imploring look.

"First, he insulted her," Gregar answered flatly. The lack of his normal joking winks and grins sent Rhaekhar's hand down to grip his *rahke*. "He called her an outlander whore."

"And he still lives?" Rhaekhar roared. Khan snorted and reared, his ears laid flat and teeth bared at the warrior on the ground. "Why didn't you kill him without delay?"

"The other women were upset," Shannari stepped closer to lay her hand on his thigh. "Besides, no one needed to die for a simple insult."

"Simple?" Rhaekhar struggled against the swirling rage

pulsing through his blood. "He implies I have no love for you. He implies you will never carry my honor. For those words alone, I shall see him dead."

"There's more," Gregar said softly. "He planned to touch her. Kiss her. Molest her in some way with witnesses to spread tales."

Utter calm swept through Rhaekhar. He unsheathed his *rahke*, smiled at Sontache, and raised his gaze to Lyell. "Death is too good for you both. Instead, I shall make you live to regret this insult every single day for the rest of your long, miserable lives. Join your khul and let the *kae'don* begin."

He didn't hear Shannari's hurried questions to Gregar, nor her pleas. He didn't hear *Kae'Shaman's* ceremonial words. He didn't see his forty nine warriors line up for the charge. All he saw was two warriors, nay, two curs, that would take all his control and concentration not to rip limb from limb.

*Kae'Shaman's* hand dropped and the warriors whooped. Grimly silent, Rhaekhar released Khan and charged at both his opponents. The ground rumbled beneath the warhorses' hooves. With a slight touch to the flank, Rhaekhar directed his stallion to strike Lyell's mount while he sliced a long deep cut down the other warrior's chest.

Khan lunged beneath him, powerful forelegs striking out, and the other horse squealed. Whirling, the stallion let rear hooves fly at Sontache's mount. Rhaekhar took the opportunity to flay Lyell's right cheek open to the bone. Another strike to his other cheek. Then a stripe down his chest to match his Second's.

Feeling Khan's subtle shift of warning, he jerked to the side and slammed his elbow back into Sontache's face. Unbalanced, the warrior slid off his warhorse and fell beneath Khan's hooves. A few deliberately well placed stomps broke both an arm and a leg, but Rhaekhar reined the stallion away before he could smash the warrior's skull open.

Returning his attention to the khul, Rhaekhar urged Khan

into a formidable display of force. The stallion reared to his full height, clawing the sky and screaming with fury. Already pale as cream, Lyell cast his gaze left and right as though he thought to flee. Eight of the Blood closed around Khul's chosen opponent. Not to interfere, for that would damage his honor; they prevented Lyell from fleeing before Khul was finished.

Blood pounded through Rhaekhar's body, throbbing in his head, his heart, his groin. The thought of another warrior laying a hand on his woman awoke a fierce urge he hadn't felt in years.

Bloodlust. A warrior's nightmare. Gritting his teeth, he fought the rising urge and concentrated on his opponent. He'd planned to slice every inch of Lyell's body open, but the longer he fought, the more the bloodlust would take him.

"We meant no harm, Khul." Lyell swiped a hand across his face, wiping blood from his mouth. "Sontache was merely to—"

"You would have shamed her!" Red pulsed through his vision, urging him to pound this cur to a bloody pulp. Unfortunately, he would then turn to Shannari for a different kind of pounding, and she would likely fare just as poorly in his hands. He breathed hard, deliberately sheathing his *rahke*. "Take your Camp and go."

"Forgive me, Khul. I've offended you, much more than I intended. Surely—"

The faint scent of spicy flowers floated on the breeze. Shannari. She was close. The pounding urge rose in him. The urge to reclaim what was his and release this fury in uncontrollable need. "If I see your face again before the Summer Gathering, I shall give you formal challenge. I won't kill you, but I'll drain you to the point of death over and over and over. All the blood in your body couldn't remove my anger."

Lyell dismounted and knelt on the ground beside his groaning Second. "Kill me, then. I cannot live with such dishonor."

"Live every day and know my love for Shannari. Know my

honor." Despite his best efforts, his voice was thick and raw with the need for blood, for her. Praying that perhaps Gregar had sensed the rising bloodlust and sent her away, Rhaekhar turned his head, seeking her.

Shannari stood at the edge of the ring made by the mounted Blood, her gaze locked on him. Gregar stood beside her, and he shook his head imperceptibly. She wouldn't flee, not her.

*Not even when I will hurt her.*

"Know *her* honor."

G rim-faced with eyes blazing like the sun, Rhaekhar turned his stallion toward her. He'd beaten the two fools easily. He'd embarrassed them. No one had died. So what was wrong?

"You should have run when you had the chance," Gregar said mildly.

"I never run." For the first time in her life, though, she seriously considered it. The look in Rhaekhar's eyes... The stallion shook the ground beneath her feet. He was coming straight at her. Through the bond, she felt only vicious, pounding anger.

No. Not anger.

Lust.

Fire doused her from head to toe. The barbarian had gone from battle lust to simply lust in a heartbeat. From the look on his face, he was going to take her as soon as he got his hands on her.

Her first instinct, again, was flight. *Shannari dal'Dainari never ran from anything, let alone a man.* She raised her chin, stared him right in the eye, and dared him.

The massive stallion that had trampled a man moments ago brushed past her. Barely bending down, the barbarian snatched her up with him, and they galloped away from the battlefield.

His hands, so hard. His body, hard muscle, slick with sweat and blood from his opponents, steaming with heat and need. His mouth, aggressive, unyielding, commanding. He inhaled her, his teeth hard against hers, his tongue halfway down her throat while he gripped her head just so for his attack.

Distantly, she heard other horses following. The Blood were never far from their Khul. Yet when he drew the stallion to a sliding halt and fell to the ground on top of her, she couldn't bring herself to care.

He pinned her wrists above her head and jerked the under-cloth away from beneath her Sha'Kae al'Dan clothing. "I... can't... wait... any... longer."

His hand gentled somewhat. He cupped her and growled, his chest vibrating against hers. She knew what he found there. His raw need blazed through the bond into her, making her nearly as desperate as he.

She thought he would sink into her immediately and slake some of the brutal lust blazing in his body. She even arched up against him, urging him to greater speed. Instead, he slid down her body and buried his face between her thighs.

Teeth, tongue, as hard and demanding as his hands. Within moments, she clawed at his hair, shuddering beneath him, her cry echoing in the silence of the Plains. Blinded with crushing need, it took her a moment to realize he'd left her.

Bewildered, she let him haul her to her feet. "What are you doing?"

"Fight me." He unsheathed his knife and jerked his head at her sword. "Challenge me. I need it. Those dogs couldn't draw my blood to save their lives, but you can. You will."

At her hesitation, he raised his right hand to his mouth and pointedly licked his fingers. "This was just an appetizer. Now I need to bleed before I can continue driving you mad with pleasure."

"You want me to challenge you. Now? You actually want me to bleed you?"

He bared his teeth in a vicious smile. "I welcome you to try."

He leaped at her, *rahke* flashing. Dodging aside, she drew her sword. He lunged again, and she barely blocked his strike. He was serious. Deadly serious.

Heart pounding, she crouched lower and concentrated on protecting herself. She wasn't afraid, not exactly, but the risk was great. What if he managed to arouse her own blood hunger? She might actually gut him or slice his heart open.

He gave her no time to contemplate strategies. The knife darted high, snuck low, as fast as she could twist the sword in her hand from side to side. Back-pedaling, she blinked sweat from her eyes, already breathing hard.

Unlike before, he didn't spare any of his phenomenal strength. "Come on, woman. You can do better than this. You're faring no better than Lyell."

Whirling away from the arcing blade snaking toward her face, she felt the first burning slice high on her shoulder. Surprised, she couldn't stop him from putting another long shallow cut on her other arm.

"You cut me. You actually cut me!"

"Of course I did." He inhaled deeply, his nostrils flaring, and he gave her a look of arrogant satisfaction that made her grind her teeth. "I want to smell your blood and your need. And then I'm going to taste both again."

She knew better than to allow any emotion to skew her concentration during battle, let alone anger. Or desire. The bond blazed between them, searing the cool calm lake shining in her mind until it boiled with storm-tossed waves. Blood pounded in her veins, surging with fury, desire, frustration. A need so fierce, so primal, so overwhelming, she threw off her last hesitation and attacked him with every skill she possessed.

Using her longer weapon, she forced him to give her more breathing room. When he dodged inside her defenses, she elbowed him square in the chest hard enough his next breath wheezed, and followed up with a kick to his shin. He grabbed at her and she twisted away desperately. If he got those big hands on her, she'd be finished. In more ways than one. And she had yet to draw his blood.

She swung at him again and he knocked her blow wide with his forearm. Staggered off balance, she saw the wicked knife gliding so gracefully toward her chest. Too late to change direction, too late to bring her sword up, there was nothing she could do to prevent the knife from sinking into her heart.

Her trapped breath exploded from her lungs when he missed, or so she thought until she felt the breeze on her bare skin. The vest sagged open, baring her breasts. The close call froze her in a moment of sheer shock.

*He could have killed me. He could have sunk the knife to the hilt in my heart, just like Devin.*

Molten gold eyes locked onto her breasts and a rumbling growl rolled from deep in his throat.

"You want my heart?" She whispered, her breathing ragged. "That's as close as you'll ever get again. I'll cut your own heart out and feed it to Varne."

The barbarian laughed. "As I said, you're welcome to try."

Cold fury ignited in her. "Maybe I should try Gregar instead."

Ah, that blow struck home, if the smoothing of his face to granite was any indication. "You've already cut out my heart, *na'lanna*, and you use Gregar's ivory *rahke* to accomplish the task."

She refused to feel guilty for something he'd forced upon her time after time. She refused Gregar's attention. She refused to discuss any "arrangements" with Rhaekhar. What more could he want? She couldn't help the strange, dangerous attraction to the

Shadowed Blood any more than this desperate, aching need for the Khul. He was the one who'd left her with the wicked Blood, insisted he protect her at all times, and nearly thrust her into the other man's arms.

The fierce pounding need she felt from Rhaekhar lessened, as though he regretted his words just as much. Playing on his emotions, she turned partially away and let her shoulders droop. She allowed the sword tip to sag to the ground. "I should never have come here."

"Na'lanna, my heart, forgive me. Please—"

She snapped the sword up toward his throat, catching him beneath the chin. He jerked backward, but her blow was true. Blood dripped freely down his neck to his chest.

Stunned, he searched the wound with his fingers to check the severity. "You could have slit my throat."

"Aye," she answered mockingly, letting fury flash in her eyes. "You know my fear for your safety, the Shadow I carry. Yet you play with fire every time you challenge me to these fool fights. This is all fun and games to you, isn't it?"

He took a step toward her, stretching out his empty hand imploringly. "Shannari..."

"Don't. Just don't." She averted her gaze, determined to refuse him fully. The scent of blood and sweat was thick in her nose, drowning out the scent of the Plains. "Let me go, Khul, before it's too late for you."

He seized her, wrapping those mighty arms around her and pinning her arms to her side. "You're mine, Shannari, Rose of Shanhasson. I refuse to let you go!"

Furious, she screamed and drummed her heels against his legs, but his thighs were like massive oaks. With her arms pinned, she couldn't get her sword up. "Bastard! Let me go!"

Instead, he squeezed harder, making it impossible for her to breathe. The sword fell from her numb fingers.

"What do you want from me, Shannari?"

Right now she was so angry she wouldn't be satisfied with simply nicking his throat. She'd take his head off. "I want nothing from you!"

"Nothing?" He growled in her ear, grinding his groin against her. "Your scent says otherwise. You smell like smoldering flowers and steaming summer nights. What can I do to earn your love?"

"I'll never love you!"

"My heart is yours. My Camp is yours. My own Blood is yours. What else can I give you?"

She sagged in his arms, trying to unexpectedly drop her weight through his arms. He wasn't fooled. "I don't want you, let alone your Blood!"

His anguish sliced through the bond, choking her. Fighting back tears, drowning in remorse and guilt and fury, she slammed her skull back into his face. He grunted and released her, momentarily dazed.

Scrambling on hands and knees, she tried to flee, to find her feet, but he slammed into her and carried her to the ground. Her head recoiled on the packed earth and she tasted blood in her mouth. Crushed beneath him, she couldn't breathe. Darkness threatened.

He wrenched her head around so he could plant his mouth on hers. He sucked on her split lip, his chest rumbling against her back. Her blood rekindled the fierce driving need in him. In her. The bond kept no secrets from her. From him. His desperate fear he would lose her sliced viciously through his emotions, but the need for blood and sex was stronger. Her need for him was stronger than the Shadow festering in her heart.

He forced her face up beneath his chin, smearing blood on her mouth. "From the start you wanted me to act the dominant herd stallion, to take so you wouldn't have to choose to give yourself of your own accord. You wanted bloodlust. Now you have it."

His blood fired through her body, just as hers stirred him to greater lust. Lady help her, she wanted him so badly. She wanted his blood pouring into her mouth while he took her savagely. She sank her teeth into his throat, gnawing at the wound, his skin.

"Aye. Tear me up." Shifting against her, he plunged hard and deep. "Shred me as you shred my heart."

She screamed against his throat, her neck aching with strain to keep her mouth pressed to his wound. He took her viciously, his body slamming against hers, forcing a guttural cry from her with each thrust. His jaw locked on her shoulder so hard his teeth broke the skin and dug into the muscle beneath. A shudder wracked his body against hers at the taste of her blood.

Pinned beneath him, she quivered and cried with pleasure until her throat was raw and darkness claimed her at last.

## 22

R haekhar struggled to open his eyes, trying to remember where he was. Why he was asleep with the sun glaring so harshly into his eyes. Why his entire body ached and yet hummed with sensuous pleasure at the same time.

Why he tasted blood.

Sweet blood.

*Shannari.*

Jerking awake, he started up only to find her staring down at him. She leaned over him, draped across his chest. Blood and dirt streaked her face and her lip was split and swollen. He might be mistaken, prayed he was, but the shadow of a bruise darkened her chin and jaw line.

Yet she smiled at him with a satiated gleam in her midnight eyes. Lazily, she stroked fingers through his hair. "I thought you might not wake until nightfall."

"Forgive—"

Pressing her fingers against his mouth, she shook her head. She traced his lip, staring at his mouth with such tenderness...

Terribly afraid he'd injured her, he sat up and gently shifted her onto his lap. Heavy limbed and languorous, she let him arrange her to his wish, draping herself loosely on him, which only alarmed him more.

"Shannari—"

She nuzzled his neck, clinging to him when he tried to hold her away enough so that he could examine her for injuries. "So that was bloodlust."

"Did I hurt you?"

"Some."

His heart stuttered, drowning in remorse. A warrior never hurt a woman, let alone *his* woman, his heart. Bloodlust was unforgivable. He couldn't bear the dishonor.

Clenching his jaw to keep back the cry of anguish, he reached up and began unbraiding his hair. He would strip his *kae'valda* and submit to her judgment. He would accept nothing less.

"What's wrong? It was wonderful."

His chest ached as though Khan trampled him. "I hurt you."

"Not seriously. I'm fine, really." She tugged his hand away from his hair. "Did I hurt you?"

He began to answer negatively, but then realized he did bear injuries. The cut on his throat burned like the Three Hells, and his jaw felt tender when he opened his mouth. Injuries she'd dealt him.

Details of their challenge flooded him. Her courage. Her pride. Her rage. Why had she been so angry?

"You did something no other man has been able to do. You looked my Shadow in the eye and resisted its call." Her voice trembled and she buried her face tighter against his neck. "You didn't try to kill me."

Gently, he tilted her face up to his. Tears shimmered in her dark blue eyes. She smelled as soft and fragile as a new spring blossom kissed by rain. If love had a scent...

Heart racing, he stroked his fingers carefully along her face, lightly so as not to frighten her away. "I would sooner slit my own throat."

"You don't understand, do you?" She smiled sadly, turning her cheek into his caress to rub his palm more fully against her. "Not even your wicked Blood could have done it. You were enraged with bloodlust, possessing none of your normal phenomenal control, and you still didn't put your *rahke* in my heart."

Horror choked him and he squeezed his eyes shut. He couldn't even begin to comprehend her pain. The betrayal. Never able to trust. Doubt justified again and again as yet another tried to kill her. Even lovers. So that was how she received the scar on her breast.

"I've finally found someone I could trust. Someone I could... love."

His eyes flew open. For such happy words he'd longed to hear with all his heart and soul, through the bond he felt only grief.

"I must leave you."

Tightening his grip on her, he glared with all the fierce love roaring in his heart. "How can you even think of leaving me now?"

She kissed him lightly, her lips trembling against his. "Have you ever felt bloodlust before me?"

As a lad not yet a warrior, he had thought to never outgrow the great shame he'd brought himself. "Once, a very long time ago."

Carefully, she touched his neck, flinching at her handiwork. "Like this?"

"Not exactly." He frowned, trying to understand her worry. "I wasn't yet a warrior, but my Father was Khul. I grew up with great responsibility and hope for the future. A woman wanted to be a part of that future, but I didn't return her affection. She deliberately involved me in a dispute with another lad, and somehow..." Despite the years, it still shamed him to admit the truth. "I lost control at her insults. Enraged, I nearly killed the other lad who defended her. I still pay for that mistake this day, for Tehark is my greatest opponent. The young woman we fought over is now his mate."

"Did you make love to her?"

"I never touched her. I had no desire for her. I lusted for blood, though, and nearly killed her mate in my rage. Father drilled me ceaselessly for months after and worked me to exhaustion day after day so I couldn't even lift a finger against another. He prided himself on making me into the warrior I am, but in all honesty, it was a vision of you that saved me."

She laughed uneasily. "You couldn't have known of me so many years ago."

"I was so ashamed that I couldn't face the Summer Gathering and instead camped alone in the foothills of Vulkar's Mountain. I hunted and sat on a rock mostly feeling miserable, until one afternoon I found an unusual trail. Hoofprints unlike any I'd ever seen before or since. I followed them to a strange green valley where I saw..."

Reverence filled him. He saw again in his mind's eye the mighty Stallion trotting across an ocean of fire. His Mare shimmering in a rainbow of moonlight with Her black mane and tail like a velvet night sky. "Both Vulkar and His Beloved Dark Mare spoke to me. She promised me a love like no other. You, Shannari, the Rose of Shanhasson. I saw a deep red flower dripping blood, locked within impenetrable shining white walls. Heavy, thick shadows hung all around, but you... I smelled your scent, and I hungered for your blood, for your love, even then."

Shannari bowed her head. "Even in your vision I carried

Shadow. Don't you see? I'm tainting you. I'm tainting your Plains. I bring you blood hunger and suffering, I worsen your enemies, and I ruin your friendships. You must let me go before it's too late."

Forcing down the driving instinct to dominate her into acceptance and surrender, he fought for a reasonable tone of voice. "There's no taint. Why would Vulkar send me to your Green Lands if not to love and protect you?"

Her brow creased. "Even if this were true and your God did send you to me, why torture us with happiness that can never be permanent?"

"Who says it cannot be permanent? Live on the Plains, Shannari. Become my Khul'lanna. Carry my honor and my children."

"And let my people rot and die of starvation and disease? Eventually the Shadow will spread beyond the Green Lands. Even here to your Plains. Do you want your Camps falling into eternal darkness? Alea and Drendon wasting away with some horrible disease? Your warriors starving to death, ill, murdering each other for a loaf of bread? That's what will come if I don't wear the Rose Crown. I told you my destiny from the beginning."

She pressed her face against his chest and fisted her hands in his hair. "I... I care for you too much to tarnish your honor. To break your Camp. To destroy your people. If not for your own sake, then for all Nine Camps of the Sha'Kae al'Dan, you must send me back to the Green Lands."

Heart aching, Shannari tightened her arms around Rhaekhar. His scent in her nose, his skin like velvet against her mouth, his arms so protective and demanding around her. Every warrior instinct he possessed told him to fight, rage, and refuse to let her out of his sight for a moment. To sink into her, claim her body so hard, so furiously, that he would claim her very soul.

Yet his hands were incredibly gentle on her back. His blood sang in her veins, drawing her closer to him. Tying her to him.

Freeing herself would tear her apart and leave her empty and wounded. Again.

"You don't have to leave me, *na'lanna*." He stroked a big hand through her hair, his voice low and soft against her ear. While through the bond, his heart roared and screamed and fought to keep what was his. "I'm warrior enough to keep you safe."

"I'm not worried about me."

"You should be. After everything you've told me about your Green Lands, the cur your father would have you mate, you should be very worried. Why would you willingly return to such a trap?"

Dread strangled her throat. He was right, so right. She couldn't wed Theo before she'd known this barbarian's love and tenderness. Could she now marry for politics, no matter the necessity?

"They'll chain you, *na'lanna*. They'll dishonor you. They'll try to murder you, break you, kill your spirit. You would be forced to hide the strength of your heart, deny your courage, suppress your sweet passion. You would live a lie every single day."

"I have no choice!" Her words came out in a wail, muffled against his chest.

"Think of the love we've shared, my heart. Think of the blood. Every time you shared blood with me, your heart drew nigh to mine. I know your body. I know your very heart. My heart lies open to you every moment of the day."

"Please. Don't do this to me."

*:I love you, Shannari, with all my heart and soul. I cannot bear to let you return to such a cage. I cannot bear to let you face the Shadow alone.:*

Lifting her head, she stared into his burnished gold eyes. *So much honor. So much love. I don't deserve it.*

"Stay with me," he whispered against her lips. "Love me."

Staring into his eyes, breathing the very breath from his lungs, she wanted so desperately to make it so. To let the fragile emotion in her heart burst forth. Hope. Love. Trust. Ideals she'd murdered long ago in her fight for the High Throne. She didn't even wear it yet, but the Rose Crown was so very, very heavy.

"I—"

"Khul." Grim as ever, Varne approached. "A messenger arrives from Dalden Bay."

That could only mean one thing. Trouble. She saw the immediate urgency in Rhaekhar's gaze. The determination. Plans she'd set in motion what seemed an eternity ago were now coming to fruition.

Swallowing the words threatening to shatter her resolve, she pulled away and stood, albeit stiffly, clutching her vest closed. She felt like a herd of horses had trampled her.

Rhaekhar stood just as stiffly, for he'd fared no better than she in their battle. "No one will take from me what I've claimed for the Sha'Kae al'Dan. No one. You're mine, Shannari dal'-Dainari, Rose of Shanhasson."

She said nothing. Couldn't refuse him, couldn't agree. Agony seized her lungs in bands of iron. How could she leave him? How could she live every day knowing he was alive and lost to her?

His jaw clenched. His right hand reached for the *rahke* that was missing on his hip. "Fight the chains of destiny, Shannari. Don't let them put you in a cage."

Gregar silently offered Khul's *rahke*, which he'd lost in their challenge. Rhaekhar sheathed it yet kept the handle gripped hard in his right hand. He made such an impressive figure standing in the hot noonday sun, surrounded in a brilliant nimbus of light, so fierce and proud and invincible.

"Fight them as you fought my love, Shannari."

"I lost that fight." A tear slipped down her cheek, burning like acid. Gregar offered her sword to her, his dark eyes pools of Shadow against his Khul's light. "I've lost every fight with you. But this one I must win. I must return to the Green Lands and uphold my destiny."

Rhaekhar seized her chin, his voice rumbling with violence. "You are welcome to try."

## 23

After riding all afternoon and through the night, the warriors drew rein to survey the green field below with a new dawn breaking the horizon. A wide, fast river snaked through the barrens along the desert and dumped into the distant bay. Already attacking, the outlanders chose the desert side for battle. Rhaekhar counted at least ten fists of outlanders facing the one fist of warriors he'd left to protect his claim on the village.

Although his warriors held his own against them, Athgart hadn't yet defeated the challengers. A small group of outlanders were mounted on fleet ponies this time. They were no match for the *na'kindren's* sheer bulk, but they darted in and out fast enough that the warriors couldn't crush them as easily as the men on foot.

"Pella," Shannari muttered.

Although she sat in his arms before him, she'd never felt so far away as this moment. Drawing on the bond, Rhaekhar read only a hard, blank emptiness. The closer they came to her homeland, the more that emptiness spread through her heart. Now, she was numb, frozen on the inside.

Which frightened the Three Hells out of him. "This is the great enemy you spoke of?"

"One of them. Not the worst."

So flat, her voice. His heart clenched with worry. Fury he could help her release by instigating a fight. Fear he could laugh and challenge away. Desire, well, he certainly knew how to ease her longing. But how to break this frozen emptiness spreading through her heart? "What's wrong, Shannari?"

She stared down at the unfolding *kae'don*, her mouth a hard slant of resolve. "It's over."

Gone. In her heart, she was already lost to him. Urgency and rage pulsed through him. Tenderness on the ride to these Green Lands had failed to break through to her. *Perhaps I should resort to warrior dominance and aggression. If nothing else, I'll rouse her fighting instinct.*

Deliberately, he made his voice harsh, echoing with command. "Nothing is over, *na'lanna*, until I say it's so."

She flinched but refused to look at him. "I fear this battle may go badly for you."

Arrogance steeled his voice. "You've defeated Pella numerous times. This day will be no different, for I shall surely defeat him too."

Wordlessly, she nodded. But her heart throbbed sharply and she gave a little gasp of pain that sent his blood boiling higher. Why her heart? She would find it impossible to convince him to allow an outlander's intentions to be made known. Impossible! "Do you have feelings for Pella?"

She laughed bitterly. "Only hatred and disgust."

Listening to her bond, he felt a sharp pain as though a *rahke* plunged into her heart, twisting and grinding on bone. Furious, he gripped her chin and jerked her head around to study her face. Blank. Cold. Smooth as granite. But through the bond—

Grief. Sorrow. Regret. All emotions tumbling through her, slamming into him in fast succession.

And love. At last. But the *rahke* in her heart twisted deeper.

"Watch out for the pikes," she whispered. A single tear trailed down her cheek. "If you charge him straight on, his troops will square up with pikes on the outside. They'll butcher your horse if you're not careful."

"*Na'lanna...*"

She smiled, but her chin quivered. "He'll have a reserve, too. Light cavalry, the quicker to flee the battlefield if things go badly. They're likely on the high point above the river. His soldiers always fold easily. His Captain is feared but not respected, and they'll fear you more."

Leaning down so close his nose to.uched hers, he let all the love and determination in his heart roar through the bond. "I love you."

Her voice rasped and she shuddered against him. "Take care of yourself. While they lack courage, Pellans fight dirty. They've been known to poison their blades."

"I fight for your love, Shannari. I fight for you. You will return to the Plains with me."

She broke eye contact, dropping her gaze to his mouth. "I can't."

"You can, and you will. I'm warrior enough to find you wherever you go. I'll drag you kicking and screaming all the way back to the Plains, where I will earn so many white *kae'als* you'll nigh never walk again."

Nothing. No spark of fury in her beautiful eyes. No tightening of her mouth with rage. Not even a hint of color on her pale cheeks. She didn't reach for her sword or threaten him in any way.

"Try walking away from me, *na'lanna*."

A sad, fragile smile softened her lips. "Good bye, Khul."

He wanted to throw his head back and howl. If his honor didn't depend on defending what he claimed for the Sha'Kae al'Dan, he would wrap her tight to his heart and ride for the Plains at a dead run. "I challenge you to love me, *na'lanna*."

"I'll never forget you."

His heart thudded in his chest so loudly, so hard, he thought he would surely die. How could she refuse him now? How could she reject his love, his honor, his protection, after all the love they'd shared on the Plains?

"Look at me, Shannari. Where is your heart?"

Hoarsely, she whispered, "My heart is dead. It always has been. I told you, I warned you, I begged you to leave me here before it was too late for you."

Gripping her shoulders, he shook her hard enough her teeth slammed together, trying to find a spark of her courage—even her anger—that he could flame into passion.

She stared back at him with dull eyes. His proud, strong warrior woman was defeated. She'd stood against his warriors, fought courageously, survived Death Riders, battled him toe to toe. Yet she stared back at him now, broken and defeated as he'd never seen her before.

"Your warriors need you. Go, Khul."

"I shall come for you wherever you go. Against all outlanders, against all Nine Camps, against your father, your enemies. Great Vulkar help me, against your Blessed Lady if needs be. I shall come for you against any and all who stand against me. Do you understand?"

"I understand," she said softly. Another tear fell.

Vulkar help him, he was tempted to throw her to the ground here and now and ravage some sense into her. If needs be, he would order Gregar to assist him. Surely between the two of them they could convince her to fight this destiny suffocating her very heart.

"Let me go, Khul. Before I break you. Before you lose your honor. Before those *kae'als* fall from your hair. Let me go. I'm not worth fighting for."

He drew her close for a hard, searing kiss, a domination of teeth, a promise. "Never. I'll die for you, *na'lanna*."

He let her slide to the ground, but it was the hardest thing he'd ever done in his entire life. "I'll leave Gregar—"

"Nay." Gregar stared down at the *kae'don*, his face and voice just as flat as hers. "She's made her choice. Let her live or die with it."

Tightening his grip on his *rahke*, Rhaekhar contemplated cutting out the Blood's heart. Fury and fear warred in him. While she stood there, shoulders slumped, head down, tears dripping onto her chest.

*It will kill me to leave her.*

*But the Blood's right.*

He laughed harshly. It was better than weeping. "I want all of you, all of your heart, all day, all night, for the rest of your life. Until you want me the same way—"

Swallowing back a curse, he touched his heel to Khan's flank and galloped for the *kae'don*. But the greatest battle of all raged in his heart.

S hannari couldn't bear to watch him ride away. It took all her control and determination to stifle the entreaties and apologies screaming in her heart. She wanted to run after him, screaming at him to come back, that she—

Swallowing painfully, she brushed away the tears. *Blessed Lady above, it's so hard. So hard to hurt him, to refuse him, when I want what he offers with all my heart.*

Duty weighed heavily on her shoulders.

She heard the horses coming, lighter than the mighty warhorses. She knew exactly who approached, so she didn't bother to turn around.

"Princess Shannari, imagine meeting you here." Stephan laughed softly and reached down his hand to haul her up in front of him. "Would you like to be rescued?"

Reluctantly, she looked up into his face. A small, smug smile quirked his lips. Clean shaven, his hair queued at his neck, dashing in a brilliant blue coat, the sight of him turned her stomach. Fighting back the sobs threatening to overwhelm her, she ignored his hand and grasped the back of his saddle, hoisting herself up behind him.

"I love your ensemble. It'll be all the rage at Court, I'm sure."

The thought of his pale, filthy gaze on her skin—so much skin—made her ill. She longed for a tub of steaming water, stiff bristle, and soap strong enough to burn her eyes. She doubted she'd ever feel clean again after touching him.

Refusing to remark or react in any way to indicate her discomfort, she chose inquiry. "How many troops did you bring? From what I see, you won't hold the field for long."

Stephan led his men away from the battlefield and Dalden Bay. She had no idea where he would take her. Shanhasson? Surely not yet. "Trust me."

Her stomach heaved and a sound of disgust managed to escape her clenched lips.

"I have a few surprises planned for the barbarians. Did you know the libraries in Shanhasson indicate the Crown Prince Raulf was held captive by the Sha'Kae al'Dan in the last invasion? He managed to escape and return home, minus a few fingers and all his sanity, I'm afraid. In his journals, he wrote that the barbarians possessed absolutely no armor. They have no defense against, say, archers."

Instant worry flooded her. He was right—archers could stand well off the field and pick Rhaekhar's warriors off one by one. Before she stopped to think through the consequences, she reached for him through the bond.

A throbbing wall of black and red blocked her. Fury, terror, shame, desperation, sorrow roiling in a storm of agony.

*I broke his heart. I defeated the greatest warrior on the Plains who'd never lost a challenge, never lost a* kae'don, *until me. I abandoned him.*

Gregar, too. The Shadowed Blood had sworn no blade would ever touch her, as long as she allowed him to stay at her back. Simply thinking of him brought a killing frost to his bond, the icy aloneness of the coldest winter night. She'd refused him, too, when he'd taken a knife for her. When he would give his life to protect her.

*Lady, forgive me.*

Blinking back another wave of tears, she pulled herself together as Stephan halted before a small stone chapel. A cold ball of dread lodged itself in the pit of her stomach. Silently, she dismounted. With another sly little smile, Stephan followed and offered his arm to escort her inside. Suppressing a shudder of revulsion, she lightly laid her hand on his arm and walked into the Lady of the Bay Chapel.

Father Aran stood before the altar. Tears flowed again. He was shrunken, aged, so small and forlorn. She'd abandoned him, too, disregarded his premonitions. She'd harshly rejected his counsel. What had he said when she left Dalden Bay? *Sometimes the Lady washes our eyes with tears. An ocean of tears.*

"Father, I would like to make this lovely woman my wife."

Father Aran raised his sorrowful, ancient gaze to hers. "Is this the man you want, Daughter of Leesha?"

His pain and regret tied her heart into knots. No "Your Majesty," but Daughter. Daughter of the Lady. The Blessed Lady of Peace and Love. *Love. The one thing I refuse to give.*

Sobs wracked her throat, shaking her shoulders.

"Does the Lady's Moon shine in his eyes?"

Squeezing her eyes shut, Shannari could only smell baking bread, sweet hay and flowers, horses, warrior. Her warrior. She felt again the hot velvet of his skin, the hard press of his invincible strength against her, the tenderness in his big, rugged hands, the golden blaze of the sun in his burnished eyes. Not the moon, exactly, but filled with such boundless love she knew the Lady would approve.

A hint of dark rich caffe flavored his sweet hay. Wicked laughter, shining obsidian eyes like the night sky filled with flaming stars. The Lady would approve of the Blood, too.

Her blood pulsed in her veins, leaping with longing, screaming with loss. Their blood was hers, now. How many times had they offered blood freely and gladly? Even now, she tasted the rich, smoky taste of them both in her mouth, the metallic salty sweetness rolling on her tongue. She felt the blaze of heat in the pit of her stomach, the clench of her inner muscles, the bitter ache of her heart.

"Search your heart, Daughter. Answer truthfully. Is this the man you wish to wed?"

Heart pounding, she saw the lake in her mind from her dreams. A full moon hung over mirrored waters; a jagged peaked mountain glowed red in the distance. Only a dream she'd created in her mind to allow her to escape her duty? Or a true message from the Lady?

*WE SENT HIM.*

*DO NOT BE AFRAID TO LOVE.*

"Only love can use the Rose Crown. Only love can defeat the Blackest Heart. Only love can shine against the Shadow."

*Love, the greatest gift of all. And the greatest sacrifice.*

Father Aran's voice trembled with strain. "Will you sacrifice for Stephan, Duke of Pella?"

She saw again the *rahke* coming for her heart, Rhaekhar's golden eyes gleaming with bloodlust and his unshakeable love. *I'd rather die at his hands than live without him.*

If the price of her life was required, she'd pay it for him. She would give him blood. She would give him her body. She would give him her loyalty, her knowledge of politics and strategy.

*I would give him my love.*

Even if it meant dying. Even if it meant losing everything. *A way is provided. A way to love, even for my scarred, shriveled heart.*

*:I love you.:*

"This isn't the man I'll wed." She opened her eyes and smiled through the tears. "The Lady's Moon shines in Khul Rhaekhar's eyes. I'll marry him and no other."

"The barbarian?" Stephan laughed, a murderous edge in his voice. He seized her arm, hauling her up against him, his ghastly eyes flashing. "Have you forgotten the High Throne, Shannari? Who else can give it to you but me?"

"The Last Daughter needs no one to give her the High Throne or the Rose Crown." Father Aran stood straighter and his eyes gleamed with luminance. The smile of joy and pride on his face warmed her heart. "The Lady has washed your eyes with tears, Your Majesty, so you may See."

Cold water suddenly overflowed from that still lake in her mind, startling a gasp from her. Ice dripped down her spine, cutting like razorblades. Her stomach heaved so hard she vomited. Her knees collapsed, and the only thing holding her up was so foul, so tainted...

Slowly, she turned her head. Blackness swirled about Stephan. Touching her. Stroking her. Screaming for her death, blood, and agony. Instead of his face, a naked skull leered at her, snakes of evil curling from his mouth like repulsive tongues.

"Make your choice, Shannari. Marry me, or go to Theo in

chains. Imagine the rewards he'll give me for bringing you to Shanhasson at last."

"Never," she gasped. *My sword. Kill him. Before—*

Her arm wouldn't move. Fighting back the darkness sucking her down, she rolled her head, trying to see, trying to fight. Soldiers. They held her arms.

She jerked and thrashed, fighting the foulness that seeped into her with each breath, but they shackled her in chains so heavy she could hardly move. Father Aran closed his eyes, his mouth moving in a low prayer. Before the Lady could intervene, Stephan casually backhanded him with the butt of his dagger.

The aged High Priest staggered and went down, so still she wasn't sure he breathed.

"Well, well, well." Stephan stepped over the puddle of sickness, the jeweled dagger in his hand. "You were so close to deposing the Crown Prince. I would have been delighted to be of service to you in your quest. Now, I'm afraid I must be the instrument of your defeat."

One of the black snakes writhing from his mouth licked her cheek. Cringing, she turned away, but she couldn't escape the Shadows touching him. Touching her.

"Such a waste to give you to Theo. He'll delight in ruining such loveliness." Stephan reached into a pocket inside his coat and slipped a silver cap on the end of his index finger. "My... tastes... aren't quite so... scarring."

Shame and horror suffocated her. She should never have come here. Such a betrayal. Rejecting Rhaekhar's honor and love, for this... this... monster. *How could I have been so stupid? So foolish? So blind?*

Love had been there in her heart all along. If she'd only opened her eyes, her heart, as the Lady willed, then she could have struck down both Stephan and Theo with her power.

Instead of standing here defeated and chained, vulnerable before such utter evil.

*Now, it's too late.*

Stephan pointed the silver cap on his finger at her, waving it up and down, side to side, so she saw the vicious point on the end. A nasty smile twisted his face. "Before surrendering you to Theo, I want a small memento of our broken alliance. I believe I'll be the first to taste this rich, royal blood."

Her breathing hitched, terror clawing her throat. The end of the cap was a needle. A silver needle. Desperate, she struggled against the chains and the men holding her. "You won't be the first."

She couldn't free her sword, couldn't even work her hand over to touch it. Slamming her skull back, she smashed a soldier's nose so hard he bellowed.

"Hold her!"

More soldiers stepped in to assist. Someone threw a length of chain around her throat, crushing her windpipe.

Stephan touched the fresh bite mark on her right shoulder at the base of her neck. "Ah, I see the barbarian has indeed beaten me to the task."

Agony sliced through her. Sagging in the chains, she fought to remain conscious. Cold sucked her down. So dark.

"What a hulking brute to simply bite you, albeit effective. I'll be much more..." He smiled widely and lightly tapped the needle against her cheek. "Creative."

Terror shrilled through her, her head throbbing in agony with the Lady's warning. Pain drove some of the darkness away, allowing her to think. Sharp but not long, the needle scratched a path toward the vein pumping frantically in her throat. Blood welled in a delicate puncture. Not too deeply. Not yet.

*He'll be careful not to kill me, but then he'll be able to sense my thoughts and emotions.*

*A piece of my soul will be his. Forever.*

Oh, Lady, she couldn't bear to let him corrupt what had become so sacred to her. So intimate. Ruined forever by this instrument of evil.

The mirrored lake in her mind shattered. Icy water bubbled up inside her, building pressure until she opened her mouth to scream.

*:RHAEKHAR!:*

Water poured from her mouth, spraying Stephan in the face. Screaming, he clawed at his eyes and stumbled away.

Choking, drowning, her lungs full of water, Shannari fell into a yawning cavern of darkness.

## 24

T rampling outlanders should have been at least entertaining. After hours of doing just that while his every instinct bellowed at him to charge after Shannari, Rhaekhar quickly wearied of the game. He kneed his stallion straight into the last surviving fist of archers, cursing and growling beneath his breath. *One last surge, and I'll be free to gallop north. To Shannari.*

Warriors whooped and galloped ahead, chasing each fleeing outlander and running them down beneath punishing hooves. He let them have the small honor. He had more important worries on his mind and heart.

His skin blazed with urgency, flesh trying to crawl off his bones. Again, he sought her through the bond but met only blackness. No dream, no thought, no emotion. He hoped she was merely injured, perhaps knocked unconscious. Better than dead or lost to Shadow entirely.

"She isn't dead." Gregar rode up beside him, his face grim. "You would know."

"*We* would know."

Gregar refused to meet his inquiring gaze. "She spoke to your mind, your heart, Khul. She admitted her love for you. I'm more pleased than I can say."

"She thought of you, too. She felt your bond."

"Aye. But she'll never admit more."

Vulkar knew how hard Rhaekhar had fought to hear those three words. *I love you.* And now this horrible emptiness where her bond should be.

Varne drew up beside them. "Dalden Bay is yours once more, Khul. Shall we ride for the Plains?"

Gregar reached over and broke off the arrow embedded in Varne's thigh. "We ride north."

Varne grunted but his face remained inscrutable. "She made her choice. Let her live or die by it. Is this not what you said?"

"Aye." Gregar shrugged and winked at Rhaekhar. "She changed her mind. Khul won't leave *na'lanna* behind."

Rhaekhar turned Khan north without a backward glance. Her bond was still a dark void, but he could feel that emptiness. How far away, exactly, he couldn't say. With a shrill whistle, he drew Athgart's attention. "Take another fist and secure the village!"

The remaining two fists fell in behind him, speeding their *na'kindren* to a hard trot to keep pace with him.

"Are you sure two fists are enough, Khul?" Varne frowned, scanning both sides of the wide well-traveled trail they followed for danger. "We may encounter resistance."

"Then I'll crush them." Why didn't she awaken? Who inspired such fear in her, such sickness? His stomach twisted and rumbled at the memory of the final moments before her bond had gone so still. "I shall kill whoever harms her."

The first twinge of her bond drew a shaking breath from him. Relief flooded him and he shared a wide smile with Gregar.

Until she screamed in his mind.

:RHAEKHAR!:

:Na'lanna, *I'm coming for you.*:

:*I'll be dead by then.*: Calming at his touch, she sent wave after wave of regret to him. :*I'm so sorry. I was wrong, terribly wrong. I love you, and I wish*—:

:*Hold that wish in your heart, na'lanna, and I shall make it so.*:

:*Tell Gregar*—:

:*Tell him yourself.*: Rhaekhar watched his Blood closely, waiting to see a sign that she did so.

:*I can't. He can't hear my words.*:

:*He doesn't need words, na'lanna. Feel for him, let your heart call to him. He'll hear you.*:

Squeezing his eyes shut, Gregar shuddered and drew his *rahke.* He rolled it back and forth across his palm, his hand shaking.

:*Pella took me to Shanhasson.*: Rhaekhar felt her trembling, her dread. :*He's taking me to Theo, the new High King. Unofficially, since Father Aran hasn't coronated him yet. He will, though, in an attempt to buy me time.*:

:*What will Theo do?*:

Her silence was the answer. Grim and deadly.

:*We'll reach you in a few hours. Hold on, na'lanna.*:

:*No time.*: Her fear escalated, shredding at his control. :*We're going in now. Besides, you can't breach the Shining Walls.*:

:*If you're held beyond, then I shall.*:

Someone jerked her, wrenching her shoulder. For a moment, the bond blazed so strongly that he saw her: heavy links of chain wrapped around her delicate wrists, neck, and ankles; bruises darkening her skin; midnight eyes huge in her pale face; chin and head up as they dragged her into a cavernous room full of fancily dressed outlanders.

"She walks... into a place of such... Shadow." Gregar rasped, his breathing labored. "We must—"

"Khul!" The forward scout reined his *na'kindre* to a sliding halt. "Outlanders hold the way ahead!"

"Great Vulkar! How many?"

"Nearly forty fists."

Rhaekhar pounded his fist on his thigh. Any other day he would be interested in trying such odds, but not while *na'lanna* was in such dire danger.

*:I'm sorry it took me so long to give up the fight.:* Wry amusement and heartache shimmered in her bond. *:I surrender to your challenge.:*

*:Don't give up,* na'lanna.*:* Rhaekhar seized her chin through the bond, sending all his pride and honor to her, his confidence in her heart and courage. *:Fight. Stay alive. Help comes.:*

*:Good bye. I love you.:*

Thinking fast, he turned to Gregar, who straightened expectantly. "Can you slip through these outlanders unseen?"

"Aye, easily."

"Can you find her in this place of Shadow and bring her out?"

"Aye, Khul. They'll die before they see me."

"Ride, then. I shall continue as I'm able once I win this *kae'don*."

"My blood is yours, Khul, and my blood is hers. It's an honor to serve you both." Gregar touched his heel lightly to his *na'kindre's* flank and the black leaped ahead. The Blood had flown through the air to save her before. Would he reach her in time once more?

"What will you do with these outlanders?" Varne asked.

"Whatever I must to win passage northward. I shall challenge their khul or cut a path straight through them to the Three Hells and beyond. I won't remain far behind Gregar."

Looking northward, he scanned the horizon. Gregar and his black *na'kindre* were gone. No thundering hoof beats, no hint of thickening shadows, nothing but a faint hint of ice trickling down his spine. Rhaekhar felt a predatory smile twist his face.

*I shall fight Shadow with Shadow. Fly, my Shadowed Blood.*

Shannari's father had always compared Shanhasson to a pit of vipers, and the welcome Stephan received at the Palace confirmed it. She'd been unconscious for most of the rapid trip up the river, but she took careful note of the lords who bowed and scraped to Stephan as he dragged her to the High Court.

The Steward swung open the heavily carved and gilded doors. "Princess Shannari dal'Dainari of Allandor and Father Aran, Our Blessed Lady's High Priest, escorted by Stephan, Duke of Pella."

Silence fell in the High Court. Nobles lined up between the massive marble columns. Staring at her, some were shocked. Some horrified. All of them planned how they could use her defeat to their advantage. They were like a pack of starving hyenas, ready to turn on each other for a scrap of the downed doe.

Shuffling and clanking with each step down the red-carpeted aisle toward the dais, Shannari struggled to keep her head high despite the chains dragging at her. Despite the foulness rolling off the man grasping her elbow in a mockery of escort. Despite the pulsing black miasma cloaking the High Throne ahead.

The lake shimmered in her mind, smooth and undisturbed once more, but she couldn't forget the flood of water, the brittle, cutting ice. Stephan's right cheek was puffy and inflamed, streaked with red, and his eye was swollen shut entirely. As if she'd spewed acid on him.

The Lady's power. Love was in her heart at last, so why not? *If only I can figure out how to use it to protect myself from Theo.*

Father Aran stumbled along beside her on her left. Dried

blood streaked his elderly face and he'd remained unconscious right up until they walked into the High Court. Gasping, he fell against her.

She caught him awkwardly despite the chains.

"Power awakens," he whispered urgently. "Through you, Our Blessed Lady shows Her love and light in the world. Power doesn't come every time, though. Some—"

The Pellan soldier yanked him away. Shannari kept her gaze locked on the gorgeous stained glass window in the wall far above the High Throne. The blood-red glass roses cast a mosaic of light on the white marble. So beautiful. And on the Great Seal beneath her feet, made of stone instead of glass, more roses and rampant lions to match the lions arched above the High Throne on either side.

Reluctantly, she raised her gaze to her fiancé and concentrated on not quaking like a leaf in a hurricane.

Theo dan'Regis dan'Rikard lounged in the High Throne, his face shadowed by the massive lion statues pawing the air high above him. His shaved head gleamed in the fading sunlight filtered through the lions' paws. A thick cord of ebony hair growing from the base of his neck hung over his slender shoulder. Gleaming with oil, his prince's lock was banded with gold at various distances to represent the length at each of his twenty birthdays.

He leaned forward, revealing his face, and her skin crawled. Blue eyes like her own, only cold and hard, like the eyes of a snake. Or was that merely her imagination?

Theo was her cousin, descended mostly from the same royal line. Yet the twisted sneer of malice on his face spoke of hatred and cruelty that she didn't—couldn't—understand. A byproduct of living in Shanhasson, twisted by the Blackest Heart, Lord of Darkness, who was imprisoned somehow deep beneath the

Palace? Or had Theo been born with a thread of shadow and evil that only grew over time?

*Born from the same blood as me.*

Her teeth chattered and goose bumps prickled up her arms, making her shiver. The air was thick and foul, musty and rotten like a corpse. Breath shallowly, she tried not to draw that taint into her lungs. Would she be as corrupt as he if she'd grown up locked within these Shining Walls? Or was it already too late for her, as she feared?

What of the grand throng, the rest of the nobles who lived and dined and played politics in the High Court? How could they not see the madness in Theo's eyes? The evil? How could they not smell the rank odor of corpse that choked her?

In his oh-so pleasant voice, Stephan said, "Kneel before the High King."

Straightening to her full height, Shannari refused. "The Crown Prince hasn't been coronated by the High Priest."

"He will be." Still pleasant, Stephan jammed his fist into her lower back. Gasping, she fell onto her knees, barely catching herself before planting her face on the marble. "Right, Father? Because if you don't coronate the Crown Prince, it will be my grim duty to slit the lovely Princess's throat. She's a traitor after all, plotting to steal the High Throne for herself."

Pain pulsed deep inside. For a moment, she feared he might have jabbed the silver cap into her back. Wheezing on her hands and knees, Shannari watched jeweled slippers come into her line of vision and pace around her.

"Why Stephan, my old friend, how can I reward you for at last bringing my fiancée to Shanhasson? Naughty, naughty Princess to have left me waiting so very long." A wooden heel trod on her hand, and Theo twisted his foot to grind her finger hard against the marble. "Well, Shannari. Shall we proceed with the ceremony?"

Nausea roiled in her stomach, burning her throat. "I regret to inform you that I broke our engagement."

The sound of their laughter shrieked on her nerves like metal on metal. "Oh, Shannari. You surely know that if you don't marry me, I'll execute you."

"And if I marry you, you'll execute me any way."

"But of course. You've proven untrustworthy."

"You have no idea, Your Majesty. Why, Shannari even tried to lure me into marrying her, offering me the High Throne if I would help her."

The jeweled slipper flew at her head and the diamond tip sliced across her cheek. Twisting away, she rolled onto her back. Hot blood tracked down her face. Her head buzzed and the world felt very distant, thin, stretched as if from a great distance.

*Blood is the key. Blood is the key. Blood is the key.*

Reverberating, the words pounded in her skull. Agony splintered through her. Another kick.

*:Na'lanna:*

Not Rhaekhar's voice in her head. Gregar's. Her heart ached with his admission of love. My beloved.

*:Don't let that cur kick you again or you will owe me two kisses.:*

Laughing raggedly, she blinked away the pain. Theo's foot came at her again, and she threw her hands up and twisted, trapping his ankle in the chains. Mustering all her strength, she jerked her hands up over her head and Theo fell, narrowly missing her. She pushed to her feet and backed away. "Try kicking me again and eat some chain."

Red-faced with fury, Theo scrambled to his feet. "I want her dead. Now."

Soldiers came at her again. What could she do, unarmed and chained? *Nothing but act like the Princess I am.* Holding her head up and her gaze steady, she stared at Theo wordlessly, ignoring the men who grabbed her.

"Over here. On the Great Seal."

They dragged her back to the mosaic. So beautiful, the roses could be real blossoms grown into the stone. Forced to her knees, she felt blessed peace roll over her as Theo sauntered over to her. He wrapped a fist in her hair and jerked her head back, baring her throat.

:Na'lanna!: Rhaekhar's rage poured into her, his fear and frustration sending a shiver through her. She saw him low against Khan's sweating neck, urging the stallion to greater speed. Too far away.

Gregar, too. He was closer, his black horse barely skimming the ground in a dead run. Too far.

*Blessed Lady, thank you for letting me feel love before the end. Take care of them.*

A drop of blood rolled down her cheek, splattered on her breast, and slid in a slow, hot trail.

"Give me a sword." Theo leaned down over her, his face a twisted mask. Softly, he whispered, "It's a shame to kill you so quickly. I had such lovely plans for you, Shannari."

His voice caught on a soft sound of arousal that sent a shrill of dread screaming down her spine. His eyes, so dark, so vile, so black. Flat and dead and drowning in Shadow. He traced a finger down her cheek, smearing in the blood. Closing his eyes, he raised her blood toward his lips.

A drop of her blood fell onto the Great Seal.

Power rippled outward, a shockwave of chilling water, pure moonlight, joy and light and love. Theo jerked back. Eyes wide, he stumbled off the Great Seal and scrubbed his hand on his powder blue breeches. "Did you feel that?"

Stephan stood at the edge of the Great Seal, carefully not touching even the tip of his gleaming boots on the mosaic. "Feel what, Your Majesty?"

Father Aran's voice rang out in the High Court. "Only Our Blessed Lady may judge one of Her Children fit for execution!"

"This is my Court, my Throne!" Theo snarled, his fear making his rage all the worse. "I'm the Crown Prince, and the High Throne is mine! Leesha holds no power here! Shannari dal'-Dainari must die!"

The marble floor rocked beneath Shannari's knees. Several nobles cried out in fear. Theo's gaze darted from her to Stephan to the High Priest, his desperation mounting. Like a rabid cornered animal, he might leap in any direction. Who would he attack first?

"The High Priest is right." One of the nobles came forward, King Challon of the North Forest. Why would he stand forward in her defense? She didn't know and really didn't care, as long as she kept her head awhile longer. "Princess Shannari is the Last Daughter, the only one who may wear the Rose Crown and live, let alone wield its power. If you want to be High King alone, then I suggest you choose your Champion for a Trial by Blood."

Stephan stood beside Theo. With narrowed gaze, he studied his uncle, but nodded thoughtfully. "King Challon speaks wisely. Imprison the Princess while you choose your Champion, Your Majesty."

Hatred twisted Theo's face until he looked like a demon. Sweat beaded his upper lip and his hands clutched repeatedly. He pulled on his prince's lock so hard his head jerked sideways. Fingering that long hank of hair, he got a nasty look of smugness in his eyes.

He waved a Lion Guard over and pointed at her. "Drag her over here by her hair."

Sliding across the floor, trying to keep the tears of pain back, she dropped her weight to the side in an attempt to jerk out of the soldier's grasp. But the Lion Guard merely yanked harder until she knelt at the Crown Prince's feet.

Theo tugged her hair away from her face. The hair that had never been cut, a sign of her royal blood. She didn't think it would bother her, but it did. He took her hair, jagged cut by cut, until her once royal mark hung hacked and rough about her face.

"Take her to the dungeons." He gathered her shorn hair into his hands and lifted it, breathing deeply. A shudder swept through him. Lust darkened his eyes—not for her body, exactly, but with his need to maim and torture her. His breeches strained at the front with his obvious desire.

The thought of how close she'd come to being trapped in marriage to such a foul, perverted monster made dark spots dance before her eyes. Lightheaded, she couldn't stand when the Lion Guards tugged on her arms. They dragged her, stumbling, out the side door, through a narrow hallway, down stairs and more stairs and more, deeper into the bowels of the earth.

The dream that haunted her. Blood thundered in her ears and her stomach rolled. *The Blackest Heart of Darkness waits down here.*

*For me.*

## 25

L eaving the warriors lined up to charge as in a *kae'don*, Rhaekhar rode forward with only his eight remaining Blood. Time was of the essence. He had no doubt he could win this *kae'don* as any other, but how long would it take? He could ill afford any delay.

A group of outlanders on ponies rode out bearing a white flag on a pole. The two parties drew to a halt.

Valche, Shannari's father. Shaking his head, Rhaekhar dismounted. As much as he disliked this outlander, she wouldn't appreciate him dishonoring her father or butchering her soldiers. What did the man hope to accomplish by delaying him from reaching Shannari in time to help her?

"Khul."

"King." Rhaekhar gripped the hilt of his *rahke* but left his sword sheathed. He hoped to avoid bloodshed, for this outlander wouldn't understand such honor. "Why do you delay me when your daughter's very life hangs in the balance?"

Valche started and then narrowed his gaze. "Stephan, the

Duke of Pella, marched on Dalden Bay with nearly every soldier he possesses. I decided to take advantage of the situation and attack the victor. Why would Shannari's life be in danger? Where is she?"

"Pella took her while I was occupied in the *kae'don*."

Valche's face paled and he sagged with dismay. "Blessed Lady! Where is she? What did he do with her?"

"I don't know, other than she suffers great pain and is in the gravest danger imaginable. She's somewhere north of here."

"North? He must have taken her to Shanhasson." Valche ran a trembling hand through his hair. "Not yet, not yet. Damnation. I don't have enough allies yet! Not enough troops!"

"I ride north with all speed. Do you ride with me or against me?"

"Didn't you hear me? We don't have enough troops to take Shanhasson! We can't—"

Rhaekhar contemplating shaking some sense into the outlander. "I don't need troops. I don't need you. I simply thought Shannari would like to see you again."

"Why are you doing this? What do you hope to gain?"

He smiled and mounted Khan. "I do this for *na'lanna*, my beloved, my heart. I do this for my future Khul'lanna. I do this for a love like no other. I do this so Shannari might live. Now get your outlanders out of my way before I kill them all."

"Khul'lanna? Like your queen?"

"Her wish will be second only to mine on the Plains."

Valche arched an eyebrow, a gleam of interest—or greed—in his eyes. "How many warriors can you raise for her?"

Rhaekhar gave him a hard, vicious smile. "Thousands."

Valche brightened. "Like these?"

Rhaekhar nodded.

"Theo and Stephan will try to kill her."

"I shall kill them first." A sudden wash of terror made him

growl. Drawing his *rahke*, he stared northward. *Shannari*. Danger approached once more, such dire danger she thought she would surely die. *Fly, my Shadowed Blood!*

F ighting back her terror, Shannari stood to the right of the cell door. With her back pressed tight against the dank stone, she gripped a femur in both hands over her head. It was the only weapon she could find here in the darkness.

Deep in the bowels of the earth, there wasn't any light except a flickering torch down the hall. Damp and foul, the chill air smelled as musty as a grave. Muck and slime coated the floor, dusted with moldering straw.

This was the horrible nightmare of Shadow that had tormented her all these years.

The heavy door rattled, ramping her heartbeat even higher. At least the guards had removed the chains before shoving her into the tiny cell. In her weakened condition, she wasn't going to be able to put up much of a fight. Was this Theo's assassin? Or the nightmare coming true at last?

Her stomach heaved with the memory of shadows writhing down her throat.

The door creaked open. Tightening her grip, she gathered her waning strength. *I must strike first.*

"Your Majesty?"

Startled, she jerked the bone aside, barely missing the elderly priest. "Father Aran!"

"Hurry, there's not much time." Strong and sure, the High Priest pushed a coarse monk's robe over her head and pulled the cowl up to hide her face. "Come with me and speak to no one."

She let the bone club fall from her numb fingers and crept after him. When she'd been locked in the forgotten cell deep in the earth in those dreams with the Heart of Darkness coming for her, no one had ever heard her screams. Let alone helped her.

She certainly never expected Our Blessed Lady's own priest to come for her. *Perhaps the Lady truly has heard my prayers.*

A guard led the way down a dark passage that tunneled even deeper beneath the castle.

"How much farther?" The High Priest's soft voice barely reached her.

"The maps are very old, Father, but we should be almost be there. Yes, here it is."

They paused before an offshoot tunnel to the right. Water dripped somewhere. Wet and slick, the clay floor hinted at an underground spring or river nearby. The heat had risen so high that she swiped sweat out of her eyes.

"This tunnel bypasses the mineral springs that supply the Palace's hot water and should take you outside the inner walls. Keep going straight and don't take any of the branches."

"Very good, Ilko. May Our Lady bless you for your help tonight."

The guard bowed respectfully to them both and then turned back the way they had come. "I must return to duty before I'm missed. Goodbye, Father, Princess."

The escape tunnel made for slow going. Treacherously slick, the clay floor sucked at her feet until her calves ached. She slipped several times and almost fell flat on her back in the muck. The heat worsened, as did the smell of something rotten.

Retching, she resorted to clamping her nose shut. "I heard about the mineral springs beneath the Palace of Shanhasson, but I never dreamed they smelled so bad."

Father Aran halted in the middle of the tunnel. With his eyes closed, he listened intently, turning his head back and forth.

She listened but didn't hear anything but the occasional plop of water. "Father?"

"The mineral springs don't smell like this."

Then she felt it, too. Her skin itched and crawled with urgency as something slithered down a side branch toward them. The odor of decay intensified and her ears rang with the clamor of her internal alarms. Thick, oppressive shadows congealed in the tunnel like a huge blob of oily night.

"Keep your feet on the chosen path, Shannari dal'Dainari, Daughter of Leesha, destined High Queen of the Lady's Green and Beautiful Lands." His voice hummed with growing power. Opalescent moonlight danced around him, soft and pure and so sweet it hurt her heart. A beautiful, piercing of sweetness like the faint, haunting strain of flute or harp. "Run, Your Majesty."

Automatically, she dropped her hand to her sword, but it was gone. "No, I can't leave you here to fight this alone!"

"This is my choice, my willing sacrifice, for you, Your Majesty. I do this with Our Blessed Lady's love in my heart. I give my life that you may live. Run, Child of Leesha, and Shine against the Shadow!"

Rooted with dread, she watched as the light flared brighter in the tunnel, illuminating the creature of Shadow that approached. When it hesitated at the ring of silvery light, her eyes couldn't make sense of it. As tall and wide as the tunnel, the shapeless mass had arms and legs and snouts and heads too many to count. Too many...

"Run toward the Moon that shines in your eyes. Run to your beloved Evening Stars. Run!"

Unable to tear her stricken gaze away, she stood there trembling. Paralyzed. The monster's faceted eyes glinted at her, the whole multitude, black and hungry and empty. Mouths gaped, opening and closing on a garbled string of grunts and wails she didn't want to understand.

"Sha...RI...Nnar...SHA...Ri...."

She screamed soundlessly in her head. A rumbling roar rolled and crashed inside her, breaking whatever invisible bonds held her immobile. Flinching as shards of glass splintered inside her head, she jerked away from the advancing creature.

A flash of brilliant light shot from Father Aran into the shapeless horror of melted bodies. The gentle rainbowed light became a blinding weapon of pain. Both the creature and the High Priest began to scream.

Galloping toward her with all speed, Rhaekhar gripped her through his bond, dragging her step by shaking step away from the magical battle. His formidable will clamped like an iron fist about her heart. *:Run! Run as you've never done before, na'lanna. Run!:*

Gregar filled her mind, deliberately using his bond to stroke velvet and seductive shadow through her thoughts. *:I'm near, Shannari. Run to me.:*

The Blood was so close. She could almost smell him over the rotten stench of death clogging her nose. Stumbling, slipping, sobbing, she ran with her right hand on the slimy wall of the tunnel and her left wavering at head level to make sure she didn't crash into something. She ran toward the light that must exist somewhere outside this tunnel. She ran toward the beloved barbarian galloping toward her with all speed. She ran toward the wicked laughing Blood who swore no blade would ever touch her.

It was coming behind her. She could hear it, the slurping sound of slime oozing through the tunnel. The horrible legion of voices howling her name in pain and hate. Suffocating shadow of Death stealing her breath, choking on rotten flesh and offal....

Arms snaked around her, holding her fast to a muscled, bare chest. Silken skin against her cheek, satiny heat warming her cold and numb limbs as powerful, gentle hands gathered her close.

With her face pressed into that warm haven, she took a deep, blessedly clean breath. The sweet hay of the Plains mixed with strong and distinctive caffe. She sank into the Blood's embrace and wrapped her arms around his neck.

E nfolded in Gregar's gifts of Shadow and Death, Shannari heard only the steady, comforting beat of his heart. He ran effortlessly through the twisting, slippery tunnel without a single misplaced step, taking her further and further away from madness and hate. She could feel the sweet promise of the light growing, until he burst out of the tunnel into a moonlit clearing.

Breathing rapidly but not winded, he knelt in the circle of dappled moonlight. She fisted her hands in the long fall of hair about his shoulders, trembling. "Oh, Lady! Monsters! The High Court is full of monsters!"

"You're safe, Shannari."

"The monster in the tunnel knew my name! And Theo...." Just remembering the perverted pleasure in the High King's eyes made her stomach heave.

Grabbing the back of her head, Gregar pressed her face deep into the hollow of his neck and shoulder beneath his sable velvet hair. His strong, distinctive scent enveloped her, driving away the horrors. He smelled so good and strong and familiar, her heart hurt.

*Run to your beloved Evening Stars.*

Even Father Aran knew the truth she struggled to deny.

With a low cry, she lifted her mouth to Gregar's. He froze, barely breathing, his hands still on her back. She caressed his lips, tracing them with her tongue, enjoying the fine trembling spreading through his body. When she slid her tongue deeper, tasting the darkest recesses of his mouth, the dam broke.

Rumbling against her mouth, he clutched her hard. He took possession of her mouth, tugging her bottom lip with his teeth, nipping, stroking his tongue against hers and the roof of her mouth.

Now they both panted as though they had run on foot all the way to Dalden Bay. Laughing softly, he pressed his forehead to hers and simply held her. "This is not the day of my death, *na'lanna.*"

"I thought it might be the day of mine." Hearing him call her beloved made her heart hurt all the more. Rhaekhar. She loved him; at last, she could admit it. How could she do this with his nearest Blood?

*:I know your heart,* na'lanna.: Despite the miles between them, Rhaekhar's heat pressed against her back, his big arms wrapping around her in a hug that blended with the Blood's. *:I've been waiting for you to realize the truth. You had to admit your love for me before you could admit your love for Gregar.:*

She felt like weeping. *:I'm sorry.:*

"Why?" Gregar found the slice on her cheek. His fingers dug into her back and he rumbled with pleasure. He licked the dried blood from her skin, carefully cleaning the wound without reopening it. "Love comes as it wills, *na'lanna*. Think you Khul longed to fall in love with an outlander with no understanding of the Sha'Kae al'Dan, when the Nine Camps are slipping further apart day by day? Think you I ached to fall in love with my greatest mark, to face the constant temptation that I would commit such an atrocity, violating the sacred gift Vulkar gave me?"

Swallowing hard, she fought back against her old fears. "You know how I feel about... love. About trust. I can't—"

*How can I say I don't love them both when I do, so very, very much? How could I possibly choose?*

Rhaekhar whispered through the bond. *:I never asked you to choose. You may have us both. I'm warrior enough to allow it.:*

Confusion swept through her. How could he be so... so...

calm? About sharing her heart with another man? If Gregar didn't anger him, what would push him over the edge into a jealous rage?

His answer—a dark rage—rumbled through her body. :*Stephan and Theo push me over that edge, na'lanna. They die as soon as my eyes behold them.*:

She couldn't argue with that oath.

Gregar tensed and drew his ivory knife, shielding her with his body.

A stranger trotted up on a sturdy mount, a priest by the look of his scarlet robes. Tears dampened his cheeks, but he smiled at her shyly. "I'm Josef. Father Aran charged me to see you safely out of Shanhasson, Your Majesty. Leesha weeps with joy as She welcomes him home."

Such a sacrifice. She heard again the High Priest's screams. While she ran. Shame and regret spilled from her eyes like scalding rain. For the first time in her life, she'd run from a fight, and someone else had died.

*It should have been me.*

Gregar's fingers settled on her chin and forced her face up to his. His shadowed eyes flickered with flames. "Even you cannot fight every *kae'don*, let alone single-handedly and unarmed."

She pointedly stared at his vicious knife. "Not single-hand-edly—I have you."

When the Blood's hand tightened on her chin and tilted her mouth up toward him even more, her breath caught in her throat. Need swirled in her abdomen. Longing. And danger.

"Aye, you have me forever. The question is will you actually take me. Will you take *all* that I offer?"

Staring up into his eyes, she felt heat curling in the pit of her stomach, tightening, desire rising. Forbidden desire.

"Not forbidden," he whispered against her mouth. He didn't

kiss her, merely allowing his breath to mingle with hers. Her desire escalated until she groaned out loud. "Ask him."

:*Not forbidden.*: Rhaekhar's bond glowed in her mind, golden and warm like his eyes. She felt only immense relief from him that she was safe and well, mixed with satisfaction. He was actually glad that she'd kissed his Blood. :*I'll never deny you something you need. And you need him,* na'lanna.:

Shame choked her. She squeezed her eyes shut, trying to squeeze her heart shut as well, but it was too late. The barbarian charged toward her, unswerving in his love and honor. He would find her anywhere, ride through anything and anyone, to reach her. Even after her adamant refusals. Even after she'd turned her back on him.

*While I dally with his Blood, one of his best friends. How can he forgive me this unfaithfulness?*

:*There's no shame in the love of your heart,* na'lanna.:

:*I love you.*: Her words came to him in a wail, a cry of anguish.

:*I know.*: Rhaekhar swamped her heart with so much love and joy, that tears burned her eyes. :*And you love him, too. Now get on his* na'kindre *and ride to me as quickly as possible so I may show you exactly how much your love means to me. How much your love means to us both.*:

Gregar was already standing, drawing her up with him. His black horse whuffed, nodding its head and pawing the ground. "Aye, Shaido, we ride hard and fast."

Shannari started to laugh at the thought of conversation with a horse, but then she looked into its gleaming eyes. Luminescent as the moon, and frighteningly intelligent. The horse winked at her, and she swore it was laughing.

Mounting quickly, Gregar leaned down and offered his hand. A wicked gleam flashed in his eyes. Would she ride in his arms as she allowed Khul to carry her? Or would she refuse him, riding behind as she'd done with Stephan?

Grumbling, she took Gregar's hand and let him haul her up

before him. He wrapped her close, pulling her up beneath his chin and shaking his hair down around her. The sable pelt was heavier than Rhaekhar's hair, more like velvet. Sinful velvet. "Wasn't Drendon supposed to provide my own mount?"

Gregar chuckled and turned his mount south, setting the pace to a hard trot. "Aye, but finding your perfect *na'kindre* has proven difficult. Khul is very choosy and hasn't been able to find what he wants for you yet. Drendon was quite insulted and nearly challenged him to another *kae'rahke*."

Father Josef reined up beside them. "What think you of our self-proclaimed High King, Your Majesty?"

Shannari had to push Gregar's hair out of her face so she could speak. "I think the Green Lands are doomed to darkness under his rule."

"We've been praying for Theo's removal from the royal line for quite some time." Father Josef admitted. "Our Blessed Lady knows the heart of every man and woman, Your Majesty. Theo's been careful to keep most of his cruelty hidden from everyone, but we saw, and we heard, and we prayed for your safe return to the Green Lands."

"As long as he lives, there's no safety in the Green Lands for me." Remembering Theo's hatred and perversion made her skin crawl. "Besides, I—" She sighed, struggling to find the words. How could she tell the holy priests who prayed for her safety that she planned to abandon them?

"Father Aran agreed wholeheartedly, Your Majesty. He regretted the manner in which he sent you to safety on the Plains, but it was the only way."

*A way will be provided.*

WE SENT HIM TO SAVE YOU. WE SENT HIM TO LOVE YOU.

Her throat clogged with tears. All this time, she'd clung to duty and politics, what she'd assumed Leesha's will must be. While Our Blessed Lady had sent her the love she needed to gain her magic and safety from Theo's minions. *And I fought every step of the way.*

"Our Lady's will isn't easy to understand, Your Majesty." Father Josef reached out to her, hesitating at a low warning rumble from Gregar. "We're only human. We can only do our best, pray for guidance, and follow our heart."

*Follow my heart—all the way back to Rhaekhar.*

The Blood tightened his arms around her and dropped his chin against her shoulder. She sighed. After so long, she'd feared, even hoped, she'd never love again. Now she had not one but two obstinate, arrogant, demanding warriors to deal with. "And to you, too."

Wicked pleasure surged through his bond, followed by a dark, aching longing that stole her breath. Instead of following through with that yearning, Gregar eased his grip and straightened, his bond hardening with determination. Her body screamed danger, threat, death at her back, her blind spot, but she ignored it and wiggled deeper into his embrace.

A rock-hard erection dug into her lower back. Heat flooded her, clenching her thigh muscles and making her stomach flutter. Hadn't he told her he was above such feelings as Blood?

*:Not when you look at me and feel such desire. I'm not made of stone, na'lanna. Not even a Blood bond could prevent a warrior from responding to you.:*

For a moment, she felt a sharpness in his bond. Bitterness? Jealousy?

*:You have corrupted me entirely.:* His bond wound through her, stroking like his incredible hair and tightening her body even more. He laughed in her head, so wicked and dangerous and utterly irresistible. *:I beg you, corrupt me some more.:*

The priest gasped softly. Grateful for the interruption, Shannari searched his face. "What is it?"

"I See—" His eyes were soft and dreamy, his voice gentle.

"When I first saw you, the Rose Crown was on your head, just as Father Aran told me long ago. Now, though, I also See a dark green cape about your shoulders and a white knife in your hand. I don't know what they mean."

"I do," Gregar replied, his voice smug.

Irritated at the leap of her pulse and the immediate hope and joy flooding her heart, she retorted, "I can't be both Khul'lanna and High Queen at the same time."

Gregar deliberately pressed his groin tighter against her back, grinding against her until she made a sound unfortunately close to a whimper. "Who says you cannot?"

Damned Sha'Kae al'Dan clothing. *What I wouldn't give for a full suit of armor.* "I must rule the Green Lands from the High Throne."

"That's not entirely true," Father Josef said slowly. "Our Blessed Lady dictates that only a Child of Her Blood may rule from the High Throne, true. But Her protection and blessings on the land come through the Rose Crown, not the High Throne itself. Theo can't touch the Rose Crown. If he did, you would no longer be in danger, for he'd drop dead immediately."

Shannari's mind whirled with strategy and politics. The Green Lands were too loosely aligned to allow a successful rule from a distance. Not long term, at least. But if she made regular trips to Shanhasson... She'd have to talk through things with her father, but they might make it work. "What exactly do you recommend?"

"I See the green cape on your shoulders, as firm and solid as the Rose Crown. Once you eliminate Theo—" Father Josef shrugged and smiled. "You're the Rose of Shanhasson, Your Majesty. The Last Daughter. None will be able to refuse you."

"Why didn't my mother take the Rose Crown then? Why did she live in exile in Allandor, only to die at the hands of an assassin?"

Father Josef's face tightened, grim grooves lining his mouth. "Rikard never allowed her near the Rose Crown. As she came into her power, she fled Shanhasson and swore to never return. Why, I don't know. But I assure you, Your Majesty, once the Rose Crown is on your head, none will stand against you."

---

Pointing to the southwest, Father Josef asked, "What's that?"

The night sky glowed red. Unless an entire village was on fire, the only thing she could think of that would create such a glow was—

"Campfires, a great many of them." Gregar drew his horse to a halt, his voice grim. "Friend or foe, Shannari?"

"We're still in Shanhasson, so foe. But Theo doesn't have that many troops, does he?"

"The entire Shanhasson Guard only numbers a few hundred troops," Father Josef replied. "He wouldn't send his whole force away and leave himself vulnerable."

"I have a very bad feeling about this. Gregar, can you get close enough to see what flags they carry? Their exact number?"

"Will you kiss me again?" He whispered against her ear, his voice husky. "I want your hands in my hair, your tongue wrapped around mine, your scent in my nose, your body aching with need. For me."

Clenching her jaw, she fought back her automatic retort. She wanted what he asked for just as badly. She nodded once, sharply, and he breathed heavily into her ear. "Wait here. I'll be back in a few moments."

He slipped to the ground and almost immediately disappeared. Cold chills raced up and down her arms, ice trickling down her spine. She hated the thought of Shadow tainting him, corrupting him even more than she'd already done.

*:The taint doesn't touch me any longer. Not with your love in my heart.:*

She didn't reply aloud, but he could feel her relief and longing through his bond. She stole a glance at the priest, wondering what he would think of such a relationship. Wondering what the nobles would think. Bad enough their future High Queen would wed a barbarian. Let alone take two savages to her bed.

Rhaekhar suddenly spoke in her head, his voice low and rough. *:Aye, both of us, at the same time.:*

She jerked with shock, both at his constant surveillance and what he'd suggested. He definitely wasn't angered or outraged at the picture that formed in her mind. Gregar solid against her back; Rhaekhar staring into her eyes, his golden gaze blazing like the sun. He thrust hard and deep, stealing her breath, drawing a cry from her, while Gregar—

*:Stop it at once!:*

*:That was your desire,* na'lanna. *I merely made the suggestion. You supplied the delightful image.:*

"The Moon is quite lovely tonight." Father Josef stared up at the silvered crescent rising to the south. "And the stars, so bright." He turned to her and the sudden intensity in his gaze snagged her attention fully. "I See stars blazing about you, Your Majesty. They glow so brightly, with you blazing in the center, that you might very well set the world on fire with your love."

Tears filled her eyes. Smiling, she whispered, "My beloved Evening Stars."

"With great love comes great power, Your Majesty." Sympathy flickered over his face. And pain. "Our Blessed Lady has blessed you indeed."

How many times had Gregar spoken of the day he would die? Agony pierced her heart so hard she rubbed her chest absently. "Love, the greatest gift of all."

"And the greatest sacrifice." Out of the night, Gregar appeared on her left, scaring her to death. "I counted at least six fists of men on foot and two fists of ponies staked out on lines to the east of their camp. The two cloths waving in the center of their tents were of a gray four-legged animal and a pink flower."

"The rampaging Boar of Pella and the Rose of Shanhasson," she replied slowly. "Well, now I know where Stephan's reserves are."

"What does that mean?" Father Josef asked, frowning.

"It means we'd better ride hard for Fort Walton and raise the alarm. Shanhasson and Pella have united and will strike the fort at dawn. And if Fort Walton falls, all of Allandor will quickly follow."

A s the northernmost fort closest to Shanhasson and the ever-present threat of the royal family, Fort Walton had grown over the years to be the mightiest fort in Allandor. Instead of well-manned walls and sharp, experienced sentries, Shannari found a nearly deserted post.

A familiar face met them in the courtyard. "Captain Fenton! Where is everyone?"

Fenton saluted her and handed her a beribboned letter bearing the Allandorian royal seal. She scanned it quickly and then turned away to stare out over the wall. *Oh, Father, what have you done?*

The letter ordered all but a handful of the fort's once mighty contingent to ride south. King Valche wrote of Pellan plans to take Dalden Bay from the barbarians. He wrote of driving the barbarians back or wiping out Pella's infantry once and for all with the full might of Allandor.

While he left their northern border completely unmanned.

With Shanhasson's aid, the Duke of Pella's small force—no doubt made up of his finest divisions—would ride to the heart of Allandor unmolested.

Her father would return home to find the gray boar flying over Rashan.

Shannari reached for her sword, grimacing when she remembered it was gone. "Nearly five hundred soldiers wait just over the border to invade at this empty Fort. Damnation!"

"I objected as much as I was able, Your Majesty," Fenton said, pacing back and forth. "He left me with a skeleton force, fully expecting me to hold it until he returns with my men. You could have made him listen to reason, but he waved my concerns away."

"What is it, Your Majesty?" Father Josef asked.

"It's a trap." She cast out her senses, reaching for Rhaekhar down their *na'lanna* bond. He was coming, a furious, urgent force of unstoppable love. She trembled with that brief brush against his heart and soul. But would he arrive in time? Would he even care about this Green Land battle?

*He will if he must ride through Pella's troops to reach me.*

"Nay." Gregar wrapped steely arms around her to crush her against him. "You will not do this. You will not risk your life."

:*Nay!*: Rhaekhar bellowed in her head so loudly she winced. :*Ride to me without delay!*:

"I'm the Princess of Allandor and the Last Daughter of Our

Blessed Lady." Her voice was muffled against Gregar's chest, but he would still hear. "I can't abandon my countrymen to Pella and Shanhasson, not after what I saw in the High Court."

"No matter. Khul shall challenge me if I allow you to risk your life for outlanders who know nothing of honor. And I would let him drain every drop of blood in my body if any harm came to you."

Rhaekhar's bond tugged on her, straining with fury. *:If he allows you to do this, I shall kill him.:*

She pulled back enough to look up into Gregar's face. Grim and chiseled from granite, the Blood glared down at her with the cold Shadow of Death in his eyes. He felt every ounce of Khul's fury; he didn't need to hear Khul's threat. "Please, Gregar. Remember *my* honor. Not Khul's, but mine. I can't leave these men to die while I ride to safety."

Still, he hesitated. One of his big hands cupped her cheek and his other hand kneaded her back while he considered her request.

"I can't run again."

A tremor shook him from head to foot and he finally nodded. "You will tell me all your plans. If I decide your life is endangered too greatly, you must retreat to safety without delay."

Her smile wobbly, she nodded. "Of course."

Gregar leaned down close enough that his breath wafted against her face. "Before Khul challenges me and I allow him to kill me, will you invite me to Khul's blankets just one time? I want very much to expand on the image you created for him."

She ground her teeth with frustration and cursed her flaming cheeks. Was there no such thing as privacy any longer? Where she could have a sinfully tempting thought without one—or both —of these annoyingly demanding warriors knowing of it? "Bloody hell."

"Is that aye or nay?" Gregar pressed his mouth to her ear,

laughing huskily. "My death will be worth such a reward. Only I wish for you to look into *my* eyes while Khul pleasures you."

Shoving him in the chest, she whirled away and concentrated on battle. On trying to save a besieged fort with a handful of soldiers. That was easier than facing the flames blazing in the Blood's eyes and his devilish smile.

Thankfully, he didn't press for an answer. Or worse, declare a challenge. Facing Rhaekhar would be enough of a challenge after feeling so much for another man. Let alone his fury that she'd refused to continue riding toward him. His bond was a cold, hard blade, gleaming in her mind like fresh steel. And very, very silent.

"Fenton, how many men remain under your command here?"

"Less than one hundred, Your Majesty. As King Valche ordered, the main force marched south last week."

"Gregar, how many warriors ride with Khul?" she asked without turning around to look at him.

"Two fists."

She turned and looked Fenton in the eye. "Three divisions of Pella's infantry and one of Theo's cavalry will strike the fort at dawn. Can you hold the fort against them until my Khul arrives with his warriors roughly an hour later?"

"If you're with us as Captain, then we can hold. The men will hold against Lygon Himself."

Shannari sighed. *:Forgive me, Rhaekhar, but I must do this.:* "I'm with you, Fenton. Now, let's prepare for battle."

Shannari walked the top of the wall to survey the approaching enemy troops. Whole sections of the wall remained unmanned, but she'd worked with Fenton the last hour before dawn to devise a plan. The enemy would know exactly how diminished their force would be—that was Stephan's true purpose all along in attacking Dalden Bay. His contingency plan, so to speak. Even if she failed to marry him, he would take Allandor by force from the north and win the new High King's eternal devotion by handing her over to him at the same time.

Brilliant, actually. And he'd come terrifyingly close to pulling it off.

She didn't need to hold Fort Walton forever, though, and that was the key her enemy wouldn't know. They knew nothing of the impressive force led by one very furious barbarian. That he was furious with her made no difference. He'd mow them down in his haste. What he would do when he reached her, then, was another question entirely.

Shivering, she touched Rhaekhar's bond again. Ominous silence.

"I don't believe I've ever felt him quite so angry before," Gregar said thoughtfully. "Not even when he learned of Sontache's plan to deliberately embarrass you. Not even—"

"I know," she broke in, shooting a glare at the Blood. "I do what I must. I'll apologize when he gets here."

"I say you'll do a lot more than apologize." Gregar winked suggestively. "Perhaps he'll wager with me again regarding how many times he can make you scream. As angry as he is now, I believe he could drive you insane for hours and hours before..."

Shannari climbed down the ladder as quickly as she dared.

The Blood jumped and landed effortlessly on his horse's back. "What keeps these outlanders from merely marching south to take your main Camp?"

"Nothing but us. If we put up a good fight, they'll hesitate here long enough for Khul's warriors to arrive. Once your warhorses crash into Captain Maldani's lines, he'll never be able to reform them again."

"And when they swarm your outer walls?" Gregar's tone was still light but his eyes darkened, swirling with Shadow. He knew very well how quickly she'd lose the massive but unarmed wall to the enemy.

"Then we retreat quickly and orderly to the inner keep. We can hold it for days, and I only need to buy an hour or two at most. Does that meet with your approval?"

His mouth quirked with amusement at her sarcasm. "Aye. What says Khul of these arrangements?"

"He won't speak to me."

"Ah." Gregar nodded, the dreadfully wicked gleam returning to his eyes. "He'll want a private discussion with you, then."

After all the times she'd begged for privacy, this sounded quite foreboding. "What does that mean?"

:It means I shall hold you down, prevent you from so much as touching me, while I lave every inch of your skin with my tongue and you shout yourself hoarse.: Rhaekhar growled in her head. :And then I shall do it again. And again. And—:

:You're welcome to try.:

Hard amusement trickled through his bond. :I'm warrior enough, na'lanna. I accept your challenge. Though Gregar is not warrior enough to protect you from yourself.:

:If you were here, you wouldn't be able to stop me either.:

Rhaekhar didn't answer, but his bond vibrated tighter, straining to pull her away from danger with nothing but his love. It very nearly succeeded, especially when he softened his touch, his inner voice, and trailed ghostly fingers through her heart and mind. :I love you, Shannari. It drives me mad to think of you in danger. I beg you, my heart, run to me, now, as you ran to Gregar.:

Impressive warrior. He would use every weapon at his disposal, including her guilt at her betrayal with his Blood. :You had best ride harder, my heart. The Pellan and Shanhasson forces have arrived.:

At first, she felt rather useless in her hurriedly assembled armor, even with a sword hanging at her side once more. On the borrowed horse's back, she couldn't see the battle let alone participate. The wave of scaling hooks were too numerous for the handful of troops on the wall to knock away, and soon soldiers wearing the gray of Pella engaged her small ground force.

All too quickly she saw a handful of mounted soldiers wearing the rose of Shanhasson, so the gate had been compromised as well. Little pockets of Allandor's blue and gold stood firm but well outnumbered.

More and more enemy soldiers crowded the inner courtyard, and her defensive pocket tightened. She'd already lost five men in her own group, and if she wasn't careful, her own retreat would be blocked. Gregar reined his black stallion closer and jerked his head toward the keep.

Nodding, she thrust her sword forcefully, taking a surprised soldier in the throat, and then spared a quick glance for Fenton.

His force had indeed given up large sections of the wall, but their retreat progressed orderly. A few more minutes, and all of his men would be safely in the keep.

A horn blared outside the walls, and fighting everywhere paused as the enemy soldiers waited for the order.

Rhaekhar. She felt him close, still silent, hard, unswerving in his determination to reach her. His warriors slammed into the rear of the enemy's force and the horn frantically called again.

The fighting redoubled around her, and even Gregar's black was hard pressed to keep the soldiers from collapsing their little pocket of safety. Fighting their way back to the keep's iron gate, she glanced over her shoulder and saw Fenton fall. An arrow took him in the leg. He fought on the ground, crippled, bravely slicing at the crush of enemy soldiers around him.

His blue stood out alone in a sea of gray.

Jerking the horse's head around, Shannari went for him. Gregar bellowed, his horse neighing a challenge to her own. She kneed the reluctant horse hard, forcing it out into the melee, carelessly running down any enemy who stood in her way. She wouldn't leave one of her men—let alone Fenton, her Sergeant all these years—to die for her father's mistake.

With a final leap, her mount cleared the last of the soldiers surrounding Fenton. Leaning down, she grabbed his bloody hand and hauled him upward. He bit back a curse, struggling to get his wounded thigh swung over the horse's back.

Too late, Shannari saw the sword coming from underneath.

Despite an obviously very broken leg, the soldier leaned upward and plunged his blade into her side.

"Nay!"

"Na'lanna!"

Rhaekhar yelled from one direction, Gregar from the other.

Soldiers flew through the air in all directions as Rhaekhar barreled toward her with his warriors close behind. Behind them were more soldiers in blue. Dazed, she couldn't figure out how so many more Allandorian soldiers had arrived.

Fenton slipped from her grasp, groaning when he landed hard on the ground. Her horse reared, confused, and whirled back toward the keep. Too much. Her grip on the horse slackened and she started to slide from its back.

For one long, endless second, Shannari hung in the air, slipping down the horse's sleek side. She had time to feel ashamed that both Rhaekhar and Gregar would see her fall from her horse. She even had time to look down at the ground and estimate how hard she'd hit. She closed her eyes when the ground loomed just inches beneath her, but pride made her open her eyes.

Crushing the last of the soldiers between him and his goal, Rhaekhar hung nearly upside down as his great golden stallion galloped toward her. Fiercely bared teeth gripped the *rahke* in his mouth. His long brown hair dragged the ground. Clamping a hand on her so hard she cried out, he snatched her to his chest before she hit the ground. With one hand fisted in Khan's mane and the other clutching her tightly, he hauled them both upright. The stallion exploded with a burst of speed, hooves clattering on the stone tiles as they pounded into the safety of the inner keep with Gregar right beside them.

"*Na'lanna!*"

Hands ripped the chest plate away. She could feel the wound in her side gushing blood like a fountain. One of them pressed his hands against the wound in a desperate effort to staunch the flow. But she didn't feel any pain. It didn't hurt at all. *It must be bad.*

Rhaekhar's voice shook with urgency. "Nay, *na'lanna!*"

Sweet hay, baked bread, caffe, warrior. Hair fell in her face. Arms clutched her desperately. Her beloved Evening Stars.

"You cannot die before me, *na'lanna.*" Gregar, so fierce, so adamant, his voice ringing like deadly steel. "Do you hear me? I've seen the day of my death and this isn't it! You don't yet carry my ivory *rahke!*"

The lake formed in her mind, mirroring the brutal black mountain with jagged peaks. A full moon loomed over the water, crystal clear, cold, and so sweet. So very sweet. A horse neighed, urgently, screaming her name.

*Blood is the key.*

*Love, the greatest gift of all. And the greatest sacrifice.*

She pushed at the chest pressed so tightly against her. Fought the arms trying to hold her down. The sacred spring welled up inside her, cold water flowing in her veins, raging through her body. Power rose, freezing her bones. She couldn't bear to hurt one of them as she'd done Stephan. She tried to speak, but water trickled from her mouth, choking her.

*:Let me go.:*

Rhaekhar growled, wrapping her tighter. *:Never!:*

*:Magic. I must—:*

He stood, pulling her up to brace her against his powerful body. One of his big hands pressed against the wound, but everything in her demanded blood. Sacrifice. Prying his fingers away, she stood straighter.

*Blood. I need blood. On the ground. Can't waste it.*

She caught blood in her left palm and cast it out, sprinkling the ground. With each drop that hit the earth, a rolling echo of power sank deep, sparking life. Cold, pure water bubbled out of her like a sacred spring, washing away the Shadow embedded in her homeland.

Stumbling, she headed for the battle. Rhaekhar caught her arm, supporting her, but he didn't try to stop her. *Gregar. Where is he? I need—*

Immediately, he took her other arm. With the Lady's magic rolling from her, she could feel his gift of Death from Vulkar.

Drawing on his bond, she drew a hoarse cry from him as she dragged his shadowed power into her own, poisoning the pure water flowing through her.

Death spread among the soldiers.

For a moment, she panicked, terribly afraid she would kill her own people. But the whisper in her heart soothed her, a gentle touch from the Lady, a reminder. The Lady's magic would never harm one of Her own.

Enemy soldiers shrieked and writhed on the ground. Allandorian soldiers fell to their knees, stunned and afraid. The Sha'Kae al'Dan horses whinnied, adding to the magical melody in her heart, and distantly, she heard that horse call again.

*:I'm coming!:*

The outflow of power ebbed, gently receding.

Sagging against Rhaekhar, she tugged her left hand free of his grip and raised bloody fingers toward his mouth.

Golden eyes gleamed, caught fire, and he groaned raggedly. "Are you sure—"

She ignored his hesitation and pressed her hand to his mouth. His eyes fell shut and he tasted her sacrifice. Her blood. Full of magic, full of love.

Raising his head, he tightened his arms around her, shifting her toward Gregar. The Blood backed away, his eyes wild. "Nay, I cannot—"

The lake called to her. Floating, floating, with the moon so full, so large in the sky.

Leesha's voice came from a great distance away. *:IT IS ALLOWED. YOU MAY SHARE THE SACRIFICE AS YOU CHOOSE WITHOUT FEAR.:*

"Gregar," Shannari called weakly. Her knees trembled and she could no longer hold herself up. "You must. I need you. I need your bond."

"Khul—"

"Do as she says."

The Shadowed Blood of Death came to her side as Rhaekhar lowered her to the ground. Sliding deeper into the lake of chilled water, she couldn't seem to lift her head or arms. Rhaekhar held her on his lap, his warmth soaking into her, making her eyes drowsy.

She fought unconsciousness.

"Hurry," she whispered. "Our Blessed Lady's touch is leaving me."

Trembling, Gregar took her hand.

"No, no, not enough." She struggled against the heaviness dragging her under. This might very well be the only time Gregar tasted her blood, and she wanted to remember it. She wanted to feel his reaction through his bond, feel her blood flowing in his veins, tying him to her. "Wound."

He made a low, rough sound, likely sharing a questioning glance with Khul for approval. Rhaekhar lifted her higher in his arms, tugging the linen shirt she wore beneath her armor aside to better bare the wound.

Silken lips grazed her ribcage. She looked down her body, at his sable hair spread across her. As if he knew she looked at him, he rolled his gaze up, shifting so his eyes met hers. Obsidian, flickering flames, moonlight, those shining dark eyes fell shut and he closed his mouth over the puncture wound in her side.

Pain, now, but not bad, not as though she were dying. Enough, though, that she moaned, and Rhaekhar growled a low rumble of warning. Through the bond, she felt the Blood's quickening pulse and the surge of his desire.

Gregar shuddered, licking the wound, drinking the blood as fast as it welled. The flow, thankfully, had lessened to barely a trickle. He pressed his mouth tighter, daring to probe with his tongue, to suck a little harder.

Pain speared through her. *Sacrifice. For him, for Rhaekhar, I'm more than willing.*

A muzzle touched her face. Blinking, she tried to focus on the horse. Not the brown one she borrowed. Not black or gold. This one was as silver as the Lady's Moon.

*:What's your name? Where did you come from?:*

*:My name is Wind. I came for you.:*

Darkness fell, water closed over her head, and she sank into oblivion like a stone in a bottomless lake beneath the shining full Moon.

Gripping the *rahke* on his hip so hard his fingers cramped, Rhaekhar stared down at her face, so pale and strained, as she slept. Shadows ringed her eyes. A bruised cut marred her cheek. Bruises on her ribs, her back, from that cur who'd dared to kick her.

And that horrible, gaping puncture wound in her side.

The young holy man knelt beside her cot, his head bowed in prayer. Gently, he laid a hand on her forehead, the other over the terrible wound, while he prayed. Endlessly, it seemed, but when he sighed wearily and lifted his head, the wound in her side was closed, fragile and pink, but Healed, as was the scrape across her cheek. The scars remained though, a testimony to her courage.

*Vulkar, I came so close to losing her.* "I shall ride to those Shining Walls this very day and kill the cur who calls himself High King."

"Impossible," Valche said, shaking his head. "You can't just waltz into Shanhasson and kill our King, no matter how evil he is. No matter how invincible you believe your soldiers to be. This must be done carefully and most importantly, legally."

Rhaekhar growled beneath his breath. "I care nothing for your laws. All I care about is ensuring she never suffers another moment's unease or pain or fear from that monster's hand."

"Agreed. But razing our royal seat to the ground isn't the answer."

"I agree, Khul." The young priest stood, wobbled, but brushed Valche's steadying hand aside. "Our Blessed Lady wants Theo removed from Her Throne. On that we all agree. But She wants to denounce Shadow at the same time. She wants all the world to see Her message of love. Simply killing Theo and shoving the Last Daughter onto the High Throne by force is not Our Blessed Lady's will."

"We must do this legally," Valche insisted. "Give me a few months to form new alliances. Few of the other nobles will be pleased to hear that Shanhasson and Pella united to attack Allandor. The land is locked in a heat wave unlike anything we've known in generations. The crops are burning up in the fields. It's raining now, but the drought is so bad—"

Shannari stirred, a sound of pain escaping her lips. Forcing her eyes open, she whispered, "It rains in Allandor because of my sacrifice."

Relief eased the strain in Rhaekhar's shoulders. Releasing the *rahke*, he flexed his fingers and crouched beside her. She smiled up at him, and his heart swelled with so much love he couldn't breathe.

"Yes," Father Josef said. "Your sacrifice broke the drought in Allandor, and your blood blessed the soil and unlocked the weather. But the rest of the countries will continue to suffer. It's unfortunate and hard for us to understand, but Our Blessed Lady has a great yet dire purpose in mind. The people must suffer to understand her message."

"Tears," Shannari whispered.

"Yes, Your Majesty. She washes Her people's eyes with tears. Rest now. You shouldn't be awake so soon."

"Too much to do." She struggled up to her elbows, her face tightening with pain. Rhaekhar sat beside her and gingerly pulled her up against his side. Closing her eyes, she leaned against him, pressed her mouth to his skin, and breathed deeply. "You smell so good. Lady above, I love you."

"Your Lady's Moon shines in your eyes, *na'lanna*."

Startled, she jerked her gaze up to his, a pleased and tearful smile on her face.

"Think you a barbarian can't learn the proper way to tell his woman he loves her in the manner of her people? You're my my beloved Evening Star. I shall guide my life by your light."

Tears flowed, then, but her smile was so beautiful his heart ached. "The Lady's Moon shines in your eyes, Rhaekhar, Khul of the Nine Camps of the Sha'Kae al'Dan." Her smile sobered, the joy slipping from her face. She looked about the room and her gaze fell on Gregar.

The Shadowed Blood still looked shaken. He sat against the wall, his dark gaze locked on her, the ivory *rahke* rolling on his palm. She held out her hand to him, and he flinched.

"Gregar, come here."

Frantic, the Blood looked to Rhaekhar, pleading, for what he didn't know. The Blood had tasted something sacred, something he thought never to have. Why he wasn't more joyful, Rhaekhar couldn't understand. "Do as she says."

Silently, Gregar knelt at their feet, placed his *rahke* on the ground before him, and took her hand. Rhaekhar swore the Blood was trembling.

"Are you going to challenge him?" Shannari asked.

Startled, Rhaekhar jerked his gaze to hers. Hadn't she accepted them both? Why else would she torment him with her vision of both of them loving her? "Nay, *na'lanna*. We'll come to whatever arrangement you desire."

Her cheeks flushed and she shook her head. "Are you going to kill him as you threatened for allowing me to risk my life?"

Slowly, Rhaekhar answered, "Nay."

Instantly, Gregar drooped against her, his head in her lap and his shaking hands clutching hers.

"Your Lady approved of your choice and your sacrifice, so who am I to punish him or you for doing Her will?"

Shannari combed her fingers through Gregar's hair soothingly. "He couldn't bear to die so soon, not after—" Her voice broke. "Not after coming so close to his heart's desire and finding honor instead of murder and darkness."

Resolve firmed Rhaekhar's jaw. He'd given her plenty of time to adjust to her feelings for both him and the Blood. It was time to fully ease her worry and guilt and begin a life of love. He turned to the young *shaman*. "Are you the one who would approve the Last Daughter's choice for marriage?"

Father Josef blinked and straightened. "I am."

"Then you heard my oath to her. I would have her hand in marriage."

"King Valche, do you object?"

Shannari glanced at her father worriedly, but Rhaekhar recognized the gleam of greed in his eyes. Not for titles or riches or whatever outlanders valued, but for the warriors such a joining would bring his daughter. Rhaekhar didn't mind, as long as none opposed. She wouldn't be pleased if he had to beat some sense into her father.

"I don't object."

Shannari cupped Gregar's cheek and turned his face up to hers. "The Lady's Moon shines in Gregar's eyes, too, Khul's own Shadowed Blood."

Barely breathing, Gregar looked to Rhaekhar, his dark eyes swimming suspiciously.

"I accept Gregar at my Khul'lanna's side."

Swallowing, Gregar looked back into her eyes. "Shannari, Khul'lanna of the Nine Camps of the Sha'Kae al'Dan, is my beloved Evening Star. I shall guide my life by her light until the day I die in her defense."

His smile of love made Rhaekhar's own heart squeeze in sympathy and dread. *It will break her heart when Gregar dies.*

Shannari couldn't stop the happy tears, and joy welled up in her heart. Love, two warriors to love, when she'd thought her heart was dead. *Thank you, Blessed Lady. Thank you.*

"Very good," Valche said, smiling.

Her father must be too enamored with the barbarian horde she'd have access to as Khul'lanna to think too carefully about the oaths she'd just taken with two different men. "How did you get here so fast? Fenton said you were far to the south with our main army."

"Your brilliant idea of fast Keldari horses." King Valche replied proudly. "We only had two hundred horse, but we doubled up on each mount and we were able to keep up with your Khul for the most part. Now give me a few months to peacefully dethrone Theo—"

"No, Father. Theo must die."

Cold shadows trickled down her neck. Where before the Blood's eyes had been dark with misery, now the Shadow of Death hovered in his gaze. The Death Rider waited for the word from her. One nod, and he would ride to Shanhasson.

*:No.:*

*:Are you sure, na'lanna?:*

She felt immense pleasure from Gregar at the simple touch of her mind and her words through a bond he'd never let himself hope to feel. Not with the temptation of her blood always tormenting him.

*:I shall relish the chance to terminate him.:*

"Not yet," she said aloud. "Our Blessed Lady has a purpose that I don't yet understand."

She hesitated, trying to understand. She'd chosen so poorly last time, blinded to the Lady's true will.

"Trust your heart, Your Majesty." Father Josef kindly patted her shoulder. "Our Blessed Lady will never fail to guide your heart."

She took a deep breath, listening to her heart so full of love. All she wanted to do was fall asleep with Rhaekhar's heart beating against her cheek. To smell her beloved warriors, feel their heat warming her, their hair covering her, their love protecting her. She wanted to ride for the Plains immediately.

Rhaekhar's arm tightened around her. *:Your wish is my—our— command, na'lanna.:*

Which reminded her of the silver mare. "Where's Wind?"

Rhaekhar shared a solemn, reverent look with Gregar. "Your *na'kindre* waits for you outside with my Blood. How do you know her name?"

"She told me." She turned to her father and the priest. "Make sure the news of Theo's betrayal of Allandor spreads across the land. His threats to kill me unlawfully. His declaration that Leesha has no power in Her own High Court. Meanwhile, I'm leaving with Khul as soon as he desires to ride."

"Our Blessed Lady will Call you when it's time."

Her stomach rolled with fear. Facing the Shadow in Shanhasson alone was much easier than contemplating her beloved warriors dying to protect her.

Rhaekhar gripped her chin, his fingers hard. His eyes gleamed with determination. "You won't face Shadow alone. I offer all that I possess to help you fulfill your destiny. My Camp, my warriors, my Blood's life, my own life. What would you have me do?"

"I want the Nine Camps united beneath their Khul."

Her supreme warrior smiled. "With you as my Khul'lanna I can do no less."

So much love. Smiling through the tears, she rubbed her cheek against his fingers. Without looking away from his burnished golden gaze, she reached out her hand. Gregar took it, nipping the heel of her palm teasingly. "Let's go home."

J erking against the chains, Theo wailed. *"It's just a dream! A dream!"*

Then why could he hear the air slicing as the lash descended on his back again? Why could he feel the blood tricking down his sides? Why were his wrists raw from trying to free himself from the chains that bound him flat on his stomach on cold, unforgiving stone?

THE COST OF FAILURE IS BLOOD AND PAIN. SHALL IT BE YOURS, SERVANT? OR HERS?

"Hers! I swear it! Give me another chance, Great Lord, I beg you!"

DO YOU UNDERSTAND WHAT YOUR FAILURE HAS DONE? I FELT HER KNEELING ON THE GREAT SEAL. I TASTED HER FEAR AND HER BLOOD. YET SHE ESCAPED YOUR DUNGEON AND MY GUARDIAN. EVEN THE HIGH PRIEST'S DEATH CANNOT REMOVE THIS STENCH OF FAILURE.

NOW SHE WILL MATE THE HORSE KING AND SPAWN

MORE FOALS OF THAT HATED BLOOD! MORE BURNING BLOOD TO BLAZE AGAINST MY DARKNESS.

Whistling through the air, the lash descended again and this time vicious teeth bit into his back and buttocks. Howling with pain, he thrashed helplessly when chunks of flesh tore away.

YOU LIKE THE PAIN, SERVANT.

Panting with fear, he twisted against the chains desperately. *No, not pain. Not blood. No!*

Trapped between his stomach and the stone floor, his erection throbbed in agony. Black tendrils of shadow stroked his skin, tasting the blood.

YOUR TAINTED BLOOD IS SWEET, SERVANT, BUT NOT AS SWEET AS HERS. IMAGINE HER BLOOD PAINTED ON YOUR SKIN. IMAGINE HER BODY BENEATH YOU AS SHE WAILS WITH PAIN AND HORROR. IS THIS NOT YOUR HEART'S MOST SECRET DESIRE?

"Yes! Oh, Lady, forgive me!"

The oppressive weight of silence warned him.

FORGIVENESS? YOU BEG her FORGIVENESS?

Shrieking rage blasted through him, squashing him against the floor like a spider beneath a manure-encrusted boot. Crashing waves of agony and torturous hate hammered him again and again, while the many-mouthed lash ripped meat down to the bone. Drilling, merciless pain filled him while he screamed without sound.

KILL HER! KILL HER! KILL HER! KILL HER! KILL HER! KILL HER! KILL HER! KILL HER!

"I will! I swear it!"

*KILL HER!*

*AND THE SUN WILL NEVER SHINE AGAIN!*

Hands scrabbling through the tangled sheets, Theo jerked awake. Pain seared every inch of his shuddering body with the final spurt of his seed into the mattress. Gasping for air, he brushed the silken strands of her hair out of his face. Her unforgettable scent of roses had nearly faded from the shorn hair, but not from his memory.

Roses, hot and tantalizing and forbidden.

Would her blood smell as good? Taste as good?

He gathered her hair beneath his cheek like a pillow of black, fragrant silk.

*Shannari.*

# SNEAK PEEK INTO THE ROAD TO SHANHASSON

Keep reading for a sneak peek into The Road to Shanhasson, book 2 of The Shanhasson Trilogy

*Blessed Lady above, thank You for bringing me home.*

Shannari drew rein and paused her mare at the top of the hill. Rolling waves of golden hay stretched off into the distance. The scent of baking bread and warm earth filled her nose, a visceral reminder of the warrior on her right. Not the home of her birth, perhaps, but the Plains had definitely become the home of her heart.

Rhaekhar, Khul of the Nine Camps of the Sha'Kae al'Dan, had defeated her heart as well as her army and she was sure would admit the former had been much more difficult a battle. His tousled golden-brown hair hung well down his shoulders, begging to be combed by her fingers. The braids at either temple were heavy with colored beads, golden rings, and other symbols of honor he had won over the years. His skin gleamed like polished bronze in the summer afternoon light, tight over his powerful arms and shoulders. Looking at him made heat unfurl deep in her stomach.

The breeze picked up enough to flutter her cropped hair into her eyes. Irritated as much by the stinging pang to her vanity as the tickling hair in her face, she swiped at the unruly mess. She missed the heavy weight of hair down her back but she was extremely lucky Theo hadn't taken her head as well as her hair.

"In a matter of hours, I'll be making you my Khul'lanna." Rhaekhar's voice rumbled, thick and tight with desire. "Do you desire Gregar to participate in your claiming?"

She opened her mouth to respond, but she really didn't know. Did she want Gregar? Definitely. Did she want a complicated relationship that made her uncomfortable, let alone with Rhaekhar and such an extremely dangerous man? Not really. Especially in this so-called claiming, where Rhaekhar's whole intent would be to make her scream as many times as possible while everyone outside the tent listened.

"Even if you asked, I would refuse."

Jerking her attention to the Blood, she listened carefully to his bond. His heart ached with longing, even while a darker need twisted his own *rahke* in his heart.

"You're still my greatest mark, *na'lanna*. I refuse to risk you. I won't rush you into asking me to Khul's blankets."

"Are you saying never?"

"Great Vulkar, nay." Gregar laughed shakily. "You'll be Khul'lanna; the honor of your claiming is rightfully Khul's. My time will be later, if you so desire."

"I shall declare you co-mate before the Camps," Rhaekhar said to his Blood, his voice ringing with command. "If you want to participate, she shall ask you, or I shall order you."

Shannari felt heat sear her cheeks at the thought. "No ordering. If it happens, it happens."

"*When* it happens." Rhaekhar cupped her chin in his palm and tilted her gaze up to his. "His blood is mine to command, and he offers himself to you. You want him. You will have him. Our honor is greater than this doubt you carry." His eyes darkened, turning smoky amber. "Besides, I want very much to expand on that delightful image you created for us. I want to see the pleasure in your eyes when he touches you."

"And I want to see your pleasure when Khul touches you," Gregar said.

Both warriors laughed at whatever expression was on her face.

Another gust of wind drew her attention to the sky. A storm brewed in the distance. Clouds scuttled toward them, thickening on the horizon. Shadows raced across the hills. Despite the two warriors so close and the army of mounted barbarians behind them, she shivered and touched the sword at her hip. She'd come so close to dying in Shadow. Could she ever see a shadow stretching across the ground and not remember the madness in Theo's eyes?

Both warriors crowded their horses closer to hers: Gregar at her left, his heat searing her back, Rhaekhar on her right, his hair tumbling into her face. Their scents filled her, sweet hay and flowers, warrior and leather, accented with dark, rich caffe and the smell of baking bread. Her heart ached, clutching with fear. Eventually, she'd have to go back to Shanhasson. She'd have to face Theo and exact Our Blessed Lady's justice, and when she did ...

Either one of them could die.

"I won't stay you from your destiny, *na'lanna*." Rhaekhar sighed heavily, and through his bond, she felt a fierce surge of warrior instinct to wrap her up in his arms and carry her far to the south where he'd never let her face danger again. "But I care nothing about those honorless curs in your homeland. Your own people would have stood by and watched Theo kill you. I say let them writhe in agony in the Three Hells forever."

"As long as Theo lives, he'll try to kill me and any children we have. I refuse to live in danger the rest of my life, and I certainly won't let him destroy the Lady's Green and Beautiful Lands."

Gregar whispered against her ear. "Let me stay tight at your back, and as long as I live, Shadow shall not touch you again."

*:You won't die. You can't.:*

*:The day of my death is closer than ever, na'lanna. Do not wait too long to ask me.:*

Straightening, Rhaekhar guided his horse down the slope, and Wind automatically followed, with Gregar close behind. "We must discuss the arrangements of our co-mating."

"Shall I stop drinking *drakkar*?" Gregar asked. "Just in case?"

*Drakkar* was the warriors' method of birth control on the Plains. Shannari's hands clutched the reins but she didn't dare look back over her shoulder. She was sure to see a big smirk on the Blood's face.

"Aye. All children, whether mine or yours, shall carry my honor."

"Agreed."

The awful reality of the position she'd put Rhaekhar in twisted her stomach into knots. The greatest warrior on the Plains might be faced with the task of raising children not his. His honor, which she had only begun to understand, would surely be lessened. How could he let this happen? "Don't I get a say in this?"

Rhaekhar ignored her. "When she asks you to my blankets, I'm First. I reserve the right to impose limits if she is unable to do so."

"Actually, I insist you do so," Gregar replied, his voice hard and brittle with ice. "I have no limits. If the dreams I've had over the years are any indication, she has none either, at least when it comes to me."

Years before she'd ever known him, she'd dreamed of a man wrapped in shadow, lying in wait for her. In these dreams of darkness and death, they'd battled and loved and killed each other, over and over. Those gruesome dreams still haunted her.

Evidently, they haunted Gregar, too. "My honor is yours, Khul. I ask that you make one solemn oath to me."

Rhaekhar drew his golden stallion to a halt and turned to face his Blood. "Anything, my friend."

"If she bleeds at any time, you must kill me."

She gasped and reached out to Gregar immediately. His forearm was corded, his fingers white on the reins. His eyes glittered like obsidian.

"I'm not to be trusted if I catch the scent of her fresh blood. Don't let me slide into bloodlust, or I may—" His voice broke. "I have no limits," he whispered hoarsely. "Don't let me—"

"On my honor, I shall kill you first."

The tension bled out of the Blood and he nodded. "My thanks, Khul."

"You can't be serious." Heart pounding, she looked from one warrior to the other. "I love him. You can't kill him. You promised!"

Rhaekhar stared at her, his eyes dark, his face grim. "I'll do whatever I must, *na'lanna*. You want him, you have him, but I won't let him hurt you."

Shivers crawled down her spine. Ice crept around her heart.

"Much," Gregar whispered softly.

Rhaekhar growled, his hand dropping to his *rahke*.

"She'll like a little, Khul. Just rein me in."

"We shall see." Rhaekhar turned his gaze to her, his eyes almost as dark as his Blood's, his voice thick. "Together."

Heart pounding, she stared at him, trembling. "I'm sorry."

He shook his head, a small smile playing about his lips. "Are you up for a *kae'rahke* this night, Gregar?"

The two warriors rode ahead, leaving Shannari staring after them with dread pounding in her veins. A *kae'rahke*? Challenge? Sometimes they fought to the death.

"Aye, I'm up for many things, Khul."

Rhaekhar laughed, a dark masculine sound of arrogance that made her grind her teeth together. "I bet you are. Good. I'll declare you co-mate before the claiming. What do you want for terms?"

Groaning, Shannari tried to think of a way to distract them. Short of ripping her armor and clothes off, she didn't think much would distract them from their goal of blood.

Gregar winked at her. "I would certainly enjoy another kiss. This time, I want a proper kiss."

"Oh, aye," Rhaekhar replied, giving her a smoldering look over his shoulder. "Do you want her tongue in your mouth, or yours in hers?"

"Preferably both."

Very firmly, she turned her attention to her horse. Wind's ears flickered back and forth, listening to the warriors. Her head was up, her muscles tight beneath Shannari's thighs. The mare's entire manner was alert, whether to flee or charge Shannari didn't know. She stroked the sleek silvery neck and fingered the moonlight mane that was as soft and fine as Rhaekhar's hair.

Deep inside her, Shannari felt a ripple in the still waters of the Lady's lake she carried. Wind was not just a horse. Perhaps Wind was the Lady's horse as well.

Clucking to her, Shannari urged the mare to canter ahead of her warriors, determined to put a little distance between them and all their "arrangements." She felt both relief and regret at Gregar's words. She wanted him ... but that desire was fraught with danger, blood, and turmoil. She hated putting Rhaekhar through such conflict.

Yet something dark and raw quickened in her heart at the thought of exploring those bloody dreams with the Shadowed Blood.

Tightening her grip on the reins, Shannari leaned lower over the mare's neck. *Faster,* she thought. *Let's outrun them. Outrun the doubts and guilt. Outrun the darkness inside me.*

The mare's ears flickered back as though she heard. Lowering her head, she tore off across the Plains at a gallop so smooth that Shannari barely felt the thud of hooves on the baked earth. Her hair whipped her face, and grass snapped at her thighs in sharp whips that made her thankful for her leather pants. For once, she was free, not chasing her destiny or fighting a losing battle. She was running away, and it felt ... good.

She glanced back over her shoulder through streaming eyes. The golden and black warhorses chased after her, but they were no match for Wind's speed. The mare was truly a gift from the Lady. She could outrun them and escape.

If she wanted.

Ah, that was the catch. Because she didn't want to lose them, not even if it meant she failed her destiny and lost the High Throne forever. They each held a rein on her heart, and although they could have, they didn't use their bonds to slow her or draw her back. Her own heart held her captive.

Wind slowed to a more manageable canter that allowed the warriors to catch up. Shannari kept her gaze straight ahead and didn't make any apologies. As soon as she'd run ahead into the Plains unprotected, she'd felt the immediate clutch of fear in Rhaekhar's heart and Gregar's surge of icy shadow. It didn't occur to them that she could never be unprotected now that the Lady's gift welled in her heart. All they knew was the strength of their blades and the weight of their honor.

Whatever either warrior had been prepared to say was interrupted by a hail from the top of the next hill. They'd been sighted. Now the Camp would empty to come and greet the returning warriors, and they'd want news of the battle. How many of them would be disappointed to see her still with their Khul?

"It doesn't matter," Rhaekhar replied to her thought. A glance at him confirmed the arrogant slash of his mouth, the hard line of his jaws, and the determination glittering in his eyes. He was Khul and he'd beat sense into anyone who objected. Such a display of arrogance made her mouth quirk with amusement.

They galloped up the next hill. People already lined the other side of the slope, cheering as their Khul made his appearance. Drendon and Alea led the foray. After the rocky start to their acquaintance, the woman would likely be furious to see the outlander still at Khul's side. Shannari searched the other woman's face for dismay but oddly enough, she thought that Alea looked rather pleased.

"Welcome home to the Sea of Grass, Khul," Drendon said. "You were victorious, of course."

"Aye, but in the end, the greater battle was for the Rose of Shanhasson," Rhaekhar said without resentment. In fact, the look of stark possession in his eyes damned near curled her toes. "Both are mine. In fact, I have an announcement."

The crowd quieted expectantly.

"I, Rhaekhar, Khul of the Nine Camps of the Sha'Kae al'Dan, hereby claim Shannari dal'Dainari, the Rose of Shanhasson, as my Khul'lanna. Anyone who dares challenge me for her, let him come."

Most of the people roared with approval, but not all. Shannari scanned the faces carefully, watching for a flicker of anger, hatred, or secrecy. The mix of negative and positive emotions seemed relatively balanced. *Great*, she thought. Only half of her soon-to-be husband's people hated her.

Of course, tight-lipped and silent, Varne, Khul's nearest Blood and the last line in his defense, looked like he'd swallowed a bellyful of *rahkes*.

Gregar's voice rang out, "I challenge for her," and she nearly fell off her horse.

People whispered excitedly, looking back and forth between the two warriors like they'd break out knives and fight to the death here and now. Braced for condemnation or outrage that both warriors would claim her—and Khul's own Blood at that—she was shocked to find the glares and grumbles at Rhaekhar's announcement disappearing beneath genuine excitement.

"Fun and games," she whispered, shaking her head. Now Rhaekhar's acceptance of another warrior at her side didn't seem quite so far-fetched, although she still battled her Green Land sensibilities.

Rhaekhar drew out the silence, staring at his Blood with the grim, implacable glare of the Khul, weighing and considering, as though he tested this warrior's honor *kae'al* by *kae'al*. Each moment's threat of bloodshed only improved the mood of the crowd.

Gregar might not wear any beads in his hair now that he was Blood, but she knew that everyone must remember what he'd been before Rhaekhar became Khul. Death. Shadow. Assassin.

Fun and games indeed, and in true Sha'Kae al'Dan fashion, a great deal of blood and honor were promised in Khul's silent examination. The watching warriors were nearly jumping up and down with glee at the prospect.

"She loves *me*," Rhaekhar growled. "What claim do you have on my woman?"

How much of this was playacting, and how much was torment for both warriors? Her own emotions were in too much turmoil for her to be able to understand what she was receiving of theirs. Shannari's heart pounded, her palms sweaty. It was all she could do not to draw her sword or turn the mare and run back across the hills. She didn't know where she'd go, but if she weren't here, this couldn't happen.

Gregar flashed his trademark smirk. "She loves me, too."

Alea gasped out loud and the whispers increased until Rhaekhar turned to look at Shannari. Silence fell, as though the whole Plains listened and waited.

"What say you, *na'lanna*? Does my Blood speak the truth?"

Bloody hell. She sent a dark surge through their bond, allowing him to feel her irritation. Surely he could have prepared her for such a public and sudden announcement. Gripping the sword hilt on her hip, she lifted her chin and squared her shoulders. She could do this. Rhaekhar already knew the truth, as well as Gregar. They'd known long before she'd admitted the truth to herself. "Yes. I love you both."

The crowd erupted into cheers again.

Rhaekhar smiled and it was like the noonday sun shining down on her. "Then I accept your challenge as co-mate, Gregar. Let us offer blood this night to bind our oaths to Shannari."

"Agreed, Khul. My blood is yours; my blood is hers." Gregar's eyes swam with shadows and glittering obsidian. "She will taste us both."

Concentrating on breathing, she closed her eyes a moment. She'd promised Gregar that she'd taste his or Khul's blood whenever they offered, no matter where they were, no matter who watched.

"Can you wait a few days so we might contact the rest of the Camps?" Drendon asked. She scanned his face and posture, trying to guess if Rhaekhar's best friend were pleased, shocked, or horrified at this development. She didn't know Drendon that well, but his reserve surprised her. She'd expected his reaction to be more blatantly obvious, either for good or bad she didn't know. "I'm sure many would like to be present. It's not every day that a Khul claims his Khul'lanna."

"I'll not wait a single night." The tone of Rhaekhar's voice was low, rumbling bass.

"Neither shall I." Gregar's voice was cold with shadows, sending goose bumps racing down her arms.

*:I thought you refused to participate.:*

*:I did. Yet I will feel Khul's pleasure as his Blood, and your pleasure as na'lanna.:* Gregar's voice wound through her mind like black, thick velvet, stroking where no hand could ever reach. *:The two of you will likely kill me, but I shall ride to Vulkar with a smile on my face.:*

She swallowed hard and scrubbed her sweaty palm on her leathers. *:This is not the day of your death.:*

He laughed silently, but beneath the amusement echoed heart-rending sorrow. Her heart stuttered in response. *:Not yet, na'lanna.:*

The silvered lake in her mind rippled briefly, disturbed by small plops on the surface like tears. Shannari's throat constricted. If the Lady wept ...

*Please, Blessed Lady, save him. Don't take him from me.*

*:Do not weep for me, Shannari,:* Gregar whispered in her mind. *:Dead or not, I shall never leave your back unprotected.:*

Rhaekhar touched her knee, drawing her attention to him. He'd dismounted and offered her a hand down. The sympathy and even grief on his face—because she loved and ached at the thought of losing another man—made the tears shimmering in her eyes fall down her cheeks.

She slid down into his embrace and wrapped her arms around his neck. *:Is he right? Will he die?:*

Rhaekhar's voice through the bond was somber. *:Only he knows what visions Vulkar gave.:*

Unless Gregar was mistaken, one of the men she loved more

than she'd ever thought possible would die because of her, because he loved her. Yet he had no reason to lie.

Guilt and agony flooded her. Her grip tightened on Rhaekhar's hair, and she fought not to reach for her sword and challenge him, just to make herself forget that awful finality she sensed on the horizon. *:I can't bear for either of you to die for me.:*

*:My life is yours, my heart. His life is yours. It will be our greatest honor to die to keep you safe.:*

His scent filled her, bread hot from the oven. The thought of him laid out on the white marble of the High Court, gasping his last breath, sent a shudder through her so fierce she actually cried out.

Gregar, bleeding, dying, and Rhaekhar ... It was her worst fear.

All these years, she'd told herself she couldn't love because of Devin, the lover who'd tried to kill her in her own bed years ago. Perhaps she'd been lying to herself. Perhaps the reason she hadn't wanted to love had been another reason entirely, because it would kill her to lose either of these warriors who walked beside of her.

Oh, Lady, why? Why give her love greater than anything she'd ever hoped to feel, and then take it away so harshly?

Resolve tightened her grip on the sword and firmed her chin. Nobody had died yet. She had the skill to fight and protect herself, as well as the Lady's power filling her heart. Surely it would be enough, no matter what vision Gregar had received. *I will kill to keep them safe.*

Thunder rumbled across the Plains.

"Come on, Shannari." Alea grabbed her arm as it began to rain. "I'll prepare the steamtent for you and then you can rest awhile. I'm sure you're exhausted." She hurried Shannari off toward the camp.

Ill at ease, Shannari couldn't relax in the thick clouds of steam, even as the heat soaked deeply into her muscles. She'd never had a true female friend, and she and Alea had certainly gotten off on the wrong foot before. The other woman must be nearly bursting with questions about Shannari's complicated relationship, and she had questions of her own. Alea obviously knew both warriors better, and had known them longer, than she. Part of her wanted ask for details that would help her deal with them easier, but the other was afraid she'd learn too much. She felt poised between two pawing, snorting horses that were ready to tear off in opposite directions, ripping her limb from limb.

"I see you have a new injury."

Shannari flicked her gaze up to the other woman's face. Surprised, she realized Alea was actually concerned, not appalled at all the various scars Shannari had earned over the years. "I took a wound in battle, but one of Our Blessed Lady's priests was thankfully nearby and Healed me."

True, definitely, but she didn't admit she likely would have died if not for the Lady's intervention as well as Her priest's. Her blood had spilled on the ground to break a curse of Shadow, and she'd killed several hundred troops at once without lifting a weapon, with Gregar's unwilling help.

*:Not unwilling. I was more than pleased to assist you.:*

*:Quit eavesdropping.:* Shannari closed her eyes and listened to the bonds, trying to estimate how closely both warriors listened. They hovered inside her mind, listening and feeling everything. She knew where the pawing, snorting image of horses came from as soon as she touched Rhaekhar's bond. He was like a warhorse screaming a challenge as he crushed his enemy beneath massive hooves.

Gregar laughed in her mind, making her shudder. *:Be quick with the bath, woman, or Khul may decide to start the count before our kae'rahke.:*

Shaken, she concentrated on toning down that raging, pounding stallion leaking from Rhaekhar's bond. :*What's wrong with him?*:

:*He leads the Nine Camps for Vulkar. Is it any wonder that the Great Wind Stallion would walk in his body when Khul claims his Dark Mare?*:

Shannari wished she understood their religion better. The Dark Mare sounded rather ominous, and yet fitting, too. She was definitely dark, and mare to Rhaekhar's stallion. She'd never thought of it that way before. Perhaps there were more parallels between Our Blessed Lady and this Dark Mare than she'd thought. If so, that made Gregar ...

:*I am Shadow. I am Death.*:

Yet Lygon, Lord of Darkness, had never felt such over-whelming sorrow and love. She didn't believe it one moment. :*And you're mine.*:

Startlement shimmered through his bond, making Shannari smile. Alea blinked and smiled back hesitantly, which only made it funnier. :*Stop it. Even Alea thinks I'm trying to be her friend now.*:

"I know we started off ... awkwardly," Alea said, her face and eyes warm and sincere. "But I see how much Khul loves you and you him, and I'm more happy then I can say. If you need any assistance as Khul'lanna, please ask."

Shannari studied the woman, looking for any hint of duplicity or falseness, but her gaze remained steady and her eyes open. "You truly do care for him like a brother, don't you?"

"Aye. I hope we can be friends, Shannari."

What would it be like to have a friend, a real friend, someone she never had to suspect of a plot to entrap her? Could she truly trust Alea? Listening again for any ripple in the magical lake that welled within her, Shannari sensed no reason not to trust her. She smiled more openly herself, relaxing some of the ever-present guard that she kept about her heart and mind at all times. "Let's bury the hatchet ... er ... *rahke*, then. What can you tell me about this claiming business?"

Alea gave Shannari a bright, eager smile. "The very first *kae'rahke* ever recorded on the Plains was between two warriors who desired to claim the same woman."

Shannari's stomach knotted and she clenched her hands so tightly her nails dug into her palms. "What happened?"

The other woman shrugged. "They fought, they bled, and they came to an agreement. The first *kae'rahke* led to the first co-mates. It's even rarer than *na'lanna* bonds but you're not the first woman to love two warriors."

Pushing strands of wet, clinging hair off her face, Shannari asked, "What does Drendon think?"

"I didn't speak to him, but if I know my warrior, he's more concerned about Khul's protection. If he falls, the responsibility of all Nine Camps falls to my mate, and with one of Khul's Blood otherwise occupied ..." Alea gave her a rather lecherous wink that sent a wave of embarrassment hotter than the steamtent flooding across Shannari's face and neck. "Did I mention that not too many years ago, a claiming was a very public event?"

Shannari shook her head, though she could imagine. The moist heaviness in the air weighed on her chest and she felt like she couldn't get a deep breath. Suddenly anxious to get some fresh, rain-slick air, even if she got wet and cold, she stood up to leave the tent, but swayed and almost lost her balance.

Alea jumped up to steady her. "Are you well?"

Weariness suffused her limbs and Shannari was grateful for the other woman's arm. "All of a sudden, I feel rather tired."

With halting steps, she exited the steamtent into Khul's adjacent tent where Gregar immediately took her other arm. She yawned and nearly cracked her own jaws.

"Well, no wonder," Alea exclaimed. "It's a long ride to Dalden

Bay and back. The ceremony won't begin for at least an hour, so you have plenty of time for a nap."

Gregar lowered her to the cushions. "Why don't you rest a while?"

Her eyes were so heavy, but she fought to stay awake. "Khul —" She slurred.

"He'll wait, *na'lanna*. Rest."

She tried to say more, but the words wouldn't come.

# ABOUT THE AUTHOR

Joely Sue Burkhart has always loved heroes who hide behind a mask, the darker and more dangerous the better. Whether cool, sophisticated billionaire, brutal bloodthirsty assassin, or simply a man tortured by his own needs, they all wear masks to protect themselves. Once they finally give you a peek into the passionate, twisted secrets they're hiding, they always fall hard and fast. Dare to look beneath the mask and find love in the shadows with Joely on her website, www.joelysueburkhart.com.

If you have Kindle Unlimited, you can read all her indie books for free!

Wondering what's next? Sign up for her newsletter and receive exclusive free content.

ALSO BY JOELY SUE BURKHART


**Blood & Shadows, erotic fantasy**

Free in Kindle Unlimited

THE HORSE MASTER OF SHANHASSON


*The Shanhasson Trilogy*

THE ROSE OF SHANHASSON

THE ROAD TO SHANHASSON

RETURN TO SHANHASSON


*Keldari Fire*

SURVIVE MY FIRE

THE FIRE WITHIN


**Their Vampire Queen, reverse harem vampire romance**

Free in Kindle Unlimited

QUEEN TAKES KNIGHTS

QUEEN TAKES KING

QUEEN TAKES QUEEN

QUEEN TAKES ROOK


**Zombie Category Romance, paranormal romance**

Free in Kindle Unlimited

THE ZOMBIE BILLIONAIRE'S VIRGIN WITCH

THE MUMMY'S CAPTIVE WITCH

**Mythomorphoses, Paranormal/SF Romance**

Free in Kindle Unlimited

BEAUTIFUL DEATH

**The Connaghers, contemporary erotic romance**

Free in Kindle Unlimited

LETTERS TO AN ENGLISH PROFESSOR

DEAR SIR, I'M YOURS

HURT ME SO GOOD

YOURS TO TAKE

NEVER LET YOU DOWN

MINE TO BREAK

THE COMPLETE CONNAGHERS BOXED SET

**Billionaires in Bondage, contemporary erotic romance**

(re-releasing in 2017 from Entangled Publishing)

THE BILLIONAIRE SUBMISSIVE

THE BILLIONAIRE'S INK MISTRESS

THE BILLIONAIRE'S CHRISTMAS BARGAIN

**The Wellspring Chronicles, erotic fantasy**

Free in Kindle Unlimited

NIGHTGAZER

**A Killer Need, Erotic Romantic Suspense**

ONE CUT DEEPER

TWO CUTS DARKER

THREE CUTS DEADER

**A Jane Austen Space Opera, SF/Steampunk erotic romance**

LADY WYRE'S REGRET,free read prequel

LADY DOCTOR WYRE

HER GRACE'S STABLE

LORD REGRET'S PRICE

**Historical Fantasy Erotica**

GOLDEN

**The Maya Bloodgates, paranormal romance**

BLOODGATE, free read prequel

THE BLOODGATE GUARDIAN

THE BLOODGATE WARRIOR

Made in the USA
Las Vegas, NV
07 March 2022

45221394R00197